WILD

Also by Eve Langlais,
Kate Douglas, and A. C. Arthur

Growl

WILD

Eve Langlais   Kate Douglas   A. C. Arthur

St. Martin's Griffin ⚹ New York

WILD. Copyright © 2016 by St. Martin's Press.
"Catch a Tiger by the Tail," by Eve Langlais. Copyright © 2016 by Eve Langlais.
"Wild Passions," by Kate Douglas. Copyright © 2016 by Kate Douglas.
"Her Perfect Mates," by A. C. Arthur. Copyright © 2016 by A. C. Arthur.

All rights reserved. Printed in the United States of America.
For information, address St. Martin's Press,
175 Fifth Avenue, New York, N.Y. 10010.

www.stmartins.com

The Library of Congress Cataloging-in-Publication Data
is available upon request.

ISBN 978-1-250-07859-9 (trade paperback)
ISBN 978-1-4668-9106-7 (e-book)

Our books may be purchased in bulk for promotional, educational, or business use. Please contact your local bookseller or the Macmillan Corporate and Premium Sales Department at 1-800-221-7945, extension 5442, or by e-mail at MacmillanSpecialMarkets@macmillan.com.

First Edition: October 2016

10 9 8 7 6 5 4 3 2 1

CONTENTS

CATCH A TIGER BY THE TAIL

Eve Langlais

CHAPTER 1

Having nine lives was well and good in theory, but when a woman straddled a man—fully clothed unfortunately—held a gun to his head, and said, "What are you doing in my drawers?" it probably wasn't a smart thing to say, "Hoping to lick some delicious cream."

Broderick could blame his stupid statement only on the fact that his mother claimed he'd landed on his head instead of four paws more than was healthy for a kitten.

He could also blame hormones for his ill-advised statement because it took only one look at the curvy redhead straddling him, and a single sniff, to realize the goddess threatening his life was his mate.

Meow. And he meant "Ow!" as she dug the barrel into his skin, not at all impressed by his compliment.

"Give me one reason why I shouldn't shoot."

Apparently, "Because I'm pretty sure we're soul mates" wasn't the right answer.

"Listen, smarty pants, I really don't want to have to blow a hole through your obviously empty head. However, I will if you don't give me some answers as to what the hell you're doing in here. This area is off-limits to patrons."

"And are you off limits, too?" Too late it occurred to him how that might sound. *I think I might have just implied she's a prostitute.* Maybe she wouldn't take it the wrong way.

Judging by the way her lips pursed, she did. "I am not for sale."

"I didn't mean to say you were. Ah hell, this isn't going too well. Do you mind if I get up so we can start over?"

"Not until you explain how you got in here and why you're going through the bar's files."

"I came in through the door."

"The locked door."

"Was it?" He gazed at her with his biggest, most innocent, kitty cat eyes.

They didn't melt her one bit. "I know it was locked, which means you broke in."

"Or had a key." He held up the shiny silver object.

Her gaze narrowed. "Who gave that to you?"

"Your boss." His, too, but no use getting into details about that now, given she still held a gun to his head.

"Why would the bar owner give you a key?"

"So I could do my job. I'm an auditor."

Long lashes blinked. "Excuse me, you're what?"

"An auditor, not an IRS one in case you're wondering. I work for a privately operated company that does a lot of subcontract work for the city and law enforcement."

"And you're here because?"

"Congratulations, you've been selected out of hundreds to have your business dealings perused and your bank accounts monitored for illegal activity." His game show announcement and brilliant smile fell flat.

"I've got nothing to hide."

"Then this will be a painless process, especially if you don't shoot me."

"I guess since you're here on official business that people know you're here?"

"Tons of witnesses."

"It's your lucky day then," she said with a smirk.

Brody couldn't determine if she joked or not. Either way, the gun lifted from his temple.

The lovely redhead moved away—a shame—and dropped with a sigh onto a worn office chair.

Broderick picked himself up off the floor and brushed himself off. While not as meticulous in his appearance as his friend Gavin, as a feline, he couldn't help but groom himself.

"Now that we've ascertained I'm here on valid business, I think we should start over. Hi, my name is Broderick Fredrickson with the 123 Audited Agency. I've been hired to go through all your accounting records in order to reconcile certain discrepancies that have come to light." The city and the cops weren't the only ones looking for an answer to mismatched funds. His secret boss, the Lycan alpha of the city, also wanted to know. *"Who the hell is screwing me over?"* were his exact words.

Only an idiot would think they could steal from Fabian Garoux and get away with it. Brody hoped that idiot wasn't the woman in front of him. If she proved culpable, then fate surely screwed with him, leading him to his mate only to have her taken away, because if there was one thing his alpha boss hated, it was thieves.

"I'm not aware of any discrepancies."

"And you would know this because?" He arched a brow.

"Because I'm the one who, for the last few weeks, has been filing the receipts, collecting the monies, compiling the employee pay records, and submitting them to the accountant."

"Who was doing it before you?"

"Ricky."

"What happened to Ricky?" Brody already knew—strangled and fed to the fishies—but wondered what she'd say.

She shrugged. "Damned if I know. No one does. Ricky disappeared. Didn't show up for work one day, and a week later, with girls threatening to quit if they weren't paid and distributors refusing to deliver, I kind of took over until they could send in a replacement."

Broderick frowned. "The guy managing this place disappears and upper management didn't send someone to look into it?"

"Yeah, they sent Frank, the guy who collects the money and stuff for the accountant. He's the one who told me to keep doing what I was doing."

Curious. When they'd questioned Frank, he said the accountant, Larry, had put her in charge because she had hot boobs. She really did, a perfect handful, confined by an awful bra.

We should rescue her breasts.

Any other time he would have attempted, but Brody was here to solve a mystery. He couldn't allow himself to get distracted by a lovely redhead.

"Are we done here? I left Nancy alone behind the bar, and given that the after-dinner rush hour is about to start, I should get back there."

Done? Oh, they were far from done, and Brody didn't just

mean because of his job. His kitty wanted to get to know her better. Starting with her name. "Who are you? I never did get your name."

"Because you never asked." Then, almost begrudgingly, "Lulu."

"That's it? Lulu?"

A heavy sigh left her. "Lulu Lamontaine."

A made-up name if he ever heard one, but he didn't push it. Lots of people had reasons to change their names. Some to escape their past. Others to ensure a brighter future. He wondered what Lulu hid from. "Nice to meet you, Lulu. What time do you finish work?"

Her brows crinkled in suspicion. "Why do you want to know?"

"I thought we could grab dinner." And then hit somewhere a little more private for *dessert*. Meow!

"Why would we do that? I've already told you everything you want to know."

"Oh, we're far from done. I'll have many more questions for you, but the real reason I asked is because as I said, when we first met, you are my soul mate." He presented his claim with his biggest smile, the one that popped both of his dimples.

Instead of swooning in pleasure, she laughed, and pointed her gun again.

"Not a chance, numbers guy."

"We prefer the term *geek*." Sure, he wasn't the classic thick-rimmed-glasses-wearing, pasty-skinned nerd portrayed in movies, but Broderick definitely belonged more on the geeky side of things, where numbers and equations brought a thrill of excitement.

"Whatever. Geek, nerd, I don't really care; we're done. Now get out of my bar."

He'd leave, for the moment. However, she was delusional if she thought they were done. Lulu had caught the eye of the tiger, and no way was he letting her escape.

Step 1: Woo her with his incredible charm.

CHAPTER 2

Lulu didn't move for several minutes after the attractive male in his rumpled suit left. She didn't move for a few reasons.

First, finding the guy snooping in her office had taken her by surprise. On his knees and sifting through her filing cabinet, he was rocking along to the music piped into her office and didn't hear her approach.

She almost shot him. Surely no good could come of someone spying. But she'd restrained herself. Too many questions from the cops. Once she'd ascertained he was there on legal business, she decided he was harmless. An accountant, snort. Or so he claimed. Like an idiot, she'd forgotten to ask for identification, but then again, the fact that he produced a key and a plausible explanation for his presence seemed to indicate he was there on real business.

I wonder why no one warned me about it. Surely, whoever gave him the key could have spared a quick warning call.

And that was just the first set of reasons keeping her mentally spinning.

The second was she needed a minute to process his claim that someone was cooking the books, with an unvoiced accusation that she was to blame.

Not me. Lulu wasn't a crook. It would have never even occurred to her. Stealing was never okay. Murder under the right circumstances though . . . Her parents had an interesting ideology that she struggled with now that she'd left home.

But who cared about her traumatizing childhood? Someone thought she was pocketing dough. Never. Every dime the bar made went to the accountant. She barely did anything more in her job as manager than hand over the cash and credit card receipts for their daily sales. With company checks, which left a trail, she paid the distributors and did payroll. So okay, she was pretty involved with all the money aspects surrounding the bar, but that didn't mean she was the culprit if numbers didn't add up. The knowledge that something illegal was happening, on her watch, didn't sit well.

I better not be getting framed.

The final reason she lingered in her office, the most surprising reason of all, was because of her unexpected reaction to Broderick. He'd told her they were soul mates, and for a moment, a stutter from her heart, and a warmth she'd never thought to feel again after the betrayal of her ex, floored her.

Attracted to a numbers geek who practically accused her of stealing? Never.

Although, when she said *geek,* it should be noted the guy was anything but. Forget a scrawny, pale-faced wimp lacking confidence and good posture. This self-referred geek was extremely attractive with his golden brown hair, teasing amber eyes, and a panty-dropping grin.

Oh yes, she'd noticed the power of his dimples at work, but she'd learned how to hide her inner self a long time ago and thus betrayed nothing in her expression. Add in the attractive package a body that moved with smooth grace, and it had her wondering what kind of physique hid beneath his suit.

Not that she'd ever find out. She wasn't interested in a relationship with anyone. However, now that he'd left and she was all alone, she could perhaps admit a certain attraction to the white-collared guy with his engaging manner and tempting smile.

Admit, yet never act upon. He couldn't know about her secrets. Especially not given who he was.

The best thing to do? Avoid him. But how? If he had been mandated to examine the books, then she'd have no choice but to see him again.

Next time, I'll make sure it's in public. This would prevent her from shooting him if he annoyed her too much—and from doing something even more foolish, like succumbing to his charm.

Exiting her office, Lulu took a brief moment to scan her bar. Not really hers—she simply managed it—but since she currently set the rules, and kept a strict eye on the place, a certain sense of ownership came naturally.

Her career at the Tail Waggers gentlemen's club had begun a few months back as a waitress. A hard worker, Lulu didn't hide her ability to handle patrons, money, or responsibility. It wasn't in her to do a half-assed job, nor did she ever let anyone pull a fast one on her. Given her work ethics, and the fact that she always showed up on time, she quickly jumped from waitress to bartender, courtesy of Ricky, the currently missing manager.

Then when Ricky went missing, Frank, whom she'd gotten to kind of know on his several-times-a-week pickups, temporarily assigned her to take over.

The patrons soon learned to respect her. A woman in charge didn't mean a pushover. It only took her ordering the bouncers to toss a few of the troublemakers out, literally on their ears, to ensure they didn't try anything with the girls who danced at the club.

See, Tail Waggers was more than just a bar serving drinks and pretzels. It also provided entertainment. The type that came with a stage, a pole, and the least amount of clothing allowed by law. Which, in this state, meant the panties stayed on, but some of those scraps held together by string barely squeaked by that mark.

Right now, on the red-carpeted stage, Bindi was doing her thing. Wearing a saucy nurse's uniform, she strutted her stuff to the tune of "Witch Doctor" sung by David Seville but juiced up to give it a modern appeal. The silver pole, washed in between sets because Lulu had a thing about keeping things clean, didn't wobble as Bindi grabbed it and swung her legs around, flashing white panties where the crotch area had a red cross stitched on the front. It matched the pasties on her nipples.

Lulu had long ago become indifferent to the sight of boobs and naked buttocks flashing, but that didn't mean Lulu underdressed. On the contrary, she showed as little flesh as possible on the job, usually wearing form-fitting jeans, which hugged her curvy hips, and T-shirts with cartoons printed on them like the one of the moose with the giant set of antlers she currently sported that said STOP STARING AT MY RACK OR I'LL POKE YOU IN THE EYE.

Lights flashed, and the music blared as Bindi bent over to grab the bills tossed onto the stage. Her movements delighted the crowd sitting behind her, who got to see where the G-string on her ass went.

"I love you, Bindi!" a particularly excited fan shouted.

Nothing new, not around here.

Satisfied that things were running as they should, Lulu took her spot behind the bar. The after-dinner crowd was arriving, thirsty for more than just the entertainment.

For the next several hours, Lulu managed to forget her odd visitor, but when she locked up for the night at one A.M., early since it was Tuesday, mid workweek, she couldn't help but wonder what would have happened if she'd accepted the auditor's invitation to dinner.

Would he have seriously returned to meet her this late at night?

A white-collar guy like him was probably in bed by ten and in the office by nine A.M. The complete opposite of her, who usually didn't roll out of bed until noon, or later, hitting the bar around three or four to open it.

As Lulu stepped into the practically empty parking lot, well lit by her insistence in order to provide safety for the girls, she scanned the darkness at its edges.

Force of habit. In truth, Lulu did not fear the dangers that might lurk in the dark, but it always helped to see them coming—so she could shoot it.

Before anyone got the impression she was a trigger-happy, violent freak, it should be noted that she'd never shot anyone who didn't deserve it. And it wasn't that many times. Only seven, five of whom lived. Not because she'd missed—because, see, her daddy had taught her well. A self-defense excuse worked best if a girl didn't aim for the heart. In most cases, when a threat was needed, just a simple wave of her Browning 9mm Luger was enough to deter most criminals. In the cases where it wasn't, a well-aimed shot that whistled by their cheek made them see the light.

But sometimes there were cases when a lesson had to be taught and a gunshot would cause too many questions. When she didn't want the law involved, she resorted to hand-to-hand combat. There were ways of hurting people without leaving a bruise.

Try going to the cops with the claim that sweet little me beat the hell out of you with no proof.

It was her jujitsu training mixed in with dirty street fighting that she employed when she heard the steps rushing from behind. Before the unknown person could reach her, she whirled and took in a glimpse of the situation—guy in a navy blue hoodie brandishing a knife.

Piece of cake—the chocolate kind, drizzled with rum, whipped cream, and a dab of cherry sauce.

Mmm. How long since she'd eaten? She'd figure that out after she took care of the ill-advised mugger.

"Give me your purse, bitch!"

"How about I give you a lesson in attacking women instead?" she snapped back. The idiot rushed in with no finesse, relying on his puny knife. A knife he couldn't hold on to when she kicked his hand, sending it spinning to clatter somewhere behind him. But she wasn't done. Lunging forward, she snared his wrist, yanked him toward her, and head-butted him in the nose. His high-pitched scream made her smile in grim satisfaction, but he hadn't yet learned his lesson.

Down came her foot, stomping the top of his with as much force as she could muster. Then she wrapped an arm around his neck to yank him down and kneed him a few times in the midsection.

The screaming went to hiccupping sobs and gasps for, "Mercy. Sorry. I won't do it again."

"Damned right you won't," she snarled, giving him one more vicious slug to the jaw before sending him staggering. She planted her hands on her hips and glared at the would-be assailant. "Don't let me catching you loitering around here again, or next time, I will get rough."

His eyes widened as he wiped at the blood trickling from his broken nose and split lip. He nodded vigorously and winced before he took off, limping as fast as he could.

The sound of someone clapping startled her. One would-be criminal thwarted, and already another waited to take his place?

She pivoted on her heel and pulled her Luger. She had it aimed and cocked before she noted whom she faced. "Not you again."

But it was. Broderick had returned, more casually attired in slim-fitting blue jeans and a T-shirt that said GEEKS DO IT BY THE BOOK AND NEVER SKIP ANY CHAPTERS while clutching a bouquet of flowers and sporting a brilliant smirk.

"I say, bravo. That was freaking awesome. The way you took that fellow down and made him cry, beautiful. Absolutely beautiful. I only wish I'd thought to tape it."

For the second time that day, she stared at the surprising Broderick and wondered what the hell was wrong with him.

What sane man thought her beating up another man was

awesome? What sane man showed up bearing flowers at one in the morning and seemed undaunted by a pointed gun?

Apparently the same kind of guy who simply had to show up for her heart to go pitter-patter and her nipples to tighten. *He came back.* But why?

"What are you doing here?" she asked bluntly.

"Courting you."

Of all the expected answers, that one had never made the list. "I think you've got your definitions skewed, office boy. Stalking is not courting."

"Stalking? I beg to differ. Stalking is defined as harassing someone in a way that makes them uncomfortable or afraid. I, on the other hand, am admiring you and expressing my ardent interest in taking things to a more personal level."

"Take your expression elsewhere. I am not interested."

"You think that, but you'll see," he said, striding toward her, ignoring the still-pointed weapon. "We are meant to be together. I can feel it in my whiskers."

"You're clean shaven."

"I'm talking about my hidden ones." He winked.

She frowned. "That better not be some sly reference to your pubes because that's just gross."

The graceful Broderick stumbled, and she almost laughed, especially given the expression on his face. He didn't say anything to her remark, so she couldn't help but tease, "Cat got your tongue?"

"No, but if you're not careful, this cat will take yours."

"I'd like to see you try." She'd put him flat on his ass—*then straddle him and kiss those tempting lips while*—

Stop. Nope. Not happening. Broderick might appeal to

her womanly side with his assertions that she was his soul mate, but she wasn't falling for his lame pickup lines. He should work his wiles on someone more gullible, someone she could easily intimidate. *Because he's mine. Don't touch.*

The sudden spurt of jealousy took her by surprise. She barely knew the guy. Why would the thought of him chasing after another girl bother her?

"I brought you flowers." He thrust out his hand, and she noted with surprise the arrangement of yellow roses. And not the wilted kind bought on a street corner for five dollars a bunch. He'd actually procured fresh roses, the yellow buds just starting to open and emitting a lovely perfumed aroma.

No one's ever brought me flowers before. Tickets to a sporting event, yes. Takeout so they could eat in and tumble into bed happened more often than she liked. Oh, and the suave idiots who thought a box of extra-large condoms would impress her. That guy never even made it to second base. But flowers? How old school and cute.

While Lulu didn't take them, she did lower her gun. After all, there was no point in keeping it aimed when she knew she wouldn't shoot it. The guy was weird, maybe a little too ardent, but so far, harmless.

And if he wasn't, she'd do to him what she'd done to the mugger.

"You can keep your flowers. I don't want them." She didn't even own a vase to put them in. Not to mention, accepting them might encourage him. Men always seemed to think they were owed something if a girl said yes to anything.

"What about the chocolate?" His free hand yanked a small box, tied with a ribbon, from his pocket. The Godiva name caught her eye.

Chocolate.

Quality chocolate.

No. Must resist. She stuffed her hands in the pockets of her jacket lest she snatch the temptation from his hand. Her traitorous stomach gurgled, but surely he didn't hear it.

Judging by the amused tilt of his lips, he did. "They've got creamy centers."

Evil man. Up came the gun. "Move away with your deadly chocolate."

Still smiling, he lifted both hands laden with gifts, high enough that the fabric of his T-shirt dragged up and over the waist of his low-hanging jeans.

Her gaze was drawn to the narrow band of flesh exposed, the glimpse of taut abdominals and a thatch of hair, arrowing down to . . .

"Are you seriously getting a boner right now?" She couldn't help her incredulous inquiry. "You do realize I am pointing a gun at you."

"And it's awfully sexy. I don't suppose once we become a couple that you'd mind if I rented you a sexy cop-girl uniform? You could arrest me. Maybe frisk me. Then strip search me for evidence."

She almost went cross-eyed at his blatant proposition, less because of the audacity but more because she could picture it. With the addition of cuffs.

"We are not going to be a couple." Tired of spinning in circles when it came to talking to Broderick, and even more tired of trying to resist his damned charm, she spun and headed to her car, a late model Mazda 3, a perfect little commuter car for a girl in the city.

She didn't know he'd followed her—which bugged her

because she prided herself on her acuity—until he braced an arm on her car as she opened the driver's side door.

"So, when can I see you again?"

Did this guy never give up? "Never."

"Never say never, especially since we have to meet again. You know we still need to talk about the bar's books."

"If you have business to conduct with me, then you will do so during business hours. In public." With witnesses to keep her from doing something rash, like kissing him when he leaned in close and whispered to her.

"Until tomorrow then, sweetheart. And just so you know, being in public won't stop me." He dropped the flowers and chocolate in her lap before stepping away from her car. His wink just before he departed seemed to imply so many things—most of them naughty.

And much too intriguing.

I can't get involved with him. She repeated this mantra over and over. And over again as she caved to temptation and sucked on the chocolate. Despite his allure—*mmm creamy caramel*—she'd have to do her best—*oh god, a truffle*—to resist him. She couldn't afford to get involved with him. Now she just had to enforce it—right after she finished the chocolate.

CHAPTER 3

Leaving Lulu—not by choice but because his mate was proving stubborn—Brody found himself at a loss as to what to do. He'd truly, in his misguided mind, expected things to go much differently. He'd offer her the flowers, and she'd blush and accept them. He'd then dazzle her with a smile and chocolates, she'd thank him with a hug, and then they'd end up naked somewhere.

In retrospect, he was probably a tad optimistic. *Try unrealistic.* His tiger thought he should have acted a little more aggressively. Maybe roared a time or two or peed on something to show his manhood.

Somehow he doubted that would have worked either, but what would?

She's my fated mate. As in the one and only woman for him. It was how it worked in the shifter world. Once a fellow met his lady: wham, bam, mated, shazaam. The human and, in this case, her tiger would live happily ever after.

Except his human soul mate wanted nothing to do with him.

Impossible. He knew she was the one. His inner tiger chuffed and meowed most pitifully when she was around.

His body became aware of her every move. His entire being urged him to touch her. *Lick her. Bite her.*

Wait a second. Maybe that was the problem. He hadn't yet touched her. Perhaps the whole insta-love thing required contact to jump-start. If that were the case, then he'd resolve that issue at his earliest convenience when he met with Lulu on the morrow.

Which was too many hours away. Bummer.

Needing to kill time, he decided it was a good time to check in with his boss, and he didn't mean the one for his legal day job. He was talking about his position as go-to guy for the city's alpha and mob lord, Fabian Garoux.

It was Fabian who'd ordered him assigned to this case, a case that came through his company office as a part of the city's and law enforcement's investigation into businesses they felt were shirking their taxes through creative accounting. Fabian had certain friends in strategic places, which was how he'd wrangled getting Brody in charge of the audit.

Who knew a double agent job—and yes, Brody liked to equate his life in terms of being a secret spy—would lead to meeting his future mate?

To think the request to investigate had started so innocuously.

"I think my new bar manager is fudging the numbers," Fabian had announced when Brody answered his phone a few days back.

Given he was in his cubicle at work, Brody kept his voice low when he replied. "And this concerns me because?"

"For one, because the city decided to launch an impromptu investigation. Secondly, because you're my numbers guy, and this involves money. My money to be exact, which makes it important."

"To you."

"And even more important to you if you want to keep what's left of your lives intact."

Seeing as how he had only four or five left—he wasn't too sure on one of them on account of the concussion and amnesia after he discovered drunken tigers didn't always land on four paws—he thought it prudent to perhaps humor his alpha overlord.

"Who's skimming the kitty?"

"I'm thinking it's got to be the new broad Frank put in charge of Tail Waggers."

"Isn't that your strip bar downtown?" Brody knew of it but had never gone. He never saw the point of paying for overpriced beer while staring with a bunch of guys at boobies. Personally, he preferred to meet women who wanted to get naked for him and not just anyone with a dollar bill.

"It's a gentlemen's club, thank you very much. And a classy one, too."

Good thing his boss couldn't see his smirk. "If you say so, boss."

"I do, and it's also a decent moneymaker, or was until a few months ago. The numbers have been dipping. A lot. Larry, who's the one handling the financial paperwork and crap, doesn't have any answers as to why. He says he's just working off the receipts and invoices the broad running the bar is giving him. Something isn't right, and I want you to find out what the hell is going on."

"What are you going to do if it turns out someone is skimming?"

"The less you know, the better." Ominously said, and yet Brody knew Fabian wasn't as bad as he liked to make himself sound. While he might keep a heavy hand on the shifters under his domain, and an even firmer one on his empire, Fabian wasn't a man prone to undeserved violence, nor risk.

He might skirt human law, but Fabian always stayed within it. Much to Gavin's disgust.

Brody's lawyer friend had long wanted to nail Fabian's ass to a wall, legally of course, but alas none of his investigations had borne any fruit. And now that Gavin had hitched himself to Fabian's cousin, Gavin had to reluctantly give up the dream of retaliation against the man who'd made him into a wolf.

Brody often wondered if he'd feel the same urge to retaliate if he were to ever meet the tiger shifter who'd made him. Probably not, given Brody had been a tiger for as long as he remembered.

Bitten when he was just a child, his father killed during the same tiger attack incident, Brody had never known any other life. He was always both a boy and a cat, something his mother—who would love the very tough Lulu—had to learn to deal with without any help or knowledge—but lots of flea baths—until Fabian came into their lives.

The crime lord, only a teen himself at the time, caught her trying to coax a tiger cub from a tree. He did so love to climb things. He'd just sucked at getting down. Problem was his mother didn't dare call anyone for help, lest they take the tiger cub away. Some parents threatened their kids with jail. His mother told him to behave or she'd give him to a zoo.

But threats didn't work that day, and Brody refused to

change back. Seeing her dilemma, the young Fabian stood under the tree and put on what Brody called his alpha face, which, seeing as how Fabian was only a teen at the time, wasn't all that impressive, unless you were a wee cub who'd met his first predator in human skin.

Curious, like most cats, Brody crept down to sniff at Fabian, who grabbed him by the scruff, hauled him up, and caught his eye. "Cubs listen to their mother. Or else the alpha will deal with them."

Back then, it was Anthony in charge of the pack, the man who'd made Fabian who he was. And a scary bastard, too.

Not that Brody saw Anthony much. After Fabian pulled him into the pack, the other shifters left him pretty much alone, except for Fabian. He'd taken on the role of teacher and big brother to Brody. He was the one who'd taught him how to hide who he was. Who taught his mother to maintain a firm hand on him—and use a wooden spoon if needed.

Brody owed a lot to Fabian. So why didn't he work for him directly?

Because Fabian was practical. When he took over as alpha of the pack, and inherited the ownership of the businesses, he decided his business interests were better served by having key people in positions of power. People loyal to him and the pack who weren't susceptible to a bribe that could be traced or countered by a larger sum.

Thus did Brody, and many others within the pack, get mundane jobs with the humans. Most of them government-type positions that gave them access to records and inside news that could benefit Fabian.

Most times, Brody didn't mind. His job as an accountant might not sound exciting, but the truth was that Brody did enjoy working with numbers, and there was a certain smug excitement in knowing he led a dual life. Accountant by day, mobster's right-hand man by night, and wild cat when the moon was full.

And now he'd get to add to his list of identities: lover. One who went to bed alone that night.

Sad meow.

But he consoled himself with the thought that he'd get to see Lulu in a few hours, and this time, he would touch her, and she would recognize him as her mate. Shazaam!

CHAPTER 4

Sizzle.

That was the sound the bacon made in the pan, which meant the heat was just right and the time to flip the strips almost here. Savory, salty protein, crisping to perfection, making her taste buds water, which meant she was more than irritated when someone pounded at her door.

"Go away. You are not ruining this." She turned the pieces over, yelping as hot, fat drops splashed her.

She yelped again as a voice from behind said, "Are you all right? I thought I heard you cry out in pain."

Whipping around and wielding a plastic spatula while wearing only a long T-shirt and panties might not prove the most fearsome of appearances, but was it necessary for Brody to snicker and lift his arms with a mocking, "Don't hurt me with your wicked spatula. Actually, on second thought . . ." He whirled and braced his hands on the wall. "Beat me, sweetheart. I've been bad."

"I'm sure you have," she muttered, tempted to give him a swat. But smacking his buttocks took a backseat to something more important. "How the hell did you get in here? I know my door was locked."

"Was it?" Big innocent eyes peered innocently at her over his shoulder.

Ha. As if she'd fall for it. She doubted Brody ever had an innocent moment in his life.

"I know it was. What are you, some kind of cat burglar?" He certainly knew how to move stealthily.

"Nothing so petty. If I were to be anything, I'd be an undercover tiger." He seemed so pleased with this answer, and yet she couldn't see the appeal.

"Why would you want to be a secret tiger?"

"Because they are the most wonderful and ferocious felines in the world, of course. And quite handsome, too."

"While I'll admit they make nice patterns on faux rugs and they're cute to visit at the zoo, I don't see why anyone would want to be one. I mean, apart from the fact that the only place they could roam are protected reserves or cages at the zoo, what else do they have going for them?"

He gaped at her. Sputtered a little as he said, "They have lots going for them. They're excellent hunters. Stealthy. Fast."

"Lazy, and always sleeping. Oh, and they pee on things to like, mark them. And exactly why are we still talking about this? I still want to know what the hell you're doing at my place, breaking and entering I might add, at an ungodly hour of the morning."

"It's ten."

"Exactly. And I just got up. The last thing I want to deal with is you and—"

"Burning."

How did he know about the burning inside her? Wait, he didn't mean that burning. He meant—"My bacon!"

The black smoking things in the pan no longer belonged

to the bacon family. She could have cried, especially since they were the last four pieces. Her breakfast would now consist only of toast and eggs. Bleh.

He must have caught some of her depression because he tried to apologize. "Oops. Sorry my awesomeness distracted you. Let me make up for it by taking you to breakfast."

He'd barged into her apartment, uninvited, engaged her in ridiculous conversation, and now tried to invite her to breakfast? "Fine. But I warn you, I have a very healthy appetite."

And not just for food.

A sane part of her insisted she throw him out on his ear, and threaten him if he ever came around again, but another part of her was curious as to his true intent. What was he really after? Surely he wasn't so suddenly besotted with her as he kept implying? He had to have some ulterior motive. Did it have something to do with the audit? Was he trying to get close to her to find out things not in the books?

Is he looking to discover my secrets?

Two could play that game. In the game of cat and mouse, she thought it was time to flip the roles. Starting now.

"Give me a second to throw something on. Clean this up, will you, while I get ready?" She thrust the spatula at him and then sauntered away, the tingling between her shoulder blades assuring her the extra waggle in her step had an audience. Just before the opening to her room, she noted the afghan she kept on her couch had fallen to the floor. Knowing he watched, she bent over, fully aware it made her T-shirt ride high and presented her butt. She wore full-bottomed panties, practical cotton ones, but Broderick was a man. She heard him whimper and mutter, "So wonderfully cruel."

And wicked. So utterly brazen and wicked. She straightened and left the living room. Entering her bedroom, she shut the door and leaned against it.

What am I doing? Teasing and taunting the poor guy. She could argue all she wanted that it was revenge for his own actions; however, the truth was she enjoyed teasing him way too much.

His mere presence ignited her. He was nothing like the guys she usually dated. For one, he wore a suit, with a tie! However, his white-collar status didn't stop her from lusting after him and wondering what it would be like to slide his jacket off his surprisingly wide shoulders. To unbutton his shirt and run her hands over his defined chest. To—

"Need some help in there?" he called out, a hint of amusement in his query.

Did he know she was thinking about him, or did he just rightly guess? Didn't matter. Lulu needed to do something about this insane attraction she had for Broderick.

Do him and get him out of your system.

Such a dirty solution. A fun one. A viable one, too. Perhaps if she did allow him to seduce her, she could better control herself around him, and in return, control him and his digging.

Or fall even worse under his spell, which with every minute that passed was seeming less and less worse.

CHAPTER 5

Broderick had never felt worse. And it was all her fault.

Breakfast, especially the all-day kind served in a greasy spoon where everything was plastic or vinyl, including the menu, wasn't supposed to be arousing. A woman chewing on bacon wasn't supposed to give a guy a hard-on, yet it did.

In his defense, Lulu did it on purpose. What woman popped a crisp piece of bacon into her mouth and closed her eyes while uttering happy sounds? Sounds that should be made only with less clothes and a lot more touching.

Speaking of touching, he'd yet to manage to touch any exposed parts. He'd managed a brush of her arm, covered in her jacket, a brief palm in the middle of her back as he held the door open to the restaurant and guided her in. Yet no actual skin-to-skin contact.

How to manage it short of lunging across the table and—

"What are you doing?"

"Eating bacon." He held her hand to his lips, the shock of contact almost rendering him speechless. There it was, the zing he'd expected, and he wasn't alone in feeling it. Her breathing grew shallow, a faint pink hued her cheeks, and her scent changed, growing muskier, richer, as arousal claimed her.

He nibbled the tiny bit she held until he reached her fingers. He took the tips in his mouth and licked the salt from her skin. She sucked in a breath and yanked her hand away.

"Eew," she exclaimed as she scrubbed her hand, and yet she couldn't hide the fact that her cheeks now bloomed, and beneath her long-sleeved T-shirt—which read PINCH ME AND DIE—the bra she wore couldn't hope to hide her protruding, erect nipples.

He leaned back in his seat. "Sorry. I couldn't resist getting that last bite."

"It was mine."

"Better get used to it, sweetheart. What's yours is mine. What's mine is yours, and . . ."

"Hold on there, tiger. I am not your sweetheart. And my bacon is mine. Always. Nonnegotiable. Actually, touch any of my food again, and I might seriously hurt you."

"Really?" Perhaps he shouldn't have sounded so intrigued, but he did really like the fact that Lulu wasn't a shivering rabbit.

She sighed. "You are incorrigible."

"Thank you. I do my best. Now, I hate to end this delightful lunch, but I didn't just show up at your door this morning—"

"Don't you mean conducted a home invasion?"

"—to get jealous of the way you eat bacon. I was actually looking for you so we could get together at my office and go over some of the financial statements in question."

"Why aren't you doing this with the bar's accountant? He's the one I send everything to."

"Ah, but see, he's claiming you're the one submitting false stuff. Inflated receipts, fake ones, too. Employee paychecks for nonexistent folks."

"What?" Her eyes widened, her indignation real. "I did no such thing."

"Let's try and prove it then. Come and check the stuff out and let me know what seems familiar or not. Someone, somewhere, is lying."

"It's not me. I've nothing to hide."

If only she'd not averted her gaze from his as she said it. Lulu was hiding something. Something she didn't want to come out. He could only hope it wasn't enough to get her in serious trouble with his boss, either of them.

A life on the lam wasn't how he'd pictured his future.

After some arguing, Brody drove, alone, to his office with Lulu following. She refused to get into a car with him. His mate certainly had a solid independent streak. They met up again just outside the main doors of the building where he worked.

"Do you always just wander in to work at any hour you choose?" she asked as they went through the security checkpoint armed with metal detectors.

Taking the visitor badge from the on-duty guard, Brody took it upon himself to pin it to her shirt. He behaved. His fingers didn't brush the swell of her breast. However, her indrawn breath indicated she'd expected him to.

Could he hope she was disappointed he hadn't?

He led the way to the bank of elevators, his access card in hand, before he answered. "Given that some of the businesses I need to audit don't keep regular hours, and I can work from home, my schedule is pretty flexible. So long as I get the job done in a timely manner, my boss isn't too worried about what time I clock in and out."

"Must be nice. My job requires me to be around before the rush starts to make sure things run smoothly. I often work ten-, twelve-hour days just to keep on top of things."

"So why do it? Why not find a less stressful job?"

"Says a guy with a degree or two I'll bet under his belt. Not all of us have the benefit of picking and choosing where we'll work. Rent has to be paid. Food has to be bought. Manager of a gentlemen's club might not be considered respectable by some people's standards, but it pays decently."

"You say you found yourself managing it because the last guy disappeared. Was a police report ever filed?"

She shrugged. "No idea. I mean, in this line of business, people come and go all the time. It's not an industry that keeps people long term."

"So no foul play is suspected?"

She eyed him suspiciously. "Do you know something I don't?"

Actually he did. "Your old boss, Ricky, was found dead a few days ago. Floating in the river, his throat ripped open. The medical examiner's report says he probably died about a month ago, about the time you took over." He watched her for a reaction. Most people would act surprised at hearing about a death. Except Lulu wasn't shocked at the news, even if she faked it well.

She already knew. But why lie?

"That's awful. Any idea of who did it or why?"

"The cops think it might have something to do with the audit."

"So he cooked a few books. Why kill him over it? Wait a

second, you don't think his murder is related to Fabian Garoux?"

"Why would you say that?"

"Well, because Garoux heads the corporation that owns the bar. If someone was cheating him out of money, it's a safe bet to assume he didn't like it, and given his reputation, did something about it."

Except Fabian swore up and down, growled a bit, too, that he'd had nothing to do with the murder. His boss was pissed actually that someone had dared to kill one of his employees. If a man cheated him, then Fabian preferred to kill him with his own two hands—or four paws.

The elevator dinged as they arrived at his level. Exiting, Brody and Lulu walked into chaos. Or at least an accountant's version of it. The maze of cubicles hummed with conversation.

He caught snippets as he strode toward his dedicated space.

". . . no idea what was taken, but they were looking for something."

". . . Sally from the mailroom said she heard Tammy from the precinct claim there's a bounty on his head."

". . . so are we on after work for that beer?"

The snippets didn't make much sense until he arrived at what was left of his once-tidy cubicle. Papers lay strewn all over it. Some shredded. Some crumpled. Others soaked in . . . his sensitive nose twitched: urine.

Bear urine.

Not anyone he'd ever met or knew about, which meant they were here clandestinely since Fabian didn't let any of those clannish teddies into his city or pack.

Bears causing shit? His boss needed to know, and he didn't mean the human one in his office. However, notifying Fabian would have to wait. His human employer spotted him and poked his head out the door. Unlike a shape-shifter, who would have bellowed for him to get his hairy ass in his office, Perry, in a modulated voice, said, "Brody, could you please come here for a moment? These officers have questions for you."

"I can see you're busy. We'll have to do this another time." Lulu used the scene of the crime to slip away, and there wasn't a damned thing he could do about it.

Except roar silently in his head as her pert butt walked away from him.

You might think you've escaped me, but I'll be back. You won't rid yourself of me that easily, sweetheart. And the next time they did meet, he'd leave her with something to remember him by.

CHAPTER 6

Lulu couldn't leave fast enough. She'd done her best to avoid the glance of the cops in the manager's office, but the last thing she needed was for one of them to inadvertently say something in a show of recognition.

Broderick would surely have even more questions and suspicions if he realized she wasn't a stranger to law enforcement.

Just like she had more questions. It didn't take a genius to figure out the destroyed cubicle belonged to him. Someone was trying to hide something, and she couldn't help but wonder if it was connected to the audit of the club.

What exactly had Ricky done, or hidden? Did his death, which she'd heard about through the grapevine, have anything to do with the problems with the bar's books? Lulu certainly hadn't seen anything suspicious since she'd taken over. In an effort to familiarize herself, she'd pored over the ledgers, but nothing jumped out at her. She'd compared the receipts and payroll numbers since she'd taken over with previous ones and didn't notice any wild swings up or down in dollars. So where was the corruption occurring, and who was behind it?

Wondering if she'd missed anything, she drove straight to work, parking in her usual spot and using her key to get in. She locked the door behind her just in case some patrons decided to ignore the posted hours and pop in.

Immersed in her perusal of the saved documents detailing expenses, she couldn't help but startle when someone cleared their throat in the open doorway to her office. She also had her gun out of its holster bolted underneath her desk and pointed.

Aim first, ask questions later. That was her motto. Especially when someone sneaked up on her.

As she perused the man in her office doorway, she wondered how she'd not heard him approach. Lulu prided herself on having keen senses. She needed them to stay safe in her line of work. But much like Brody, this man, whom she recognized from images, crept about on silent feet and thought nothing of opening locked doors.

Given she couldn't exactly shoot him—unless he gave her just cause—she lay the gun down on her desk. "Mr. Garoux," she said as she rose from her seat. "This is an unexpected visit." And a first, too, since she'd taken over. The city's mob lord didn't often deign to visit the bar, or at least he hadn't since she'd begun working here months ago.

"You must be Miss Lamontaine. About time we met since you've been the one managing the club since Ricky's unfortunate disappearance."

"Don't you mean his death?"

She waited to see if he showed any surprise, but his expression remained smooth. The man himself was the height of slick. In his early forties, he wore an expensive suit the color of steel. He wore his dark hair short, but not short

enough to hide the hint of silver at his temples. Broad shouldered, and yet not fat, a man with a face carved from granite
and about as much emotion as a rock.

"Poor Ricky. I heard about his demise from some friends
at the precinct. And you are his replacement. How . . .
convenient."

"I am." No point in denying it, even if she didn't like his
inflection when he stated it. "Is there something I can help
you with?"

"As a matter of fact, yes." The male, with a slinky grace
that raised all the hairs on her body, flowed into the room
and settled himself in the chair before her desk. Impecca-
bly attired, down to his polished leather shoes, he was the
perfect image of a gentleman. But everyone knew it was but
a thin veneer.

The man ruled the city and its underworld with an iron
fist. Or so the rumors claimed. Garoux had yet to be caught
or charged with anything, and yet the gang problems plagu-
ing other cities didn't crop up here. As soon as any kind of
organized group tried to move in, they quickly found a reason to move out. Drug dealers didn't own the streets at night,
and hookers didn't flock to the corners.

But they had to be somewhere. Drugs, sex, and other
vices were a fact of life. All cities had them, although if this
city did, then Garoux kept it where no one could see it.

"So what did you want?" She didn't simper at him but
kept true to her belligerent self. This wasn't a man who would
respect weakness or false flattery. His flat eyes stared, long
enough that Lulu had to force her itching fingers to stay away
from the gun she'd placed on the desk.

All her instincts screamed danger, and yet Garoux hadn't

done anything threatening. Just a businessman checking in with a few questions, or so it appeared on the surface, but Lulu didn't believe it. One only had to look into the man's eyes to note the cunning and distrust simmering.

Beneath the suave veneer lurked an animal. A man not afraid to get his hands dirty—or bloody.

Tense, she held herself ready, certain at any moment he'd lunge over the desk to grab her in a choke hold or slam her against the wall. Instead, in a mellow voice, he merely asked, "Are you cooking the books?"

"No." The answer left her lips without hesitation.

"Stealing money from me?"

"Never." She might skirt the edge of right and wrong sometimes, but she wasn't a thief.

"Do you know who is?"

"No."

"Care to take a guess?"

"The accountant? Frank the middleman?" She shrugged as she tossed out suggestions. "I really don't know. I didn't even know there was a problem with the books until some city guy showed up claiming he was here to perform an audit."

"So you've met with Mr. Fredrickson?"

"Yes."

"Good, I expect you to comply with his demands."

Not all of them. Work ones yes, but the demands he seemed determined to make of her heart and body? Not happening. "You're not afraid of what he'll find?"

"You'll find, Miss Lamontaine, that I am afraid of nothing. On the contrary, I eagerly await the results. It takes either someone with incredibly big brass balls or very limited intelligence to think they can screw me. I hope you won't make that mistake."

She almost said "You don't scare me," her usual reply to anyone who threatened her, but in this case, she held her tongue, partially. "What will you do if you find whoever is stealing from you?"

A cold smile, his first real expression since he'd invaded her office, pulled his lips wide. The predator in the man rose for a moment to the surface. "Best you don't know."

With those enigmatic words, Garoux left, but questions lingered. It seemed the corruption wasn't something he'd mandated, or so he wanted her to believe. If that was the case, then who was stupid enough to think they could screw him? And who seemed determined to make her look guilty?

Thus far, Lulu had yet to see any of the supposed evidence damning her, but judging by what Broderick had said and Garoux implied, a lot of the blame was being shifted by the accountant to her.

I wonder if I need to pay him a visit. Lulu had never met the man. Only Frank knew who he was. Lulu liked Frank, big and shy, and she had a hard time imagining him plotting such a devious theft. But then again, what better façade to fool them all?

A noise at the door had her raising her head. Expecting it to be Garoux coming back to ask her something, she was caught off guard by the big man leering at her from the doorway. He might have proven handsome if it wasn't for the menace he exuded.

"Well, well. I guess my source who claimed this place would be empty was wrong. Looks like I found myself a Goldilocks."

"My hair is red, moron. And the bar's not open yet. So, turn yourself around and get yourself back outside."

She kept her eyes locked on his as her hand inched toward her gun. But he must have caught the movement because he lunged, and damn, for a guy his size, he was freaking fast!

Lulu just managed to wrap her fingers around the grip of the weapon when he hit the desk, hands outstretched to grab her.

The chair scooted back, the wheels rolling with the momentum, but not far, as her seat hit the wall with a hard thump. Cigarette-tinged breath washed over her face as her attacker grabbed her by the upper arms and tried to immobilize her arm. While she didn't have a great shot, she relied on the element of noise and surprise to favor her.

She fired the gun and was rewarded with a yelped, "Bitch! You shot me."

Nothing vital unfortunately. The angle meant she'd only nicked his leg, but it provided enough distraction for her to jerk herself out of his grip and shimmy out of the chair. She didn't make it around the desk before he was towering over her, his entire brutish frame bristling, his lips curled in a snarl.

"You'll pay for that."

She aimed the gun at his chest as she inched to the open door. "You'll be dead before you reach me," she promised, finger on the trigger.

What she'd not counted on were the arms that wrapped around her from behind and said, "Wrong. You're the only one dying today."

CHAPTER 7

The cops didn't have a clue who had ransacked his cubicle. Neither did Brody. However, it didn't take him long to deduce why.

Almost all of the receipts gathered and given to him for the Tail Waggers' account were gone. Either the thieves had taken them, or they were soaked in urine—and no, he wasn't about to handle those tainted pieces of paper to check.

For sure taken were the printouts of the numbers, the lovely digits lined into neat columns with various mathematical sums keeping them organized. Don't mock him because he geeked out over cool equations. Mock him because he proudly displayed a replica bust of the great Greek mathematician, Pythagoras, in his living room.

The handwritten notes, made with different-colored sticky sheets—coded by question or observation—were MIA as well, but he didn't tell his boss or the cops that. He wasn't in the mood to try and catalogue exactly what the thieves had taken.

Pretending befuddlement proved easy, and he didn't have to fake at all his repugnance as the strong urine stench drove them away from the scene of the crime.

The cops promised to file a report, and his boss ranted—in other words, Perry flushed red and took a deep puff from his inhaler after saying, in a louder tone of voice than usual, "Targeted by tax evaders."

Why else would someone steal receipts and audit reports? In Perry's eyes, the club went from suspect to guilty.

But Brody wasn't as sure.

He relayed nothing of his suspicions aloud. Instead, he echoed his boss. "Those darned thieves." Congratulate him. He managed not to snort. Barely. He could just imagine the color of Perry's face if he told him shape-shifting bears had infiltrated their cubicled haven and destroyed the paperwork in an attempt to weaken the Lycan mob lord's hold on the city.

It sounded crazy even to him.

What surprised him almost as much as the brazen attack was his cell phone didn't have a single voice mail about the incident. Not even to check if the targeting thugs had come after him.

I feel so loved. Not. Worried about his welfare or not, if it were Fabian running this office, he'd have fetched his feline ass himself, probably by the tail, and dragged him in for a peek while growling and promising retribution.

How different the humans handled things.

So different, that when Perry told him to take the rest of the day off, no wait, make that the rest of the week: "Work from home while we get your cubicle sterilized and re-outfitted," Brody didn't argue.

That sounded like a fine plan to him. For one, a certain lady needed tracking down. And two, he did his best work out of the office anyhow.

This unexpected turn of circumstances led to him hitting the club in search of Lulu. It was still really early in the day, and a few hours before it was slated to open, but he drove by the parking lot in case she'd decided to start work early. His intuition proved right. Her car was the only one in the lot.

Sliding his own vehicle alongside, he exited and scanned the area, force of habit for predator shape-shifters. Another tidbit taught by his mentor. Always remain alert. Danger could strike anytime, anywhere. Be prepared.

A glance at the street didn't show anything amiss. Cars parked alongside the curb. A few people roaming the sidewalks. Not many this time of day, given the area only truly came alive at night when the bars opened up.

Nothing jumped out at him, and yet the nagging sense of something amiss wouldn't leave. The front door of the club yielded to a tug, which surprised him given the posted schedule said it wouldn't open for another two hours.

Perhaps Lulu had left it unlocked for expected staff or deliveries. Maybe.

He didn't trust it, especially since he knew how easy it was to slide past most basic defenses. One of his pastimes, which more than one girlfriend had labeled nerdy, was the study of locks, mainly the mechanism behind them. The intricate turn and tumble of pieces to allow access to places and things fascinated him. He made a study of it, and in turn, his knowledge meant he was an expert lock picker, talented enough that he'd even entered and won the competition at the annual Cat Burglar Convention. Open to real cats only.

The most concerning aspect to the unlocked door, though, was the distinct scent, still fresh, and highly recognizable.

Intruder, growled his cat. *Bear.*

The same bear, Brody would wager, that had pissed on his desk and computer.

A bear, here in the club, with Lulu. *Grrr.* He took in a deep breath as he entered, chest filling with protective urgency.

Must find our mate.

Indeed, Lulu might find herself in grave danger if the bears visited with nefarious purpose in mind. *Or she's in cahoots with them.*

Surely not. He didn't believe it for a second. Surely Lulu had told the truth when she claimed to have conducted the business affairs for the club in a responsible and honest fashion.

Although I'm one to talk about honesty. It wasn't as if he'd come clean with the revelation that he worked for Fabian on the side. Sure, Lulu worked in a sense for Fabian as well, but in a much more distant capacity.

I work for the mob. It wasn't every woman who could handle that.

The inside of the club proved quiet. Too quiet. It was also only dimly lit. The entrance was dark, and he didn't get any illumination until he passed the second inner door, also unlocked, and stepped into the main area of the bar. A faint light over the bar shone weakly against the streaked but clean surface of the black granite. The stage, with its red carpet and gleaming silver-plated pole, proved empty of entertainment and nudity.

I wonder if Lulu knows how to dance with that thing. Perhaps she'd give him a private performance.

Once he convinced her to give him a chance.

At the far end of the seating area, a red EXIT sign provided a beacon, but it was the thin sliver of daylight around the door that bothered him. Someone had left the door open.

Sniff. It seemed he'd miscounted—the horror. His nose now discerned the distinct aroma of two bears. They'd come in through two of the entrances. Were they the only ones?

What did they do here? What did they want? Did he need to guard against them, or were they somehow on his side? Perhaps Fabian had sent them, which would make them—

His tiger stopped his circling series of questions with a very simple summation of the situation. *Bite if enemy. No bite if ally. Bite if touching mate.*

Trust his feline to get to the heart of his choices.

In order to make that determination, he needed a better handle on what was happening. At the far end of the bar was a door marked EMPLOYEES ONLY. The handle gave, and he swung it open on well-oiled hinges to reveal an empty hall with a few doors. One labeled DRESSING ROOM, another SUPPLIES, a third door marked as RESTROOM, and the one on the end, OFFICE.

About eight feet from the door, his ears perked as the rumble of voices came to him. Given that the scents he followed grew stronger the closer he got to the office, the more it seemed safe to assume he faced just two male bears.

He paused to strain and listen.

". . . hand me those zip ties for her ankles and wrists. We don't want her escaping in case she wakes up."

"I say we kill her now. Make sure she doesn't wake."

"Remember our orders. No signs of foul play. We have to make this look like an accident."

"Won't the medical examiner notice the bump to her noggin or the fact she was tied?"

Brody tensed at the mention of his mate getting knocked in the head. If she was unconscious, that would explain her silence.

"She'll be at the heart of the fire we're starting in her trash bin. There won't be evidence of nothing except she tried to burn some papers. The fire marshal will rule the flames got out of control and torched her."

Burned alive? Brody winced. Even by bad-guy standards that was pretty darned cruel. Good thing he'd arrived in time to rescue his mate. The thing was, how should he proceed? Outnumbered by bears and him without a weapon. Not that many shifters carried weapons. It was considered unsporting.

As he saw it, he had only a few choices. Waiting until they set the fire, left the office, and came at him in the hall, a narrow passageway that would allow him to tackle them one at a time. Good for him if they were tough, bad for Lulu, as it meant giving the flames a chance to spread and for toxic smoke to choke her.

Another option was to charge into the office. Him against the pair. He'd be at a disadvantage in hand-to-hand combat against the two men. If he remained human. As his tiger, though, he could totally have some fun.

Play with the bears. His inner tiger practically chased its tail in excitement. It did so love teddies, especially when he got a chance to rip out their stuffing.

As a teen, Brody used to go to the county fair, and with his quick reflexes and honed aim, manage to win the giant stuffed animals the carnival games offered. He'd drag the giant blue gorillas home, or the ridged dinosaur painted purple and green. Then he'd swap skin and let his tiger go wild. *Meow*.

Such fun, except when it came time to clean up the fluff. To this day, his mother still swore she vacuumed up bits.

These bears would have the gooey stuffing, which would prove messy. And loud, probably. Here was to hoping Lulu didn't regain consciousness during the battle, or else it might be kind of hard to explain how two bears and a tiger came to be fighting in her office.

Unsure of how much time he had before the bears set the fire, Brody stripped quickly.

He set his things aside, wishing he'd worn track pants and a T-shirt instead of a full suit today. Then again, when he'd woken this morning, eager to see Lulu, he'd wanted to impress her with his white-collar status. He'd not expected he'd have to wear his tiger suit at one point.

Naked, Brody paused for a listen. His breathing stopped as he heard the distinctive click of a lighter. Out of time.

Or not.

Bumbling bears bungling their burglary. Say that fast five times.

"Stupid lighter." *Click. Click. Click.* "I think it's out of gas."

"What do you mean 'it's out of gas'?"

"It hasn't worked in a few days."

"And yet you kept it in your pocket."

"Give a hoot, don't pollute, man. And you know what Smokey says."

"Yeah, he says you're an idiot and a disgrace to bear-kind."

"Got any matches?"

"Why the hell would I carry around matches? Some of us respect our bodies and don't smoke. What happened to that other lighter you had, the green one you've been lighting those cigarettes with?"

"It's in my pack of smokes, which I left in the car."

Slap.

"Ow. What was that for?"

"Being a moron. Get your fat ass out to that car and grab it."

"I'm gonna tell the boss you hit me."

"Go ahead. He'll probably hit you, too, for whining."

"Asshole."

Naked, but still very human, Brody had only seconds before the bear exited the office.

And boy was that thug surprised when he saw a huge Siberian tiger waiting for him with a smile full of sharp teeth.

Brody didn't make a sound. Tigers rarely did on a hunt, but they did so love to pounce.

His front paws hit the man in the chest, and they went down with a hard thump. Unlike a human, though, the man he attacked didn't stay surprised for long. Nor did he remain human. Clothing tore as his opponent's big brown bear burst free.

Teddy! His tiger made a happy chuffing noise.

Now that was more sporting. Brody did so enjoy a challenge. Snarling at the bear's mini roar, they exchanged swipes of their paws. Of course his did more damage. Brody's retractable claws were much sharper and deadlier—he kept them honed on a salvaged piece of wood he kept in his living room that he told visitors was a unique sculpture. Funny what a person could pass off as art.

As he and the bear snarled and snapped at each other, he could hear the other attacker shout, "What the hell is going on out there?"

What were the odds he wouldn't come and see?

Zero.

The other thug stuck his head out of the door. The whites of his eyes widened. "A fucking tiger. Shit. I heard about him. That's Garoux's man. You can't let him leave. Take care of him while I take care of the girl."

The first was laughable. If anyone was gonna get schooled in this battle, it was the bear who squirmed underneath him. But the part that chilled him was the reference to Lulu. Like hell was anyone taking care of her other than him.

Ignoring the furry toy beneath him, Brody sprang for the door, in time to see the other bear furiously shaking and clicking a lighter. Before Brody could pounce, a feeble flame flickered, not much, not long, but enough to ignite the piece of paper held to it.

The thug waved the lit sheet in front of Brody as he stalked closer. "Stay back, furball, or I'll drop it on the girl."

Look who was calling who a furball. Another time, he would have taken the time to get offended and draw the bout out. Given the office reeked of whiskey, an accelerant, this probably wasn't the time. The last thing he wanted in here was a fire.

So he did the only thing he could.

Surrender?

Hell no. He blew.

In his mind, it seemed like the right thing to do. It always worked on his birthday cakes, even as the number of candles increased every year. But on a burning, flaking piece of paper?

Embers scattered, the force of his breath actually brightening them as they drifted, much like dust motes, to settle on the desk and all around. Under usual circumstances, they would have flickered out, a paper firefly run out of fuel. But alcohol was a superfood when it came to feeding flames. Drop even the tiniest ember into a puddle and *whoosh*.

The instant ignition created immediate heat and smoke.

Worse, the alcohol allowed the fire to spread wide and fast. In no time, the flames licked the entire surface of the desk.

Dancing and hot. Very hot. He needed to grab the extinguisher from the hall, but that meant leaving Lulu here with the bears and the flames. He needed to get her to safety first before he attempted to fight the flames.

Who was he kidding? By the time he solved the bear dilemma, got his mate to safety, and returned, the fire would have spread too far.

At this point, the only logical thing left to do was escape.

With Lulu, who thus far lay slumped on the floor still clear of flame, but how long would that last?

It seemed the thug saw his dilemma. "What's it going to be, alley cat? You gonna waste time trying to take me out or save the girl?"

There was never any question. Lulu came first, and yet at the same time, he didn't dare turn his back on the other shifter. He couldn't help Lulu if the bastard clocked him from behind.

Sensing his dilemma, the thug laughed. "Guess we're at an impasse."

Brody snarled and took a step toward the shifter. If he tore the guy's throat out quickly, then he could still change shapes and grab Lulu, making sure they both escaped the spreading flames.

A plan that might have worked better if he'd not assumed the brown bear in the hall would take off.

A heavy body hit him from behind, driving him into the flame-ridden desk. He hit it hard enough that it tilted first away from him then rocked back, spilling some of the burning fuel onto his lovely striped coat.

No.

The burn on his skin, and the retched smell of singeing hair, had him dropping to his side and smothering it. All animals, even shifters, had a healthy fear of fire. A throwback to times when a forest fire could wipe out herds and clans.

While he made sure he didn't turn into a literal tiger, tiger burning bright, the bears left, slamming the door shut behind them.

While he would have liked to chase them, because now he really wanted a bear rug, make that two, for his place, Lulu needed him more.

But she needed a man to carry her out, not a cat.

However, a cat was what she'd get. During his tussle with the bears, or just after, she'd regained consciousness. Big eyes peered at him through the thickening, smoky air.

"What the hell is a tiger doing in my office?" She didn't say anything else as she coughed. Coughed again. She drew the collar of her shirt up to cover her mouth and crawled to the door, smart girl keeping low while muttering, "If you're real, please don't eat me."

If she could get out of here on her own, then he'd have no

reason to reveal his true self yet. Perhaps she'd pass his presence off as a hallucination.

More bad luck. The bears hadn't just closed the door. They'd wedged something under the handle. No matter which way she pushed and pulled and turned at the knob, the damned door wouldn't open.

"Are you freaking kidding me?" she cried, banging open-handed on the door, frustration bubbling. An inhalation of breath had her coughing and doubling over.

Since he couldn't exactly tell her to get out of the way, he head-butted her.

She jumped.

"Holy cow, don't tell me you're real?"

Real enough and big enough that he could throw his body at the door, and while whatever was wedged under the handle didn't give, the frame did.

Which proved good and bad.

Good, she could wrench the door out of the way, the chair beyond it toppling. Bad because all that fresh air got sucked into the room, and the fire behind them whooshed as the smoke billowed.

Lulu slumped, overcome by coughing. He nudged her, pushing her to move up the hall, but she staggered, her steps uneven, her breathing raspy.

She slid down to the floor, her head lolling to the side.

He nosed her.

She didn't get up.

He licked her.

She grumbled but crawled, coughing all the way. His own lungs were getting tighter, and he knew they needed to stop wasting time. He swapped bodies.

Just in time because she slumped to the floor again. Rolling her onto her back, he bent over her to grab her just as her eyes fluttered open.

Puzzlement made her brow crease. "Broderick?"

"Hold on, sweetheart, I got you." Slinging her over his shoulder, he snagged her and did a one-handed grab at his pile of clothes as he moved rapidly up the hall. Shoving open the door allowed fresh air to rush into his starved lungs. But the air in here wouldn't remain clean for long. Of the bears, there was no sign.

The EXIT sign still glowed red at the back. However, the sliver of daylight was gone.

Brody didn't want to emerge onto a street with curious eyes, so he chose the back exit. Before opening the door, though, he took a moment to throw on his pants and his shirt, which he left unbuttoned, but no shoes. His mad grab had netted him only one, and he'd probably look dumb walking around in just one loafer.

And there was no time to go back.

The employee door slammed shut behind him, yet he could still smell the smoke. Was that lit strip coming from under the door the glow of flames?

Time to blow this joint. Flinging Lulu over his shoulder once again, fireman style, Brody hit the bar to the exit door and then cursed as he bounced back.

"Bloody bastards. Don't tell me they blocked this entrance, too." Should he assume they'd probably done something to the front doors as well?

He couldn't really waste time finding out. He gave another shove at the exit door and was gratified by a groan of metal and the appearance, if brief, of daylight. He shoved again, really putting his shoulder to it, and the metal bin placed against the door screeched as it dragged across the concrete ground. He put Lulu down to the side and out of the way before he took a running start at the stubborn door.

He hit the portal, and the bin went sliding with a god-awful sound. But at least he'd gotten them an exit.

Quickly, he scooped up Lulu and carried her out. Luckily, the alley proved clear, and he made it to his car without getting unduly noticed. Even he would have been hard-pressed to explain his half-dressed state, smelling of smoke, and carrying an unconscious girl. Those kinds of stunts he'd left behind during his college days. Good times.

He lay Lulu along the backseat of his practical sedan. Yes, he drove a Cadillac, one inherited after his grandfather died. Some of his friends mocked him for keeping it. It wasn't exactly a cool car for a tiger of his caliber. In his defense, the thing drove like a dream, had all the bells and whistles, and the trunk was big enough for two bodies.

And, yes, he knew this fact from experience.

Right now all his trunk held was an emergency stash of clothes, protein bars, and a blanket. He hopped into the running shoes, sockless to save time, and snagged the woolly blanket. He tossed it over Lulu, hiding her from the casual onlooker. He needed to get her out of here without anyone seeing.

It was pretty clear at this point that—whatever was going on with the club, between the audit and the bears—she was considered dispensable.

Not to him.

But where could he take her to keep her safe? Her place was out of the question. She needed to hide while he sorted things out. His place? Probably not a good idea either since he should also lay low. The bears had intended for them to both die in there.

Their boss wouldn't be too happy when they found out not only Lulu but also a direct link to Fabian had survived. Those bears might come after him again.

Fun. His tiger didn't mind, but he did. Safety for Lulu came first.

So with the most likely spots vetoed, what did that leave?

Less than a half hour later, his boss's bellow was probably heard across a few states: "You mentally defective feline. You brought a human here!"

There went his employee-of-the-month steak dinner.

CHAPTER 8

Waking to find herself in an unfamiliar place was bad enough, but to wake to a man yelling, making the pounding in her head worse? Yeah, she might have lost her cool for a minute.

"Would whoever is shouting shut the hell up? I've got a bloody mariachi band drumming through my mind, and your lack of control over your temper isn't helping it."

The haranguing stopped, and a velvety-smooth voice that sounded kind of familiar said, "Are you seriously telling me to be quiet in my own home?"

Peering with one gritty eye, Lulu could have groaned as she noted the unsmiling countenance of one mob lord. "Not you again." Probably not the most diplomatic thing to say to her boss. "How did I end up here?"

"He"—Garoux jerked a thumb behind him—"brought you. And he's now going to leave with you."

From behind Garoux stepped Broderick. "You know we can't leave. Where would she go?"

"Home."

Broderick shook his head. "I don't think that's a good

idea. I get the impression those thugs from the club were targeting her."

"I happen to agree, but just because she's gotten mixed up with unsavory elements doesn't mean she can stay here."

"Hold on. Back up a minute." She went into a deep coughing fit as she tried to speak. *What's wrong with my throat?*

Last thing she remembered was getting conked on the head. No. Wait. There was more. She remembered fire. Smoke. A tiger?

Her memories were hazy, and she wanted answers, but she could hardly ask questions while hacking up a lung.

Someone thrust a cloth in her hand and said, "Spit."

She did, the awful taste of ash making her grimace, and yet it was seeing who held the cloth that made her cheeks burn bright. Nothing screamed sexy like hacking up something gross in front of a cute guy.

"Better?" Broderick asked, not seeming to mind her less-than-ladylike act as he smoothed the hair from her brow.

Not trusting herself to speak, she nodded.

"That might feel better, but I'll bet your throat is super dry after that smoke." Broderick craned his head and said, "Can I get a glass of water? Make that two. I could use something to soothe my throat, too."

"Here. Try this."

It was a glass of white wine, but parched, Lulu grabbed it. Thirsty, so thirsty. She gulped it, but the strong flavor hit her hard, and she choked, spewing out a large mouthful . . . right on Broderick.

The wine dribbled in wet streams down his soot-covered

face. He grimaced, but his expression held mirth. "I think we should have waited for the water."

"No kidding. That was a Louis Jadot. Not a mouthwash meant for gargling and spitting." Garoux took back the glass, affronted at the waste. "I'll go get some water. Try not to spit on the carpet. It's a lot more expensive than the wine." Garoux left the room as Broderick continued to stroke the hair from her forehead.

If she wasn't feeling so weak, she might have slapped his hand away. It was a rather intimate gesture. However, she was feeling kind of benevolent toward him at the moment. And she liked his gentle touch.

Voice still rough, but somewhat soothed by the wine, she rasped out, "What happened to me?"

"I'm not sure what happened before I arrived. I got to the club, and you were collapsed in the hall. I carried you outside."

Something nagged. Something he'd said or not said. Whatever it was tickled the edge of her mind and took a backseat to a more pressing truth. "You came into a burning building and saved me?" Tough as nails or not, Lulu was girly enough to find pleasure in that. When she forced her brain—and ignored its pounding protest—she managed a vague recollection of seeing him before he lifted her to his shoulder. He had carried her out. But that vague recollection was nothing compared to the much more vivid memory of the giant tiger in her office who'd smashed down her office door and then licked her when she'd taken a break from crawling to escape. "What about the tiger?"

"Tiger? What tiger?" Brody uttered a small laugh. A false one.

"The one that helped me escape."

He averted his gaze. "Wow, you must have really inhaled a lot of that smoke. There was no tiger there."

"What about those guys? The ones who clocked me?" The ones he'd alluded to, and yet, by his own words, hadn't he arrived after they'd left? How did he know about them? And what about the club? Was the fire contained?

"The bar?" She sat up. "Is it all right? Did someone call 911?"

"The fire was put out, and they think the building was saved, but the bar won't be open for a while. The fire gutted the back end of it pretty good. We won't know the true extent of the damage until the place cools down and the inspectors can get in to assess. They'll need to check the structure to see if it's safe to renovate."

"Was anyone hurt?"

Brody didn't immediately answer, using Garoux's reappearance to stall. Lulu eagerly took the glass of water offered, the tall glass tumbler cool in her hands. The liquid was cold and refreshing as it slid down her burning throat. The water held a hint of mint and an almost medicinal aftertaste.

Is Garoux trying to drug me? She forced herself to stop drinking to ask, "What's in the water?"

"Nothing nefarious, I assure you. Simply a healing brew we keep on hand."

"On account of he likes to yell a lot and give himself a sore throat." Broderick's mock whisper and accusation almost made her giggle—which was totally out of character. A fear it would send her into another coughing fit had her biting her tongue instead.

What she did ask, again, was, "Did anyone get hurt in the fire?"

"Not exactly."

"What's that supposed to mean?"

Broderick shot Garoux a look. Why would he look to the other man in the first place? Exactly how did they know each other, and why would Broderick bring her here? It occurred to her rapidly clearing brain that the pair seemed well acquainted. Well acquainted enough to share a secret. Her gut insisted there was something afoot here. Was Broderick working for Garoux? But in what capacity?

What use could a mob lord have for an investigative accountant?

What about bribing him to look the other way if he finds something?

Was Broderick a criminal? She sure hoped not. Criminals belonged behind bars, not featured in her lusty fantasies.

"No one was technically hurt," Broderick finally replied. "However, given your car was found in the club's parking lot and that you haven't checked in, for the moment, you're presumed dead in the fire."

Now there was an unexpected answer. "I can't be dead!"

"Calm down, sweetheart. You won't be dead for long. Once the fire investigators get into the building, they'll soon realize there's no body."

"Or even quicker than that, we can call someone and let them know I'm alive."

Again, Garoux and Broderick shared a look. "Or not."

"What do you mean, 'not'?"

A "bah!" sound emerged from Garoux. "Use your head, girl. Someone was out to kill you."

"We can't be sure of that. I wasn't supposed to be there. Maybe their goal was to burn down the club, and I just happened to get in the way."

"Perhaps," Garoux conceded. "In that case, why don't you call the cops to let them know you're okay and then go home? Give me a call in the morning if you're still alive."

"What's that supposed to mean?"

Broderick shifted to block Garoux from her line of sight. A much better view, even if his dirt-striped face wasn't his most attractive look. "What my boss is not so eloquently saying is if we let the world at large know that you're not dead, and you were the target, then those thugs might try again."

She finished the summation. "But if they think I'm dead, then maybe we can draw them out and have them arrested?"

"Yeah, something like that. Except without the 'we' part. You won't be doing anything but laying low."

She struggled to a sitting position. "You are not going after these guys yourself. They're criminals. Murderers. And you're a . . ." She stalled on what to call him, a name that wouldn't emasculate him. Yes, Brody had some awesome qualities, bravery coming to mind, given he'd saved her at obvious peril to himself. But it was one thing to act the hero and another to play the part of hunter.

A numbers guy, Broderick was better suited to office shenanigans than violent ones involving unsavory sorts. Yet she seemed to have forgotten Broderick didn't work alone.

"Brody's a wily cat. He'll land on his four paws. Or lose another life. Either way, I have the utmost belief he can take care of himself and track down these unsavory bears. I mean, bastards."

Bears? Funny how Garoux's slip of the tongue brought

back a fuzzy recollection of two furry bodies wrestling out in the hall by her office.

A tiger and a bear? *I really should get myself to a hospital and get checked for a concussion.*

And she really needed to get to a phone to let someone know where she was. Certain people would get worried when she didn't check in.

And Daddy's never been good at keeping that itchy trigger finger of his still.

CHAPTER 9

It didn't take a genius to see the questions clouding Lulu's green eyes. Nor did it take much of a whiff for him to recognize they both needed a shower. And, no, it wasn't an ulterior motive to get her naked. Mostly.

"You know what, why don't we get cleaned up? Refresh ourselves and we'll talk about this when we're not so gross."

"Is this your way of telling me I stink?" She arched a brow at him.

"No, it's my way of getting you naked." He winked at her round O of surprise. He didn't ask permission as he slid his arms under her knees and upper body. As he lifted her from the couch, she made a protesting sound but at the same time flung her arms around his shoulders.

"What are you doing?" she asked.

"Yeah, what are you doing?" Fabian asked.

While Brody had filled his boss in on a few key facts, he'd forgotten to mention one. He did so over his shoulder as he took Lulu from the room. "Taking my mate to the blue room to get clean." And then dirty, if he was lucky.

However, that would depend on Lulu. She seemed mostly recovered from her smoky mishap, if still hoarse. The sexy growl to her voice, though, just rendered her more attractive.

Except when she used it for speaking things other than sweet nothings. "Why are you carrying me? I am perfectly capable of walking."

"But you don't know where you're going." A good answer that she poked a hole in.

"I could have followed."

"It's quicker this way. And besides, your shoes are filthy. You wouldn't want to make more work for the cleaning staff."

Even she couldn't refute that logic. "I guess. Why are we here, Broderick, in Fabian Garoux's home?"

"I think you've known me long enough to call me Brody."

"How about Fluffy because you're just as annoying as my neighbor's bloody dog?"

"A dog? You're comparing me to a dog?" The horror.

"Well, you do act like one at times. Always sniffing around me. Making dirty suggestions. Panting with your tongue practically on the floor the few times we've been together."

"Since when is it a crime for a man to display his interest in an attractive woman?"

"It's not. You were just asking why I compared you to a dog."

"I think I've got more in common with a cat."

"Because?"

"I always land on my feet. I've got feline grace. Awesome fur. And if you stroke me the right way, I might purr."

"I changed my mind. You're a pig."

"And you're a brat?" He growled, hoisting her from his arms up over his shoulder in one fell move.

She let out a squeak. "Put me down."

"No." He followed his refusal with a slap to her round bottom.

Another squeal left her. "Don't you dare do that again."

Slap. "Or?"

"I'll hurt you."

With what, the worst case of blue balls ever? Too late. He already suffered from those. He couldn't help it. He gave her another smack and then a smooth caress of his hand over her cheeks.

She squirmed but couldn't escape his grip. "Oh, you wait until I get my hands on you."

"I'd love your hands on me. You could start by stripping me. Then, when we're both naked, we could wrestle. If I pin you, I get a prize."

"You're impossible." She groaned. She hit him with a closed fist against his lower back. It might have really hurt a punier man . . . or a human.

Brody just laughed. "You'll have to do better than that," he teased.

So she did. For a moment, he almost stumbled, giving lie to his claim of feline grace. But then again, the fact that she lifted his shirt and exposed his skin and then placed her mouth on it seemed a good reason in his mind. She touched him, with her mouth.

So she could bite him!

"Ow!" he bellowed, his body twisting at the hard chomp, more out of shock than actual pain.

"I'll bite you again if you don't put me down."

"What about I put you down if you do promise to bite again?" was his reply as he finally located the door he wanted. He spun the handle and opened the portal, stepping into the plush blue room, which he used on the occasions he spent the night and wasn't in the mood—or a state—to drive home.

With one foot, he kicked the door shut. Privacy, at last.

"You want me to bite you? What is wrong with you?"

"Too many things to list." He let her slide down the length of his body, setting her on her feet before him but keeping his hands on her waist so she couldn't go anywhere.

Her breath caught, a stutter that had nothing to do with the lingering effects of the fire but more to do with the arousal surrounding her in a musky scent. "What's your relationship with Garoux?"

There was an unexpected question. "He's my mentor."

"I heard you call him your boss."

"That, too. I've known Fabian since I was a child. Since I didn't have a father growing up, he kind of provided a role model."

"A mob lord as a role model? And your mother allowed it?"

"You just know the Fabian that the media paints."

"Are you going to deny he runs the city's mob?"

"Yeah, he's leader of the pack, but he's not a bad guy. Tough, yes, but not evil like some other dudes out there."

"And that's supposed to make his illegal activities okay?"

"Who says he's doing anything illegal?" Brody countered. "Why this interest in my boss? What you should be more concerned with is whether I'm going to kiss you or not."

The change in subject had her eyes widening. She opened her mouth to . . . protest? Accept? He didn't know. Didn't care.

He stole the words by kissing her. To his delight, she kissed him back!

Soft lips parted and let him suck on tender flesh. He nibbled her mouth, inhaled her stuttering breath, wrapped her tightly in his arms.

How right she felt, a soft, plush armful of woman, his woman, a woman who tasted of ash.

It occurred to him that the only thing better than kissing Lulu would be kissing Lulu naked under massaging hot jets of water.

Not breaking their embrace, he lifted her from the floor by keeping his hands on her waist and straightening. She was tiny next to his larger frame. Tiny, yet tough.

She nipped his lower lip. "Where are you going?"

"Hot shower." Two magic words.

One big reward. Her tongue. Sinuous and slippery, her tongue invaded first, stroking across his and drawing a groan. As he fumbled for the water control knob in the shower, she sucked on him, stringing his desire for her so taut he thought he might explode from the tension.

As the water spewed forth, cold initially while the warm stuff made its way, he let his hands yank at the hem of her shirt. She unlaced her arms from around his neck and allowed him to peel it from her.

As he flung it to the side, his curious cat couldn't help but ask, "Are you okay with this?" If she said no, he might lose a life in the process because he'd surely die if he didn't get to touch her.

"A smart girl would slap you and leave. But I barely passed my classes with Cs and a girl's got needs. Consider this your lucky day."

Lucky? He'd hit the damned jackpot. He couldn't believe

she wasn't arguing or forcing him to resort to his most seductive tricks.

On the contrary, their roles had almost reversed. Now it wasn't only him kissing and touching and stripping. He couldn't help but stiffen when her hands reached for the waistband of his track pants just as he reached for hers. He almost shuddered in delight as she tugged the cottony fabric down over his hips, getting caught on his shaft. She worked it free, and his cock sprang out, slapping her tummy in the process. She laughed as she caught it with one hand.

"Eager?"

"Since the moment I met you, sweetheart." So true. He'd not been able to stop thinking of her since their first meeting.

She stroked a slim hand up the length of him. "I should lie and say I don't want you."

"But?"

She sighed. "While I find myself often irritated by your antics, I am still stupidly attracted to you."

"Because it's fate."

"Or a sign I let my lack of a sex life go on too long."

Mine. No other man would ever touch his woman. From here on out, Lulu would have the most active sex life imaginable, and since theirs was a true mating, the craving would only get stronger.

Stripped of clothing, they stepped into the shower, the hot spray striking at the top of their heads and sluicing down their bodies. Numerous jets fired, rotating streams, pummeling their bodies from two directions at once.

Lulu laughed. "Oh my god. This shower is amazing."

Not as amazing as her. She tilted her head back into the water, closing her eyes, letting the water stream over the creamy skin of her face. Her usually curly red hair straightened in the wetness, the bright red darkening in hue and stretching down to almost tickle the top of her ass.

A water nymph with the most glorious set of breasts. The perfect globes called to him, and he cupped the pair, weighing them in his palms as his thumbs stroked the tips to erection.

A soft sigh parted her lips, and she arched her upper body, offering herself to him. He wasn't about to refuse.

He bent his head and took the tip of a nipple into his mouth. A tremor went through her. He latched on, his mouth sucking at the erect bud, his teeth grazing her sensitive skin.

She clasped his head against her breast while making moans of encouragement. He switched to the other side, lavishing it with the same attention, but this time, wrapping an arm around her waist to steady her as her knees weakened and she wobbled.

He pressed her against the wall with the alcove for soap and shampoo, an anchor to prop her that he might continue his exploration. Down his lips traveled, away from the berries that tasted so sweet, farther down to the cream he could smell and wanted to lick.

A nuzzle of her mound had her twitching her hips. They were past words, but it didn't mean the shower enclosure remained silent. She panted. She moaned. She sucked in a breath when he flicked his tongue against her pussy.

"Spread your legs for me." The softly murmured command had her spreading them, not arguing for once. Why argue against something they both wanted?

Exposed to him, her pussy beckoned. It needed a lick. A nice, long lick.

"Oh."

A longer lick with a flick.

"Oh." More deeply uttered.

A rapid back and forth against her pleasure button and he almost got knocked backward as her hips thrust forward. But he kept his balance, in no little part because she aggressively held him by the hair, anchoring him in place, making a very clear demand that he not stop.

As if he'd stop licking her so soon. He'd just started, and his plan was to not stop until she came. Given the tension in her body and the raggedness of her breath, it wouldn't take much more to push her over the edge.

The flavor of her enticed, a womanly ambrosia like no other. It aroused him, and his cock pulsed between his thighs while his sac hung heavy.

Her keening cry went well with the shuddering of her body as she climaxed against his mouth and tongue. He reveled in the way she trembled, giving herself to him, trusting herself with him. How beautiful she appeared in that moment.

Despite her evident pleasure, he did not stop the flicks of his tongue. He kept her quivering and crying out. He flicked her swollen button and caught it with his lips. Her fingers tore at his hair, her hips bucking in his grip.

He could wait no longer.

Rising, he lifted one of her legs, wrapping it around his hip and opening her to him, exposing her to his cock. He nudged the entrance to her sex, pushing against the swollen, trembling flesh and sucking in a breath at the tight suction of her channel as he drove his shaft in.

Tight. Hot. Pulsing.

It was almost more than he could bear. But he pushed on, pushed in, deeper, sheathing himself fully in her glorious body.

She murmured small words of encouragement, dirty words that only raised his frenzied level of excitement.

Soon, he found himself pounding her soft flesh, sinking to the hilt. Her sex fisted him delightfully, the muscles of her channel gripping him so tightly. In and out he thrust, and while their lower bodies connected, so did their lips.

He knew she must taste herself on him, and yet she didn't pull away. She embraced him back just as fiercely, her passion still wild and beautiful. A passion for him.

She's mine. His woman. Oh yes.

The thought had him leaving the glory of her mouth for the soft hollow between her neck and shoulder. The skin felt like silk under his lips. He latched onto it, sucking his chosen spot, even as his hips pistoned, driving his cock in and out of her welcoming body.

Her fingers scrabbled at his back, clawing at him as her own pleasure reached its peak again. And when she came that glorious second time, he joined her, his whole body rigid in that moment, frozen within her as his seed spilled forward.

And his teeth sank into her skin, breaking it. Marking it. Claiming her.

Mine.

Rawr.

CHAPTER 10

Waking on the plush bed, Lulu stretched, muscles pleasantly sore because she'd had sex with Broderick.

Damn. I had sex with Brody.

What was I thinking?

She was thinking it felt good, and right, and amazing. Even now, with her mind clear, her body sated, she couldn't regret the bout of passion they'd shared first in the shower and then the bed. The man was a tiger in the sack.

She even had the bite mark to prove it. At least he'd done it on her shoulder, which meant she could easily hide it. However, she hoped she could wipe the silly grin from her lips, an annoying side effect it seemed, which happened whenever she thought of him.

What a ridiculously girly reaction, but she couldn't help it. The guy was too cute to hate, too fun to hurt, too sexy to resist.

He was also a criminal working with the city's mob.

Aw, hell. What did I get myself into? Trouble, for one. She rolled onto her stomach and buried her face in the pillow then uttered a deep groan.

Stupid. So stupid. How could she have allowed herself to

get involved with Brody? Hormones weren't an excuse. She should have had better control, but in her defense, she blamed him for her insane attraction. Stupid jerk was just too freaking cute, and to add even more fuel to that fire, how could a girl resist a guy who asserted they were soul mates? Meant to be together. Forever.

It was enough to make her groan again, not because of his clingy assertion but more because she kind of wished it were true. While not usually given to fantasy wishes of a happily and totally romantic ever after, pragmatic Lulu couldn't deny its appeal.

How would it feel to be the focus of one man, a man she found equally attractive? Wait, she already knew. It felt great. Wonderful. She never wanted it to end.

Sigh. But that would never happen. They came from two vastly different mind-sets. His secret was damning, but then again, so was hers. Once he found out what she hid, he'd ditch her faster than she could bend over to distract him.

It amused—and flattered her—that Brody was distracted by pretty, shiny things, or in her case, naked and inviting. She'd discovered her power over him the previous night when she left the bed to use the bathroom. In the midst of talking to her, telling her, of all things, about the time he'd streaked naked through his neighborhood and then for weeks after put up with seventy-seven-year-old Mrs. Hinklesmith winking at him, she emerged from the bathroom, still completely bare skinned. Spotting her shirt, which somehow got kicked out of the bathroom, she stooped to snag it. She flashed him big time, and he reacted by stopping midsentence and staring. Then crooking a finger.

She never did find out if Mrs. Hinklesmith stopped her flirting.

However, the knowledge of how to throw him off track proved valuable. But would it be enough to diminish her secret if he ever found out?

Speaking of secrets. Right now the world still believed she'd perished in the fire. Even if they didn't, no one knew where she was. Not good. If she didn't want Daddy going on a rampage to hunt her down—and he would, possibly accidentally killing people in the process—then she needed to get to a phone. *Except my phone is back at the club in my office where the fire started.* She sighed as dread slumped her at the thought of calling and filling out the necessary paperwork to cancel bank and credit cards, as well as getting a new driver's license issued.

Lacking a purse with her stuff didn't mean she still didn't want a phone. Surely there was one around here somewhere.

Rolling to her side, she took stock of the room. She didn't sense anyone around, but it never hurt to take a peek, especially given how quietly the men she'd met over the past few days moved. It didn't take long to confirm she appeared alone. No sign of the growly sexy Brody. A shame.

Wrong answer. It was good he'd left. She had calls to make. Calls he shouldn't hear. She also needed to find a way to put distance between them. She needed to fight his allure, a task that would prove a lot easier if she wasn't naked when she met him.

When she sat up, the soft linen sheet fell to her waist, baring her upper body and triggering an automatic reflex to cover her boobs with her arms. Nakedness wasn't something

Lulu indulged in much. At home, she always wore at least a T-shirt and panties.

If people were going to be around, then she covered up, which some might find ironic since she worked in a strip club. But never mind where she worked. She always felt better and more prepared when armed with clothes.

Of course, clothes weren't something she spotted as she peered around. Even her dirty shirt from the night before seemed to have vanished. Brody tidying up before leaving?

He didn't seem the type. First of all, he was a guy. The guys she knew were pretty lazy when it came to housework. Lulu once asked her mother why she didn't shove her dad's straying socks into his mouth while he snored at night. Her mother laughed and said boys will be boys. A pushover? Not really. Mother got him back in more devious ways.

Relaxing at home for the Super Bowl? Aunt Henny came over with her three little boys, who were in a cops-and-robbers phase that involved lots of siren noises.

I wonder what bad habits Brody has if dirty laundry is off the list. She'd need something to use against him.

A startling thought, given not a moment ago she'd made a vow to stay away from him. The geeky mobster had a way of slipping under her defenses and disarming her.

Focus on the now. She needed to contact some people and let them know she lived. On her second glance around the room, she spotted a cordless phone nestled in a charging cradle on a side table across from the bed.

It took her a moment to decide. Should she streak naked across the fifteen feet or so to make her call—and possibly still be naked when Brody walked in? Maybe he'd take her in his arms and . . .

Clothed it was. She peered at the soft sheet pooled in her lap. She dragged the hem to her neck, covering her upper body. It would do.

She mentally apologized to whoever would have to remake the bed, but she wasn't comfortable wandering around without a stich on in a mobster's house—in the hopes of seducing a certain geeky one—and she certainly couldn't imagine calling her contact while in the buff.

Wouldn't the boys who knew her have some choice things to say? Until she punched them in the face to make them eat their words, or outshot them on the range. Don't judge her too harshly. Her father had wanted a son. He got Lulu. She didn't really mind. Her dad loved her. However, given his expectations, it meant Lulu had to be twice as tough. Not everyone could handle it. Her mother certainly tried to get her to swing in a more girly direction. However, with her wild red mop and her lack of interest in fashion or makeup, Lulu often missed the girly-girl mark. But, for her mother, she'd made an effort, and now that she was older, was glad her mother had encouraged a softer side to her persona. A softer side that emerged naturally with Brody. Not that he seemed to care which side he got. He always smiled around her.

Except when he was saving me from that fire. The grim determination she recalled was possibly even sexier.

Distracted again. Argh. *Get your butt moving.* Sheet wrapped toga-style, she shuffled to the phone, cursing as her feet tangled in the large swath of fabric. She plopped into the velvety, blue, corduroy-covered club chair perched alongside a square wooden table. She couldn't help but run a finger along its shiny wooden surface. Someone had polished it so well it reflected her appearance.

Straggly hair with swollen lips from too many—not enough!—kisses. In other words, a mess.

Good thing no one could see that on the other end of the phone. She dialed the memorized number, and the line rang four times before someone picked up.

"Sal's Pizzeria. Home of the best deep dish in town."

Not even close. Her aunt Cecily owned that place, but she wasn't calling to argue the claim. "Is Sal there?" she asked the unfamiliar voice who answered. As she held the phone pressed to her ear, she found herself constantly glancing in the direction of the door leading to the hall. It remained shut, which begged the question: Was it locked? Guarded? Or was she exaggerating her situation because of what she thought of Garoux?

This situation was unique. Exactly how did a guest, and still technically an employee of a mob lord, get treated?

And where had Brody gone?

As she waited on the phone, her glance strayed to the left, where the door to the bathroom gaped wide. She'd not checked in there before dialing. Could Brody be in there, perhaps brushing his teeth?

Taking only shallows breaths, she strained for the slightest sound. Nothing. However, not hearing anything didn't mean he'd left the room. Or that eyes didn't watch.

Shit. Secret cameras. Too late to worry about those now, given what had happened the night before, but the possibility that they watched her now, maybe even listened, meant she needed to maintain extreme caution. Until she better understood her situation, she should play it safe.

A scramble of a phone getting handed off yanked her attention back.

"Sal here. Who is this?"

She recognized the gruff voice. "Hey, Sal. It's me, Lulu."

"Lulu!" The shock in his voice said it all. Nobody knew for certain she was alive yet. "Where the hell are you? The boys have been out looking for your ass in case you weren't in that fire."

"I'm all right." Barely, but she didn't expound on that. "A friend of mine came to my rescue at the club and took me to a safe place."

"Safe where?"

"I can't say." Not out loud, a precaution in case electronic spies recorded. "I just wanted to let you know I was okay. Mind passing the word around and letting everyone know?" Most especially, her father. Daddy dear wasn't always rational when it came to his daughter. In that respect, he treated her like a princess. He liked coming to her rescue, and then, once he got her home, paced and lectured her, asking how she could have avoided the situation in the first place.

The only way to avoid this situation was to avoid Broderick. What a crappy plan.

"I'd feel better if we saw you were fine for ourselves," Sal replied.

"You'll have to take my word for it. Tell you what, when I get out of here, we'll get together for some Italian. But not that place with the spicy sausage. I want the mellow one." Code for: I'm currently guesting with the mob, but I don't think I'm in danger. Or was the clue too subtle for Sal to pick up?

Apparently he did grasp her reference. "Italian? Bah, I'm more in the mood for some Greek." A less polite way of saying: Do you need us to screw someone?

"We'll figure that out later, Sal. I gotta go. Say hi to the gang for me, and I'll be around soon." She hung up before Sal could argue and sat for a moment in the chair, wondering about her next move.

Broderick seemed intent on keeping her at Garoux's house. While the mobster might have great security, Lulu was more concerned about him. Brody seemed to imply she had nothing to fear, and yet she'd heard the stories about the guy. Everyone had. The newspapers loved him because he provided fodder like that big case last year.

A gang from out west came to town. And they weren't quiet about it. Robberies went up overnight. Gun violence sparked. People feared walking the streets.

But not for long.

It wasn't long before certain gang members went missing. Rumors swirled about a wild pack of dogs being sent to kill. Attack dogs under Garoux's control, used to scare people into line, a bold claim supported by several supposed witnesses, and yet not a trace of those canines was ever found with any of the search warrants.

The media outlets went wild with the news that wild wolves with big bite radii were on the loose, cleaning up the criminal element. Whatever the real truth was, the deaths stopped after a few months, the gang tucked tail and left town, and the crime waves stopped. Garoux remained the uncontested king of the city.

A man like that might hide behind a veneer of civility, but he wouldn't hesitate to act. But what about Brody? Did he have that same hard core?

A core I also have. Lulu also knew how to act with ruthless determination. She just stopped short of deadly force to get her point across.

But nothing had worked against the two thugs who'd accosted her in her own office.

How it galled that they'd managed to surprise her. Took her down with barely a fight. It made a girl want to shave her head in shame. Not that she would. The last time she did that, when she was nine, her mother had the salon weave pink braids to cover the bald streak.

Back to the thugs though. Their attack made no sense. She took a moment to remember what had happened, to try and see if she'd missed a motive.

As far as she could recollect, they'd made no actual demands. A usual robbery would have gone after cash, or her purse. Perverts would have restrained her for rape. But these guys seemed more intent on destruction, and focused it on her office. And they made sure she was in it.

What were they after? Did they truly seek to kill her like Brody claimed, or was it simply a matter of her being in the wrong place at the wrong time?

Now that I've seen their faces, am I truly in deadly danger?

The answer to that would allow her to know if she could safely leave or not.

Speaking of leaving, I wonder if that door is locked or not.

In her sarong-sheet dress, she minced to the door and turned the handle. It opened, so well oiled there wasn't even a hint of a squeak as she swung it open.

She poked her head out and noted the sun-dappled hallway lined with closed doors. Not a soul stirred, but she still ducked back in.

Shutting the door, she leaned against it and debated her next move. Not a prisoner. Knowing she could leave took a load off her mind. It also made her itch to leave the room and find out what the heck was going on.

Aren't you forgetting something? She peered down. *Oh yeah, my awesome dress.* She couldn't wander around in a sheet. That was too weird even by her standards. Maybe there was a robe in the bathroom, or she'd find her clothes.

She poked her head in the bathroom. Nothing to see except towels. Fresh ones. The wet ones they'd used and dropped on the floor in their hurry to make it to bed were gone, probably in the laundry chute she found when she yanked on a handle in the wall.

Cool. She didn't know anyone with one of those. What a bummer it was too small to fit her. Not only might it have provided a discreet escape route—with possible clean clothing at the end—but it might also have proven fun. At least it always looked awesome in the movies. *Whee.*

Funny part was she could practically picture Brody teasing her to try it.

Wandering back into the room, she eyed the sliding door to the closet. As a guest room, it probably wouldn't have anything. But it didn't hurt to check.

Aha!

Sliding it open she came across shirts hung neatly, pants folded on the creases and suspended, with matching jackets: a full-on suit for the nerd-on-the-go. Lucky for her, though, the closet wasn't just packed with business attire for a man. The shelves at the side contained more comfortable gear, soft cotton T-shirts and track pants, both of which proved too big when pulled on.

Cinching the waist tight only served to bunch the fabric oddly about her waist, but then again, the rolled cuffs on the legs wouldn't help her win any fashion competitions.

The T-shirt fit a bit better, still large but the cotton material had room for her breasts. Now if only her nipples would stop reacting to every slight sensation. Brody had enjoyed himself a lot with them. The soft cottony rub had them peaking to attention.

So it was with nip-ons, straggly bed head, and lumpy pants that she met the perfectly attired Broderick, who took one look at her and laughed.

CHAPTER 11

So perhaps it was not the brightest thing to laugh at a woman he'd spent the night worshipping.

But seriously, when he opened the door, the last thing he expected to see was her, dressed in ill-fitting clothes, striking a battle stance with her hair standing out in every direction in a wild halo of red.

She looked adorable, which, in turn, made him happy. Until he recalled the phone call she'd just made. Guilt twinged him a little for spying. However, it wasn't targeted specifically at her but part of the entire house's security measures.

So, yes, he'd listened at his boss's behest. While appearing innocuous on the surface, he didn't need to see Fabian's tight lips to know the entire conversation was a sham. Lulu hid something, and he'd been tasked with finding out what.

"Where have you been?" she asked, her gaze focused on the tray. His cat meowed with indignation. Nice to know the food he carried caught her attention more than him.

He truly was a besotted idiot. Now if only he could say the same of her. While he had fate making it easy for him to succumb to his feelings, she was human. She'd need seduc-

tion the old-fashioned way. While sex and conversation provided a good start, keeping her happy ranked as the most
important.

"I wrangled us some food. Hungry?" He waggled the
offering and felt a bit like a pied piper as she followed him
to the table flanked by club chairs. Setting it down, he tried
to think of a way to broach her phone call without letting
on that he knew about it.

"So when are you going to ask me who Sal is?" she asked
as she finished chewing on a piece of toast.

He spewed out his mouthful of orange juice, thankfully
not on her. The drapes, however, behind the table didn't fare
so well.

"What do you mean? Who's Sal?"

"Oh, come on. You've been fidgeting like a cat on a hot
tin roof since you came in here with the food. It's obvious
you're uncomfortable about something. You know I made a
call."

"Are you accusing me of spying on you?" Did he look as
guilty as he sounded? Suave amongst predators, but in front
of her, he was a clumsy kitten.

"No, I don't think you set out to spy on me, but your boss
would, and I'm going to wager you both heard my phone call
and he asked you to find out who Sal is."

Was there any point in hiding the truth? "Just so you
know, bugging the phones is standard with all of his homes
and businesses. Fabian is a tad paranoid about his security."

"And nosey."

"Yeah, he's nosey all right." And more accurate than a
bloodhound. "I gotta admit, though, he's got a point being

suspicious. I mean, you didn't exactly call a family member or something to let them know you were alive. You called a pizza place at ten in the morning."

She took another bite of toast and chewed slowly before answering. "It's complicated. And I wish I could tell you more, but—"

The wail of sirens had her eyes widening.

He knew that sound. "What the hell are the cops doing here?" Brody leaned over to peek out the window and watched a trail of cop cars, and even a SWAT team truck, come screaming up the long driveway. But he didn't clue in on the truth until she said, "I told them I was okay. They weren't supposed to come here."

He whipped around to face her. "What do you mean you told them? You called the cops? Why? I told you that you weren't a prisoner. The damned door was unlocked."

"I know. Like I said, they weren't supposed to come. I just had to let them know I was okay."

"When the hell did you call them?" Then it hit him. "Sal. The pizzeria. It's a front, isn't it?" She couldn't meet his gaze, and the rest of the truth hit him harder than the time he fell out of a tree and hit the driveway. "Oh my freaking god, you're a cop, aren't you?"

He waited for a reply, wondering what it would be. However, it turned out Lulu didn't need to say a word. It was written all over her slumped body and the first time Brody had ever seen her so defeated and by the most unexpected weapon of all, the truth.

It blew him away. "I can't believe I didn't know. Shit, Fabian is going to kill me. I brought a cop into his house. How could you hide this from me?" Yeah, he might have sounded a little betrayed there.

"I was undercover. I couldn't tell you."

"Oh, this is bad. I'm involved with a cop." This time he said it with more of a bewildered air. Talk about unexpected.

She took offense at his words. "This wouldn't be a problem if you weren't associated with a mobster," she snapped, her momentary docility at getting ousted vanishing beneath outrage. She'd found her inner fighter.

Good. He didn't like to see her cowed.

He'd also like to keep seeing her alive, which, given police were outside and the doorbell was ringing, would probably put Fabian in a foul mood.

"Fabian isn't a mobster or a criminal." *He's a werewolf.* He kept those words to himself. Would she think that Fabian's being a Lycan was better or worse?

Forget asking her right now. Until he knew where she stood, he couldn't tell her any more. To reveal life-changing secrets at this point, as she was about to get reunited with her brothers in blue, didn't seem prudent. The last thing he and other shape-shifters needed was her spilling about their existence until she understood the importance of keeping their secret.

"Even if he's not a hardcore criminal, he's not exactly pristine."

"Name someone who is." She opened her mouth, but he didn't let her speak. "And don't tell me you are."

"I am a law-abiding citizen and an officer entrusted to uphold the rules."

"Ha." He snorted. "This from the girl working in a strip

bar who took out a guy in the parking lot the other day. I'm going to wager you've bent your fair share of the laws. Even cops sometimes skirt the edge of legal."

"For the greater good."

"And who's to say that the actions Fabian takes aren't also for the greater good, a good I'd like to tell you about, but right now might not be the best moment. We've got company."

He could hear them pounding on the front door demanding entrance. Fabian was a smart one. A true survivor with a glib tongue. He'd handle the cops at the door. If they proved reasonable.

The rumble of voices came to his acute hearing, but no signs of violence—yet. However, tempers could too easily flare with the wrong actions. How desperate were the humans downstairs? They'd certainly wasted no time getting here. Were they looking for an excuse to get rough and blame his boss?

If they are here on a mission of rescue, then there's one easy solution. One both man and tiger didn't like. In order to diffuse the situation, Lulu needed to show herself.

She came to the same conclusion. "I guess I should go present myself and prove that I'm okay."

Easy enough to do, but then what? Cover blown, Lulu had no reason to stay, and Garoux certainly would expect her to go.

One big problem with that. Brody didn't want her to leave, and not because of the bears who'd threatened her. She was his mate.

She was a cop.

Still didn't change anything. *She's mine.*

And damn, my grandma is going to have a fit.

CHAPTER 12

Lulu could have happily throttled Mahoney. Her father's best friend stood in the front hall conversing with Fabian, certainly not arresting anyone and acting much too chummy with the crime lord for her liking.

The worst part was she couldn't demand Mahoney arrest him. In all her time working for Fabian undercover at the club, and now within his home, she'd never caught him doing anything underhanded. It was the biggest mystery the precinct had ever handled and one that drove them insane.

Everyone could see there was something different about their city compared to neighboring ones. They hunted and tried to track the seedy underworld that existed in every place in the world where too many people gathered and brought along bad habits. Thieves, drugs, even the sex trade were things cops dealt with in other cities. It occurred in the city where Lulu had been raised. It was a fact of society, except for here.

The common theory was the man behind the oddity was Fabian. To all appearances, he was the man with the power, a power unchallenged until a few months ago. That was when the subtle campaign to smear Fabian came to light.

Anonymous tips were made to the precinct, things that would supposedly cause Fabian grief. None of the tips panned out, and what they found wasn't concrete enough to act.

Word came down to try harder. As part of the operation to nab Garoux, Lulu was sent in undercover to try and ferret out his secrets. Working at a strip club, known dens of vices, should have provided fodder, especially when she got the managerial job. But the place was clean.

Until the audit.

The audit was the first real criminal link. However, Lulu really had to wonder where the corrupted link was—the accountant who brought it to Fabian's attention or the go-between blaming the new girl?

Speaking of blame, she peeked over at Brody. He stood on the main floor, leaning against the wrought-iron balustrade for the staircase, the image of nonchalance in his suit.

Suave perfection to her Raggedy Ann state. What did he see in her? Or had he known all along and merely played her? Despite the situation, she had an urge to pull him aside and ask.

She tried to read his body language or expression. It told her nothing other than he didn't feel ill at ease at all. Yet, for some reason, he didn't meet her eyes. He'd also barely said two words to her since they hit the main level. It wasn't that he kept quiet. He just conversed with everyone else.

It shouldn't have miffed her. It shouldn't have hurt. But it did.

While everyone laughed about the misunderstanding, she told the rookie who took her statement how the guys who attacked her at the club had escaped. They were still on the loose.

But did they still pose a danger to her? She doubted an incident like this would go unnoticed by the media. Soon everyone would know of the undercover cop revealed. Those thugs who attacked her would know she didn't work for Garoux. Only a moron would dare to harm a cop.

"You ready to leave, Lulu?"

Startled from her thoughts, she realized they were the last ones left, the other police cruisers and the special team's van gone. She turned to Mahoney. "Yeah. I guess so." But oddly enough, she didn't want to go. She cast a glance at Brody. He met her eyes for a brief second, his expression inscrutable.

Say something. Do something. Anything, a part of her silently begged.

He didn't move.

Mahoney drew her attention. "My car's this way."

Since she could think of no good excuse to delay—*but I want to stay*—she followed Mahoney out. She felt somewhat awkward, given her oversized attire and bare feet. However, she wasn't about to beg for some better clothes.

What she would demand, though, were answers, starting with a whispered and irritable, "Why the hell did you come raiding in there, *Sal*?" Now that they were away, she referred to his code name. "I said I was okay."

"There was concern you might be under duress and forced to say that."

"It was code-speak. They wouldn't have known what I was saying."

Except they had suspected, and the look of betrayal on Brody's face stung more painfully than expected.

She'd known her being a cop would throw him. It would

throw most people—especially those who didn't obey the law.

"Whatever the case, the order was given to extract you from a possible hostage situation."

"Since when does extraction for a hostage invite sirens and fanfare? Next time, let's really go all out and add a little writing in the sky or a Twitter announcement."

Mahoney didn't immediately reply as he ducked into the driver's side of his car. She slid onto the passenger seat of the police sedan. The interior appeared much like an office on wheels with stubs of paper stuck to the dash, brown envelopes stuffed between the seats, and a laptop mounted on an arm projecting from the dash.

She lifted a sheaf of papers from the seat before slipping in.

"We didn't mean to come in with sirens blaring. The signals got mixed, and the crew came in hot instead of stealthy. Don't worry. Someone's head will roll for this."

"So long as it's not mine. I was in his house, Mahoney. Who knows what I might have found or heard?" And what if it incriminated Brody? Could she truly jail a man who brought her such pleasure?

A man she'd probably never see again.

How depressing. She and Mahoney continued debating the case.

"What happens now?" she asked. "My cover is totally blown. Who else do we still have working the case?"

"No one. This is it."

"What do you mean, 'this is it'?"

"The plug is being pulled. Too many months spent watching and for nothing. If Garoux's not clean, then he's hiding it perfectly. The department doesn't have the money to keep on investigating a man whose worse crime thus far is eating those hellishly good dogs down on Main by that bank."

"We should arrest that hot dog guy. It's his fault I gained five pounds over the summer," she grumbled.

"We could make a better case against the hot dog dude than Garoux."

"I can't believe this is it. That brass is just going to shut it down and assume Garoux's clean." Did that mean she could no longer think of him as a mob lord?

Does that mean Brody isn't a criminal? Maybe not a bad guy, but he was doing something unethical in handling the audit of the club while working undercover for Garoux.

"What about those guys who attacked me in the club? Do you have a lead on them?"

"We didn't even know you were attacked until you gave your statement. We'll head to the station and fill out a—"

Bang!

The other vehicle slammed out of the side road into the front of the police sedan, sending them spinning, which, on the two-lane blacktop bordered by a thin line of fir trees, meant they ended up off the road. Branches snapped against the undercarriage as they careened before slamming to a halt against a sturdy tree.

Lulu snapped forward, smooshed into the air bag, and then bounced back. Her brain rattled around inside her head. The car shuddered and came to a stop on its side. Her seat belt held her mostly in place, as did the air bag, but gravity still tugged.

She heard a groan beside her and tried to peer sideways,

the bright mocking sunlight streaming through her window making her blink.

"Mahoney?" No reply. "Are you all right?"

A groan this time. While sore, she could move all her body parts, and her wits were fast returning. She needed to get out of the car and call for help.

Leaving her buckle intact so she wouldn't land on Mahoney and squish him, she pushed at the door. It clicked and shifted, but the darned thing wouldn't budge farther. It was heavier than it looked.

Crunch. Someone walked outside.

"Hey. Anyone out there? Can you help me with my door?"

Too late did it occur to her that it might be the driver of the other car, the one that had intentionally rammed them.

But why?

For a second, she thought she'd perhaps hallucinated hearing steps outside until the car wobbled as something lit atop it. She braced her hands and feet before daring to unclip her seat belt. She squinted through the sunshine-filled window.

She couldn't see much. Legs encased in jeans. Black boots. She'd just described a good portion of North America's population.

The door to her side was wrenched open. Opened, torn off its hinge, and then tossed to the side.

What. The. Hell.

Leering down at her was the thug from the club, the same guy with the friend who'd knocked her out and then set her office on fire while she was in it!

Not good.

Some women might have quivered in fear. Some might have begged for their lives. Lulu got pissed.

"You!" she shouted. "You've got a lot of nerve showing up again after what you did last time."

"Don't remind me of my failure," the dude snapped. He reached in and grabbed her by the arm and yanked her from the car in a show of strength that impressed even her. "Because of you, I lost out on a great condo because I didn't get paid. Although, now the client is offering a bonus to bring you in alive. So in a sense, I guess this is a better deal."

What a waste of a handsome face, although his mug provided a good spot to plant her fist.

Before she could think twice, she reeled back and popped him one in the nose. Something crunched, making it totally worth the sore knuckles.

A satisfied grin stretched her lips as he bellowed, "You bitch. You broke my damned nose. Do you have any idea how annoying that is to fix?"

During his tirade, he kept one hand clamped around her upper arm, an immovable vise. His free hand grabbed his crooked nose and yanked. It cracked again but straightened, and as she watched, got straighter, the redness of her blow fading.

However, it wasn't the rapid healing that totally freaked her out. It was the . . .

"My, what big teeth you have."

The thug, with the suddenly pointed dentition, sighed dramatically. "And see, it's comments like this that prove my theory that 'Little Red Riding Hood' was originally written about a bear."

Say what? "No, it wasn't."

"Because you've been brainwashed to believe otherwise."

"No, because that's how the author wrote it like a zillion years ago. Little Red Riding Hood was stalked by a wolf while the bears got Goldilocks and a much better ending."

"Bah. 'Goldilocks' is a joke. It has been perverted from its original intent and commercialized into something feel-good. In the true version of the story, the bears ate the girl. They didn't become lifelong friends."

How utterly serious her wannabe murderer seemed. "Are we seriously debating fairy tales while you dangle me from a wrecked cop car? What exactly is your plan for me?"

Because she doubted he'd gone through the trouble of smashing into her car to say hello.

"I told you. Taking you in for the bounty."

"There's a bounty on my head?" How astonishing. "What for?"

"Because of who you associate with."

"You mean because I'm a cop? How do you figure kidnapping me and attempted murder are going to benefit you? I mean, is there seriously enough money to account for the hassle this is going to cause?"

"There is." His smile was too charming. So she punched it, and then screamed as, in retaliation, he jumped from the top of car, dragging her with him. It wasn't a long span, but unexpected, and tethered to him by an iron grip, it made her landing awkward.

Forget breaking free and making a run for it. Freaky guy with the teeth was not letting her go, and he'd brought a friend. She noted another guy standing by a pickup truck, the same truck with a thick grille that had rammed them only moments ago.

"You're the one who hit us."

Dude actually rolled his eyes. "Well, duh. We needed your car to stop. It seemed like the fastest way."

"We could have died."

"Yeah, that would have sucked, given my new bonus is contingent on you being alive. Now could you get your ass moving? Places to go. People to see."

His buddy by the truck fidgeted. "Damian, would you stop yapping with the broad? We need to hurry and get out of here. We are way too close to his land still."

"What, are you turning into a 'fraidy cat?" her captor mocked as he tossed her into the truck. The bench seat meant she got the middle, squashed between the two arguing men.

"No, but I'm not stupid, either. Let's drop her ass off, get the money, and then go on that vacation."

"Or you could just let me go now, and I contact a few friends and we see what we can do to help you."

The one called Damian snorted. "Darling, I'm a hired mercenary. We only work for the mighty dollar. Not plea bargains or tears or big pleading eyes."

"And steak."

"We do not work for steak, Bubba. We buy the whole damned cow for the right price. God, I wish I hadn't promised your mother I'd let you work with me."

The surreal arguing had her almost giggling, and not just because of hysteria at her situation. The pair of them were hilarious, especially all their references to bears and wolves and even a tiger.

"You guys are way too obsessed with the animal kingdom," she interjected at one point.

"Says the girl associating with tigers."

"I don't know what you're talking about." Or was Tigers the name of Garoux's gang? Had she finally stumbled across their identity in the underworld?

"She's got his mark," Bubba remarked, a stubby finger tugging at the collar of her T-shirt.

She slapped his hand away, but Damian couldn't be budged when he hooked the neckline to cop a peek.

"Do you mind?" she snapped.

"Who bit you?" he asked.

"None of your damned business."

"Actually, given you smell like a cat rubbed all over you, I'd say the accountant fellow."

Before she could ask him how he knew what Brody smelled like, the truck slowed to a stop. Their destination proved a big shock.

"This is my building. Does this mean you are letting me go?"

"You know, I almost wish I could. You're an interesting chick for a human. But in this business, once you give your word, you kind of have to keep it."

An apologetic hit man. Had the whole world gone mad?

No one stopped them as Damian frog-marched her in. Not a soul was around to hear her scream for help. Both Damian and Bubba proved adept at avoiding her stomping feet. They'd gotten wise to her violent tricks.

The elevator ride proceeded silently. She eyed the numbers as they lit up, ascending to what: her doom? *Dum-dum-dum.*

To her surprise, they skipped past her floor and kept

going. When the elevator deposited them on the eleventh floor, she debated yelling for help.

Middle of the week, in the afternoon? The upper floor with its four penthouse suites catered to the white-collar business-men. There would be no one home to hear, so she refrained, but she did eye with interest the various doors.

Which of them would lead to whoever had paid to have her killed?

As it turned out, none of them. They skipped all the doors and headed to the end of the hall, where an EXIT sign led them out to the stairwell. But they didn't go down. Up they climbed, one last level to the roof deck, a supposed oasis in the city.

Imagine a concrete balcony featuring a bolted pergola providing false shelter placed over a communal barbecue and outdoor seating area with some wilted plants in big clay urns. A rooftop paradise for yuppies.

Movement drew her eyes as a man dressed in jeans and a black silk shirt turned from the parapet. Lulu could not help but stiffen upon seeing him. *He seems so familiar.*

While handsome, with his tanned skin complemented by his longish ebony hair and piercing blue eyes, there was a coldness in the gaze that perused her from head to toe.

"Welcome, Jack Lamontaine's daughter."

At the mention of her dad, everything in Lulu froze. Espe-cially because she suddenly recognized the man in front of her. Although young at the time, she recalled seeing his photo on the front page of the newspaper years and years ago. His mug was plastered everywhere as media groups touted the arrest of a known serial killer—with a grudge against her dad.

Uh-oh.

CHAPTER 13

Someone pounded on the front door of his boss's mansion. Sulking on the divan, Brody couldn't bother himself to answer it—which irritated Fabian to no end.

"Are you going to get that?"

"Why bother? It's not going to be Lulu because she left. No 'Hey, see you later.' No 'Why don't we go finish breakfast?'" No "I love you and can't stand to be separated from you" theatrical moment that would have involved kissing—lots of it, with tongue.

He did so like to lick things.

But Lulu had left. Without a second glance, she'd walked out the door, and now he didn't know when he'd see his cop mate again.

Meow. Such a sad sound from his tiger. As for the man, he moped.

Fabian shook his head in disgust. "I still can't believe she was an undercover cop. And you're shackled to her. Ha. Too funny." Fabian snorted. "Have you told your grandma yet?"

"No one knows yet. I only found out a little while ago myself. I'm still working on processing it all."

"What's there to process? She's your mate. So what if she's a cop? That fact won't change."

"Hold on a second. Does this mean you're not mad she's working for law enforcement?"

His boss shrugged. "I might be an asshole at times, but even I know you didn't purposely set out to screw me over by bringing trouble into the family. We'll adapt to it. We always do. It's how the pack works."

Ah yes, the pack. The secret he'd not had time to divulge. Because she'd left! "I guess it will only be a problem if she comes back. Do you think—"

Bang. Bang. Bang.

Brody snapped. "Would you quit banging like that? I'm trying to have a bloody conversation," he bellowed in the direction of the front door.

A moment later a gun went off, and the door was kicked open. Fabian never moved from his position of nonchalance against the fireplace, but anyone who knew him would see the coiled tension in him. He was ready to spring if what entered the house proved a threat.

Brody, on the other hand, sprang to his feet and held himself ready to attack, but it was just the older cop called Mahoney who staggered in, looking battered and disheveled.

"You shot my door," Fabian observed.

"You should have answered it."

"I thought we were done with our pleasant chat."

"We were. But I need help."

Fabian arched a brow. "You're asking for my aid? That's priceless. What makes you think I want to do anything to help you?"

"Because it's not for me but that girl you had working for you."

"Lulu? Wait a second, you're the cop she left with. Where is she?" And why did the man looked so abused?

Brody couldn't help but move closer, nose twitching, but he didn't scent anything untoward.

"A truck smashed into us less than a mile from here. Whoever it was did it on purpose and took her," Mahoney said.

"Who took her?" Brody practically roared as he circled around the man and came face-to-face with him.

"Some hired thugs from the sounds of it. They had orders to deliver her to another party."

"Where?"

The cop shrugged.

It made him want to roar again. Brody also wanted to shake the cop. *The man needs to give us answers.*

When Fabian reached out to offer Mahoney a clear glass filled halfway with amber liquid, the cop didn't refuse. He took a sip, grunted in appreciation, and took another. Took his damned time. Meanwhile Brody breathed through his nose in an attempt to calm himself. It didn't work too well. Calm wasn't an option, not with Lulu a prisoner.

Danger. Our mate needs us.

Indeed she did, but where was she taken?

"Where did this happen? Take me to the scene of the crash," Brody demanded.

"There's nothing there. They took off in a truck, the same one that ran us off the road I'd wager."

Forget holding on to humanity. The culmination of facts just piled on top of each other. Brody ran out of the house, ignoring Mahoney's surprised, "What the hell is he doing?"

What, had Mahoney never seen a grown man strip before? Brody shed layers as he streaked across the front lawn. By the time he hit a copse of conifers, he was hidden enough from view to change skins, adopting the lankier stride and hunting ability of his tiger.

As his feline, he could also properly roar his frustration.

Since Fabian eschewed city or suburban living, and hated neighbors, the land he'd purchased, acres of it, provided a privacy Brody couldn't have hoped for anywhere else. It meant he could run, wild and free, springing from rock to rock, streaking through the bush. He didn't have a scent trail to follow as yet, but he paralleled the road out, trusting it to lead him to the scene of the crash, which, according to Mahoney, was less than a mile from the property. A crash on the pack's lands. The blatant evidence remained at the scene, the sedan laying on its roof, the passenger door entirely missing.

A shifter was here. Brody slowed his pace and slunk around the wreck, sniffing the scene. He caught the distinct aroma of a bear. However, any further details, even confirmation it was the same one as before, proved impossible, as gas fumes tainted the trail and made his eyes sting.

With a huff through his nose to expel the dizzying miasma, he backed away from the sedan. What clues were to be found?

Studying the dry gravel lining the road and judging by the crushed foliage, a second vehicle had pulled over. Big tire treads, but not a ton of weight on the back judging by the shallowness of the rear tire tracks. More than likely a pickup truck, but that alone wasn't enough to give him a trail to follow. And Lulu was most certainly in that truck.

He noted the scuffmarks on the ground, paired with larger steps. Clear evidence of someone reluctantly being moved along by brute strength and size.

They'll pay for that.

With their lives, his cat agreed. In his world, things were pretty easily categorized. Good or bad. Stays alive or dies. What was funny about this philosophy was Brody had never truly encountered it before now. Something about Lulu, though, yanked at his protective instinct. It brought out the animal in him. The hunter.

Rawr.

The beast in him, and he didn't just mean that of his tiger, but the one that worked on emotion, urged him to act. To find.

To protect.

He'd love to if he knew where the fuck they'd taken her.

He roared. It didn't help the situation. Neither did retracing his steps and seeing the wreckage of the car. Parked behind was Mahoney, and even from a distance he could hear the yelling.

He headed in the direction of the house, keeping close to the side of the road, only moving out of hiding when a black Humvee slowed to a stop. Fabian rolled down the window, his expression hidden behind a set of silver-lensed aviator glasses. "Get dressed." A bag came whipping through the window of the truck, and Brody barely dodged it. He hissed.

"Stuff it, furball," his boss snapped. "Get your ass moving. We've got somewhere we need to be."

Asking where wasn't happening in his tiger form, so Brody

shifted, the pain of melting from one shape to another barely noticeable now since he'd done it so many times.

As he pulled the athletic pants on, a navy blue pair of Adidas that offered ease of movement—and quick removal—he asked, "Where are we going exactly? Did Mahoney cough up a lead??"

Fabian shook his head. "I still have no idea who your girlfriend's enemy is, but apparently the bear hired to kidnap her had a price, which I agreed to, so expect it to come out of your paycheck." Cheap bastard. But Brody forgave him when he said, "I have a location."

"Yeah. Yeah. Brothers in the fur and all that, yada yada. Where is she?" Brody slid into the passenger side of the truck.

"The rooftop of her apartment building."

Not exactly an inspiring location. "Well, come on, boss. Put that pedal to the metal. We have to rescue my mate."

"You do know rescuing a cop goes against several of my moral grains? Having her around will probably come back to bite me" was Fabian's dry reply. The truck lurched, throwing Brody against his seat as Fabian peeled off down the road.

"Boohoo. So you might have to follow a few more laws. Like you said, she's my mate. She's family now."

"I really should have you made into a rug."

"But then who would you go on a wild adventure with? Now move it, old man. We have a sweetheart to save."

Brody teased his boss, even though Fabian had already broken the posted limits. Hopefully Mahoney would ensure they weren't stopped by his subordinates. Speed was of essence.

While false bravado veiled Brody's exterior, inside, he churned a great big ball of worry. Time ticked just to mock him. Fabian did his best. They couldn't move any faster, and yet each second they took was another one in which she was in dire danger.

I'm coming to save you, sweetheart. Hold on.

CHAPTER 14

I don't know how much longer I can hold out.

Lulu held the chair in front of her as a shield while Peter, or as her dad liked to call him, "That murdering son of a bitch," tracked her movements with his eyes. The gun he held down at his side never twitched. A man determined to not show fear—or common sense.

She hated when people didn't take her seriously. "Why are you after me?" Distract him with small talk. It worked in the movies. Why not real life?

"I am not after you, princess. I want your father. We both know what he did to me. Putting me behind bars like a fucking animal. Keeping me from the one I loved. Because of him, she died, a victim of a home invasion, because I wasn't there to protect her."

A little girl at the time of the trial, she'd not heard of the details, just knew her father had caught the bad guy. "That wasn't his fault. Blame the people who killed her."

"I did. It was the whole reason for my killing spree. See, I'm not talking about the second time he caught me, but the first. Your dad put me in jail for public intoxication and a bar fight. But see, he didn't put the ones I was fighting in there with me. Nope. He left them loose, and those mongrels decided to hurt me. Since I was out of reach, rotting in a cell, they went after Ariel."

"So for revenge you stole me? I had nothing to do with it."

"No, but you are one of the people he loves most. What better way to punish him? You see, once I knew you were joining me, I put a call in to your father telling him to come join the party. I can't wait to see his face when I toss you, hopefully begging and screaming for your life, from this building."

A cold shiver worked its way down her spine. For a while there, when he'd told his story, she almost felt bad for him, and then he reminded her what a maniac he was. Throwing her from a building? The man belonged behind bars. "No, thanks. I don't like heights." She really didn't. It's why she drove to places and never flew.

"Would you prefer I shoot you?" Peter, such an innocuous name for a killer, drew her attention to his gun.

Asking her how she'd like to die? How to handle it? She stuck to answering with the truth. Her shoulders lifted in a shrug. "I'm not crazy about holes in my body, either. Heck, I don't even have my ears pierced. I don't believe in tattoos either, and yet I see you have a few." Yeah, she blabbered, but she couldn't resist as the expression on his face went from murderous to baffled.

Keep the opponent off balance. A rule drummed into her at a young age by her dad.

"Has anyone ever told you that you are vastly annoying?"

Despite the situation, her lips twitched. "Often."

"Your cutesy thing won't work on me, princess."

Cute? How warped was this murderer's mind?

"Get your ass over here." Peter waved the gun at a spot too close to the railing for her comfort.

Wild red strands flew as she shook her head. "I think I'll stick to where I am."

"Move now or your father will arrive to find your corpse. You choose because I really don't care. You're starting to really irritate me. Dead. Alive. I don't think I really care how he sees you. Either way, your father hurts."

"This grudge you have for my dad isn't healthy." Neither was this conversation. However, the longer she stalled, the better. Not because she expected the cavalry to come to the rescue. Her dad had too much pride to call for help, and it would take him a few hours to get here. His determination to single-handedly save her himself meant she couldn't rely on his timely intervention.

Good, because it meant she still had time to extricate herself from the situation and prove to all her male relatives that a girl cop was just as good as a boy one—even if she couldn't write her name in the snow.

"Blame the grudge on the fact he jailed me for a second time before I was done with my vengeance. I had one more person left. The pack leader of the miscreants who attacked my woman."

She didn't need his hissed "Fabian" to guess who he meant.

"I take it he's next."

"My plan for him is multifaceted. It's not just enough to kill him. I want his position. I will be the new alpha, which means playing the power game with the pack."

"So the whole audit thing and the murder of Ricky, even

my attack, is part of a ploy to undermine him and take over his gang?"

"Precisely. Chip away at his empire so I can swoop in, vanquish the old wolf, and take over."

"Why is it most wars happen because of power?" she muttered as she jabbed the chair at him, more to remind him she paid attention than anything.

"Power is everything. Jail taught me that."

"Weren't you supposed to be in there for life?" she remarked, inching slowly backward in the direction of the rooftop door.

"There isn't a cage that can hold me, princess. I'm a beast."

She snorted. "You say that like it's a good thing."

"Because it is. In the animal world, the strongest prevail. And I am strong." He practically snarled the word. "Enough talk. No more stalling. I am done toying with you."

Peter lunged, darting so fast across the space separating them that it felt as if she had only a second to blink before he was almost upon her.

Move, you idiot!

Instinct took over, and she swung the chair. It connected with a satisfying thud that jolted her arms. A good solid hit, but it didn't stop his momentum. A foot kicked out and knocked the chair from her grip, sending it clattering.

Retaliate. Her fist shot out, fast enough that she managed to glance a blow off his chin—to no effect. His head didn't budge an inch.

He caught her second punch, encasing her fist and squeezing hard enough to have her gasp in pain. An iron band wrapped around the bicep of her other arm. No amount of tugging could set her free. She was getting mighty tired of being disarmed by brute strength and men with as much training as her father—in other words on par skill-wise with her.

Matched in skills, what did that leave her?

Use your head. She could practically hear her father's chiding voice. What could she do to maybe extricate herself?

No weapon. No free hands. Flailing, useless feet. That left her only one thing in her arsenal.

"I can't believe you fucking bit me!" he yelled.

Neither could she. Even worse, it didn't set her free.

As Peter dragged her to the parapet, mumbling about gagging her vicious human mouth—because Mr. Sociopath seemed to think he was a whole other species—she truly began to wonder if she'd make it out of the situation alive. As a matter of fact, much as it galled her to admit it, she needed help.

If only someone would come to her rescue. Maybe like that tiger she'd hallucinated at the bar during the fire. She could use a furry champion.

Or how about a real hero? Nope. No such luck. She got a cute and courageous dumbass called Brody.

CHAPTER 15

What the hell does Brody think he's doing? Who comes to the rescue unarmed and without backup?

Indeed, Brody emerged onto the roof deck, hands spread and open, palms empty, his T-shirt snug enough to show he didn't have a holster, and nothing appeared tucked into his pants.

"Are you stupid?" she yelled. "Get out of here." Before he got hurt.

"Is that any way to greet your rescuer?" he teased, his tone light, but his eyes, ooh those intent and dangerous-looking eyes of his, never left Peter. How at odds with his genial nature. But sexy.

"So the wolf sends his second. I don't know whether to be flattered or insulted," Peter mocked.

"You'll be dead in a moment so it won't matter," Brody growled. In that moment, he appeared so dangerous it sent a thrill through her, which was totally inappropriate to the situation. Apparently she was more of an adrenaline junkie than she knew.

Still, though, Brody threatened a man with a loaded

revolver. Was he suicidal? "How do you expect to rescue me without a weapon?" she asked.

"It's not sporting to bring a gun to a shifter fight."

Lost again in the weird gang terminology she'd encountered the last few days. She really needed to brush up on today's terms. When had city gangs turned to using animal terms to describe their turf and differences?

"Does the kitty want to fight? A fine idea. My bear could use a snack."

Peter's grip on her arm loosened, and she wasted no time snatching her limb free and taking a few steps away. Only to freeze in utter disbelief.

There were times in a girl's life that proved momentous. The first time Daddy let her fire his Luger. Her first period arriving on the day she wore faded blue jeans and a short top. Losing her virginity in the front seat of a Mini Cooper—not easy, she might add. The newest life-changing moment? The what-the-hell-is-going-on morph of a man into a tiger.

A fucking tiger.

Holy shit, Brody is a tiger!

She didn't mean the small, cute, and cuddly kind either. There was nothing gentle about Brody, or did he have another name when he turned into a giant feline? Whatever the case, he stood on four paws with a massive frame that must have measured at least eight or more feet. His fur bore the classic stripes of his kind, an orange-blond sliced with distinctive slashes of black. Oddly enough, his golden fur matched that of his hair when he was a man.

Oh my god, when he was a man. Now there was something a girl didn't say often.

Brody's change into a giant jungle predator was only the tip of the series of messed-up things happening. It seemed that vengeful, violent Peter wasn't human either. Hello, big black bear.

How the hell had she gone from a life dealing with criminals who wielded knives and guns to giant predators sporting claws and sharp teeth?

Numbly, she stared, not daring to jump into the fray to help. She wouldn't stand a chance. But standing by, doing nothing, galled as well. How her fingers itched for a weapon.

A pity she had nothing, but Peter did. Where did his gun go when he changed shapes?

She dove for his clothes, scrabbling at the pile as the snarling behind her continued.

When she finally found the gun, she pulled it free with an "Aha!" She whirled in time to see the bear and tiger wrestling by the rooftop ridge. She didn't think, nor did she hesitate. She raised the gun and aimed.

Fired.

The bear roared as her missile hit him in the shoulder. Pain and rage gave Peter the strength to fling Brody from him.

Lulu should have shot again, but she stayed her finger as the fur shrank, leaving behind bare skin, muscle, and a sluggishly bleeding hole in his shoulder.

"Give yourself up, Peter. Don't make me shoot." Then again, maybe shooting would solve all their problems? *I am an officer of the law. It's my duty to arrest him.*

Peter winced as he rolled his wounded shoulder. "That smarts."

Recovered from his crash landing, Brody growled and took a step forward.

"You want me? Come and get me." Peter hopped onto the edge of the parapet, wobbling a little. "I'm not afraid to die. Are you?" Peter crooked a finger at Brody just as a strong gust of wind caught him. His arms windmilled, and for a moment, concern stole his cold expression.

Then his features smoothed. "Fuck it. See you in the next life." Peter took a step back into open space just as Brody lunged, his paws swinging and jaw snapping, trying to grab ahold. He managed it, gripping Peter's upper arm.

However, this unwieldy snare yanked Brody against the parapet with his upper body leaning over the retaining wall, a precarious perch. It didn't help that Peter twisted in his grip, trying to unbalance him.

Brody's rear paws scraped at the rooftop, the claws scrabbling for purchase. Gravity pulled. It dragged him, without mercy, forward.

"Let go," she whispered, not wanting to shout out of fear of ruining his concentration.

The jaws released their grip, but Peter was ready for that. His free hand clung to Brody's foreleg. Brody tried to pull back but couldn't escape the pair of hands that wrapped around his paw. Peter chuckled as he held on. "If I'm going down, you're going with me."

Are you just going to stand here and watch the man you love die? Move.

Dropping the gun, she ran the few yards separating them and dove forward as the rear haunches on the tiger coiled in a last-ditch effort to stay on the roof. Her fingers sought purchase. Any body part would do.

She grabbed ahold of his tail.

He roared and flung his head.

She yelled, "Sorry about this," not really, as she sat down hard on the rooftop to brace herself, an anchor in the game of tug-of-war.

Rawr!

Brody flung his head again, and his teeth tore a line across Peter's arms.

With a loudly uttered "Fuck!" Peter let go, and all the weight dragging them disappeared. Lulu tumbled back as she lost her grip on the slack tail. She couldn't catch her balance, and her head smacked against the rooftop surface, leaving her stunned for a moment.

And not just stunned because of the blow.

A very naked, and human again, Brody stood over her. He didn't seem happy judging by his lips drawn into a frown.

"What the hell did you think you were doing?"

"When?" A lot had happened. "Are you mad I shot him while you were wrestling? I assure you, I'm a good shot."

"Not that. The whole grabbing-my-tail thing."

"You know what they say, catch a tiger by the tail."

"And if they holler let them go."

"No, that's if you catch them by a toe."

"Whatever," he yelled. "You could have died."

"Are you mad I saved you?"

"You did not save me. I rescued you."

She snorted. "Whatever. Shouldn't you be doing something, like leaving right about now before the cops show up?" Wait, she was a cop and already here, although she really didn't know how she'd write this up in a report. They'd send her away for evaluation for sure if she talked about tigers and bears.

"The cops ain't coming. Why would they? There's nothing to see."

"What do you mean, nothing to see? A man just jumped from the building."

"Did he?" He arched a brow. "Let's just say he never made it to the sidewalk. And even if he had, it would have been taken care of."

"By Fabian?"

"You really ask too many questions."

"I think I'm entitled. Especially now that I know you're a tiger."

"Is that a problem?"

Was it?

CHAPTER 16

The question hung in the air, and Brody tried not to tense as he waited for her answer.

When he'd changed back into his man shape, a part of him almost feared turning around to face her. He loved his cat, thought his tiger side was amazing, but what would Lulu think? Sure, she hadn't run screaming from the battle, nor had she shot him when she had the chance. However, could she accept the fact he was both man and beast?

He had often heard it preached that fated females could handle anything, even the fact that their males liked to pee on things, scratch at trees, and shed on the couch.

The silence lengthened as he waited to see what she would say. Would she accept him, or would he have to seduce her until she forgot he liked to chase giant yoga balls wrapped in twine in grassy fields?

Her expression betrayed nothing as she finally gave him a reply. "I can't believe you're a freaking tiger. I mean, how the hell does that happen?"

"I was bitten as child."

Her eyes widened in shock, and he could pretty much

anticipate her next question. "You bit me. Does that mean I'm turning into a tiger?"

"No. Surviving the virus is rare, and the change only happens to men. Scientists theorize it's because of our Y chromosome."

"People have studied you?"

"Can we talk about this later? I'm still waiting for your answer on accepting me how I am."

"Why does that matter?"

"Because you're my mate."

She ducked her head, choosing to break their locked gaze. She struggled still with the concept but tried to hide it. "I guess now all those corny jokes you kept spouting make sense."

"I tried to tell you."

"No, you didn't. Comparing yourself to a tiger isn't the same as saying, 'Hey, Lulu, I'm a shape-shifting feline.'"

"Complains the girl who neglected to tell me she was a cop working undercover to get dirt on my boss."

"I eventually admitted it."

"Just like I showed you my cat. So are we even?"

She shrugged before grinning. "I guess. But, now what, Garfield?"

He didn't even try to hide his shudder. "Are you comparing me to a domestic breed? I'll have you know I'm a Siberian tiger. A rare and majestic species."

"With a giant ego."

"And tail." He winked.

"Speaking of ego, are those dark roots I see at your temple?"

His fingers brushed the area in question. "I kind of have a stripe on the side. I've had it since I was a kid. I get it dyed to look normal."

Lulu snickered. "Normal. There's nothing normal about a geeky tiger in an accountant suit."

"You forgot to add who's mated to an undercover cop."

"About that whole mate thing. I like you, but that doesn't mean we're like married or anything."

"Are you going to torture me with dating?"

"Yup. And family dinners. By the way, did I mention all the males in my family are cops?"

He swallowed hard. Oh, would Fabian and the others have a field day with this. "You mean your whole family might try to arrest me?"

"Not my whole family. Only those who think you've committed a crime in their jurisdiction. My daddy, though, he won't arrest you."

"That's good."

"Because he'll probably try to kill you."

Great. Just great. And enough.

The adrenaline from battle still hadn't worn off, and there she stood, defiantly eyeing him. Or was this her way of seducing?

Her eyes sparkled, and her lips tilted in a challenging smirk.

The minx.

He pounced and flipped her onto his bare shoulder. Completely bare-assed, he marched her to the stairs, pausing only a moment to snag his clothing as he went.

How nice of the bear to make their final confrontation somewhere close to a bed.

Picking the lock to her apartment wasted too much time, enough that he almost died—leaving him with very few lives—as Lulu, far from fighting his grasp, nibbled at his back.

"Can you hurry up?" she mumbled against his flesh. "I'd much rather be kissing something else."

Those were the kind of words to make a man lose all sense as blood rushed to one zone.

He wasn't sure how they got into her apartment or how he ended up pressed against the wall. His mate sure had an aggressive streak. *Meow.* Whatever her methods, he certainly wasn't going to argue with the sight of Lulu on her knees, sucking the length of him with evident pleasure.

Eyes shut, her face flushed, her lips slid back and forth against the taut skin of his cock. The suction and pull of her mouth had him sitting on the brink, struggling not to spill too soon.

She braced her hands on both his thighs, the tips of her fingers digging into his flesh as she bobbed her head.

Pure torture.

Absolute pleasure.

He couldn't handle any more. He dragged her to her feet, plastering his mouth to hers, stealing her breath with a hot kiss.

Her arms wound around him, tight, and her tongue met his in a wet clash. He hoisted her, loving her softness against him but loving even more burying his hardness within her.

She took him with a cried, "Brody." How sweet his name sounded coming from her lips. How hot she wrapped him within her sheath. How decadently she rode him, bobbing her body on his shaft, a friction to make him dig his fingers into her buttocks.

Together they rocked and shuddered, their breathing coming in fast pants. He'd already marked her once, but he couldn't resist placing his mouth against his previous claim.

"Bite me," she urged. "Bite me as I come."

How about when he came? He thrust one last time into her heat, clamped his teeth, and rode the wave of his orgasm, an orgasm that was almost painful in its infinite glory.

It went on and on, probably because she came at the same time, the quivering of her sex pulsing around his cock, fisting him and drawing every ounce of pleasure it could manage.

And to his surprise, it wasn't Brody or his tiger that whispered, "Mine."

Lulu had finally succumbed to fate.

CHAPTER 17

Waking up with a gun pointed at your face? Never good, especially when the naked woman beside you squeals, "Daddy!"

Shit. Especially since the father of his mate seemed none too pleased at finding him in her bed.

"Who is this?" Father dear, with the cropped red-and-gray head, flinty, cold eyes, and I'm-going-to-kill-the-defiler-of-my-daughter stare, didn't lower the gun. He cocked it.

"This is Brody. My, um, fiancé," she said, a touch too brightly.

Her father didn't buy the act either. "What the hell is going on, Lulu? First I get this call from that murdering A-hole that busted out of jail that he's got you. Then I get here to find you, instead, in bed with some guy you're calling your fiancé?"

"Peter was taken care of, thanks in large part to Brody here."

"This boy took Peter down?" Dubiously said. The other man eyed him, and Brody got the feeling he didn't fare well in the assessment. "What precinct does he work out of?"

"He's not a cop, Daddy. He's an accountant."

"A what?" The gun, which had dropped, rose again. "What the hell are you doing getting engaged to a numbers guy? You know a pencil pusher isn't going to save you when the apocalypse comes."

"The apocalypse?" Brody couldn't help but question.

"Yeah, did I forget to mention that not only am I descended from a line of police officers but they also think it's just a matter of time before the zombie apocalypse hits? You should see the storerooms they have on their properties." Lulu couldn't help a hint of red in her cheeks as she told him.

Meanwhile Brody bit his inner cheek, lest he laugh as her father elaborated. "It's coming. Scientists are eyeballing that meteor, the one they say is going to miss earth by a sliver, but I know better."

And to think he worried she'd find his tiger heritage hard to accept. She came from even crazier roots than him. "So the zombies are coming? Well then, I'd better make sure I stock up on supplies, sir. I wouldn't want Lulu here to go without."

"My girl needs more than food. She needs a man who can protect her." The disdain was clear.

Brody refrained from rolling his eyes, but he did get defensive. "I can protect her."

"You look like you're fit enough, but still, trust my baby girl to a yuppie?"

"Brody's not a yuppie. He's a tiger wearing accountant's clothing." Lulu snickered.

Tired of the aspersions on his virility—because of his geeky addiction to numbers—Brody sprang from bed. Too quick for human reaction, he twisted the gun from Lulu's dad's hand and tripped him so he hit the floor. He pointed the weapon at the man's forehead.

Then he held his breath as he waited.

Would the guy freak for getting taken down by a white-collar nerd or would he . . .

Laugh. "Well, I'll be damned. He might not be a useless pencil pusher after all."

Lulu, who'd come up behind him and draped a robe around his shoulders, chuckled. "Oh, you'd be surprised at what he hides, Daddy. There's a tiger under that skin."

A tiger indeed. *Rawr.* He might hide his awesome feline from most of the world, but not Lulu. His mate now knew all of his secrets, just like he now knew all of hers.

The fact that he was mated to a cop might make life challenging, but love didn't care what side of the law she was on, and neither did he. Lulu had caught this tiger by the tail, and he, for one, hoped she never let him go.

EPILOGUE

Strolling along the riverbank after the cleanup at Lulu's place, Fabian silently cursed. The damned bear behind all the shit happening had gotten away. Even worse, he apparently had a grudge against him.

Problem was Fabian didn't understand why. Perhaps that cop Lulu would have some answers, but that would happen only once Brody let the girl out to breathe.

The tiger was pretty upset at her capture and was now focusing on reaping the rewards of rescue.

As for Fabian, as twilight descended, he had his driver drop him off by the river that ran through the city, out to the outskirts where it flowed through his property. He often used this river route to clear his mind and see if he could puzzle things out.

Only rarely did he come across people, the occasional fisherman or picnickers or couples making out by the water in the moonlight, so he didn't think much about the murmur of voices from around the bend. Usually he would have avoided them by detouring through the woods, except something they said caught his attention.

"Just toss her in the river. Let the fish have the body."

Toss something into his river? Fabian had donated to too many charities and community events to clean up the water to have some miscreants ruin it with their murderous pollution. Not to mention, the last thing he needed on a midnight swim was to bump into a corpse.

Also, who the hell had sanctioned a kill and disposal on his turf?

My town. My rules.

Sniff.

Damned bears again. They were cropping up all over the damn place.

Two of them against his wolf?

Sounds like good exercise. His inner beast did so like a challenge, and Fabian liked to personally remind encroachers not to mess around in his town.

Slipping off his shoes, he treaded on bare feet toward the voices. A stand of trees and a slight hillock blocked his view of the speakers, but at the same time, the foliage and incline provided concealment as he sneaked and stripped his clothes.

"Shouldn't we kill her first before dumping the body?"

"Why bother? With her hands and feet tied, she'll sink like a rock."

Speaking of rock, one rolled out from under his foot. He'd let himself get distracted, and now the repercussion was the noise alerting them to his presence.

"Someone's out there."

"Or it's just some forest creature. This is protected parkland."

"Whatever, let's get this done. Toss her in the drink, and let's hit the bar for some beers."

"Sounds like a plan."

Before Fabian could barrel from the shadows, there was a splash, and he faced a choice. Go after the miscreants or save whoever sank in his river.

He played the part of Good Samaritan.

And to think the rag sheets call me a cold bastard.

Definitely cold. The water wasn't exactly warm when he hit it. Nor was it illuminated. He dove from the top of the hillock into the spot where the ripples radiated, relying on luck to help him find—

Aha! His fingers brushed spidery strands of hair. He stroked downward, and his hands encountered squirming flesh.

The body quieted at his touch, as if sensing he'd come to help. *Yes, help.* His wolf seemed particularly keen on playing the role of savior. Unusual.

Fabian wrapped an arm around a distinctly female waist and used his feet to flutter and scissor his way to the surface. His head broke the water, and he pulled in a fresh breath.

The woman he'd rescued gasped and coughed, expelling water and sucking in air. He tread the surface for a moment while she regained some sense of composure.

When she did finally draw in one smooth breath, it exited almost as quickly with, "Who are you?"

Before he could answer, it was followed by, "Who am I?"

And then the bullets began peppering the water.

WILD
PASSIONS

Kate Douglas

ACKNOWLEDGMENTS

I am so lucky to have an absolutely terrific crew of beta readers. Sue Thomas, Kerry Parker, Jay Takane, Ann Jacobs, Rose Toubbeh, Karen Woods, and Lynne Thomas—thank you so much, ladies, for making me look a lot better than I could ever manage on my own. If my readers knew what you see first, they'd thank you, too!

CHAPTER 1

"Everybody here?" Traker Jakes took his seat at the head of the big dining room table in the lodge and pointedly made eye contact with every other wolf who'd managed to show up tonight. Kentucky Jones, a.k.a. Dr. Tuck, the pack's vet, sat at Trak's left; Trak's older brother, Lawz, was on his right.

The rest of the single guys—Evan Dark, Manny Vicario, and Drew Miklos—had taken seats, and while there was space for Wils and Ronan and their mates, no one really expected the four of them tonight. They were currently somewhere up in Canada celebrating a long-delayed honeymoon. He'd kind of thought Brad and Cain and their mate, Cherry, would show up, but you never knew. Understandable, considering how flat-out sexy Cherry was. Trak imagined she could prove to be quite a distraction.

Those four guys had all found their mates, proof that the whole concept of Feral Passions was on target. Everyone—including Trak—had laughed at Brad when he'd first proposed the idea that they build an upscale resort for women here on the wolf preserve as a way to meet and find mates. The guys had laughed even harder when Trak reversed his original opinion and agreed that building a resort designed with the single woman in mind was an excellent way for the pack to attract available women up here to the middle of nowhere.

It wasn't as easy as it sounded for single werewolves to find lifetime mates, especially when their women birthed only male children and the guys liked to howl at the moon.

No one was laughing now, and it hadn't escaped Trak's notice that all of the guys had ended up joining the partnership of Feral Passions Resort Inc. Cherry had been the catalyst—Cherry DuBois had won their hearts when she'd fallen for both Brad and Cain, accepting not only the fact the guys went furry and ran on four legs, but also that she'd get two guys for life—a very long life—when she went furry along with them. Brad and Cain had been a pair in search of a third, and Cherry had slipped right into her place as part of a loving triad. Even better, Cherry had come to the resort with her sister and her sister's best friend, two women who'd fallen for each other as well as both Ronan and Wils, and another atypical match had been formed.

As if there was anything at all typical about women falling in love with werewolves.

But it was already the middle of August. They'd agreed they'd shut down for the season by mid-September, and there were still six wolves actively searching but still without women. Not that they hadn't had plenty of chances, but no one wanted to risk falling for a woman who wouldn't be able to handle the kind of life the pack could offer.

"Ya know, Trak, it would be a hell of a lot easier if we could tell them what we are, damn it." Evan glanced from one guy to the next. "Trying to figure out if a woman's the kind who can handle pack life without a hint of what she's getting into? Think about it."

Manny's laughter lacked a certain amount of humor. "Tell me about it. Convincing a woman you love her while hiding the world's biggest secret isn't easy. We want them to be honest with us, but we're lying to them through our very sharp canines."

Trak glared at Manny. "Armando, if that jackass Cain can do it, you can figure it out."

"Who you callin' a jackass, my exalted alpha? Good evening, gentlemen." Cain Boudin sauntered into the dining room with Brad and Cherry beside him. "Sorry we're late. I know you've missed me like crazy, Trak, but Ronan called. They're in Alberta, everyone's having a great time, and they said to tell all of you hello from the four of them. By the way, they've got a bet going that Tuck and Manny are going down this week or next. Just thought you should be forewarned."

Tuck laughed, reached across the table, and high-fived Manny. "She'd better be a whole lot of woman. We are not small men." He gave Manny an appreciative glance. "Anywhere."

Cherry laughed so hard she snorted. Trak merely waited them out while the jokes got tossed around the table. It was good to see them laughing, because there'd been a time when he feared the pack wouldn't survive much longer. When a man lived for hundreds of years, he saw a lot of changes, and the modern era had not been good to shifters. The old days had been so much easier—when you wanted a mate, you took one. Grabbed a woman and hauled her into the hills, and rarely did you find one who wasn't willing to make a new life within the pack.

Women back in the day led hard lives, treated like so much chattel with very few rights and not much to look forward to beyond popping out babies on a regular basis. Pack life was always a shared life, with women treated like royalty. Once they'd decided on a mate—because in the old days, the women were given a choice of men once they were captured—then they went through the process of joining the pack physically. A single small bite, and she became one of them with a life span to match her mate's and the chance to run as free as any other member of the pack.

Female werewolves were made, not born. A female bore only male children, all of them werewolves, but she was an equal within the pack. Before women had won equality in the modern world, it made a captive mate's changed circumstances much easier to bear. Modern women, though? They already had it all. When you couldn't tell a gal what you were offering her beyond life out in the boonies surrounded by men, it wasn't easy to make it look like a very good trade-off for life in the city and all that it offered.

The purpose of Feral Passions was to change all of that. It gave the men a chance to get to know women, in many cases intimately. That was one of the really terrific things about the modern woman, at least the ones who'd made it to Feral Passions. They really liked sex. Loved sex, in fact, and while only four men had found mates, every guy here had enjoyed more quality time with the feminine gender than at any other time in their very long lives.

Hell, he'd waited for a mate for well over a hundred years. Trak figured he could wait a few more. In the meantime, Feral Passions had turned out to be the best financial investment any of them had ever made. And they'd gotten Cherry, Christa, and Stephanie in the first season. Not bad.

He clapped his hands, and the chatter stopped. "Okay, gentlemen. Time to figure out the work schedule for the coming week. We've got six young women expecting to have the time of their lives. Three of them are nurses, two more are in finance, and the last is unemployed and looking to have 'way too much fun.' Seriously, that's what it says on her reservation." He shook his head. Never a dull moment. "It's up to us to make sure that's exactly what happens."

"The week after that, we've got a bridal party coming," Manny added. "Three bachelorettes and the bride-to-be coming to celebrate a week of freedom. Now, whether or not the bride's freedom is, shall we say, all encompassing, we'll have to wait to find out. But in case it isn't, I would suggest you manage to keep your paws off the woman while still showing her a good time." He raised one very expressive eyebrow. "The bridesmaids, however, are fair game."

"Excellent point, Manny. If the bride-to-be doesn't want a man trying to get her into the sack, all men will back off." Trak made eye contact once again with everyone at the table, including Cherry, who had the audacity to wink at him. He had a feeling she'd never quite get the concept of deferring to her alpha. He bit back a smile.

She'd definitely gained self-confidence along with her werewolf mates. It was all good.

Meg Bonner stood in the bedroom doorway, watching her boss as he slept the unrepentant sleep of the well-fucked male. He lay on his stomach with one hand draped over the side of the rumpled bed; his black hair, streaked with iron gray and usually so neatly combed, was tousled into sweaty curls around his face. With his penetrating hazel eyes hidden in sleep, the thick sweep of dark lashes left perfect half-moons against his cheeks. He was, without a doubt, the most breathtaking man she'd ever seen. And he was hers. Sighing softly, her gaze roamed his body. Sheets tangled over his perfectly formed butt, and sunlight through the window highlighted his sleek, muscular back and strong arms, teasing her with the visuals and sensations of exactly what he'd been doing with that body.

Of what that body had been doing with her body.

Muscles pulsed between her legs, released, and tightened again. Her mind filled with memories of his strong thighs between hers, the clench and stretch of rock-hard buttocks beneath her hands, his strength as he powered into her. Her breath hitched in her throat. At one point, he'd dipped his head, taken first one nipple between his lips and then the other. Her breasts, which felt so ponderous to her, captivated him.

His big hands had held her, fingers tangled in her hair as he looked into her eyes just before taking her over the edge for the most amazing orgasm imaginable.

Yet here she stood, fully dressed, hair combed, purse in hand, ready to go back to work. Even worse? She was actually thinking of looking for a new job, of walking away from him forever, even though she knew it would kill her. She was such an idiot, but he was just too . . . too *everything*. That had to be the reason for the panic, because for the life of her, she couldn't figure out where else this monumental case of cold feet could be coming from.

Her boss, her lover, and her fiancé? That last word was the one she still couldn't seem to wrap her head around. The most handsome, the smartest, sexiest, nicest—not to mention richest—guy she'd ever known wanted to marry her. No caveats, no prenup, nothing but her promise to love him back as much as he claimed to love her.

If she could actually make herself believe he really meant it.

Just like her mother never meant it. She'd made damned sure Meg knew there was nothing about her worth loving. She glanced at the sparkling solitaire diamond on the ring finger of her left hand. He'd actually gotten down on one knee in one of Portland's nicest restaurants in full view of the other patrons, asked her to marry him with promises of love forever, and then slipped it on her finger just two months ago. She'd never forget the sigh that spread across the exquisitely decorated dining room—an audible wave of pure emotion—or the applause from the other diners when she accepted, sitting there at their table in absolute shock and happy tears until Zach stood and pulled her into a loving embrace. He'd cried, too, hazel eyes sparkling beneath the crystal chandelier.

Theirs had been—and still was, for all intents and purposes—a storybook romance. The wealthy young owner of a successful company falling for his personal assistant, courting her, asking for her hand.

Storybook, as in fantasy—but that was the problem in a nutshell. Fantasies didn't come true in Meg's world.

In all that time—all the plans they'd made for the wedding, all the laughter and meals with their friends, the private times like this when they sneaked out of the office in the middle of the day and raced to the condo she shared with him for a quickie that was anything but quick—in all that time, she hadn't really believed it.

Why would anyone like Zachary Royce Trenton love a woman like her? She wasn't blind. She saw herself in the mirror every single morning, a neatly attired yet obviously plus-sized blonde with a loud laugh that matched her full-figured size, a somewhat raunchy sense of humor, and the ability to organize even the most disorganized businessman and make his office run like a well-oiled machine.

That had to be the only reason he wanted her. The sex was beyond wonderful, and he always seemed to be enjoying whatever they did, but there was a bit more of her than most men generally found attractive. Zach said she was lush, sexy, and voluptuous. She figured those were his politically correct terms for fat. She knew she didn't look horrible if you ignored the pounds that no amount of exercise seemed to affect, and she was always—as her grandmother used to say—well put together, but still . . .

Zach said he loved her, and he talked about their future with stars in his eyes, but who did he really see by his side? Did he honestly want a woman who might make him a laughingstock among his wealthy, physically attractive, and active friends? A woman who never went out in public in a bathing suit and never played golf because of the way she looked in the shorts?

Did Zach really love her? Did he love Meg Bonner in spite of her imperfections, or did he merely love what she could do for him and his very successful company?

On that depressing thought, she quietly stepped out of the bedroom and closed the door behind her. She'd left a stack of paperwork on her desk when he'd grabbed her hand and, amid his laughter and her flustered protests, tugged her out of her chair, out of the office, and into his private elevator to the parking garage.

She glanced at her watch. Damn. They'd been gone for over two hours! She really needed to get back to work, especially since she was going to be gone all next week. She gathered up her things and quietly slipped out the door.

With any luck, the upcoming week at Feral Passions Resort down in California's rugged Trinity Alps might help her find answers to her questions. She needed time away from Zach, a chance to interact with her girlfriends, to indulge in some time for herself without Zach's overwhelming presence.

It was impossible to think rationally about their relationship when he was around, though she'd managed to compartmentalize her emotional life from her work life. Personal assistant Meg Bonner kept it together because that was her job, but fiancée Meggie Bonner had a hard time questioning what the hell was going on in her personal life whenever she was with Zach.

Zach owned her heart whenever he was near, but when they were apart, it was too easy to see they really didn't have anything going for them beyond the fact she was head over heels in love with the man. Maybe Zach loved the hero worship. Maybe he needed a woman who thought he was flawless, or he had to have a woman who looked at him with open and wide-eyed lust whenever she glanced his way.

Except she knew Zach wasn't a narcissist. He was an honestly wonderful guy, but did he really love her? It was an honest question, one she really needed to find an answer to before they married next month, but it was too hard to figure out just what was going on when she was with him.

Which was why this week away was so important. Time to think without Zach clouding her thoughts. Meg had never heard of the resort before, but Elle and Jules swore that Feral Passions was the ideal place for their bachelorette getaway. Darian had agreed, so all four girls were going to spend an entire week in an isolated resort on a wolf preserve.

Wolves? Now that had caught her attention. She'd always loved wolves, but so had the rest of their "gang of four," as the parents called them. Except Meg's, of course. They barely knew she was alive, much less had friends, but those amazing friends had kept Meg on the right track for twenty of her twenty-five years. She was five when she met Jules, Elle, and Darian waiting in line on their first day of kindergarten, the only girls in a class dominated by stinky boys.

Now? Now she felt as if she paused at a fork in the road where she really wasn't certain which way to go. The boy in question was definitely not stinky. Her friends were still single—no one had a boyfriend, though Jules had gotten close to marriage about a year ago—so Meg was the first to make this journey. Except she, Megan Ann Bonner, the one who would not be stopped at anything she attempted, felt as if she paused with one foot raised and no idea where to plant it. No idea which road to take, much less how to move forward.

She hoped Feral Passions and a week of utter indulgence would help her discover if what she and Zach had was good or bad, right or wrong.

She hoped time at Feral Passions would help clear her head and at the same time give her single besties the time of their lives. While they played, Meg prayed she'd either find the strength to actually look for another job and break off her engagement, or accept the fact that Zach actually meant what he said. That he loved her. That he wanted to marry her.

That he thought she was absolutely perfect. Yeah. Right. What a joke.

Elle Marcel left her client's office and headed toward the coffee shop at the bookstore. Darian and Jules were probably getting tired of waiting, but the man she'd just spent the past hour with had needed more than the usual go-get-'em-you-can-do-it pep talk. He really was just as bad at marketing and promotion as he thought—worse, even—but it wasn't lack of confidence. It was flat-out lack of ability.

Maybe she needed to write this guy off. She definitely needed a new job. Shouldn't a life skills coach have better, well, life skills? Yep, simple. She was on the wrong career track.

She'd really wanted to be a veterinarian. Animals were much nicer than people. If her lease allowed, she'd have at least a dozen cats and dogs. Her grandmother said she had the "family gift" for healing critters, which was true. Weird, certainly, but she could actually heal injured animals. Unfortunately, she lacked any gift for advanced math, a necessity for the right studies to succeed in vet school. Like her poor marketing guy, it was her lack of ability holding her back, and didn't that just suck?

"Hey, Elle. You just getting here, too?"

Startled, Elle spun around and then laughed. "I am. Dar, you're never late. What's up with our favorite greater Portland weathergirl?"

"Don't even talk weather. The current chief talking head in news wanted me to postpone my week at Feral Passions so he can take his girlfriend to Cabo. I told him no way, that I'd scheduled this week over a month ago and the reservations were nonrefundable. However, his ego is tender, and he's the producer's favorite. It required more diplomacy than telling him to stuff it."

Elle linked arms with Dar. "You could charm the balls off a bull, sweetheart. I don't see you having any trouble charming that jackass."

"That's the problem." Dar pushed open the door to the coffee shop. "If he had balls, there'd be something to charm."

Elle snorted. "Well, that makes it tough." Laughing, she led the way into the coffee shop. "Look. Jules is already here." Elle hauled Dar across the small shop, and both of them got hugs from Jules.

"I'll go order for us, Elle." Darian went over to the counter while Elle took a seat.

"It's been way too long since we all got together," Elle said, "but I feel guilty doing this without Meg."

"Yeah." Jules sighed. "But Meg's the reason I called this little meeting."

"What?" Elle sat back in her chair, frowning. "What's wrong?"

Jules shrugged. "Wait until Dar's back. I'm worried about Meg. We need to talk."

Trak stomped out of the main dining room at Feral Passions and looked around the grounds for his kitchen crew. This week's group of women was going to be showing up for the last breakfast before checking out in another couple of hours, but the stove was cold, the coffee not made, and there was no sign of Brad or Cain. Wils and Ronan were still gone for at least another week—but Brad and Cain had promised to hang around until the other guys got back.

Unless something had happened to Cherry. "Crap." He hadn't thought of that, so he shot a quick glance toward their window upstairs. Dark. No one was home, and Cherry was fine. He knew that. Irritated and really wanting to punch something, he stood a moment longer, staring at the windows on the second floor. This had all been a hell of lot easier before the guys actually started finding mates, even if that was the ultimate reason they'd built this frickin' resort in the first place.

"Mornin', Trak."

Shit! He spun around so fast he almost tripped over his own feet. "Lawz? What the hell are you doing here? I thought you had a job over in Humboldt County this week."

Lawz merely shrugged. "So did I. They ran into some sort of snag with the county, have to do a few more studies before we can get moving. Then Brad called last night and asked me if I could cover for him. He and Cain wanted to take Cherry away for a couple of days."

"Oh, really?" Trak folded his arms across his chest. "So why didn't they ask me?" He knew it wasn't Lawson's fault— he merely glared at his brother on general principle. Lawz could be such a pain in the ass sometimes. He might be older, but he seemed to move in his own world with a totally different set of rules. Sort of like another guy who drove him nuts.

A thought popped into his head. "It's Cain, right? This was his idea."

Lawz merely laughed. "Worry about Cain later."

Trak bristled. He actually felt the tiny hairs on the back of his neck rise. "What's so funny?"

"You." Lawz grinned at him like he was the biggest joke going. "Look at you, going all alpha on me. This is exactly why they didn't say anything. Cain will never be your favorite wolf in spite of the fact he's damned good at his job. Hell, he's the only one who'd even consider doing the job. Face it, not another pack member here would consider working as your enforcer, so you'd better remember that before you blow your top."

"I never blow my—"

Lawz held up his right hand. "Look, Trak, neither one of them wanted Cherry to feel guilty for making you mad. She knows you too well, knows how fucking anal you can be about the details when we've got people coming in, and if she thought you didn't approve, she'd have refused to go. They've been mated for almost two months and still haven't gotten that honeymoon you said they could take, and the guys were feeling really bad about that. All that girl's done is work! They're gone. They'll be back when they're ready. Get over it."

Trak took a couple of deep breaths. Counted to ten. Counted to twenty and exhaled. "Okay. So who's going to make breakfast?"

Lawz hooked an arm around Trak's neck and hauled him back into the lodge. "Guess," he said.

Trak growled. But he followed Lawz back into the lodge, and that pissed him off even more.

CHAPTER 2

"So this is where you disappeared to. I should have guessed."
Zach leaned over Meggie's desk and kissed her. He loved the
way she got all flustered when he surprised her like this,
though he'd been awfully disappointed to wake up and discover she'd left the condo. Didn't she realize he'd just been
taking a break before round two?

Once they were married, he hoped she'd understand that
when he closed up shop in the afternoon, he meant it. He
owned SeaSun Integrations, and he was well aware when
they could afford to leave early. When the office was closed,
they could go play. There wasn't anything on the docket for
now, and he'd given his construction crew paid time off for
the next two weeks. As successful as SSI was and as hard
as the guys—and that included the women shipbuilders—
worked for him, it was the least he could do.

Meg shoved all that glorious blond hair back from her
face and smiled at him. "Where did you think I'd go? One of
us has to work, and besides, I hear the boss can be a real
slave driver."

"Aw, he's not that bad." He leaned close. "He's smart and

absolutely adores the woman he's going to marry. Kiss me, Meggie. I miss those luscious lips."

She rolled her eyes, but she kissed him. Maybe he really needed a private room off his private office. One with a bed. A large bed, soundproof walls, and . . . no. He'd never get anything done. He licked the seam of her lips until she opened for him, and he groaned into her mouth.

He knew he'd never get enough of her.

When they finally broke the kiss, both of them were breathing hard. Leaning his forehead against hers, he whispered, "I love you, Ms. Bonner. Cannot wait until you're Mrs. Trenton."

She reached for him, wrapped her fingers around the back of his neck, and kissed him again. "I love you, Zach. So much it frightens me."

"No need to be frightened." He couldn't understand why sometimes she sounded so unsure about them. In every other aspect of her life, Meg was the epitome of self-confidence, a strong-willed, self-assured woman, one he admired beyond measure. "Honest, Meggie." He kissed her again. "We're going to be so good together."

She looked at him with those stormy-gray eyes, and for a moment he was certain he saw doubt. He wished he knew how to reassure her without making himself look like an absolute basket case. She had no idea what she did to him. For him. No clue about the power she held over him. His life had been lost in a deep, black hole before Megan Bonner, a beautiful woman with a mind like a steel trap, came into it.

He'd barely begun to emerge from the horrible deaths of his parents and only brother in a stupid plane crash on their way to a ski vacation in Tahoe in a storm. His poor mom must have been terrified. She hated that plane, hated the fact that her husband insisted on flying even after a heart attack that had almost killed him. Zach wondered if his dad took the Beechcraft just to bug her. He'd been cruel like that, to his eldest son and the woman who loved him in spite of himself, but that cruelty was the reason Zach hadn't been with them. He'd had it with the criticism and overbearing personality that were probably why Robert Trenton had been so wildly successful.

But it was also why Zach hadn't wanted anything to do with his father's business or his money. Why he was so proud of his own success and so excited about sharing that success with a woman smart enough and sexy enough not only to understand his goals, but to help him succeed. He cupped her face in his hands, tilted her head so that she looked at him when he knew she wanted to look away. He wished he knew what she was so afraid of. He was nothing like his father. He loved her for the woman she was, and all he asked was that she love him back. "You, Meggie Bonner, are everything to me. Don't ever forget that. Please, don't ever doubt me."

Her lips parted, and her eyes filled with tears. He hoped like hell those were happy tears. If Meggie ever left him, if she walked away, he didn't think he could handle the pain.

Sunday morning
Meg checked her watch, looked at the clock, double-checked to see if she had all her luggage, and looked at the clock again. Almost five in the morning, about the time she was usually getting up, but she was ready to go and waiting

impatiently. Elle was driving, mainly because she was the only one of the four of them with a larger sedan that was comfortable for long trips. It was an older Mercedes her dad had given her—twenty years old and still ran like a dream.

They'd be sharing the driving because it was going to be a long trip—almost eight hours driving straight through, but with stops along the way for meals and breaks, they figured ten or more. It was long enough that Dar was calling it a road trip and said she wasn't even thinking about their destination—what she really wanted was a chance to get away from the guys at the station who were mostly a bunch of misogynistic, narcissistic jerks, and if the guys on the website were the ones at the resort, they were truly fine-looking men. Elle said she didn't care how good they looked as long as they were big and strong and made her feel petite. That was going to take a really big guy—she was easily six feet tall and freely admitted her proportions pushed the limits on generous. Jules had been quiet about what she hoped to find at Feral Passions. She hadn't dated much after her last boyfriend. The relationship hadn't lasted very long, but she didn't seem to miss him and hadn't had much to say about him.

Meg glanced toward the bedroom. She was going to miss Zach. She'd thought about waking him for a kiss, a chance to tell him she was leaving, but he'd worked late last night, and she hated to disturb him on his day off. It would only be a week, but they'd never been apart, not since he hired her right out of college. Not more than weekends in the beginning. Then they'd started dating, and she'd stayed at his place on a lot of those weekends and moved in after he proposed.

She figured he'd suggested it because her lease had been up. He'd said it made sense because they'd be living together as soon as they married.

Living with Zach was good. Better than good. Sighing, she glanced at the clock again. The girls weren't due for at least ten more minutes, but after all the talk about going, all the reasons she kept giving herself for wanting to get away from Zach for just a few days, the reality of what she was doing scared her. She hadn't expected that.

What if she realized that she didn't miss him, that she was happier without him? What if one of those really good-looking men suddenly looked better to her than Zach? Honestly, she couldn't imagine any man possibly matching him, much less surpassing him. She was such an idiot, choosing to leave him just to see if she really loved him.

Except that wasn't the real question at all. What she really wanted to know was if Zach really, truly loved her. What if he didn't? What if he changed his mind? What if he realized he was happier without her? Meg figured the odds of that happening were greater than her ever changing the way she felt. Heart thudding in her chest, she grabbed the back of a kitchen chair for balance, needing the stability, the anchor to keep her from running back into the bedroom, to keep from . . .

"Meggie? Is it already time for you to go?"

She spun around so quickly she almost stumbled. Zach stood in the doorway, faded sweats hanging low on his hips, his chest bare, hair all mussed, eyes squinting against the bright kitchen light. "In a few minutes." Damn, she sounded breathless, as if she'd been running. "I'm waiting for the girls to get here. I'm the last one they're picking up."

"Are you okay?" He stepped closer and wrapped his arms around her. "You're trembling. Meggie?"

"I just realized how much I'm going to miss you." Damn. She didn't want to cry, but he was warm and familiar, and she loved him, and she thought of what it would feel like if he grew tired of her one day and left. She'd already given him her heart. If he left her, he'd take it with him, but all she said was, "I was just standing here, thinking how long a week really is."

He smiled at her and then hugged her close again. "You're going to have fun. I looked at the website, and if you do even half of the outdoor activities they list, you'll be too tired to miss me." He kissed her, cupping her butt with his hands, pulling her close against his solid erection, making her ache with wanting him. "I, on the other hand," he said, nuzzling her throat, "am going to miss you like crazy."

"Mmmm. That's not fair." She nipped at his lower lip. "Teasing me when I haven't got time to play with your toys."

"I'll save them for you. I never share my toys. Not with anyone."

She laughed. "I certainly hope not. Me, neither." She kissed him again. Lights reflected off the window. "There's my ride." She slipped out of his grasp and reached for her suitcase. Zach grabbed it in one hand and slung her heavy tote bag over his shoulder with the other. "Don't forget your purse. I don't see your computer. Aren't you taking it?"

"Nope." She grabbed her purse. "They ask that we don't bring any social media stuff. It's a vacation away from everything, especially the Internet."

He frowned. "What about cell service?"

"None, though I can hook up in the main lodge to call

out. I left you a copy of my reservation with the number for the resort. I'm taking my phone for the camera, if nothing else, but if I can, I'll text." She turned when the doorbell rang. "C'mon." She kissed his chin. "If I don't go now, I'm going to change my mind and crawl back into bed with you."

He laughed as Meg opened the door. "Works for me. Hey, Dar!" He leaned close and kissed her cheek. "Are you ready for this?"

"G'morning, Zach. You have no idea! C'mon, bride-to-be. We're burning daylight."

"Burning daylight? Darian, dear, this is a lodge we're going to, not a roundup."

"Move your booty, sweetie." Dar shooed them both toward the car and opened the back door.

Jules grabbed her hand and tugged Meg inside to sit beside her in the backseat. Dar took the front passenger seat next to Elle. Zach kissed Meg, closed the door, and stepped away. Meg watched him out the back window, standing beneath the streetlight watching her, as Elle pulled away. He was still there when they finally turned a corner and headed for the freeway and the long road out of Portland to the Feral Passions Resort in California.

It was close to seven when they stopped at a little place just outside of Salem for breakfast. They trooped into the restaurant, found a table, and ordered coffee. Meg glanced at the steaming cups. "I just realized there's not a tea drinker among us."

Elle laughed. "You're just now figuring that out? We're all coffee addicts." She took a sip. "By the way, I have to say this. That is one spectacular man you left on the side of the road."

Meg laughed. "You've known Zach for months now. And you're just now noticing?"

Elle shrugged. "I've always thought he was good looking, but I think it's the way the guy looks at you, almost like you're the air he breathes. I would love to have a man look at me that way. Just once."

Meg glanced away, much too aware of that prickly feeling of tears trying their hardest to fall. "Do you really think so?"

"What?" Dar stared at her. "You mean you don't see that? Darlin', you're engaged to the man. Can't you tell he loves you to death?"

"I guess." She sort of fluttered her hands, realized she was doing the helpless female thing, and flattened them on the table. "I mean, he says he does, and he acts like he does, but . . ." She looked at the three women she'd known longer and better than anyone else. "Why am I suddenly so nervous about this?" Oh, crap, she really didn't want to turn this trip into a downer. Holding up her hand before anyone could say anything, she said, "No. Not now. I'm fine, and I know Zach loves me. It's just that he's so, well . . . I dunno. He's amazing. The best thing that ever happened to me." She took a deep breath. Laughed. "I'm just me."

"'Just you' is a terrific woman." Jules glared at her. "You've known Zach for how long now? Three years, right? I remember when he hired you. It was right after you got out of college, your very first job after graduation. You were crushing on him from the very beginning, and you've been dating now for over a year. His proposal was probably the most romantic I've ever heard of in my entire life. A man doesn't do that whole 'down on bended knee, big diamond in velvet box in a restaurant full of other people' thing if he doesn't mean it."

"That's the truth." Elle laughed. "Do you know how many people posted that on YouTube? Even shared it on Facebook? That has to be one of the most recorded, most romantic marriage proposals of all time."

Dar grabbed Meg's hand and squeezed tightly. "He loves you, Megs. No one can fake the kind of emotion in that man's eyes. And believe me, I was looking because even his eyes are sexy." Then she rolled hers, and everyone laughed.

The waitress showed up then to take their orders. At least Meg wasn't fighting down a panic attack. Once again her friends had talked her off the ledge.

"When's our group of bachelorettes showing up?" Lawz poured himself a cold beer, walked around to the other side of the bar, and sat on the stool next to Trak. He nudged his brother's shoulder. Trak merely growled. Lawz practically cackled. Why was he enjoying this so much? "Don't stress. Dinner's all planned, and it's going to be wonderful. Brad's not the only one around here who can cook."

Trak gave him the stink eye. "What are you fixing then, oh master chef?"

"Not me. Tuck's cooking tonight. He and Evan went out and caught fresh rainbow trout to go with the rice casserole Brad left in the freezer. All I have to do is stick the thawed casserole in the oven to reheat in time for dinner. Tuck's going to barbecue the trout along with some chicken breasts in case anyone doesn't like fish, Drew's got a veggie dish his mama used to make, and Manny's made a chocolate decadence I can't wait to try."

"Manny? How the hell did you get him to cook anything? He's usually a pain in the ass."

"I told him if he didn't cook, he'd get cleanup duty, and then I reminded him that women thought men who could cook were really sexy."

"I see. And that actually worked?" Trak laughed, slowly shaking his head. "I can't believe you guys might actually pull this together."

"Well . . ."

"Well, what?" Back to growling.

"If you'd quit thinking you were the only one here with a brain and accepted the fact that just because you're the alpha, you're not the only one who can figure shit out, you might realize you're surrounded by a terrific pack. None of us wants Feral Passions to fail, Trak. But a lot of the guys are a bit intimidated by your inability to see that anyone but you can manage to pull things together."

Before his brother could answer, Lawz got up and went back into the kitchen. It was time to stick the veggies in the oven, and he wondered when their newest set of guests might arrive. And he really didn't want to deal with any of this. Enough was enough.

He'd just set the oven controls when Trak stepped into the kitchen. "They're here. Should be quieter with only four this week. Two sisters had to cancel, so it's just the bridal party."

Lawz rinsed his hands and hung the apron on a peg. There'd been some really nice women who'd come through over the past few months, but not a single one had really caught his attention. Ever hopeful, he followed Trak out the front door and down the steps.

And came to a dead stop as the driver's-side door on the big Mercedes opened and the most amazing woman he'd ever seen crawled out and stretched. Tall and lean with dark chocolate skin and shoulder-length black hair, she looked like a distance runner and moved with the grace of a dancer. She'd stretched her hands high overhead once she was out and then slowly bent at the waist and flattened her palms to the ground.

His mouth went dry at the trim curve of her absolutely incredible ass. Her snug camisole top gapped at her waist, baring sleek, dark skin between her light blue pants and the cream-colored shirt, but then she straightened, turned, and caught him staring at her. Her eyes went wide. He expected a snarky comment or anger, but he scented her instant arousal. Without hesitation, he walked up and held out his hand. "Lawson Jakes," he said, smiling as she took his hand in hers. Her grasp was strong, her skin smooth as silk. "Welcome to Feral Passions."

"I'm Darian Ahlers. Dar for short. Nice to meet you, Lawson."

"Short form for me is Lawz." He smiled and then followed her around to the back of the car, where Trak and Manny were helping the rest of the women unload their bags.

"Hey, Manny. You disappeared this afternoon." He shook hands with the forester.

"Yeah, had to do a bit of scouting. You know that logging operation just north of us? I heard some gunshots over there just before lunchtime and wanted to go check. We can't risk any of the wolves getting out of the preserve. I'd hate to lose one to a hunter, but everyone's safe and accounted for."

Dar raised her head. "Would someone shoot a wild wolf? There aren't that many of them, are there? Aren't they protected?"

"They are," Manny said. "But there are enough idiots with guns who think it's their right to shoot anything that moves out here in the woods. That's why we keep the entire boundary of the preserve fenced. We've got enough property that the wolves aren't crowded, but we do our best to keep them safe."

Tuck showed up while they talked. There was no missing the fact that the pack's veterinarian was huge, and he always made Lawz feel like a little kid. At least six and a half feet tall and well over two-sixty, he was all brawn and brute strength.

Until he worked with an animal. Then he was gentle as could be and a deft surgeon when necessary, as well as a skilled artist with a paintbrush.

Interesting how Tuck went straight to the largest woman of the group, but then he'd made a quip a while back that it would take a big woman to handle him. Elle was definitely that, a large, striking woman with satiny smooth skin even darker than Darian's. She was at least six feet tall and generously proportioned any way you looked at her, but Tuck seemed to find her absolutely mesmerizing.

Manny had obviously noticed her, but once Tuck moved in on the dark beauty, Manny turned on the charm, and just that fast, the one named Jules was teasing him back with practiced ease. Manny was one of those guys women thought so sexy they often clammed up and didn't know what to say around him, but he was really just a heck of a nice guy, a little quiet but a good, strong member of the pack. Darian had walked around the sedan to speak to a tall blonde. While Lawz waited for her, he watched Manny and Jules head toward one of the cabins.

So far, the guys had learned it was easy enough to start something from the very beginning—walking a woman to her cabin often set up a pairing from the start. He heard their laughter as Jules and Manny disappeared from view where the trail led into the woods.

Evan and Drew Miklos hung back. The two of them traded off tending bar at Growl, and they'd both paired up with women last week. Nothing had come of their relationships beyond a lot of good sex, but they weren't going to move in on anyone until the other guys had a chance.

That had been a good thing about this whole resort concept. The pack had stayed strong, all of them looking out for each other. Lawz glanced up as Darian walked back and reached for her bag.

"I've got them," he said. "Ready to go?" When she nodded, he grabbed the rest of her luggage and led her away from the car, toward the cabin that had been assigned to her.

Trak usually hung back until the guys had all paired up. As the pack alpha, it didn't seem fair that he have first choice of the women when they arrived. An alpha might be the one in charge, but he'd learned a long time ago that a good alpha never took advantage of his authority.

Trak still struggled with that one.

Unfortunately, Lawz was right. Trak was well aware he could be a total pain in the ass. Too aware of his own failings, he realized Evan and Drew had gone back to work at Growl and he was the only one left, which meant that whoever was the last woman, well . . . she was stuck with him.

When she stepped around the back of the car, he almost swallowed his tongue. She was tall and built, one absolutely stacked blonde with a killer smile and sexy gray eyes framed in thick, dark lashes. Right now, she looked a little bit lost, but that made sense. All her girlfriends had abandoned her and gone off with different guys. That thought made him smile. Luckily, she wasn't alone anymore.

"Hi," she said, holding out her right hand. Her nails were painted a deep, dark red, and he had to catch himself to keep from taking her hand and kissing it as if she were royalty. "I'm Meg. Where are you going to take me?"

"Anywhere you want to go." Oh, crap! Had he just said that out loud? He must have because she was laughing, a big, fun-loving laugh that had him smiling in return.

"Sounds wonderful," she said, "but I doubt my fiancé would approve."

"Well, damn." Laughing—mostly at himself—he grabbed her bags. "You're the bride-to-be, so I guess that means I need to act like a gentleman when I walk you to your cabin. You're the one who booked the week, aren't you?"

"I am," she said. "You must be Trak."

He stopped, feeling like an idiot. "I'm sorry. Yes. I should have introduced myself. I'm Traker Jakes, and we talked a while back. I thought I recognized your voice. I hope you and your friends have a really enjoyable week with us."

"It's so peaceful here," she said. "I think we're all ready

for a break. I can't imagine not having a terrific time." She shook her head, and her expression was a bit bemused. "It's been a bit hectic, trying to get my work caught up so I could leave, planning a wedding. More stressful than I expected, so this trip is one I've really been looking forward to."

"I can guarantee you'll have a wonderful time." Trak took the tote bag she'd slung over her shoulder—it looked awfully heavy for her—and grabbed the big one out of the trunk. "I've been told there's magic here at Feral Passions," he said. "All you need to do is trust your heart, follow your instincts, and let go of anything and everything that's not letting you relax."

She laughed. He really liked her laugh. She didn't hold back at all. "It's that 'letting go' thing I have trouble with."

Trak just shook his head. "Don't we all. C'mon." He glanced over his shoulder and said, "Once you're in your cabin and settled, I imagine you'll feel a hundred percent better." Then he headed off to the left of the lodge with Meg following.

This was where the magic began. He'd had more than one guest tell him that stepping onto the trail to the cabin they'd be staying in was like walking into an enchanted forest. Sunlight filtered through the trees, but barely enough made it through the heavy canopy to lighten the shadows. Lush and green except for the occasional splash of red, there was little evidence of summer ending and fall creeping close.

"Those red leaves are so pretty." Meg paused behind him, reaching out to touch one.

He stopped her just in time. "Pretty, but as Mom used to say, look with your eyes, not with your hands. That's poison oak. It can cause a miserable rash if you're sensitive to it."

"Thank you." She pulled her hand back and stayed to the middle of the trail, but his gentle warning made her think. Even here, where everything was peaceful and calm, where it was all about the comfort of the guest, there were risks.

Was that what she'd done? Let herself get sidetracked worrying about the risks of loving Zach? More worried about failure than excited about making a new life with him?

If that was the case, she was guilty of setting up their relationship to fail.

How had she come to that conclusion, that Zach wasn't worth the risk? Or was her real worry that she was the one who wasn't worth the risk? Either way, she was putting up barriers that wouldn't exist without her building them.

Damn. She was such an idiot.

Trak paused at the top step of Meg's cabin and waited for her to join him. She'd paused where a break in the trees opened to a spectacular view of the rugged peaks of the Trinity Alps. She stood there, hands folded in front of her, obviously transfixed. That told him a lot about her—she appreciated the untamed and rustic nature of this wild country.

He hoped she'd have the same reaction to the cabin. He loved this part, showing their guests into the cabins he and his pack had built by hand. Each one was a work of art, furnished with the Shaker-style pieces he and his father and grandfather had built over the years.

Some of them featured Tuck's paintings of wolves. This one had a portrait of Brad and Cain, who were two of Tuck's favorite models, though Trak couldn't remember if that painting was still there or not. A few of the guests had asked to buy the paintings, so Tuck had quoted ridiculously high prices because he didn't want to sell them.

It hadn't worked. It appeared his art was worth the many thousands he'd asked.

Tuck was the only one who'd been surprised that anyone, especially their guests, put that kind of value on his talent.

Meg turned away from the view and walked up the steps to the door. Trak hoped she liked what she saw. Her opinion mattered to him, which was surprising. Usually he only cared if they were having a good time, but Meg was an attractive woman, and he liked what he'd seen of her in action with her friends. Caring and yet very organized. She struck him as a leader, the kind of woman who would make an excellent mate to an alpha like him.

Of course, there was that fiancé waiting in the wings.

But even if she'd been free, not promised to another man, Trak wasn't reacting to Meg the way Brad had explained his first meeting with Cherry had felt. Brad had known she was his—his and Cain's—and had set out that very first day to seduce her into loving them. Obviously it had worked or Trak wouldn't be shuffling through pack members to find guys to cover for his two wayward wolves and their new mate.

But that didn't mean he couldn't enjoy Meg's company, couldn't make it his job to ensure that she had a good time. With that thought in mind, he opened the door and stepped back to let her enter first.

She stood in the entry with her hands clasped against her chest and merely gazed at the small cabin with its tiny kitchenette, large armoire, and king-sized bed. He had no idea what she thought, hoped she approved, that she'd like the way it looked. Was it too rustic? Not what she was expecting? Finally, he stepped around her and carried her bags inside.

In a hushed voice, she finally said, "This is absolutely stunning."

She turned and smiled, and he actually felt the warmth of her pleasure. Now that was promising.

"I'm glad you like it. We've worked really hard to make each of the cabins as comfortable as we could. I'm going to leave you here to unpack, but don't be too long."

"Thank you." She walked over to the table and chairs that sat beneath a window in the tiny kitchen and checked out the small area. After a moment, she turned and smiled at him. She really was an extraordinarily attractive woman. "I don't even know what time it is," she said. "Do I have time for a quick shower before dinner?"

"Not a problem. This is your vacation. We'll do our best to accommodate you in every way possible."

He stepped out and quietly closed the door behind him. He was glad he'd paired up with Meg. He had a feeling she'd be a lot of fun without any hassles. He probably wasn't going to get laid this week, but there were other things to enjoy with a smart, funny, good-looking woman.

CHAPTER 3

Dar followed the tall, athletic-looking man who'd openly stared when she was stretching. Usually guys who focused on her ass when she was bent over in a stretch came across with a pervy vibe, but Lawz showed nothing but pure, honest, male appreciation. It was hard to find fault with that, especially when he had the look of a guy she'd really like appreciating her.

She followed him along a well-maintained trail leading away from the main lodge. It was only a short distance, but she felt as if she were walking into another world. Ferns grew thick along the trail; tall pines and evergreens hid the other cabins. They rounded a bushy fir tree, and there it was, a little log cabin with a front deck just made for sitting.

"Oh! Wow." She stood there with a stupid grin on her face, breathing in the aromatic scent of cedar. The cabin had to be new to smell this fresh, but the natural landscaping helped it fit into the spot as if it had always been there.

Lawz paused at the bottom step and smiled at her. "The architect is the guy who originally came up with the idea for Feral Passions," he said. "Brad's really talented, but this is definitely a homespun operation."

"I love it." She felt almost giddy now that she'd moved away from the car and had taken that short walk through the woods, especially after the long day of driving. There wasn't any Internet, she didn't have any bars on her phone, and the setting had her blood pressure falling and her stress levels dropping into the minus category.

Though she had to admit, the man had her hot and bothered.

"C'mon in and see the rest."

He held the door for her, and Darian walked into what was the cutest little cabin she'd ever seen. Lawz followed and set her suitcase on a stand near a large oak armoire, her smaller bag on the bed. The furniture was all very simple—she thought it was a Shaker design, but did it really matter?

Not really. Not when she was so damned aware of the man waiting beside the door, standing there silently radiating pheromones. That had to be it, the reason she was so attuned to him, to the sound of his movements, the cadence of his breathing. His scent. She never really noticed a guy's scent, at least not unless he absolutely reeked of sweat, and there were more than enough of those hanging around the gym.

No, Lawz had a scent like nothing she'd ever experienced, an intoxicating mix of pine and lemon, of herbs she almost recognized but couldn't, but whatever it was, it was taking everything she had not to turn around and go back to him and just rub herself over his body like a cat in heat.

"I won't keep you, Dar. I'm on the dinner crew tonight, so I need to get back to the lodge, but come down when you're ready and let me fix a drink for you. We do a mean margarita here, if you like them."

She turned, fully aware that she really didn't want him to leave, and wasn't that just the strangest thing? She never got like this around a man, but there was something about Lawz. He appealed to her. She meant to merely thank him for carrying her luggage, and she wasn't sure how it happened, but she moved and he moved, and they were suddenly in a clinch that had her body on fire and her breasts begging for attention.

"Holy shit," he said. At least that's what she thought he said just before he dipped his head and absolutely captured her mouth. He took her forcefully; she immediately responded.

His mouth was on hers, his lips molding to hers, and she was with him every breath, every lick and touch and taste. He feasted on her mouth, dipped his head to nip at her throat, and she bared herself to him, inviting him to taste her.

Dar was tall, but he was so much taller, and he lifted her up against him, cupping her bottom in his big hands when she wrapped her legs around his waist. He ravaged her mouth, her throat, and then dipped his head and captured her nipple through the soft cotton of her cami top.

She hadn't worn a bra for the long trip, and the suction when he wrapped his lips around her nipple had it standing hard and erect within the wet circle of fabric. He worried first her right and then her left, nipping with his teeth, tugging the sensitive nub, taking her higher, farther, faster than any man had done before, touching nothing more than her breasts.

He bit down on her nipple and tugged, and the sweet pain shot like a bolt of lightning straight to her clit. She cried out and pressed herself against his abdomen, her inner muscles spasming and clenching, climaxing from nothing more than his mouth on her breasts.

Gasping for breath, she leaned her head against his chest. Her body still rippled with her release, and her hands trembled until, from absolutely nowhere and with no intelligent reason, she started giggling. Burying her face against the broad expanse of his chest, she laughed while tears flowed and Lawz just held her. Finally, when she was fully beyond embarrassment and well into utter humiliation, he tilted her chin up and forced her to meet his eyes.

She hiccupped. He kissed her. "That was fun," he said. "Want to try it again?"

"Yes." She sucked in a breath. Her lips were actually trembling. She wasn't a giggler or a trembler, thank you. "In a bed," she said. "Preferably naked, with you as an equal participant and both of us with plenty of time. Not when you have to go cook dinner."

"Agreed." He let her feet slide slowly down his legs to the floor and held her while she got her balance.

She looped her arms over his shoulders and stared at him for a long moment. He stared right back at her without flinching. His eyes were dark, dark brown, but she saw flecks of gold in their depths. His nose was long and straight, his lower lip fuller than the upper, and she wanted him so badly it was all she could do not to drag him to the bed now.

"I'll be down in about fifteen minutes, okay?"

"That works." He leaned close and kissed her. "I don't think I've ever wanted a woman the way I want you. Please don't change your mind. And I realize begging isn't manly, but I think I'm already desperate."

She laughed. "S'okay. Desperation works. I don't intend to—change my mind, that is. I'm curious, though. Is this the way you greet all your guests?"

Slowly, he shook his head. "Never. I'm really picky about women. Don't know what it is about you, but I'm going with it."

"Good. I hope you've got protection, because I didn't bring any. I had no idea what the extracurricular activities were like here."

He kissed her quickly and stepped away. "Neither did I. I have to admit, this is a new one for me." Then he turned away and went out the door without looking back. She was glad of that. If he'd turned to her again, she had a feeling she'd be dragging him to the bed, protection or not.

She wanted him that badly.

Elle followed this mountain of a man through the woods. He'd said his name was Kentucky and told her to call him Tuck, but he didn't say much more beyond the introduction. A few words about the resort, that there was less than a month before they closed for the season. She wasn't really sure what else he'd said, because she'd stopped listening to his specific words within a few sentences, too mesmerized by the deep growl of his voice to actually pay attention to the content.

She really hoped it wasn't anything important.

Walking a few steps behind him was its own kind of tor-ture. His shoulders were so broad that she didn't think she'd ever seen a man this large, this impressively built. They tapered down to one of the finest butts she'd ever followed in her life, and it was all she could do not to reach out and touch. Realizing her fingers were actually twitching had her biting back a bad case of inappropriate laughter, but she couldn't wait to see what the other girls thought of him.

Elle thought he was the hottest thing she'd ever seen.

He led her into a small clearing, and she stopped dead in her tracks and laughed. "It looks like the Three Bears' cabin." When he turned and smiled at her, she just shook her head. "Does that make me Goldilocks?"

He surprised her then, turning and taking a step closer to her, looping a long, loose curl of her hair around his forefinger. It was naturally dark brown, but she'd added some auburn highlights last time she colored that turned it deep burgundy in the sunlight. Tuck held it up and stared at it as if this were a major decision.

"Not gold," he said, rubbing the curl between his fingers. "But it's really unique. I think you're our first guest with burgundy-colored hair. I like it. It fits you."

She stood there, speechless, shaken by both his words and her response. When he'd touched her hair, she'd wanted to lean into him. Wanted him.

Then he turned as if he'd felt nothing at all and went up the steps. Sighing, Elle followed.

The cabin was adorable, all rich-looking cedar logs with a nice little front porch, a table and a couple of chairs, and forest-green mini blinds at the windows. Practical and comfortable. Elle followed him as he opened the door and stepped aside so she could enter first. She walked through the doorway and stopped in her tracks to get the feel of the absolutely wonderful space that would be her home for the next week. This was even better than the photos on the website. She turned, and Tuck was right there, so close that her breasts brushed his chest.

They both stepped apart. "I'm sorry," he said. He dipped his head and actually flushed a deep red. "I didn't mean to crowd you."

She looked directly into his eyes—they were a dark, cloudy gray with a burst of gold, so mesmerizing she could easily lose herself in his calm gaze. "You didn't crowd me. I'm actually enjoying this unusual sense of feeling almost petite." She laughed when he smiled at her. "So often when I'm around a man, I feel like an absolute moose. You make me feel normal."

He carefully set her bags on the floor and cupped her shoulders in his big hands. "You're never going to be anything as average as normal, Elle. You're much too special. You are an impressive, beautiful woman, one I'd like to get to know a lot better."

His words startled her, but she did her best not to let it show. He was a spectacular man—big all over, with those broad shoulders and long, strong legs. His hair was dark, lying in soft curls much longer than it appeared at first glance. He was bearded, though it was neatly trimmed and framed his strong jaw in a most attractive manner. The sleeveless T-shirt he wore exposed muscular arms and a vivid tattoo that stretched around his right shoulder and upper arm. Dark hair covered his forearms, and he was, without a doubt, the most attractive man Elle had ever seen.

And he wanted to get to know her better. "I think I'd like that," she said. "Very much."

He smiled almost shyly, picked up her bags, and set the large one on a luggage rack near a simply designed armoire, like all the furniture, obviously built by craftsmen. The smaller bag went on the end of the bed. "I'm helping Lawz with dinner tonight, so I need to get back to the dining room. Take a few minutes to relax, but come back to the lodge as soon as you can. I'll fix you a drink and make sure you've got something to snack on while we get everything going. Does that work?"

"It does. Thank you." She wanted to kiss him, wanted to see what that beard would feel like against her cheeks, what his lips would taste like, but that was silly. They didn't know each other, but she smiled and realized she was biting her lips, noticed he was focused on her mouth, and she wanted him to kiss her so badly she almost ached.

He must have gotten the message. He actually groaned when he reached for her, and she moved into his embrace as if they'd been lovers for years. She'd never been held by a man as large as Tuck, never found a man who fit so well with her, who held her as if she were spun glass, a precious thing to be cared for. He kissed her carefully, his mouth coming down on hers as if he feared damaging her, and she realized that, as big as he was, he'd probably only been with normal-sized women, and it was awkward for him when a woman was so small next to his huge size.

There was no awkwardness with the two of them. She wasn't that much shorter than Tuck, yet he was so much larger than she was, a big man with a strong body, sure of himself, and yet in an endearing way, so obviously unsure of her. She loved it, loved that small sense of vulnerability in the way he held her, the way he kissed her.

And it was so unexpected, to be in this remote lodge with her very best friends, meeting a man who was her ideal—at least in size and appearance—more than any man she'd ever met.

He ended the kiss, slowly, almost regretfully, and leaned his forehead against hers. "Don't take too long," he said. "I'm going to be waiting very impatiently for you."

She watched as he left the cabin, and she didn't close the door until he disappeared along the shadowed trail beneath the trees. Then she rushed into the bathroom to get a quick shower so she could chase him down at the lodge.

Jules really wished she could get past the nerves because the man leading her through the woods was someone she really wanted to get to know better. But it wasn't going to happen, not the way she was shaking. No doubt in her mind at all, he was the sexiest guy she'd ever seen, but she figured the source of her nerves was a little like PTSD, which made sense.

She had an excellent reason to fear a man she didn't know. She'd known Andrew, and he'd still done a number on her. She'd never had the courage to tell her friends the truth about her old boyfriend. He'd looked great when she'd listed his qualities—he was sharp looking, personable, successful. They'd all liked him the one time they'd met.

They had no idea that she'd discovered the hard way that there was another side to the man. One not nearly as much fun or as likable. Now, following Armando through the woods, she wasn't certain if the chills along her spine were fear or arousal.

You'd think at this point she'd be able to tell the two apart.

They stepped out of the shadowed trail into a tiny glen, where a beam of sunlight illuminated the log cabin sitting in the middle of the woods as if it sat under a spotlight. It was so utterly peaceful, her nervousness fled and a sense of calm settled over her shoulders like a warm shawl. "This is where I'm staying?"

Armando merely turned and raised an eyebrow. "Of course. What do you think of it?"

"I love it. It's so much better than I imagined. It's peaceful. Welcoming, even." She stepped around him and walked up the front steps to the small deck.

"I actually helped build this one." He sounded justifiably proud as he carried her bags up the steps.

Jules opened the door for him and followed him inside. The cabin was small, but very comfortable with a large bed and very simple oak furniture. Everything fit the rustic setting with impeccable style. "I think I'm really going to love it here. I swear I feel more relaxed just walking through the door."

He set her large case on a suitcase rack and placed her smaller bag on the foot of the bed. "You're supposed to feel relaxed. That's the purpose of your visit, isn't it?"

"You're right. It is." She smiled at him and realized her nerves had settled to a low hum. Yeah, this was definitely more arousal than fear. The sense of relief had her smiling. "Well, that and spending a last week with our friend Meg as a single woman. She's not getting married until October 2, but this was the only week we could all swing time off."

"Are any of the others of your group married?"

Jules shook her head. "Nope. Not yet."

She might have been, she thought. Thank goodness she'd figured out what a jerk Andrew was before they got any more serious than they had. After discovering what a slimeball she was dating, she figured she'd been lucky getting away with nothing more than a split lip. As much as he'd been screwing around—quite literally—she'd been thrilled she hadn't ended up with an STD.

Armando—*Manny,* the guys had called him—laughed. "Women today aren't rushing to get married like they used to. They have the freedom to hold out for what they really want."

She sighed, running her fingers along the silky surface of the armoire. "We're not really holdouts, I don't think. Mostly just particular. I figure I'll know when the right guy comes along."

Manny nodded sagely. "I agree. A lifelong commitment to one person is a huge decision. Not one to be made in haste."

She loved the way he spoke, like a man from another time. His words were measured and calm, his voice as smooth as silk. Plus, he had long hair. Not overly long, but it was a deep, rich, silky brown that waved over his shoulders in front and curled against his shoulder blades in back. With his neatly trimmed beard and mustache and the slight widow's peak, he could have been one of the Three Muske-teers. He only needed the white shirt with blousy sleeves and a laced neckline to complete the image.

She glanced at his long, long legs. Knee-high boots wouldn't hurt, though the faded jeans and moccasins worked just as well. "Yeah," she said, responding to his comment. "I thought I'd met the one a while back. Then he knocked me out when I told him I knew he was cheating."

Shocked that she'd said exactly what she was thinking, Jules slammed her hand over her mouth. "I'm sorry. I don't know what made me say that. I never talk about what happened. Even my closest friends don't know the whole story."

She was still apologizing when Manny moved so quickly she had no idea how she ended up in his arms.

"No," he said. "Please don't apologize. It explains so much." He kissed her forehead and then held her close, comforting her in a strong but gentle embrace that brought her firmly against his chest. "I thought you were afraid of me, but if a man has treated you so badly, you have every right to be uncomfortable following a strange man into the woods. I wish I'd known. I would have made a point to make you feel safe. I'm sorry."

"It's not your fault." She was so embarrassed. She wanted to push him away, but his arms felt so good around her, and somehow hers had crept around his broad back. He was big but so gentle, and his deep, mellow voice calmed her.

"No," he said, and she thought his voice sounded terribly sad. "Not mine, personally, but sometimes I feel compelled to apologize for all the bastards who share my gender. We're not all like that, truly. I can honestly say that every man here reveres women. You are all beautiful to us for so many reasons—we respect and admire your strength and your intelligence. We love your grace, your willingness to step out of your comfort zone and come here to what must feel like the back of beyond."

She giggled against his chest, and she was not at all the kind of woman who giggled. "It's not entirely all the way to the back of beyond. You have running water, and the road was mostly paved." She raised her head and smiled at him, pleased to see he was smiling back. Sometimes her sense of humor was lost on people. Face it, it was lost on most guys.

Armando got it. "True," he said. "But you know the best thing? We have men who cook and then clean up after themselves. And this man needs to get to the kitchen."

Then he tilted his head and kissed her. She was so surprised, she gasped. He took her unintended invitation and softly licked the seam of her lips. She tightened her arms around his waist and kissed him back, opened to a man she'd barely met and yet trusted more than any man she'd ever known.

And damn, but this guy could kiss. They were both breathing hard by the time they slowly pulled apart. Jules would have been embarrassed except Armando was obviously as deeply affected as she was, his erection a solid brand against her belly, rising hard beneath his faded jeans. He was close to a foot taller than her five and a half feet and so broad shouldered and powerful he made her feel petite in comparison. He wasn't bulky at all, but strongly built with a taut, muscular body like a long-distance runner, all lean muscle and long arms and legs. She tried to imagine him naked and realized she was trembling from head to foot.

It took her a moment to recognize it as need. Pure, unadulterated need, and all from one amazing kiss. In her defense, she figured it had been a long time since she'd had any real satisfaction, especially since Andrew had left her wanting more often than not, but she took a deep breath and stepped back.

Armando's arms released her, but his hands rested on

her hips. "You need to go cook," she said, fully aware how breathy her voice sounded, that there wasn't a damned thing she could do about it, even if she wanted to. "I really have to get a quick shower and a change of clothes." She smiled, relieved that the trembling had eased. "What are you fixing?"

His smile could take a woman to her knees. And the moment that thought flitted through her brain, she wanted to go to her knees, unbutton those worn jeans, and show him just what a woman on her knees could do.

"Chocolate decadence," he said, rolling the words in a way that left her shivering.

"Mmmm. Sounds wicked."

"It is, but I don't think it's even close to how sweetly wicked you are, my Jules." Then he laughed, kissed her quickly, and headed for the door. "I want you to think about that. I'm going to want a taste. Later."

And with that, he was out the door and gone. Jules stood there, body primed, heart racing, staring at the closed door and imagining all the wicked things Armando might do on the way to getting his taste.

Meg checked her hair, decided the long skirt and tank top were appropriate for dinner, and grabbed a light sweater off the bed. She slipped on a pair of sandals and, at the last minute, and only because she felt naked without it, stuck her cell phone in the deep side pocket in her skirt. She left a light on in the kitchen area and flipped on the porch light, even though it was barely five. It would probably be dark when she headed back here after dinner.

She stepped out and pulled the door closed behind her.

Something moved in the shadows near the woods where the trail led to the lodge. She stood very still, wondering if it might be a deer, when a massive wolf stepped out of the woods.

"Holy crap." She reached back for the door handle when the wolf trotted across the open area and then sat on his butt not far from the bottom step. It watched her, ears pricked forward, tongue hanging out like it was a big dog, not something that might consider eating her.

She was already moving slowly back to slip inside the cabin, but his playful expression stopped her. He was definitely a wolf—a very large wolf—gray all over with black tips to his fur, the tips of his ears, and in a line down his tail, but he watched her almost as if they shared a private joke. She knew this place was a preserve for wolves, but she'd neglected to ask anyone if the wolves were running free on the grounds or not. Obviously, at least this one was.

Hoping this wasn't a truly stupid move, she sat on the top step and studied her visitor. He watched her just as carefully, and she wondered just how tame he was. It didn't take long before she patted the step beside her, wondering if he'd respond to a gesture most dogs would be familiar with.

He yipped and trotted up the stairs as if he'd merely been waiting for an invitation, but when he got to the top step, Meg realized just how big this animal was. With her still sitting, he towered over her, all sharp teeth and appetite. "Goodness." She backed away. "You're a big one, aren't you?"

The damned wolf yipped, almost as if he understood her. Then he sat beside her and leaned his full weight against her shoulder. Laughing, Meg leaned back. After a moment, she wrapped her arm around his shoulders, and damned if the wolf didn't snuggle even closer.

"You're incredible, and you know it, right?"

He sighed and rested his chin on her shoulder.

"And you're working me like a pro. Sorry, but I haven't got any food inside, and besides, I need to go meet my friends. Come with me, okay?"

He was on his feet and down the steps in an instant. Meg swung her sweater over her shoulders and followed him into the woods.

Sunday evening

Jules was sitting at a big round table on the front deck of the lodge when Meg stepped out of the woods. Her wolf was nowhere to be seen, though she'd followed him all the way from her cabin. Somewhere over the past dozen steps or so he'd disappeared into the thick undergrowth.

Still, she had to admit that, so far, this resort was living up to everything it promised. She felt absolutely stress-free and, other than missing Zach more than she'd thought possible, was really looking forward to exploring the area and seeing more wolves.

That had really been cool. She crossed the grassy area and waved to Jules just as Trak stepped out onto the deck and spotted her. He disappeared inside, but he was back by the time she'd found a place to sit at the table.

"Margarita?" He held out a tray with one frozen margarita and a small pitcher filled with more for the table.

"Such service. Thank you." She smiled at him and thought once again how nice he was, and how really good-looking. All the men she'd seen here were striking. Trak teased Jules about something inane, chatted with both of them a minute longer, and then went back inside.

Meg glanced at Jules. She looked ready to follow Trak back inside the lodge, and Meg laughed. "Their website doesn't do the staff justice, does it? Have you ever seen so many truly hot guys in your life?"

Jules just shook her head. "Remember that time we went to see the Chippendales? We thought they were all so handsome, and ya know what? They've got nothing on these guys."

"I dunno," Meg said. "There was one of those dancers at the club that night who was sporting some equipment under his tight little bikini shorts that I—"

Jules actually snorted. "I remember him, and I thought it looked like he'd tucked a rolled-up sock in his shorts. That was most decidedly *not* real."

And the conversation went downhill from there.

CHAPTER 4

They were both laughing when Armando stepped out on the deck and invited them inside. "We're getting the buffet set up, so dinner will be ready in a couple of minutes." He glanced at Jules and Meg. "Looks like we're missing a couple."

"I know. I wonder where Dar and Elle are?" Meg glanced toward the trails leading to their cabins just as Elle stepped out of the shadows. Darian was with her, and so was a huge, dark gray wolf walking between the two of them. He had distinctive black tips to his fur, which made him look as if he rippled when he walked.

Dar had a huge grin on her face, and Elle looked a bit shocked by her escort, but they waved as soon as they spotted Meg and the others. The wolf peeled off to the right and headed back toward the woods. Dar stopped to watch him go.

Laughing, Elle grabbed her hand and dragged her across the parking area and up the stairs.

"Is that cool or what?" Elle was too excited to sit, but she didn't hesitate to take the margarita that Manny offered to her. "I was getting ready to walk down here when he just showed up in front of my cabin. I swear he's the smartest animal I've ever seen, and when I asked him if everyone was already at the lodge, he led me to Dar's cabin." She glanced at Dar and rolled her eyes. "Because, obviously she wasn't here."

"I'm sorry. I took a shower and decided to lie down for a minute, only I went sound asleep." Laughing, she added, "Guess I relaxed faster than I realized."

"Come with me, ladies." Armando had been waiting patiently, but now it was obviously time for them to get moving.

Elle glanced around, looking for Tuck, but there was no sign of him.

The guys had set up an amazing buffet with fresh-grilled trout and a vegetable dish, what looked like homemade bread, some kind of seasoned barbecued chicken that smelled wonderful, and a rice casserole that was absolutely irresistible.

"Save room." Jules glanced at Armando as she carefully loaded her plate. "Manny said he's made a chocolate decadence for dessert." All eyes went to Armando, who swept an imaginary hat from his head and bowed with a dramatic sweep. "We most definitely don't want to miss that."

"Advice noted." Meg carefully added a few more things to her plate and walked back over to the table. She paused by the line, where the guys were now filling their plates.

"Gentlemen, I certainly hope you have some activities planned for tomorrow, because I really want to keep eating like this all week and still be able to fit into my clothes."

Trak saluted. "We will definitely help you work off any calories you consume, dear Meg. Enjoy your meal."

"Dear Meg?" Jules cocked an eyebrow at Meg as she took her seat.

She blushed. "It's just the way he talks." Meg looked directly at her. She wasn't going to take the bait because she'd noticed the courtly mannerisms of all the men she'd actually interacted with. "In fact, have you notice the speech patterns of most of the men here? Almost as if they're from another time. Old-fashioned, actually."

"I like it." Jules took a bite of her trout and groaned. "This is so good." She chewed and swallowed and then scooted her chair aside for Evan, who was coming her way with his plate loaded. "Anyway, I'd forgotten how nice it was to have a man open doors and carry heavy things." She added rice to her fork as Evan set his plate down on the table between her and Meg. "And cook," she said. Meg thought her smile at Evan looked just a bit proprietary. "Can't forget the fact these guys are great cooks."

"And they take turns," Elle added. "Drew told me that when they first opened up, the only one who could cook was a guy named Brad, who's gone this week. He's been teaching the rest of them."

"That he has." Lawz took a seat between Dar and Jules, who scooted their chairs over to make room. "I mean, we're all bachelors, so we had some rudimentary skills."

"Very rudimentary." Trak took the spot at the head of the table, closest to Meg, which brought a searching glance from Dar, seated on his left. "I think Manny was our most advanced."

"Yeah." Drew pulled a chair from another table and stuck it between Evan and Elle. "Manny had progressed from boiling water for freeze-dried camping rations."

"Hey, jerk. Give me a break." Manny took the empty seat beside Jules. He turned to her and said, "I'm a forester, so I was out in the woods and roughing it most of the time."

"You didn't let me finish, Armando." Drew drawled the man's given name. "I was trying to say you had progressed from boiling water to using a microwave."

"Don't tell me you made your chocolate decadence in a microwave!" Jules laughed, and Manny merely shook his head.

"No. I. Did. Not. Jules." He carefully enunciated each word, sniffed, and gave her a look that reminded Meg of a deeply affronted master chef. "I followed a recipe. It required a stove, measuring, and many steps to ensure my exquisite creation."

"That's the thing." Evan managed to get an extra chair in between Drew and Meg. "And for this we need to give Lawz some credit. The engineer among us discovered a cookbook, and his love of numbers and measurements superseded his fear of cooking not being a manly operation."

"What?" Elle laughed. "Every woman knows there's nothing sexier than a guy who cooks." She paused and took a bite. "Well, unless it's one who cleans the bathroom." She glanced at the rest of the table and frowned.

Meg realized the huge man who'd walked Elle to her cabin hadn't arrived yet. Before she could mention his absence, Elle's face lit up, and she smiled.

"Tuck!" Her eyes actually sparkled, until Meg realized she was smiling right along with Elle and everyone else at the table as the missing man in question walked through the front door. "I wondered if you were going to join us for dinner."

Tuck paused beside Elle, leaned over, and kissed her. Meg shared a secret grin with Dar. Obviously Tuck had done more than merely carry luggage.

"I'm sorry I'm so late. Had a trapped wolf cub that needed a rescue, and I need food. I'll be right back."

Tuck went after his dinner, and Elle grabbed a chair for him and stuck it at the foot of the table between her chair and Manny's.

Tuck was back a minute later with a loaded plate. "I was getting ready to come back to the kitchen when I heard a pup whining near the creek. There was a little guy from that late litter"—he grinned at Manny—"who'd gotten himself wedged between a rock and a big branch. Mama couldn't get him out, and his feet were in the water, so he was really chilled. I wrapped him in my vest, warmed him up, then stuck him back in the den with his two sisters. He is now his mama's worry."

The conversation flowed as if they'd all been friends for years. The guys all had wolf stories, some of them fun, a few that were sad, but it was obvious these were men who loved their lives here, loved the fact they were so close to nature.

Once dinner was over, Manny brought out his chocolate decadence, which was even better than he'd said it would be. He poured glasses of rich, dark red port wine to go with it.

Meg couldn't help but think of Zach. He would be loving every minute, and she knew he would like all the guys. She really wished he was here with her. As she watched her best friends pairing off with the men they'd met when they arrived, she felt left out. She glanced at Trak. He was sitting back in his chair, watching the interactions much the same way she was.

It was a nice way to unwind after the long drive and wonderful meal, but then Trak glanced her way and smiled and nodded toward the front deck. She wasn't sure what he wanted, but she stood and reached for their plates.

"Not your job." Trak stood and gathered everything up as if he'd cleared tables all his life and carried their dishes and utensils across the room. He left everything on the counter, took a detour behind the bar where he grabbed another bottle of the port and two glasses, and followed Meg outside to the deck.

Meg sat in a comfortable Adirondack chair, away from the light shining through the windows. Trak took the one next to her, poured a glass of wine, and handed it to her. Then he set a small tray with squares of dark chocolate on the wide arm of his chair. "This port goes great with chocolate."

She took a sip. She'd had a little with Manny's dessert. The wine was sweeter than she usually liked, but absolutely delicious, and Trak was right, it begged for chocolate. She took a piece of the dark chocolate and let it melt on her tongue. "This is so good." She smiled at him. "It's very hard not to moan when you put those two together. Moaning is so terribly unladylike."

Trak laughed. "Not always," he said, "but you're engaged, so I'm not going to go there."

She blushed. "I wasn't even thinking of that. I'm sorry. All the guys are with women who are here for a good time and whatever goes, and you're stuck with the almost-married one."

"Don't be sorry. You're supposed to relax and enjoy the break, and it never hurts to get away from someone you love, even for just a short time. It reinforces the way you feel. Tells you that you're taking the right step."

"Or the wrong one."

There was a long, telling silence. She didn't believe she'd said that out loud. She couldn't be that stupid, could she?

"Meg? What's wrong?"

She shook her head. Obviously, she was. Why did she make such an idiotic comment? She smiled at Trak. He really was a nice man and terribly sweet and good looking. And he looked honestly concerned about her. That was special, in its own way. She wondered why he was single, why no woman had snatched him up yet.

Not her business. "Just pre-wedding jitters." She smiled, shrugged. Tried not to look like such a loser. "I really love Zach. My fiancé. He's an amazing man." She took another sip of her port. "So," she said. "What are we going to do tomorrow?"

Lawz walked Dar back to her cabin. He wasn't sure how to explain the effect she had on him, the almost all-consuming sensation that he wanted to hang on to her, wanted to tell her his secrets and beg her to stay. But rules were rules, no matter how much he wanted to break them.

Brad had made a strange comment one time, how they were always told that the fantasy of finding your one true mate was just that—a fantasy—but he wondered if that was wrong. Brad and Cain had known almost immediately that Cherry was the one for them. He'd said it was like the pro-verbial lightbulb went off overhead and he knew.

Because that's sort of how Lawz was feeling about this

alluring, dark-eyed, dark-skinned woman walking along the trail beside him, holding his hand, not talking about anything, but obviously appreciating the silence and sounds of the evening, maybe the possibility of what could come next.

But what might that be? He'd told her he wanted her, and he'd definitely stuck some condoms in his pocket—just in case—but what did Darian want? He wanted to know everything about her. What she did, her likes, her dislikes, what her childhood was like. How long she'd been friends with the others. He wanted to know what it was that made her so damned special, because she definitely stood out in this group of exceptional women.

Each was smart and funny and each attractive in her own way. After a summer filled with female guests, he certainly felt as if he had a better understanding of the fairer sex. They certainly weren't anything like the women his mother's age. Hell, his mom's generation didn't come into their own until they were changed. Women had so few rights when he was born, April 12, 1861—the day Fort Sumter in South Carolina fell and the War between the States began.

He and Trak had family members they never knew who died during that war, not because they fought, but because their pack alpha had decided they should live as wolves to escape the human carnage. The women, of course, weren't able to shift if they had children, since natural-born werewolves didn't start shifting until they were about thirty.

That left their women and children the most vulnerable among them. Some had been abandoned by their mates. Those bastards had been hunted down after the war, after an accounting of who among them still survived and how they'd dealt with the upheaval. There was no room for cowardice. The women who hadn't purposefully chosen this life weren't cowards. They were the tough ones, those women who stayed in human form to protect and raise their children. Those good men who stayed behind protected their families as best they could, but too many women and children died, and too many men died trying to save them.

A few joined and fought as humans, but not for the South. Werewolves never could understand the concept of slavery. Meeting Dar, one of the first African American women he'd had a chance to get to know, being attracted by her wit and intelligence as much as her beauty, Lawz couldn't understand it, either. Of course, living such an insular life, the pack had met relatively few humans of different races over the course of their years. His years he'd spent in college getting his engineering degree had been the most time he'd ever spent around humans since he was a kid.

The tiny white lights that lined the pathway sparkled with the slight movement of the trees and shrubbery. There was a gentle breeze blowing, enough to add life to the lights and give the entire trail an ethereal quality lacking during daylight. His thoughts shifted to holding Darian, to tasting her mouth again. Tasting all of her. She was so responsive. He'd never had a woman climax in his arms before, merely from touching her breasts.

She was aroused even now, the rich scent that was distinctly hers leading him as if he were on a leash. Imagining what she'd be like when he entered her had an immediate effect on his dick. Damn, he hoped he had enough condoms, because if she was serious about what she'd said earlier, that she wanted to spend some time with him in a bed when neither of them felt rushed . . . damn. Just. Damn.

Awareness pulsed through Dar's body, the sense that she and the man behind her were somehow connected on levels she couldn't truly comprehend. But the connection was there, a pulsing, living thing. The trail had narrowed, and Lawz followed close behind her, close enough that she felt the heat from his body, imagined those strong arms wrapping around her, holding her close. She really hoped he'd brought condoms with him. She had a strict rule about sex with strangers; one-night stands were never her thing. But that was so weird about Lawz—she felt as if she'd known him for years.

All during dinner, they'd laughed. He'd say something, and she'd pick up on it immediately and turn it back to him, then he'd take off on another tangent, and one of his guys or one of her girls would pop in with a smart-ass comment, and off they'd go again.

She couldn't remember laughing so hard. Or wanting so badly. She was glad she'd decided to wear jeans to dinner because the moment Lawz sat next to her, she became embarrassingly wet and so damned needy.

They rounded a bend in the trail, and there was her cabin. She'd left the porch light burning, and suddenly her hands were sweaty and she was practically shaking with either nerves or need. Probably need. When was the last time she'd had sex? Damn, she couldn't remember. Her toys kept the edge off, but she'd had a long dry spell. Even sex with the living, breathing kind had been a huge disappointment. The fact that she couldn't remember any details told her a lot— as in the fact that none of them had been memorable.

Dar went up the steps to the front deck. Lawz reached around her and opened the door. She stepped into the tiny cabin, wondering what was going to happen next. Would he pounce? Would he want to talk? What was Lawz really like when he knew he had an open invitation?

He waited at the threshold. She turned and looked at him. "Aren't you coming in?"

He shook his head. "Only if you really want me to, Darian." He was so tall that he easily grabbed the doorframe overhead with one hand and leaned toward her. "I don't ever want you to feel as if you have to do anything you're not comfortable with. If you want to wait to get to know me better, I'm okay with that." He laughed, and at least his voice sounded strained. "Well, sort of okay. Point being, it's your call entirely."

She'd been wondering if he'd changed his mind. "I'm calling," she said. She turned and walked into the cabin, slipping her cami top over her head as she went. She was bare under the shirt, and she figured he must approve when she turned around to face him, if that look of blind lust on his face meant anything.

Closing the door behind him, Lawz toed his moccasins off and walked across the small room. She backed up at the same speed, stopping when the backs of her thighs hit the bed.

He didn't grab her, didn't grope. No, he stood there for a moment just looking into her eyes and gently brushing a loose strand of hair back from her face. Then he slowly began to unbutton his shirt and pull it free from his jeans. He slid it back over his shoulders and dropped it on the floor.

Dar's mouth went dry. He was truly magnificent, his body

long and lean, his muscles impressive. She reached for him. There was no way in hell she couldn't. He was just so . . . there were no words. Only feelings. Intense feelings, but when her palms flattened on his rounded pecs, when she stroked the taut lines of his muscular chest and then ran her hands down his sides, he tilted his head back and groaned.

Yeah. That said it for her, too.

She moved closer, lightly rubbing her taut nipples over his torso, shivering with the blatant sensuality of the move. She stroked his sides, found his waistband, and slipped her fingers beneath the button at the top of the fly. Flicked it open and then moved to the next one. She'd reached the final metal button when Lawz tipped her head up with a fingertip and laughed.

"I thought so," he said, leaning close and kissing her quickly. "You're smiling. What are you thinking, you minx?"

"Minx?" She raised her head and her eyebrows. "Sort of a dated reference, isn't it?"

"I could call you a hussy, but that's just as dated. Hell, I'm a country boy. We don't get out much. No TV here in the back of beyond, but you're redirecting rather than answering. I'll ask again. Plain English. What are you thinking while you're unbuttoning my pants, and why are you smiling?"

She tried not to laugh. Really, but that wasn't going to happen. Once she got herself under control, she gave him a saucy grin. "Well, I'm thinking that I really want to see what's behind the wrapper, to put it bluntly." With that, she grabbed the waistband at either side of his hips, pulled his jeans down, and kept shoving until she reached his ankles and worked them over his long, narrow feet. The soft knit boxers he had on hid very little, and now that she was on her knees, she decided she didn't want to miss the opportunity.

The glazed look in Lawson's eyes told her he liked the way she looked, kneeling in front of him in her snug jeans, body bare from the waist up. His look had her feeling sexy and powerful at the same time.

She nuzzled the erection tenting the front of his shorts. He sucked in a quick breath, and his hips jerked forward. She slid her fingers beneath the fabric and up his legs in back, cupped his muscular ass in both hands and pulled him close to her mouth. Covering him with her lips, she breathed warm air over the cotton knit, teasing him. Then she tugged the shorts down and off. His erection was impressive, jutting forward from a mass of dark, wiry hair, his thick length flushed with blood.

She actually salivated, staring at him, at the way blood pulsed beneath the skin along his shaft and the taut cowl of his foreskin caught behind the broad mushroom head. A tiny drop of pre-come at the edge of his slit drew her like a beacon.

She used her tongue—the very tip—to lick it off, tasting him for the first time, the salty-sweet taste that was like nothing she'd ever had before. His hands rested on her skull, gently holding her, not forcing her at all as she leaned close and licked the tip again, then slowly wrapped her lips around him. His groan made her smile around her mouthful. She felt it where her lips clasped his shaft, heard it like a deep vibration of need that was so powerful he ached.

How could she know this? Know how he felt, what he needed? It was like a storm brewing, this unbreakable connection she felt with a man she'd met mere hours ago. She often knew things about people—it was a running joke among her friends, Darian's super intuition. She knew right away if someone was lying, or if they were up to no good. The knowledge was just there. But this all-encompassing sense of knowing, of connecting with Lawz, was dizzying.

She drew on him, sucking him deep into her mouth, tasting the quintessential maleness of him, the flavors unique to Lawz and so pleasing to her. She couldn't take him all the way at first, but she found herself holding his buttocks, pulling him forward, relaxing her throat muscles and swallowing him deep.

His entire body trembled. It felt like he was holding back, trying not to fuck her mouth, letting her control how deep he went, how far she pulled him in, how tight he grasped her skull. It was almost sweet how gentle he was, how he cared for her comfort. So she gave him everything . . . and more. And when she felt his muscles go rigid, when she knew he was about to come, she didn't let him pull away but instead held him close.

This was a first. Going down on a man, letting him finish in her mouth, but with Lawson, it felt natural. Why did that knowledge confuse her even as it empowered her?

She smiled in her mind. It was crazy, but it felt right. And when he cried out her name, when she felt the powerful pulse along his shaft and she tasted his release and swallowed every drop, she was amazed at the joy she felt, the absolute sense that this man was hers, that she had claimed him with this single, simple act. On her knees, and yet stronger, more powerful than she'd ever been in her life.

He watched, transfixed by the almost mystical feeling that seemed to surround the two of them as she carefully took his last drops before setting him free, sat back on her heels, and actually licked her lips. His legs felt like rubber, but his dick was still hard. He'd come so hard he was lucky he didn't pass out, but it wasn't enough.

He had a feeling it would never be enough with Darian. He leaned down and wrapped his arms around her, pulled her to her feet, and held her close, nuzzling her throat, nipping at the soft and obviously sensitive skin behind her ear.

Her arms were around his neck, and she plastered her long, lithe body against his, except he was naked and she was still wearing jeans.

Obviously a situation they needed to deal with. He said as much. "Aren't you a bit overdressed?"

She raised her head and smiled at him. "I was sort of thinking the same thing. Aren't you going to do something about it?"

"Oh, yeah."

He couldn't believe his hands were actually trembling when he flicked the snap at her waistband. It was difficult grasping the tiny zipper tab so he could actually pull the blasted thing down. Women's clothes in this century looked hotter than hell, but damn, it was hard to get them off.

He wrapped his hands around Dar's waist and picked her up. Then he laid her back down on the bed with her legs hanging over the edge, which made it much easier to slowly peel the tight, stretchy jeans down her long, long legs.

And wasn't it a shame that her tiny little thong panties rolled partway down with her jeans, unfortunately stopping just above the juncture of her thighs. Somehow, it was even sexier this way, with them almost but not quite off. She reached for the waistband to push them down, but he stopped her. Instead, he placed the palm of his hand over the fabric covering her warm, damp center.

"Wait," he said. He went to his knees and ran his hands up her sides. Stopped at the swell of her breasts and ran his thumbs over her nipples. Her skin was soft—smooth and dark with the texture of silk. Her nipples were large and much darker than the rest of her, unlike anything he'd ever seen, and once again he realized how little he knew of the world outside, of women he didn't understand, of the many kinds of beauty he'd never seen.

She took his breath.

He'd dated in college, but he was already shifting at that point, in the late 1980s when he'd gotten his engineering degree, and he was always afraid of their secret getting out. It was even harder now, with cell phones recording everything and governments able to do in-depth identity searches. Fingerprints alone could give them away. How did you explain a set of prints that matched prints from a guy the same age in the 1920s?

You didn't. You just made sure there was no reason for the police to ever get hold of your prints. He leaned forward, prints forgotten as Dar writhed beneath his touch. She was so damned sensitive. He licked her nipple, and it tightened even further, the dark areola drawing close against the taut bud. Fascinating. He wrapped his lips around first one and then the other, moving back and forth, right, then left, then right again, sucking hard, using his tongue to apply pressure, molding her firm breasts in his hands.

He cupped them, held them close together so that he could slip from one to the other more easily. The scent of her arousal, an intoxicating musk that went straight to that primitive part of the male brain where there was absolutely no conscious process beyond *want* and *take* and *now* held him in thrall.

Still cupping her breasts, pinching her ruched nipples between thumbs and forefingers, he slipped down her body, leaving wet, open-mouthed kisses on her belly, her mons, the inner crease of her thigh. He grabbed the silky band of her thong at her left hip with his teeth and ripped, pulling the torn fabric down her right leg until it was out of the way.

He could have pulled them off gently, but that would have required letting go of her nipples. He wasn't ready for that. Her nether lips were full and glistening, her body ripe. For him. Only for him. He dipped his head between her thighs and licked from her perineum to her clit, filling his mouth with her taste, her unique flavors.

He circled her clit with his tongue, pinching her nipples harder, stretching and twisting them until she cried out, "More!" and arched her back, lifting herself. He loved that she was gasping her arousal, pressing herself against his mouth, actually begging for more. He curled the tip of his tongue against her inner walls, stroked the entrance to her sheath, probing, tasting.

He knew she was close, but she needed more. He hated turning loose of her nipples, but he had to so he could grab a condom out of his pocket. He sheathed himself and moved over her, his feet on the floor, her body at the perfect height and angle for him.

She lay there, watching him, panting, eyes wide, lips parted. He separated the damp folds between her legs, stroked the engorged head of his dick between them until he was slick with her fluids. He was big and thick, and he worried about hurting her, but she watched him with a look of pure anticipation.

"Is this okay, Dar? Are you ready for me?"

A smile split her face. "Hell, yes. Now, Lawz. Okay?"

"Oh, yeah."

Her legs came up, she wrapped them around his waist as he drove forward into her tight sheath.

"Yes!"

One word, hissed rather than spoken. Her eyes were closed, her body shivering as he filled her. She was so tight, holding him in a silky clasp that rippled along his length. Once he discovered how deep he could go, that yes, she could take all of him in pleasure, not pain, he dropped all restraint.

He thrust forward, plunged deep and hard—she wrapped her legs tighter, locked her heels at the small of his back, gave as much as she took.

He wasn't going to come alone, though it took everything he had to hold on. Reaching down between them, he found her clit and swirled his thumb over the sensitive nub. She gasped and sucked in a deep breath and then another.

He was there, so close to the edge, so caught up in the most amazing sexual experience of his life when her body tightened, when he felt the powerful grasp of her inner muscles, the rhythmic clenching along the full length of his cock.

And just like that, so simple after all, she pulled him with her over the edge.

CHAPTER 5

Jules glanced down at her hand clasped so firmly in Armando's and experienced a sense of wonder. A large, very powerful man was holding her hand, and she wasn't freaking out. Andrew hadn't been all that big—barely six feet tall—but Armando made him seem like a child. Close to six and a half feet tall and muscular enough to convince Jules he could snap her like a twig should he choose, she actually felt comforted by his presence, the sense that she trusted him in a way she'd never trusted Andrew.

"Tonight was fun," she said, thinking of the laughter, the fact that the four of them had fallen into their often silly, sometimes biting humor that never failed to lift her spirits, and the guys hadn't missed a cue. The shared laughter among her girlfriends was something she'd always been able to count on. Even when things had been horrible right after Andrew had hit her. She never felt comfortable telling her friends; the guilt and shame were too much to handle. Still, they'd been able to make her laugh.

"Your friends are terrific women." Armando gently squeezed her hand. "I love the fact that you've been friends since you were children. We often hear that women don't get along that well in groups."

She laughed. "Oh, we've had our moments, but our friendship is stronger than some of the petty things that we can find to bitch about. We can count on each other when times are tough. One of us is always talking someone down off the ledge."

They'd reached her cabin, the porch light a tiny beacon in the darkness. It threw shadows across the small front deck, but the light was warm and welcoming. Jules wondered if she was ready to invite a man inside. Specifically, this man.

Armando walked her up the steps and paused at the door. He turned and gently pulled her into his embrace and rested his chin on top of her head. "I've had a most pleasant evening. I truly enjoy your company, Jules. I hope we'll be able to spend more time together while you're here."

She loved the way it felt to be held in his arms. Safe, not at all threatening. And obviously he wasn't going to pressure her for sex. That was good. She probably would have gone along with him if he'd wanted, but pausing like this was a good thing. It was better to wait. Better to take the time to get to know him first.

She thought she'd known Andrew, but she was very, very wrong. She'd had a nagging doubt about him that never fully let her trust him. Obviously her subconscious was smarter than her working brain. It wasn't that way with Armando. Not at all. No red flags, no areas of concern.

She already knew she could trust him.

He kissed her so sweetly. "Before I go, I need to tell you that you might have a visitor later. The wolves have grown very comfortable with our guests, so if you hear someone scratching at your door, feel free to invite him in. I think they just like the chance to sleep on comfortable beds, but all you have to do is tell him to go away and he won't bother you."

"A wolf might want to sleep in my cabin with me?" She'd never imagined anything like that, though the one that walked Elle and Dar to the lodge had certainly seemed tame. "I would absolutely love that." She touched her fingers to the side of his face. His dark beard felt like silk beneath her fingers. "Thank you for walking me back tonight. Will you be going on the hike with us tomorrow?"

He shook his head. "I think I'm cooking tomorrow. Trak was still putting the schedule together, so I'll find out when I get back to the lodge. Good night, Jules. Sleep well." He kissed her once again, turned away, and quickly disappeared into the woods.

She stood there for a long time, thinking about him after he was gone.

Elle loved looking at Tuck's hands. He had such large hands, brown from the sun, and strong, but he'd said he painted, and she knew he cared for even the smallest animals. There must be a lot of gentleness in those hands. She loved the way he made her feel, not really tiny, but definitely normal. Life wasn't always easy for a large woman, especially one who towered over most of the men she dated and generally outweighed them as well. It wasn't like that with Dr. Kentucky Jones. He was large and strong, and he made her feel safe.

And he was a veterinarian. She'd learned that about him

tonight when they were talking about the wolves and some of what the men had to do on the preserve to keep them healthy. She'd wanted to say that had been her dream, to take her own special skills with animals and actually learn even more to help them, but she hadn't.

The trail opened up, and suddenly her little cabin was right in front of them, porch light shining, her sense of calm abandoning her. What would he want from her tonight? Elle bit back a laugh. She certainly knew what she wanted, and he was standing beside her, holding her hand. There was something about Tuck, the sense of so much more beneath his skin, that he could offer her an adventure unlike anything she'd ever known.

Most of her sexual experience had been with friends, guys who were misfits like she was, guys who just wanted to get off and were tired of doing it alone. That wasn't Tuck. He was focused, so strong and kind and well built that she imagined he never lacked for feminine companionship.

He walked her up the steps to the front door, turned, and, still holding her hand, pulled her close. When she wrapped her arms around him, she actually felt his sigh.

"I like holding you like this," he said. "You fill my arms, you smell absolutely delicious, and you have burgundy hair."

His soft laughter left her smiling. "I'm glad you like my burgundy hair and my hand lotion, since that's the only scent I'm wearing. I like being held by you. I'm a big girl. It's nice to have a man large enough to make me feel cosseted."

He nuzzled her hair. "It's not hand lotion I'm referring to. It's your natural scent, the one that tickles my nose and makes me want to growl. I must say, though, that I like that word. *Cosseted.* Cared for and protected. So many women today want to stand on their own. They aren't willing to let a guy go all manly on them and act protective."

She loved the dry comments he came up with. "You're welcome to go all manly on me, as long as you realize that I'm perfectly capable of taking care of myself, that I'm merely indulging your testosterone-driven need to prove manliness."

"That works. I think I'd love being indulged by you." He cupped her face in his big hands, tilted her mouth to his, and kissed her. His beard was softer than it looked, his lips softer still as they molded hers, as his tongue carefully breached the seam between them. He tasted of chocolate and the sweet port they'd had after dinner, he smelled like forest and cool mountain air, and his strength enveloped her, his long, strong arms and broad shoulders, the solid pressure of his thighs against hers.

And the thick length of him, so obvious in spite of his heavy denim jeans, pressed like a hot brand against her. She'd never wanted as much as she wanted Tuck, never needed the way she did now. He'd made her laugh all evening, had teased her and smiled with her, but now he made her want.

She was tired of wanting. Breaking the kiss, she gasped for breath, raised her head, and studied him for a long moment in time. His face was flushed, his gray eyes dark and dilated, and he sucked in one breath after another before letting out a short, sharp bark of laughter. "I'm sorry, Elle. I'm usually better mannered than this. Please forgive me."

"No," she said, but it was hard not to laugh at his stunned expression. "There will be no forgiving because it's not necessary. Forget manners. I want you, Kentucky Jones. I've been wanting you ever since you walked me to my cabin this afternoon, kissed me, and then bailed out. I'm getting tired of wanting. It's time to have something." She wrapped her arms around his neck and pulled him back down. Kissed him hard and fast. "Are you, Dr. Jones, by any chance, part of the vacation package?"

"Only yours, Ms. Marcel." He reached around her and opened the door. Held it open for her to walk inside. He was right behind her. Elle couldn't have wiped the grin off her face if she'd tried.

Tuck followed Elle through the door and into the cabin, his thoughts on a conversation he'd had with Brad and Cain shortly after they'd brought Cherry back to Feral Passions for keeps, that no matter what the old-timers said, they were convinced there really was a special mate for each of them.

He hoped they were right, because damned if he didn't think Elle Marcel was his.

She was absolutely majestic, her shoulders broad, breasts large, torso nipped in at the waist just enough and flaring out to the most amazing ass he'd ever seen. He wanted her naked. Just Elle on that big bed, her lush body ripe and ready for him.

She paused in the center of the small room, turned, and smiled at him. It was a tactile thing, that smile of hers. It touched his heart, made the damned thing pound in his chest as if he'd just run a mile. His wolf wanted to howl, but he tamped the guy down. He didn't want to blow it now. All season long, there'd been women in and out of Feral Passions, and not one of them had caught his attention. He'd been good to them, had enjoyed their company, but he hadn't felt this powerful sense of destiny. Not with a single one.

He stepped close, kissed Elle again. Held her in his arms and rested his chin on her head. "I want you, Elle. But I don't want to pressure you. We hardly know each other, but . . ."

"But it feels right, doesn't it?" She leaned back and looked him in the eye. "I saw you today when you first walked up to the car, and I felt something. I can't explain it, but it was the strangest sense that something would happen with us." Her voice dropped an octave, low and sultry. "We can get to know each other better, if you're interested."

He chuckled softly. "You have no idea how interested I am. Except I wasn't planning on this. On you. I'm not even sure if I have protection."

"The fates would not be so cruel. Check your pockets. I'll look in the bedside table." She laughed and pulled out of his arms. "I mean, it sounds plausible, doesn't it?" He checked his pockets, fully aware they didn't hold what they needed, while she walked over to the bed and pulled open the drawer on the little cabinet Trak's granddaddy had built. "What did I tell you?" Laughing, she held up an unopened box of condoms. "You guys really do take care of everything."

"I guess we do." He'd have to ask Trak whose idea it was to stock the cabins with condoms, if for no other reason than to thank him. He stepped across the room and sat on the edge of the bed, tugging Elle until she was standing between his legs. "You're sure you're okay with this?"

"Oh, yeah. What's your plan?" She planted her hands on his shoulders and smiled down at him. So often women looked like children to him. Not Elle. He loved the fact she was so tall. She wore an old-fashioned-style blouse tucked into her skirt. It had a wide neckline with a tie running through it, gathering it loosely around her shoulders, baring her collarbones, the soft curves of the tops of her breasts. When she leaned closer, her breasts almost spilled out of her bra. He cupped them in his hands, fascinated by their weight, the smooth chocolate of her skin. There was so much of her he wanted to touch, but he wanted to see everything first. He tugged on her blouse, slipped his hands beneath the hem, lifted it carefully over her head, and set it aside. He reached around her and unhooked her bra. She sort of shimmied her arms—which made her breasts do amazing things—and he helped her slip the straps over her shoulders.

He concentrated on the sleek, satiny fabric of her bra instead of her breasts. It wasn't until he set her blouse and bra aside that he turned and kissed her full lips and then turned his attention to her breasts.

They were well worth the wait. He sat there, almost afraid to touch, just staring for a moment. They were large and full, but they didn't sag at all. Instead, with him sitting on the edge of the bed, Elle stood between his thighs, her breasts displayed proudly at eye level for him, their areolas much darker than her sleek skin, her nipples tightly budded, inviting him to touch.

He cupped them reverently in his palms and reveled in their solid weight. She was a big woman, voluptuous and sensual, with curves in all the right places, a fullness to her that reminded him of a fertility goddess, ripe with promise. Holding her breasts, he rubbed her taut nipples with his thumbs, dragging a soft moan from her lips and adding more pressure against the button fly of his jeans.

He leaned close and drew her nipple into his mouth,

tonguing and sucking the right one and then the left, drawing each to an even tighter peak. Her heart pounded, loud enough to hear, strong enough to feel against his lips. He smelled the rich scent of her arousal, felt the tiny shivers racing over her skin, and he didn't want to wait any longer.

Kissing along the upper curve of her breast, over her collarbones to the soft skin behind her ear, he licked and nibbled and finally whispered, "I want you, Elle. Now. Are you with me?"

She laughed, a ragged, needy, full-throated sound that had him grinning like a fool.

"With you? Dr. Jones, at the rate you're going, I'll be finishing without you. Take off your clothes. Please? And I promise to do the same."

"Let me help." He slipped her skirt down over her thighs, taking her satiny panties with it, and she was every bit as wonderful as he'd imagined. Broad shoulders and full breasts, a waist that nipped in before flaring to full, womanly hips and thighs. A softly rounded belly, firm skin, soft and eminently touchable. Hers was a woman's body in the full flower of her prime, and Tuck knew: Elle was the one.

If only he could convince her.

She grabbed the hem of his T-shirt and tugged it up and over his head. Ran her warm palms over his chest and slipped quickly to the top button on his jeans. It was hard for her to undo them with him sitting like this, especially with the hardest dick he'd had in years trying its damnedest to get free, so he planted his hands on her hips and stood.

Laughing, she carefully undid the top three buttons. Her eyes went wide when she realized he wasn't wearing underwear, but he couldn't tell her it was just one more thing to worry about when he wanted to shift. Let her think what she might, at least there could be no doubt in her mind that he wanted her. Desperately.

He helped her with the final buttons, slid his pants down over the solid curve of his dick, and stepped out of the pants and his mocs. Most of the guys chose moccasins over boots, again for the practicality of shifting. They were easy to get off.

Handy when you were standing in front of an aroused, exquisitely naked woman.

Elle looked him up and down, eyes sparkling, lips twitching, view lingering down. Finally, she raised her head, smiling broadly, and stroked her hands across his chest. "I have to say it," she said, and she laughed. "You, Dr. Jones, are a big boy. All over."

"And you, Ms. Elle, are not a tiny woman. And for that I am overwhelmingly grateful. It tells me that the gods are happy with me—to think they've sent someone as ideal as you are for me." He wrapped his arms around her and held her close, finally experiencing the fullness of her breasts against his chest, the soft swell of her belly against his, her long, strong legs, almost as long as his. It was a revelation, this sense of meeting a woman as a physical equal, a woman who made him laugh and most definitely turned him on.

Then, without warning her, he slipped his arms beneath her legs and back and lifted her against his chest. She laughed out loud—no ladylike shriek from this woman—and she was still laughing when he carefully deposited her on the bed.

She lay there smiling broadly, arms raised in an invitation that had him over her in seconds. "I can't believe you did that." She pulled his head down and kissed him. "You could have totally blown it, you know—dropping the big girl on the floor would have been a real mood killer."

"The sexy woman on the bed who is exactly the right size for me is much too precious to drop." He reached for a condom and knelt between her legs, sheathing himself. She spread her knees for him, but instead of thrusting into her, he scooted back, leaned close, and tasted her.

The scent of her arousal had been teasing him since dinnertime, when he'd been thankful for the overhang of the table. It hid the erection he'd been sporting since he walked into the dining room and saw her looking directly at him, smiling her welcome.

She had an amazing flavor that matched her glorious scent and had him licking deep and nuzzling close to inhale. Her thigh muscles quivered, and her hands stroked through his hair. She wasn't forcing him closer, but she wasn't letting go, either.

He found her clit and concentrated on that taut bundle of nerves, using his lips and tongue while teasing her opening with his fingers. She bucked beneath him, and he knew she was close. Thrusting two fingers deep inside, he curled them forward, rewarded by her rapid breathing, the tensing of her muscles. He sucked hard on her clitoris, thrust deep with his fingers, and almost came himself as he quite literally stroked her off the edge.

She cried out, a long, keening wail that had him moving over her, needing to be inside her. He used his hand to place the broad head of his penis between her moist and swollen lips, but ahead of his thrust, Elle raised her hips and took him deep.

He slid in, slowly, carefully, working his way past her tightly clenching vaginal walls, their muscles still caught in the tremors of her climax. He filled her, for the first time in his very long life actually fitting inside a woman without hurting her, no matter how careful he'd been. With Elle, the fit couldn't be any better, their bodies meshing as if they'd been specifically designed for one another.

She wrapped her legs around his hips, and he picked up speed. So amazing, the sensations of her body clasping his, the tightness without the fear of causing pain. His balls slapped her bottom, his heart thundered in his chest, and he couldn't have stopped grinning if his life had depended on it.

This was joy. This was the connection he'd heard of but never experienced, the feeling that she was so far inside his head and his heart that she'd never break free. He was never letting her go, this woman who must have been made for him. Now, all he had to do was convince her that she wanted to spend her life with a guy who went furry on occasion, a guy who wanted her along for the very same run—on four legs instead of two.

Except he had to convince her without telling her the details. Not any of them.

His climax was rising; he had to take her with him. Leaning close, he kissed her, and she licked his lips, and it came to him that she was tasting herself on his mouth. That knowledge, that sense of connection? That was all it took. He grabbed her and lifted her close. Her arms went around his shoulders as he sat back on his heels, holding her tightly, plunging deep, hard, and fast. Her vaginal muscles grabbed him so damned tight he groaned. His climax flashed from the small of his back to his balls, from his groin to the end of his dick in a supernova of sensation.

His legs felt numb, even his toes and fingers tingled, and he knew every drop of blood in his body had gone straight to his dick for the biggest, most magnificent orgasm he'd ever experienced. Sucking air, body trembling, he carefully lowered Elle to the mattress, but when he went to roll away so as not to crush her, she hung on to him, pulled him down on top of her.

"You're not going anywhere, big guy." She kissed his throat, licked her way across his collarbone, nibbled on his earlobe. "You're covering me like a big, warm, sexy blanket. Stay here, okay? For a while, at least."

He nuzzled her throat. "For a while. Then I need to go check on that wolf cub, make sure he's okay. He's only a couple of months old, still not very tough. Which reminds me. The wolves here on the preserve have gotten really spoiled over the season. If you hear one scratching at your door and don't mind a big furry beast on your bed, go ahead and let the guy in. They're really friendly and seem to have developed a love of warm beds. Or it could be the lovely women sleeping in them." He kissed her smile. "If you leave the door ajar, you might wake up with a furry companion—that is, if you don't mind a strange guy, albeit with four legs, in your bed."

"That would be cool. I just might do that." She yawned. "It's been a long day."

He kissed her again. "It has. Now you think about wolves while I think about what I'm doing before I leave." He dipped his chin and nuzzled her magnificent breasts. This woman was made just for him. He didn't have to worry about breaking her, only about loving her.

And making her love him. He had until Saturday morning to convince her, and then, following the rules they'd all agreed on when they opened Feral Passions, he'd have to turn her loose. Let her go for at least a week before he told her exactly how he felt about her. And even then he couldn't tell her the truth, that he was a werewolf, a man who could shift and run on four long legs, a man who was already over 120 years old. And he was still considered a youngster in the pack.

A lot of things had changed in this modern generation. Women expected to be mates in all definitions of the word— equal mates in decisions and relationships. The guys agreed that modern women were a lot more interesting than the old-fashioned kind, but they were more work, too. He nuzzled Elle's breasts and inhaled a deep breath of her scent. He was going to love any work he had to do to keep Elle happy. That was a given, but he hated leading her on without telling her the truth. That wasn't a good way to start any relationship, basing it on lies. Really huge lies.

Maybe she'd be like Cherry and figure it out. That had certainly thrown Trak for a loop. The alpha didn't like knowing how easy it had been for Brad and Cain's mate to discover the men's werewolf nature. It had been all about their eyes. Cherry had quickly noticed that the wolves' eye color matched the color of the men's eyes, that when blue-eyed Wils was around, the wolf with bright blue eyes wasn't. When Cain showed up with his forest-green eyes, the green-eyed wolf was nowhere to be seen.

It hadn't taken her long, though she'd been the only one all season to make that connection.

"Whatcha thinking about?" Elle kissed the top of his

head, all she could reach with his face buried between her breasts.

He raised his head and blinked lazily, and he wasn't lying when he answered, "Just trying to figure out if you might be interested in round two. I'll check the pup later."

"If you think he'll be okay," she said. She tightened her grip on his ass.

It was quite a bit later when he finally slipped out of Elle's arms and out of her warm bed to check on the cub. Tuck shifted after he left her, after closing the door on his last view of her burgundy hair spread across the pillow, her lips swollen from kissing—and other things. His entire body felt sensitized and energized, and his wolf wanted to run off some of that extra juice.

The cub was sleeping soundly in the den down by the creek, and the mama wolf barely raised her head at the large male creeping into her home. She knew Tuck, knew he wouldn't harm her, and after sniffing noses, she tucked hers beneath her babies and went back to sleep.

Tuck thought about running to burn off more energy, but he knew morning would be coming long before he was ready. Turning away from the creek, he trotted through the woods toward his little cabin tucked into the woods near Growl, the local bar. Halfway there, he gave up on better sense, paused, turned, and ran back to Elle's cabin.

He scratched the door with one big paw.

It opened. He'd closed it tightly, which meant she had to have gotten up after he left. Must have left it unlatched. Hoping for a wolf in her bed?

Bumping the door shut with his nose after entering the cabin, he gazed across the room at his sleeping woman. Her eyes were closed, her voluptuous body covered with a warm down blanket. The nights here grew cooler this time of year.

He jumped up on the opposite side of the bed. She stirred but didn't wake. With a soft, contented sigh, Tuck curled up close beside her and closed his eyes.

It was late when Trak walked Meg back to her cabin. They'd laughed and talked about everything under the sun, and he'd warned her that she was going to get a workout in the morning. Not too early, though. They'd have breakfast before hiking up to Blackbird Lake, but she'd be working off all the calories and then some.

He paused at the bottom step. "Thank you, Meg. I've really enjoyed myself this evening." He was surprised how much he meant that. She was a lovely woman, one he could see as a friend, though he'd quickly realized that whatever spark Brad had talked about wasn't there.

"Me, too." She glanced away and sighed. "I actually relaxed and enjoyed myself." Shaking her head, she laughed. "It's a whole new dynamic for me, to be around a thoroughly enjoyable, very attractive man and relax. I think this is going to be a wonderful week. I'll see you tomorrow."

She turned away and walked up the steps. Trak waited until the door opened and she went inside. "Good night, Meg. Sleep well."

She waved, and he headed back to the lodge to get a few things ready for the morning, but it appeared one of the other guys had already taken care of things. He thought of heading to his cabin, but something made him turn toward Meg's.

He certainly didn't want her to think he was stalking her, but he worried about her. There was something she wasn't saying about her fiancé that had him wondering what was wrong, because it was obvious things weren't right.

He trotted down the trail and out into the small meadow in front of her cabin. Meg was sitting on the front porch with a cup of herbal tea and a small candle burning. He caught the scent of cinnamon and other spices, the combination of the scented candle and her tea. And then, slowly so he wouldn't startle her, he walked across the meadow and paused in the light from the front porch. It only took her a moment to pick him out of the shadows.

She was glad Trak had taken off. She enjoyed his company, but she felt so guilty spending time with him. Not because Zach would mind—he'd never shown a sign of jealousy when she'd teased and laughed with other guys at SSI—but because she felt badly that Trak must think he had to baby-sit her and she wasn't much fun for him.

She had a feeling the others were going to have sexy little romances this week. The chemistry between Dar and Lawson was off the charts, and Meg had been really surprised at the way Elle and the big guy, Tuck, had hit it off. Jules was a little subtler with the man who could easily double for D'Artagnan of the Three Musketeers. Armando was absolutely drop-dead gorgeous, but he was funny and so laid-back. He'd told them to call him Manny, so not a sexy name, but it fit his personality. He and Jules seemed to have clicked, and Jules appeared to appreciate just how hot Manny was.

A movement caught her eye, and she glanced up at the small meadow in front of her cabin. A large wolf sat spotlighted in the glow from the porch light, watching her. She was almost positive he was the same one she'd seen that afternoon. Gray with those striking black tips to his fur and the tips of his ears. "Hello, you beautiful boy. Did you come to visit?"

He stood when she talked to him and came toward the steps. Then he slowly climbed them. His ears were forward, his tail down, and if that wasn't a submissive look, she didn't know what was. She was reminded once again just how big wolves were—he was tall enough that his ears were level with her waist when she stood, which she did when he reached the porch. She held out her fingers, and he sniffed. Then he licked the back of her hand.

His tongue was warm and rough. She laughed. "I hope you're not tasting me. Trak told me specifically that it would be bad for business if the wolves ate the guests. I was just getting ready to go inside. Were you planning to stay the night?"

The wolf walked past her and waited at the door. "Trak wasn't kidding. He said you've gotten used to sleeping on the beds. Since I don't have a man in mine tonight, you're more than welcome."

She couldn't wait to tell Zach. He loved the outdoors, had been jealous of her chance to be with the wolves. Neither of them had even dreamed she'd be sleeping with one on her bed.

Meg opened the cabin door and invited the wolf inside.

CHAPTER 6

Lawz finished up everything at the lodge so Tuck wouldn't have to deal with it. The vet was always great about taking over his part of the chores, but he had a clinic in town besides the wolves here on the preserve. His schedule was crazy, so the guys all covered for him whenever they could. Besides, Tuck had walked Elle back to her cabin after dinner, and the sparks between those two were hot enough to start a fire.

It made him want to go back to Darian. Sleep beside her and see if he still felt the same when he woke in the morning.

It was easier than it should have been to convince himself.

He stashed his clothes in the spare room off the kitchen, stepped outside, and shifted. Then he stood there in the darkness, reveling in the feel of his wolf, the sense of power his human side could never provide. Senses more acute, his muscles practically quivering with the need to go back to Darian.

At least the wolf knew how to behave around an attractive woman. Trotting through the woods, he reached her cabin in less than a minute. The porch light was on, the door slightly ajar. He hoped she hadn't waited up for him, but he'd promised her a wolf. Nosing the door open enough to step inside, he used his rear to shove it closed. Then he trotted across the room, well aware of the sound of his nails clicking on the hardwood.

Dar slept on the far side of the bed. That made it easy for him to jump lightly to the near side and curl up behind her. She stirred, restless but not awake, when he finally settled down on the comforter. After a few minutes, she rolled over and threw her arm over his shoulders.

He sighed, fully aware of a sense of contentment he'd never felt, the feeling that his future lay with this woman— if they could just get past one little problem. He'd gone into the office and Googled her on Cherry's computer. Darian Ahlers was a well-known television personality, a familiar face to residents of northern Oregon. How in the hell would he ever convince her she could be happy here in the middle of nowhere with a bunch of men who occasionally turned into wolves? Yeah. That would go over well. Especially since he couldn't tell her what they were—or what she could be. A wolf, just like the rest of them. It was exhausting, keeping so damned many secrets.

He had a week. No problem. If there was one thing he liked more than a beautiful woman, it was a challenge. He would make this work.

Armando really needed this run tonight. Jules left him feeling off balance, needy in a way he wasn't too certain he liked. He wanted her in his bed, but after she told him about the bastard who'd hit her? No way was he going to push her. So he'd left her standing there with a smile on her face, gone back to his cabin, dumped his clothes, and shifted.

But she was all he could think of. Jules had a reason to fear men, and he didn't want to risk doing anything that would frighten her or remind her of that bastard who'd hurt her. He wanted nothing more than to turn his wolf loose and hunt the guy down.

He rounded a large rock outcropping and spotted Drew on the other side. Trotting up beside him, Manny raised his nose and howled. Drew immediately joined in, and a few seconds later, they heard a chorus from the valley, the wild wolves singing with them.

It took a while to get it out of his system, but eventually the wild wolves wandered off, and he and Drew sat back on their haunches, enjoying the sense of pack that was always stronger in their lupine form. Sometimes he thought it would be so much easier to live as a wolf, except the wild ones knew they were different. They accepted werewolves in their forest, but weres could never be part of the wild pack.

After a few moments, Drew shifted. Manny joined him, the two of them sitting naked on the granite outcropping still warm from the daytime sun. Drew threw his arm over Manny's shoulders.

"So, Armando, you struck out tonight?"

"I didn't want to scare her away. She needs time to get used to the idea of me." He glanced at Drew, a guy so good-looking that women practically swooned. Yet tonight, he and Evan had ended up without women, so here was Drew. Alone. "Where's Evan?"

"Evan headed down to Growl to make sure the place was

closed up tight. A couple of loggers stopped by the other night, and he was afraid they might be scoping the place out. It's not the regular crew. There's a transient group working that part of the forest north of us, cleaning up burned trees after that lightning strike last spring. Evan said he'd take a last look since Lawz, Tuck, and Trak are all spending time with the ladies as wolves tonight."

"That's what I'm thinking of doing."

"With Jules?" Drew nodded. "She's very attractive. Definitely sexy. Pragmatic, good sense of humor. I liked her, at least from what I got to know of her at dinner."

"Her last boyfriend beat her up."

"No shit? How'd you—"

"She told me. Said she still has issues with men. She flinched when I reached over her head to flip on a light. It's got to be like PTSD. I'm thinking of going back, having the wolf spend the night. I don't want her to be alone."

"No man has a right to hit a woman. It's dead wrong."

"Want to join me?" Armando had always liked Drew. They'd partnered quite a bit over the years, though with so many willing women coming to the resort this summer, there hadn't been that pressing need for sex. At least not with each other.

"You wouldn't mind?" Drew grinned. "I have actually grown quite fond of sleeping next to a warm woman who wants to hug me and rub my belly."

"Damn, you're pathetic." Manny stood and pulled Drew to his feet. "C'mon. If she left the door ajar, it means we're welcome."

They shifted and trotted down the mountain together. The door to Jules's cabin was ajar.

———

She dreamed that Manny came back, only this time he was a wolf, with long legs and sparkling brown eyes, but he wasn't alone. He'd brought that really handsome man who'd been at dinner earlier tonight, only Drew was a wolf, too. She knew it was Drew, not just because he had those smoky blue eyes. She just knew.

A soft whine woke her. Blinking, she stared at the partially open door, where two wolves waited in the dim glow from the porch light, but she wasn't awake because it was still her dream. The Manny wolf and the Drew wolf stood in the doorway. "C'mon in, boys," she said. "The bed's big, and there's plenty of room."

That was all it took. The two of them crossed the room, their toenails clattering across the hardwood, and easily jumped up on the bed. They were huge, but this was still a dream, wasn't it? She'd always had such lucid dreams, and so often they turned out to be more truth than fantasy. This one was definitely a fantasy, though. Smiling, she scooted to the middle of the bed and patted the space on her left. "Manny, you sleep over here. Drew? You stay on that side. And don't either of you crowd me. I'm used to sleeping alone."

She leaned over and kissed Manny on the nose, did the same to Drew, and then curled up between two big, warm wolves and went back to her dream.

Manny stared at Drew, who stared right back at him. How the hell had she known? She wasn't even completely awake, and yet she'd recognized the two of them. But would she remember in the morning? He did the wolf equivalent of a shrug and lay down beside Jules. After a moment, Drew did the same, but Manny wondered if either of them would actually sleep tonight.

Monday morning

Meg was awake at her usual time, in the dark. Damn it. She glared at the clock by the bed. 5:00 A.M. She was on vacation—why couldn't she just sleep in once? At least until the sun came up!

She wasn't one of those people who could go back to sleep once she was awake, and there was no way she could lie in bed all morning. Crawling out of bed, half-asleep and grumpy, she stumbled into the bathroom. A quick shower had her more awake, so she dried off and grabbed the really nice plush robe hanging from a hook on the bathroom door, combed her hair back into a ponytail, and headed for the little kitchen area where she remembered seeing a coffeemaker.

If there was a coffeepot, there had to be coffee. She found everything where it should be and stood by the front window in the dark, waiting while the coffee brewed. With the lights turned off inside, the barest hint of pale sky shimmered in the east. As tall as the mountains were, it probably took a while for the sun to actually show itself, but she did love this time of morning.

If only Zach were here to share it with her.

The coffeemaker gave out a long whoosh and shut off. As

she turned to fill a cup, movement across the room caught her eye. "Oh. My. God." Thank goodness there was a chair behind her, or she would have ended up on the floor.

"There's a wolf on my bed." She rubbed her eyes. "I thought I dreamed you. Trak did say you might show up. Have you been here all night?" She remembered a wolf coming to her cabin, inviting him in, and watching him jump up on the bed, but she'd been positive she'd dreamed it. Or imagined it.

"Well, I'm going out to sit on the front porch and watch the sun come up. Would you care to join me, or do you intend to go back to sleep?"

The blasted wolf actually wagged his tail, just like a big dog. "C'mon, boy." She looked through the cupboards and found a popcorn bowl, filled it with water, and set it out on the porch. Filling her coffee cup, she went outside and sat. A moment later, the wolf joined her.

He got a drink out of the bowl and then took off for the woods. He was only gone a couple of minutes—long enough to find an appropriate tree, Meg figured—and then he was back on the porch, curled up on the wooden deck beside her chair.

"I'm glad you're here, even though you've totally destroyed that whole vicious wild wolf thing you guys have going." She reached over the arm of the chair and rubbed his head. "I'm sure someone somewhere is going to hunt you down and take away your pack membership. You're absolutely precious, do you know that?"

He stared at her with those intelligent brown eyes, and she swore he was grinning at her stupid comments. He felt like a friend, one she could tell anything and know he'd keep her secrets. Well, of course she could—who was he going to talk to?

"I really envy you. All you have to worry about is being a wolf. The best wolf you can be. I think that would be such a wonderful way to live." She sipped her coffee. The wolf studied her, as if waiting for her to say more. "What does one talk about with a wolf? Any suggestions?" He watched her, unmoving. "I thought not. Well, I'm getting married soon. Unless, of course, I chicken out, which could very well happen."

The wolf rested his chin on her left foot. She rubbed his head with her right foot, scratching behind his ears with her toes. The silly beast groaned and leaned heavily against her leg. "The thing is," she said, staring blindly at the dark forest, "it's really hard for me to have a man like Zachary love me like he does. There's no reason for me not to believe he's sincere, but it's just so hard. He's amazing, and I'm just . . ."

She sighed, not looking at the wolf, still staring into the forest. Lighter now, or her eyes were adjusting. The trees not as dark, the sky taking on more color. "I guess that doesn't make sense without background, does it? See, I always figured my parents loved me. I mean, that's what parents do, right? Love their kids? But one night when my mother was drinking, she told me I was a mistake, that she never wanted to be a mother. She never wanted kids. Neither did my father—it's not a good feeling, to have your parents tell you that you're the result of a broken condom. A mistake that meant they had to get married. And now, when Zach is so sweet to me, I feel like such a fraud. Logically, I know there's nothing wrong with me, but inside, I don't think I'll ever get past thinking I'm not worth it. Not worth his love. I love him so much, yet I can't make myself believe I'm worth loving, that he could possibly love me the way I love him. He's everything I'm not. I'm terrified that after this week apart, he's going to realize how much happier he is without me. That's why I wanted to come here for a week. To give him the chance to find out how he really feels. It's going to kill me when he tells me he wants to cancel the wedding, but I'm positive that's what he's going to do."

Elle awoke once during the night, so warm and comfortable she couldn't figure out what had awakened her. The soft snoring beside her brought her wide awake, and the soft glow from the night-light in the bathroom left her smiling. There was a wolf in her bed. Snoring.

Snuggling close, she buried her face in the thick fur at his neck. He smelled like Tuck. Smiling, she drifted back to sleep.

Jules came awake slowly, but when she tried to roll over and couldn't, her eyes flashed wide and she bit back a scream. Then she just lay there and giggled. She had a wolf on either side of her, on top of the blankets, pinning her down.

And both of them were staring at her. "I thought I dreamed you guys, but you're really here." She stared at the blue-eyed wolf and then the one with dark brown eyes. Stroking his head, she said, "I dreamed that you were Armando." She glanced at the blue-eyed wolf. "And you were Drew. But that's not possible. Is it?"

The wolves stared at her, unblinking. She still felt as if the brown-eyed wolf was the man who'd walked her home last night and the one with blue eyes was that truly good-looking guy she'd met at dinner, which was totally bizarre.

"Or is it?" Shaking her head, she gave each one a hug. "I'm going to need to think about that one. Now off, okay? I need a shower, and then I want to go to the lodge for breakfast, and I don't want to miss the hike today."

She opened the door to let them out, took a quick shower, and then made a cup of coffee. Sitting out on the front porch, she thought about those wolves in her bed, but as much as she wanted to put her crazy thoughts aside, she couldn't. It wasn't physical resemblance, obviously, and it wasn't even the eye color. It was more an inner sense that told her the men and the wolves were one and the same.

Finishing her coffee, she rinsed the cup and left it beside the sink. Obviously, she'd been working too hard. Either that or she was merely losing her damned mind.

Dar awoke to a soft knock on the door. It was barely seven, and she'd slept better than she had in months. She'd had such a wonderful night, dreaming Lawz slept beside her, except he was a huge, silvery-gray wolf with glimmering canines and a black saddle-shaped patch over his shoulders and back. He'd been wonderfully warm, and he'd made her feel safe.

She heard the knock again, so obviously she hadn't imagined it. Yawning, she stretched her arms over her head. "Who's there?"

"It's Lawz. Are you awake?"

"I am now. If you don't mind seeing me with my eyes still half shut, c'mon in." Of course, there was damned little of her he'd missed last night. She was smiling at the thought when he pushed the unlatched door open with his shoulder and walked in, carrying a couple of cups of something smelling suspiciously like caffe mocha latte. She scooted back against the headboard, dragging the blanket up to cover herself.

"Good morning, sleepyhead. Breakfast is cooking, and your friends are already beginning to straggle in. I was getting worried."

He handed a big ceramic mug to her, and she held it to her nose. "Okay. How did you know this was my favorite?" She took a sip and moaned. "This is wonderful. Thank you."

He sat on the edge of the bed, holding the extra cup. "Did you sleep well?"

She tilted her head, stared at him, and wondered. That dream had felt so real. Smiling, she sipped her coffee and said, "Don't you know? Wasn't that you sleeping beside me last night?"

"Not me." Shaking his head, he said, "I tucked you in after you just about wore me out, but I left the door ajar the way you'd said to. It wasn't me. You had a wolf in your bed last night. I saw him leave a while ago."

She'd always been good at reading people. In fact, her real talent was lost on the job she had as a weather reporter because she always knew if someone told the truth, and Lawson Jakes was lying. She wasn't going to push him. Not this morning.

"Well, damn," she said. "And here I thought you'd come back and crawled into bed with me."

He laughed, and his eyes twinkled. "I wish it had been

me. It could have been, but I wasn't sure if I'd be welcome. Last night was a bit much for your first night here."

He still wasn't telling the truth.

"Last night was amazing, but I need to get up and get a quick shower. I'll be down at the lodge as soon as I can get there. Thank you for this." She held up the cup and then leaned over and kissed him, and it was every bit as good as she remembered.

But something was going on, and she was going to keep an eye on this guy.

As hot and sexy as he was, that shouldn't be too difficult.

Kentucky, Lawson, Armando, and Drew led the four women away from the lodge along the trail to Blackbird Lake. It was an absolutely spectacular morning as Trak watched them go. The women were laughing, the men teasing, and he should have had his camera out for pictures, because they looked like a blasted advertisement for Feral Passions, all of them hiking out along the trail through a meadow of wildflowers.

As soon as they were gone, he grabbed Evan, and the two headed for the private office behind the kitchen. "Now tell me again what Armando said."

"When Jules woke up, she looked at him in all his wolven glory and said she'd dreamed he was Armando. And then when she looked at Drew, she said that he was Drew, only she knew that couldn't be true. Then after she thought a moment, she said that maybe it was, or something like that. The guys are convinced she knows, and I swear I've never seen Manny so freaked out. Lawz had a similar experience when he took coffee to Darian. She said something about him spending the night with her, and he told her no, that it had been a wolf, but he said she didn't seem to believe him. Meg doesn't suspect you at all, but even Elle mentioned something about the wolf sleeping beside her reminding her of Kentucky. Said he smelled like Tuck. It's flat-out weird, Trak. What do we do if they have us figured out? We didn't plan for anything like this."

"No," he said, staring out the window at the mountains he loved so much. "We didn't. Maybe we should have." He turned to Evan. "I have no idea how we're going to handle this. See if you can get hold of Brad or Cain. Cherry might have some ideas. If they're not too far away, ask if they mind cutting their trip short. I'm at a loss here. I really don't get it. Cherry's the only one all season long to figure out her guys were wolves, and now we've got three women with suspicions? Not good. Not good at all."

He had no idea what the solution might be. They'd never been faced with exposure before. Not like this. Never faced the risk of giving up everything, of going into hiding.

But what alternative was there?

CHAPTER 7

It was an ideal morning for a hike. Lawz led the group, but Dar stayed back with Meg. None of them had had a chance to talk to her yet about Jules's suspicions, and while Dar honestly didn't think Meg wanted out of her upcoming marriage, there was obviously something very wrong. She should be having a blast up here, but instead she'd been introspective and quiet, which was totally out of character.

Glancing up, Dar caught Jules's eye and motioned for her to join them. She smiled, said something to Armando, and waited until Dar and Meg caught up with her. "How's it going, ladies? Legs okay?"

Meg actually laughed. "I think I'd do better in heels, I wear them so much."

Meg kept up the steady pace without getting winded. Even Dar was beginning to feel the climb.

Meg just kept moving. "What do you guys think of this place? Glad we picked it?"

Dar glanced at Jules, and they both burst out laughing.

"Okay." Meg glanced from one to the other. "What am I missing?"

"Uhm . . ." Jules blushed beet red. "I think Dar was the first of the group to lose her Feral Passions cherry."

Meg stared at Dar with her mouth open. Dar merely shrugged, but it was a struggle not to laugh.

Before Meg came up with either a question or an answer, Elle slowed until they caught up and interrupted. "If it wasn't Dar, it was me." She waved an imaginary fan in front of her face. "That man is just so fine."

"Wow." Meg lost it then, and it took a few minutes before she could catch her breath, she was laughing so hard. "I had no idea you girls worked that fast. I mean, I know you're good, but, just, wow."

Dar poked Jules in the ribs with her elbow. "Yeah, well, Jules here outdid both Elle and me. She might not have gotten around to doing the nasty, but she did have two guys in her bed all night."

"Yeah." Jules rolled her eyes. "But they had eight legs between them, so I don't think that counts."

They were all laughing when they rounded a bend in the trail, and Tuck waved them over to a shady spot beside a small creek. "Time for a break, ladies." He spread a blanket on the ground and set out a few containers of fresh berries and grapes, a tray with brie and crackers, and paper plates.

They settled in for a short feast while Manny and Drew went up the trail to make sure everything was open. There'd been a heavy rain just a few days earlier, and they wanted to check for damage. Tuck and Lawz sat on a log a few yards away, giving the women privacy, which was exactly what Dar had been waiting for.

She sat next to Meg with Jules and Elle on the opposite side. "Meg? What's going on?"

"What?" Meg looked from one to the other. "What do you mean?"

"You're not you." Dar shrugged. "We're worried about you. You don't seem at all happy about your wedding. Is there something we should know about Zach? I mean, do you still love him? Are you excited about the wedding or having second thoughts? He's not abusive or . . ."

"No. No and no." She laughed, but it was colored in sadness. Dar read that as clear as could be. "Zach's wonderful." She shrugged and glanced away.

Meg definitely wasn't lying. "Then what?" Dar grabbed Meg's hands. "Something's wrong. What is it?"

"That's it." She squeezed Dar's fingers. "That's the problem. Look at him! He's everything I want in a husband. He's smart and funny, and so damned good looking and sexy he makes me ache. He's honestly the nicest man I've ever known. He's dynamite in bed, he was rich even before he inherited a fortune, and he says he loves me more than anything in the world."

"And your problem is?" Jules's dry comment had even Meg cracking up.

"My problem is, how can he honestly love me? I mean, why me?" She pulled free of Dar's gentle grasp and twisted her hands in her lap, and it was obvious this wasn't Meg looking for compliments. This was Meg honestly afraid she'd made a huge mistake in trusting Zach with her heart. "I'm scared to death he's going to wake up next to me about a week after we're married and realize he made the biggest mistake in his life. I don't think I can handle that. He's going to come to his senses, and when he does, it's going to kill me."

"Okay. I don't see that happening, but obviously you're

worried sick about it." Dar glanced at the rest of the group. "So how do we fix this? What do you need to know to convince you that Zach truly loves you?"

"I don't know. But if any of you come up with a good idea, please share." She brushed a tear off her cheek. "I know I sound like a whiny idiot. Zach's wonderful, and he's never done anything to make me doubt him, nothing to make me doubt that he honestly loves me, but I can't shut that stupid girl up. You know, the one my parents raised who lives inside me and keeps reminding me that I'm really not much of a catch? Can't shut her up at all."

Elle turned away from the rest of them and glanced to her left toward a thick stand of cedars. "Did you hear that?"

"Hear what?" Dar looked in the same direction as Elle. "I don't hear anything."

Elle stood. "I'm going to get Tuck, see if he'll go with me. You know how I am with animals." She brushed the pine needles off her jeans and headed toward Tuck and Lawz.

Dar called out, "Just don't go rescuing any more snakes, okay? I draw the line at snakes."

They all laughed when, without turning around, Elle raised her right hand high and flipped them off.

Tuck hadn't been able to take his eyes off Elle all morning, and now, as he watched her walking toward him, he almost laughed at the immediacy of his reaction. She wore beat-up hiking boots, nylon cargo pants, and a tank top with her jacket wrapped around her waist. There was a faded Port-land Trail Blazers cap on top of her head, and the red, faded almost to pink, clashed horribly with her burgundy hair. Nothing fancy about her clothes, but even in well-worn hiking gear, the woman was sex personified—his very own fertility goddess.

Somehow, he was keeping her.

"Tuck?" She stopped in front of him. "Would you come with me? I think I hear an animal in distress, and I'd rather not wander into the woods on my own." She laughed. "I hear there are wolves around here."

That wasn't at all what he expected her to say. "What'd you hear?"

"A short, sharp bleating, like a lamb, but higher pitched. Whatever it is, it's hurt or frightened."

"Sounds like a fawn." He turned to Lawz. "Be right back, okay?" Lawz nodded, and Tuck stood. "Where'd you hear it? What direction did the sound come from?"

"This way."

She led him toward the grove of cedar trees like a woman on a mission. He felt like a tethered balloon following her. The enticing sway of her rounded hips and the way her hair bounced against her back strung him along, and the only downside was his fervent hope that they wouldn't find a badly injured animal. The last thing he wanted to do was put one down with all the women up here on what was supposed to be a fun excursion. Mentally crossing his fin-gers, when Elle dipped beneath a low growing branch, he followed close behind her.

A doe leapt out of the brush, a big mule deer with

full teats, which meant an injured fawn, most likely. The doe didn't go very far, but what surprised Tuck was Elle's reaction—or lack of one. She didn't act the least bit surprised by the doe. Instead, she headed directly toward a clump of bright orange mule's ear daisies. Then she was down on her knees, cooing softly to a fawn lying in the middle of the flowers.

"Whatcha got?" He knelt beside her. The fawn was lying stretched out in the tangle of leaves. It tried to raise its head, but the animal was obviously weak. Tuck wasn't getting a good feeling about this at all. The poor little thing was at least a couple of months old—its spots had faded until they barely showed, and the coat was mostly grayish brown.

Elle didn't seem worried by the animal's condition; right now, she was all business. He watched, fascinated, as she ran her hands over the wild creature. She crooned softly, a light, rhythmic humming that must have had a calming effect, because the fawn, while it watched her intently, showed absolutely no fear.

"The bone here"—she cupped his right front leg below the knee—"is cracked. Not broken completely, but it hurts too much, so he can't walk on it."

He didn't doubt her—she sounded absolutely sure of herself—but how the hell could she diagnose an injury like that merely from touch? Before he could question her, she turned to him and took a deep breath. "You can't tell anyone what I'm going to do, okay?"

"What are you going to do?"

She looked deadly serious, whatever it was. "Promise me."

He smiled and twisted a loop of her burgundy hair around

his fingers. "As long as you don't do something that can get you hurt, I won't say a word."

"Thank you."

"Okay. Can I help?"

"Don't let anyone come near. And you might need to help me walk back when I'm done."

Before he could question that curious comment, Elle cupped her hands gently around the injured leg, leaned close, and blew a soft breath over it. The fawn sighed and relaxed. His head went down, and his eyelids fluttered shut. Tuck was almost certain he saw a soft, golden glow over the animal's gray fur in that space between her palms. Fascinated, he watched as Elle cupped the leg, rubbing gently along the broken area with her thumbs, her soft crooning so hypnotic that it easily found its way deep inside Tuck's soul.

After a while, he heard footsteps, and knowing Elle didn't want to be disturbed, he quietly stood and walked back along the trail to meet Lawz. "Go on ahead, okay?" he whispered. "We'll catch up in a bit. Tell the girls Elle's helping me with an injured fawn. But leave a sandwich or something for her to eat. I think she's going to need it."

Lawz was obviously curious as hell, but he merely nodded and headed back up the trail. Tuck went back to kneel beside Elle once again. The fawn slept, eyes shut, his breathing even and deep. Elle didn't seem to be aware Tuck had gone and then returned, so focused was she on the injured leg.

It was close to half an hour before she raised her head and smiled at him. "It's fine now. I am so blessed to have this gift to heal. My grandmother had the gift, but not my father. It sort of skips around, but I can heal animals if the injuries aren't too severe. I need to see if he can walk before we leave. He's been like this since yesterday, so I know he needs to eat."

She turned and nodded. "Mama's over there. Can you move away a bit, maybe back up the trail about a dozen feet?"

"Why?"

She shrugged. "You have the scent of wolf about you. Mama's merely tolerating you, and Junior here doesn't know any better, but I want her to come closer to feed him. He might need some help."

How the hell could she possibly know that? "You're the boss," he said, but as he moved away, his mind was spinning. After what Lawz had told him, and what Manny and Drew said happened with Jules, he was beginning to think this entire group of women had an extra sense or two. As he backed away and Elle helped the fawn to his feet, he figured it might be an extra three or more extra senses.

The fawn was standing with his weight on all four legs, a bit wobbly but looking for his mama. And here came the doe, ears pricked forward, head low and nose twitching as she got close enough to recognize her baby. The fawn took a stumbling step toward her as Elle sat back and watched. The doe licked her baby and held still while he butted at her teat and finally latched on.

Elle watched with a huge smile on her face. And then, as if she suddenly remembered Tuck was even there, she turned and gave him a thumbs-up. A couple of minutes later, the fawn stopped feeding, and the mama and baby slipped away into the trees.

Tuck walked back to Elle and took both her hands to pull

her to her feet. She was shaky and wobbled a bit, so he steadied her. "Are you going to tell me how you do that?"

She leaned against his chest. He wrapped his arms around her.

"I have absolutely no idea. Memaw, my grandmother, showed me how when I was little. I've been able to heal injured animals since before I could remember. That's why I wanted to be a vet. I figured that with my gift and some actual training, I could be a really good veterinarian."

"I think you'd be an amazing vet. I would really like to have you go with me on my rounds one day this week, just to see you in action again."

"You'd let me come?" She shrugged and looked away. "I told you, I couldn't make the grades for veterinary school."

He shook his head, absolutely amazed by the woman he'd already decided belonged to him. Cupping her face in his palms, he gently turned her to face him. "Grades don't heal broken bones. Grades don't calm frightened, hurting animals. You have something that all my training and advanced degrees will never allow me to do. Your grandmother was right—it really is an amazing gift."

He slipped his hands to her shoulders and gazed directly into her eyes. Dark brown like that injured fawn's, but so bright they made him think of her spirit shining through. "I don't want to lose that, Elle." He kissed her then, a long, slow, sweet kiss that left him wanting so much more. "I don't want to lose you."

She hung on to his hand, thinking, as they walked slowly back to the main trail. She'd never said a word about her gift to anyone but her girlfriends, yet she hadn't hesitated to tell Tuck. She could rationalize because he'd watched her do it so there was no hiding, but that wasn't the full reason. She wanted him to know. Wanted him to see what they had in common.

They stepped out onto the trail. No one had waited for them. "Where'd they go?"

"Lawz showed up while you were healing the fawn. I told him to go ahead and we'd catch up. I wasn't sure how long it would take you, but that wasn't too long ago. They're probably almost to the lake. But . . ." He walked across the clearing and grabbed a small insulated bag hanging from a tree branch. "They left you a sandwich. I hope."

"I hope so, too." She plopped her tail on a fallen tree before she fell over. After the hike and the healing, she felt weak and half-starved, but the fawn was okay. And so was she, when Tuck opened the bag and handed a big turkey sandwich on a French roll to her. "Is there one for you?"

"No. I haven't done anything to earn an early lunch. You have."

"I'll share."

"You'll eat. And then you'll tell me why you think the doe thought I smelled like a wolf."

She'd been afraid that was coming, but it was obvious they both had secrets. "Well, I've never been around wolves before, but I had an awesome gray-and-black wolf sleeping beside me all night. I wasn't the least bit afraid of him because I sort of suspected he was you."

"Why would you think anything so—"

She held up the hand that wasn't full of sandwich. "Silly? Unbelievable? I thought at first that he reminded me of you, but I wasn't sure why. Then, when I buried my nose in his fur and was drifting off to sleep, I realized he smelled just like you. At first I thought it was merely a coincidence. I mean, men who can change into wolves? Impossible, right? But so is healing broken bones with touch, or like Darian, always knowing when someone is lying."

She laughed at the look of consternation on his face. If he was planning to deny what she'd said, she'd somehow have to hook him up with Dar to get the truth out of him, though she'd much rather he just fess up. "Believe me, Tuck. After what the two of us did last night, I know you're different. You're special. No man has ever made me laugh so much or come so hard in my life. I really want to do that again, by the way."

She finished the last few bites of her sandwich, wiped her fingers and face with the napkin that had been in the bag, and took a swallow out of her water bottle. Tuck hadn't said a word. Instead, he was staring off into the forest as if the weight of the world lay across his broad shoulders. "For what it's worth, Tuck, I don't intend to tell anyone beyond these trees about you. I understand that keeping secrets is sometimes necessary. And while I don't expect you to keep my abilities secret from the other guys here, I would appreciate the same consideration."

He sat there, forearms resting on his powerful thighs, big hands hanging loosely between his knees, not saying a word. Finally, he turned and smiled at her. "You've turned my entire world upside down, you know. And I've only known you what, about, oh . . . maybe eighteen hours?" He laughed softly. "I would like to tell the guys about your gift, if only to share how amazing you are. I can't discuss anything about your suspicions without talking to the other guys and our . . ."

He paused as if he was trying to figure out how to tell her what she'd already guessed.

"Your alpha?" She rubbed his tense shoulder when she said that. "Which means we'll need to wait until we get back to the lodge so you can speak to Trak."

He jerked around and stared at her. "But how—"

She pressed a finger to his lips. "He walks with authority, and while he doesn't say or do anything at all bossy, it's obvious that all of you defer to him. I think a couple of the others have already figured you guys out. It's okay. We won't talk."

He nodded and then stood. Grabbing the small bag off the log and looping it over his shoulder, he reached for Elle's hand. His silence spoke volumes.

A man able to shift into a wolf. It was something so far from reality it was almost impossible to believe . . . except she did believe. But did that mean there could never be anything between them? She couldn't quite see herself married to a guy who went furry while she stayed home and sulked.

And that image had her biting her lips to keep from laughing. What a bizarre conversation she was having with herself!

After a few more minutes of an easy hike, they rounded a stand of pine trees, and a pristine mountain lake glistened in the sunlight, spreading across a small valley with the towering ridges and harsh cliffs of the Trinity Alps framing the scene. Elle stopped dead in her tracks and stared for a long, long moment in time. The entire view was exquisite, beyond anything she'd ever imagined, so stunning it hardly looked real. Thick tules grew along one end of the lake, the bulrushes home to dozens of red-winged blackbirds that were obviously the source of the lake's name. Their calls echoed off the nearby cliffs. She blinked rapidly, clearing the tears from her eyes, and took a deep breath.

Tuck took hold of her hand and squeezed. His warm gaze said he understood the effect this magnificent little valley surrounded by stark mountain peaks was having on her.

Her friends were all down by the water's edge while the guys spread a cloth over a picnic table set closer to the trees and set up their lunch. A few clouds floated over; the air was chilly, but it really was a flawless day. All this and she'd even saved the life of a fawn. Smiling, still hanging on to Tuck's hand, she squeezed his fingers to get his attention. "You are so lucky to live in such a wonderful place. What's it like here in the winter?"

"Cold," he said, laughing. "Very cold, but it's even better when the peaks are covered in snow and ice."

"I'd love to see it." She turned and studied him for a moment. He looked spectacular, his dark hair in loose curls over his head, his beard not much more than a heavy shadow that defined a strong jaw and an absolutely kiss-able mouth. She knew his chest was covered in a soft pelt of dark hair, and the tattoo decorating his right shoulder and wrapping across his back was like a magnet to her fingers. She really wished there was a good reason for him to take his shirt off, just so she could feast her eyes on all that male splendor.

Instead, she voiced a thought that had been rattling around in her head ever since he'd watched her heal the fawn, something she'd not really even considered other than as an errant wish. Now, though? It was more than a wish. It was something she felt that she really needed to do. He'd praised her healing. She wondered if he'd meant what he'd said.

"Dr. Jones?"

"Yes, Ms. Marcel?"

His lips twitched, and she knew he was fighting a smile.

"I'm ready for a career change," she said. "Are you in the market for an assistant?"

The hike back down the mountain was a lot easier than going up. Jules had never really thought of herself as a country girl, but she had to admit that she loved the fresh air and the wide-open views, loved the idea of hiking with her best buds through rugged cedar and pine forests, and really loved the idea of two hot men paying her so much attention.

She might have started out with Manny, but Drew had latched on after spending the night—and there was no doubt in her mind that the second wolf had been Drew and the first one Manny—and she certainly wasn't going to tell him she didn't want him walking so close, touching so easily, looking so absolutely awesome.

He had no idea how much his scent, the mere fact of his proximity, turned her on. Her entire body was over-sensitized, her nipples hard from the slight friction of her clothing over the tips, her panties damp—and it wasn't just sweat from their hike

Good thing it wasn't illegal: hiking while aroused. Try explaining that one to a judge. On the other hand, she'd actually been wondering what it would be like to have two sexy

men in her bed. This was a vacation, after all. A chance to
play out a fantasy or two . . . or more? Dar was practically
connected at the hip to Lawz, and Elle and Tuck obviously
had something going on that already looked like more than
a vacation fling.

Which left Meg, who was engaged to be married, and
Jules with both Manny and Drew paying court. Not a bad
way to spend a week in the woods. Or in that cute little cabin.
The thing was, how did a woman go about letting two very
hot men know she was interested in sharing?

If nothing else, it gave her something to think about all
the way back to the lodge.

Meg hadn't expected to have so much fun on today's hike,
especially after she'd dumped all her neurotic angst on her
best friends, but she'd loved every minute. When Elle talked
about rescuing the fawn, Meg was reminded once again that
she had the most wonderful friends around, women who
were each so special in so many ways. But Elle? Elle was
definitely something else. They all knew about her healing
gift, but it was fun to hear her try to explain it to the guys.
The best part was the way Dr. Tuck accepted everything
she said without question.

Zach was like that. He deferred to Meg on so many things,
accepting the fact that there were some things she knew
more about than he did. She missed him. She thought of
him constantly, wondered what he would think of this place,
wondered what he'd think of her out hiking and playing in
the woods, doing things that were totally out of character
for her.

She wondered if it was bad form to invite a fiancé to a bachelorette party. The others had guys; in fact, it looked like Jules had two. Jules deserved two incredible men in her life, even if it was only for this week. They'd all figured out there had to be a horrible problem between Jules and her dentist boyfriend. She hadn't said anything, but Meg was positive she'd quit her job when they broke up, even though Jules hadn't said anything. Could her cocky dentist have been abusive?

Jules was smart and usually read people really well, so it was hard to figure out how that could have been the case.

They really needed to get together and talk. Just the four of them, no men allowed.

But not tonight. Tonight, she had a feeling she was going to sleep like the dead. She wondered if her wolf would show up.

CHAPTER 8

Zach Trenton stared at the cell phone in his hand, hoping for a text from Meggie. He missed her. He'd scheduled the annual two-week break for his company without realizing this was the week Meggie would be gone, which meant he didn't even have work to occupy him.

If only he weren't so damned worried. She'd been unhappy about something before she left, but he had no idea what it was, and she wasn't talking.

Nothing was the same without her. He couldn't put it into words, but somehow she completed all the frayed edges in his world. When Meggie was around, she kept him balanced and functional. Without her, he was a wreck. He'd never told her that. Maybe he should, except in the real world, it was supposed to be the man slaying the dragons. In his world, it was Meggie. If she knew how much he needed her, would she realize what a wimp he was?

He stared at the phone for a few more minutes. Should he or shouldn't he? This was her week off from him, a week to be with her friends. But he needed her. Plus, when he'd checked out the Feral Passions website, he broke out in a cold sweat. The guys that worked there could do a calendar and make a fortune.

Some women liked to screw around before they finally tied themselves to one guy, and Meg was ten years younger than he was. Was she looking for one last hurrah? He hoped not.

He'd realized, the moment she left, he didn't share well with others.

He slipped the phone back in his pocket. This week was his gift to Meg. They loved each other. Loving Meg meant trusting her, but . . .

He reached for his phone. Clenched his fist, left the phone in his pocket, and cursed.

Damn. He was such a wuss.

Trak and Evan had dinner in the oven, and they were both behind the bar, ready and waiting by the time the hikers straggled back to the lodge. They had at least an hour before dinner would be ready. Evan fixed chilled caffe mochas and iced spiced tea, passed out a couple of fruit juices to the tired, hot, and dusty ladies, and mixed up a margarita for Jules. Trak leaned against the bar while Evan handled the drinks, listening to the laughter, the sometimes raunchy comments, trying to judge whether or not the women were having a good time. That was something that had totally cracked him up— just how off-color a group of women could be when they got together without men.

At least everything he heard was positive about their visit so far.

He figured it would only take one bad review to destroy

the goodwill they'd been building all summer, and he worried about things going up online that he might be missing. At least Brad had called a little earlier—he'd gotten Trak's message, and since they were already headed home, they'd decided to cut out the last couple of stops and drive straight through.

That meant he'd have Cherry back at her computer, Brad running the kitchen, and Cain giving him grief. He almost missed the bastard. Almost.

Tuck leaned against the bar across from Trak and tapped him on the forehead. "What are you scowling about?"

Trak laughed. "Brad and Cherry are due home tomorrow night, and I just realized it means that Cain will be back, too."

"You just don't give that poor bastard a break, do you?" Tuck parked his ass on the bar stool and leaned close. "I've always wondered . . . what's your problem with him, anyway?"

Trak ran a white cloth over the polished surface, scrubbing at the shine with a vengeance. "Haven't you noticed? He's an alpha. A stronger alpha than I am, and yet he defers to me, doesn't challenge me. Even bares his throat when I bitch at him. What's wrong with him?"

Tuck had the balls to laugh out loud at that. Trak ground his teeth.

"Absolutely nothing," Tuck said. "He's a very smart, decent guy. Alpha or not, it's obvious he doesn't want the responsibility of the pack, but there's nothing wrong with that. And Cherry and Brad both love him, so he can't be too horrible, right? I think you've just gotten in the habit of always thinking he's out to get you."

"Decent? There's nothing decent about Cain Boudin. He's an asshole."

"He'd be an asshole if he wanted your pack. He doesn't. He does what you ask him to do and always goes the extra mile with our wild brothers. Let it go, Trak. It's not you. You're a good guy, but this private vendetta you've got against Cain bothers all of us. If he's acting like a shit, we'll call him on it, but it's reached a point where I'm afraid the guests might notice."

Crap. He hadn't even considered that. "Have I ever said anything to him in front of a guest? I don't recall—"

"Expressions can say a lot more than words, and you get a look around him that's like a scorpion crawled up your ass. It's not pretty."

"A scorpion?" He laughed at that one. Sometimes Tuck came up with the weirdest shit. "I didn't realize I was so obvious."

"Have you ever sat down and talked to him? Asked him why he submits even though you both know he's the more powerful wolf?"

"No." Sighing, Trak stared out toward the trees. "I think I'm afraid that he's going to tell me he's not really submitting, that he's pretending to, that he doesn't respect me enough to mean it." He turned to Tuck, fully aware he'd never talked about this before. Not to anyone. "Lawz resents the hell out of the fact that he, as the elder brother, was born a true beta. He feels he was cheated of his birthright. When I came along, alpha from the womb, he was outraged. I don't think he's ever forgiven me. It's come between us all our lives. Then along comes Cain, a guy who's stronger than both of us, and I think it sort of shook my sense of who I was, that maybe my leadership within the pack wasn't set in stone. I guess I'm always waiting for him to make a play for the top spot."

"Not gonna happen." Tuck took the mug of beer Evan handed him. The women had all gone back to their cabins while he and Trak had been talking. "Thanks, Ev." He turned back to Trak. "Cain's at peace. Whatever happened in his past, whatever drove him here to our pack, isn't driving him anymore. Not since he and Brad got together, and especially since Cherry came into their lives. He's got what he wants. A family, two mates who love him unconditionally. We should all be so lucky."

"He got kicked out of his pack in Idaho," Trak said, trusting Tuck and Evan to keep what he said confidential. "Do you remember when he showed up?" When both men shrugged, Trak explained. "It was shortly after World War II, and he'd served in Europe with the US Army. Buried his wolf nature and went in as a foot soldier, but he was a decorated vet when he got here, up front about getting kicked out of his pack for his overly aggressive tendencies."

"Was he a young wolf when that happened?"

"Yeah." Trak remembered the first time he met Cain. He was young and cocky and scared to death after coming out of the service without a pack to go home to. "He was born in 1910, got kicked out shortly after his first shift. He was late shifting—it happened in 1942. I guess he figured the army, with the war raging, was a natural segue, sort of trading one pack for another." It wasn't unusual for young wolves to turn aggressive shortly after their first shift, which happened in their late twenties or early thirties. It was like the power went to their heads. A lot of them didn't survive their first couple of years—they challenged older, more mature males and ended up dead. Cain had challenged the pack alpha, but the man had been a good leader, and rather than killing the young wolf, he'd exiled him from the pack.

It was the only way he could give Cain a second chance.

Cain had come to Trak's small pack after he got out of the service, humbled by the death he'd witnessed, the killing he'd been part of, and begged Trak for a spot. He'd admitted what an idiot he'd been, how thankful he was that his alpha had elected not to kill him, but rather sent him on his way with orders never to return. Trak had allowed him in, fully aware Cain was a powerful alpha, with the caveat that if he screwed up or even hinted at a challenge, he was out.

But Trak had never allowed himself to trust Cain, not even when Cain and Brad formed a partnership that was as powerful as any male-female mated pair.

Adding Cherry had made it even stronger. Trak still didn't trust him, but Tuck was right. He hadn't given Cain a chance, either. He grabbed Tuck's hand and squeezed it tightly. "Thank you." He glanced away to make eye contact with Evan as witness, then focused on Tuck.

"You're right. I never gave him a chance. From now on, I'll try." He shrugged, feeling just a bit sheepish, which wasn't a pleasant feeling at all for an alpha. "You know you'll always have my permission to tell me when I'm acting like a dick."

Both Evan and Tuck cracked up.

"You can count on it," Tuck said. "We've got your back."

"The thing is . . ." Evan glanced at Tuck as if for support, but then he turned and made eye contact with Trak, which wasn't natural for him. "Trak, we admire the job you do with the pack. You're a good leader, and other than the issues with Cain, you're always fair." He grinned and winked at Tuck. "Well, mostly fair, except when it comes to the house-keeping duties in the cabins. I want to know how you always manage to get scheduled on off days when there's no one staying."

"Not going there. I think this meeting is adjourned." He stood, swept off an imaginary hat and took a bow, and left both Tuck and Evan laughing. Now all he had to do was re-member not to give Cain any more grief than he deserved—though Trak was positive he definitely deserved at least a little.

Monday night
Jules left with Armando and Drew, Dar took off with Lawz, Elle and Tuck left hand in hand, and Meg missed Zachary so much she wanted to cry.

Trak stepped out of the kitchen, wiping his hands on a cotton towel. He set the towel aside, reached under the bar, and pulled out a large bottle. "Want to join me on the deck for a glass of port?"

She laughed. "You and your port. I see you've waited until everyone's gone before bringing out the bottle."

"Busted." Laughing, he grabbed two glasses. "I love the stuff, but it's really expensive. The guys would drink it like fruit juice if I didn't keep an eye on them. C'mon out and tell me how the hike went. I expected more conversation tonight."

"I think they're all exhausted. I know I am." Meg reached for a handful of chocolates and tucked them into her pocket.

Trak paused at the door, bottle and two glasses in hand. "Would you rather skip? If you're tired, I can walk you back to your cabin now."

She shook her head. "Honestly? I'm not ready to go back to an empty cabin, knowing my best friends are all bunking up with someone." She laughed, "Or, in Jules's case, two someones."

"Well," he drawled. "I'd offer to bunk up with you, but I don't think that's what you want."

"Thanks, Trak. You're right." She stared out the front window, at the darkness beyond and the little twinkling white lights that lit up the trails to the cabins. Then she pulled it together and smiled at him. "That was something I actually wondered. If I was exposed to a bunch of good-looking guys, would I be tempted? And it's weird, because, of any of the men here, I should be tempted by you, but there's no chemistry." She led the way to the door and held it open since he had his hands full. "I never realized before just how important that is, but I see it with our friends, with Elle and Tuck, and it's definitely there with Dar and Lawson. I guess the big surprise is Jules, Manny, and Drew. Wonders never cease."

She took a seat at one of the small tables in the shadows. Trak sat across from her and poured a bit of port into each of the glasses. Then he looked around and shook his head. "Damn. I forgot the chocolate."

He started to rise, but Meg touched his hand. "Sit. I didn't." She pulled her stash out of her pocket.

Trak held his glass out, and Meg tapped the rim of hers to his. "Here's to friendship, Meg. I'm enjoying your company, and honestly? It's nice to have an attractive, intelligent woman to hang out with and avoid all the drama." He took a sip of his port, and there was a definite twinkle in his eyes. "Okay, now that we've got that out of the way, tell me about this guy you're going to marry. And you are going to marry him, you know. I can tell by the way your eyes light up whenever you or any of your friends mention his name. You definitely have all the signs of a woman in love."

"I do love him. But . . ." And she told him. Everything about her fears that Zach couldn't love her, that he didn't really mean it, that she wasn't anyone special and he was. And when she was finished and feeling lower than dirt, Trak just stared at her with a look of absolute disbelief.

Finally, he took another swallow of his port, looked her in the eye, and said, quite plainly, "You realize that's a pile of shit, don't you?"

She snorted. Not at all attractive when she was trying to act the grown-up here, but he looked so serious and his comment was just so . . . male. Finally, she got herself under control. "Why?"

"Well, for one thing, it's usually the guy who gets cold feet, because you know we're all a bunch of pussies when it comes to commitment, and for another, none of your arguments hold water. So what if your parents didn't plan you when you came along? That doesn't make you any less valid or important. And if they're too self-centered and stupid to acknowledge the wonderful woman you are, then that's their problem, not yours. Why would their lack of parental abilities have anything to do with the woman you are now? You're an amazing woman, Meg, and obviously Zach is smart enough to have figured it out. Look, why don't you invite him here? There's no extra charge, and the bed in your room is certainly big enough."

"Do you think he'd come?"

"Of course. It's not late; it's barely nine o'clock. You said his company is closed for the rest of the week. Go into the office off the kitchen and use the phone in there. I'll wait out here and give you privacy, but tell him you miss him and the bed is real empty without him here. That's the truth, isn't it?"

Nodding silently, Meg went into the little office where she stared at the phone for way too long. She'd never taken the first step before.

Ten minutes later, Trak walked in. "You didn't call, did you?"

She shook her head. "I can't." She picked up her glass and finished the rest of her port. "Would you walk me back to my cabin now? Please?"

"If you're sure that's what you want."

She nodded and left her glass on the desk. He took her hand and led her out of the lodge and down the trail to her cabin. Walked her up to the front door.

"Are you going to be okay?"

She looked at him. Really looked. He was so handsome with his neatly trimmed dark hair and the short beard. Well over six feet tall with a lean build similar to Zach's, a fun sense of humor, and a compassionate manner. If not for Zachary, would she want an affair with a man like Trak?

What would his kisses feel like? The thrust of his cock entering her, the weight of his long, lean body over hers? "Will you do something for me, Trak? Will you kiss me?"

He ran his hand over her hair. "Is this a test?"

"In a way. I never had a serious boyfriend before Zach. I honestly have never kissed another man. I don't think high school boyfriends count. I guess I'm curious."

"I can deal with curiosity." He cupped her shoulders and looked into her eyes, then he tilted her chin, leaned close, and covered her mouth with his. His lips were firm and yet so mobile, moving over hers with gentleness that seemed the antithesis of the man she'd been getting to know. His tongue tested the seam between her lips until she opened for him, turned to meet his kiss, the thrust of his tongue, the warmth of his big hands stroking her back, pulling her close.

She felt the heat of his erection through the long skirt she wore, heard the thundering race of his heart, tasted the port on his tongue and the hint of chocolate. There was no doubt in her mind he was aroused, but as much as she enjoyed the kiss, he wasn't Zach. Her body didn't respond.

When he finally pulled away, it seemed so apropos that both of them were smiling.

"For the record, I truly love kissing you, Meg, but your body tells me your brain wasn't nearly as involved as it should be. I bet all of you is a hundred percent into whatever your Zachary chooses to do with you."

"You're right." She felt like laughing, but that would be so rude. Still, he'd answered an important question. Zach and only Zach. No one else. "Thank you. Please don't hate me. I mean, I could tell that you were . . ." She stumbled over that. Turned on? Aroused? She shrugged.

Trak laughed. "Don't worry about that. I'm a guy. It's part of our makeup. Pretty woman, soft lips, warm kisses." He paused, glanced at her chest, and grinned. "Magnificent breasts. Boners happen." He cupped her shoulders again, leaned close, and kissed her, a short, sweet kiss good night. "I'll see you in the morning."

"Do you think the wolf will come back?"

"If you leave the door ajar, he might show up." He reached around her and opened the door. "I think they go cabin to cabin, looking for a warm bed. Good night, Meg. Sweet dreams."

She watched him walk toward the forest and thought for a moment, by his measured walk and the slope of his shoulders, that he looked lonely. But that couldn't be. He had his pack and the pick of any woman who came through Feral Passions.

Too bad. This week, he got stuck with the engaged one.

Jules couldn't stop shivering. Her logical mind told her she was absolutely terrified, but her inner hussy knew the truth. She'd never been so aroused in her life, merely walking between two men.

Men she was almost positive were able to shift into wolves, but she'd decided to let that curious issue slide for now, because it was way too outrageous to really believe and she hadn't had the chance to talk about it with the others to see if they had any suspicions.

Ignoring the wolf issue, she was bracketed by two men who were not only awesomely sexy and way too hot, but smart and funny and interested in her. And in each other. She'd picked up on that vibe from the beginning between Armando and Drew. It was sweet and sensual without any heavy emotional stuff going on. They appeared to be two guys who truly liked each other and probably screwed around when the mood struck them.

Now, it appeared, they'd been struck with the mood to screw around with her. She was always the good girl, the one who played by the rules. She didn't love either man, but she certainly liked them, she was definitely attracted to them, and this week was a fantasy for her, a chance to shed that boring image she'd been stuck with.

Andrew's words reverberated through her skull, his accusations that she was frigid and uptight. The word he'd used was "prissy." No one called anyone prissy anymore, but that bastard had, even when he was already screwing the new receptionist. No wonder the turnover in his office was so high.

Tonight, though, she'd prove to herself that she was adventurous, that she could do something that, just a few days ago, would have been unthinkable. Still was, actually. How the hell did one woman have sex with two men at the same time? She glanced at Armando, and he smiled at her. Definitely a wolfish grin.

He looked like a guy who could figure it out if anyone could. She wasn't worried. No, not at all.

Well, maybe just a little. Protection! She hadn't even thought about that. She was still on the pill after that horrible affair with Andrew, but the guys here appeared to have had a constant supply of women coming through all summer, and she . . .

Well, if they hadn't come prepared, it would give her a good reason to back out. Except she really didn't want to back out, now that she'd come this far.

She took a deep breath once they reached the cabin, let it out as they walked up the steps to the front door. Armando . . . no, she needed to think of him as Manny. He wasn't all that fond of his given name, said it sounded much too pretentious, and he preferred the nickname the guys had given him.

Manny fit. She'd already figured out that while he was

so hot he quite literally took her breath, there was nothing artificial about him, no inflated ego like so many good-looking men. He paused in front of the door and wrapped his arms around her, hugged her close, and kissed her. Drew stood behind her, his hands on her shoulders, his lips tickling the back of her neck.

"This is entirely up to you, Jules," he said. "One of us can stay, both of us, or we can kiss you good night at the door and wish you pleasant dreams. We don't want you to feel co-erced or pressured in any way. It's your call. How do you want to spend tonight?"

She didn't hesitate. Tipping her head, she looked directly into Drew's smoky-blue eyes. Never in her entire life had a man as handsome as Drew been this close to her. She wanted to savor the moment. "I want both of you to stay with me." She took Manny's hand, grasped Drew's. "But only if you want to. This week is a fantasy come to life for me, but I really don't know what both of you want."

"That's easy to answer." Drew opened the door and tugged her hand, pulling her gently inside. Manny followed. Her heart seemed to lodge in her throat, pounding out a cadence that left her shivering in response. She was really doing this. She, Julia Bennett, was inviting two amazing men into her bed.

Her nipples tightened beneath her light sweater, and she was beyond damp between her legs. Drew turned on a low light in the kitchen and left the rest of the room in darkness. Manny went into the kitchen area, opened the little refrig-erator, and pulled out a bottle of white wine. The cupboard overhead yielded three wineglasses. He carried everything to the bedside table.

Filling the glasses, he handed one to Drew, another to Jules, and took one for himself. "To a night of adventure, Ms. Bennett. To you." He tapped the rim of his glass to hers and then to Drew's.

Drew took a swallow, kicked off his shoes, and stretched his long legs out on the bed, leaned against the headboard, and held his glass of wine against his chest. He was a little over six feet tall, long and lean, with shadowed blue eyes and the face of an angel. He patted the bedspread beside him. "C'mon, Jules. Sharing a glass of wine in bed with two men has to be a good way to start."

Manny slipped his hands around her waist from behind. "Not when she's wearing so many clothes."

She turned her head and gave him a narrow-eyed glance, but she honestly couldn't believe what came out of her mouth. "Not nearly as many as you and Drew."

Manny raised an expressive eyebrow. "She has a point, Drew. Strip."

Drew made a show of it, setting his glass of wine aside and doing a sensual striptease that might have been almost comical under any other circumstances. Instead, Jules felt as if he was unwrapping a gift just for her. He got down to his silky-looking boxers that did nothing to hide the impressive package behind the dark blue fabric.

Nor did they hide the fact he was magnificently aroused.

Her breath had shortened to the point where she felt light-headed, but she turned to Manny and folded her arms over her chest. This, of course, raised two of her feminine assets and caught his attention immediately. He licked his lips, and her heart stuttered in her chest. When he grabbed the hem of his T-shirt and hauled it up and over his head, her mouth went dry. Manny was a big man, tall and muscular with a light dusting of dark hair across his pecs and a darker line arrowing down and disappearing beneath the waistband of his jeans.

He kicked off his shoes—she'd noticed that most of the guys wore moccasins and she wondered if they made them themselves—and then his hands paused at the snap to his faded denim jeans. When she raised an eyebrow, he laughed.

"Just wanted to make sure you were paying attention." His lazy grin actually sent shivers across her very warm arms. "I don't do this for just anybody, you know. Not like Drew. He'll drop 'em for just about anyone."

She heard Drew snort, and she glanced over her shoulder in time to see him with his middle finger raised in Manny's direction. She rolled her eyes, and he laughed.

When she focused again on Manny, he was slipping those soft denims down his very long legs. Drew was pretty-boy handsome, but Manny was flat-out spectacular. Long, muscular legs with a dusting of dark hair, broad shoulders, muscled chest, and long, strong arms. Everything about him was oversized. She glanced at his black knit boxers that managed to hide very little, and she blinked. Definitely everything.

"Your turn."

She nodded, mouth suddenly dry, best of intentions trapped in a maelstrom of self-doubt. She was a big girl, would never be slim and svelte like Dar, but she'd never had issues about her weight, either. She was athletic in high school and college, still ran and did yoga, worked out at the gym when she had time, but she had hips and boobs and a solid build, and she'd never once in her life felt as much on display as she did right now.

But she slipped her sweater over her head and reached behind herself to unhook her bra. Drew was already there. "Let me," he said, and his breath was a warm kiss against her throat. Shivering when his hands stroked her shoulders, she was visibly trembling when his lips caressed the side of her neck as he carefully flipped the hooks and slipped the bra over her arms.

Her breasts were large, and the straps always left red marks on her shoulders, but he gently rubbed those with his thumbs before sliding his hands around to her front and cupping both breasts in his warm palms. She moaned, leaning her head back against his chest as Manny stepped closer. He slipped his fingers inside the elastic waistband on her skirt and tugged it down over her hips, leaving her in a pair of black bikini panties that matched her bra.

Drew's hands continued gently massaging her breasts, but he was plucking at her nipples now, and her desire for more rose incrementally. She didn't realize Manny had gone to his knees until she felt his warm breath against her.

Her trembling increased. No one had ever kissed her there. She had no idea what to expect, but whatever it was, she was certainly anxious to find out.

Manny knelt before Jules, his hands cupping her buttocks, his nose practically twitching from the sweet scent of her arousal. Her body was ripe and ready for him, her naturally full figure tempting in every way. Full breasts, wide hips, rounded thighs, the slight curve of her belly—his mind filled with visuals of burying himself in her sweet warmth, of sharing this bounty with Drew.

He glanced up, caught Jules watching him intently, her hands covering the backs of Drew's as he kneaded her breasts like a cat, pinching her nipples, all while tracing the line of her shoulder with his lips.

From the look on her face, it was working.

Smiling at Jules, he dipped his head and ran his tongue between her damp folds, tasting her for the first time. She was ambrosia, a feast for a starving man. Her body trembled, and he held her firmly, curling his tongue between her lips, around the slight protrusion of her clitoris.

She jerked when he found it, cried out, and arched her hips closer to his mouth. He dug his fingers gently into the cleft between her cheeks, holding her carefully so that he could tease and taste without Jules having to worry about such a simple thing as balance.

He concentrated on her clit, swirling his tongue around the tiny bud and then sucking it gently between his lips. Her trembling increased, the rate of her breathing, the thundering of her heart so noticeable to his wolf hearing.

Aroused like this, his wolf was closer to the surface, his senses so much more acute. His hearing, sense of touch, sense of smell. He inhaled, slipped his right hand between Jules's legs, and thrust two fingers deep inside her slick passage, curled them forward as he sucked even harder on her clit.

Her body jerked. She arched her back and cried out, a short, sharp scream of release. When the tension went out of her and she collapsed, it was into his waiting arms. Laughing with Drew, kissing Jules's sweet mouth, he rose to his feet with this lovely lady held tightly against his chest and carried her to the bed.

CHAPTER 9

Early Tuesday morning

It was after three in the morning when Zach gave up trying
to sleep and made his decision. Meggie might never forgive
him, but he hadn't realized how awful it would be with her
gone. He was certain she'd changed her mind, that she didn't
want to marry him.

He had to know.

He threw some clothes in an old backpack and was on
the road before four. He turned off his phone because he
knew if Meggie called she'd be totally pissed off to find out
he was heading for Feral Passions.

There was always the chance she'd be glad to see him—
at least, that's what he was banking on, but he missed her
so much he'd be happy even to have her yelling at him.

Except Meggie didn't yell. All she'd ever done was love
him with the kind of love he'd never known in his life.
Certainly not from his parents. No, he loved his work,
he was successful, and unlike his father, he hadn't had
to act like a bastard to get here, but he could trace his
growing success to the day he hired Meggie. She'd taken
one look at his cluttered office and laughed. Damn, he

missed her laugh, and it was only Tuesday. She'd left Sunday morning.

The woman was going to think he was certifiable. Maybe he was.

The hours passed quickly, but the closer he got, the more nervous he was about showing up unannounced in the middle of Meggie's bachelorette getaway. What if he pissed her off enough to cancel the wedding?

He really didn't want to think about that. Not at all.

He was going to have to . . . he was almost to Weaverville. The resort was close, and . . . a flash of brown, big and lumbering and *fast* raced across the road in front of him.

Bear! He hit the brakes, turned the wheel into the spin, missed the bear, but overcorrected, skidding in loose gravel on the side of the road. Brakes screeched, and his arms locked up as he struggled to hold the car under control. One tire went off the edge of the road, he hit the berm, and his BMW went airborne, flipping end over end before rolling and then sliding on the passenger side through brush and boulders until one much larger than the trusty old Beemer stopped him.

Stopped the car, and stopped Zach. He had a moment of abject clarity, knew the airbags—more than one—had deployed.

After that, nothing more.

Dar rolled over in the big, comfortable bed, expecting to find the wolf beside her. Instead, it was Lawz lying there, propped up on one elbow, smiling at her in the darkness. They'd made love for hours, slow, lazy love after the first rush of need was soothed, and then they'd talked. He was an engineer—she hadn't expected that for whatever reason—and he told her about building bridges and various structures around the North Coast.

He didn't live here all the time, but a job had been delayed, so he'd come home to help out at Feral Passions. He said he was glad he had or he'd never have met her. She'd laughed and said what a flatterer he was, but then she'd told him about her job as a television weather reporter for a cable news show, how she'd grown tired of the infighting among the employees, the petty politics that kept things so stirred up. They'd talked about what kind of job she could do if she lived here in Northern California, but it was all dreams and fantasies woven of moonbeams.

As insubstantial as the moonlight filtering through the window blinds, reflecting off the corner of his eye, his white teeth, giving him a ghostly but totally sexy look.

Everything about Lawz was sexy. Never, not since she'd first given it up—and that was most definitely not consensually—to her older brother's best friend when she was fifteen years old had she ever experienced true lovemaking the way she had with Lawz.

That meant that ten years of bad to mediocre sex with various and sundry males had been wiped away in just a couple of nights with the man she was lying here lusting after. Again. How many times last night? She'd lost count.

Didn't matter. She wanted to add to the number. She reached for him. He gently trapped her hands over her head in one of his. "It's the middle of the night," he said. He tapped the end of her nose with his finger. "Why are you awake?"

"Because you're here." She tried to kiss him. Teasing, he

pulled just out of reach. "I was sleeping with a wolf." She tugged her hands. He held on. "When did you change?"

"You keep saying that. I'm not a wolf." He leaned close and kissed her.

She actually tasted the lie. "I'm not going to argue with you, Lawz. Didn't I tell you that no one can lie to me? I've got like an inner lie detector that tells me when someone's not telling the truth." He raised his eyebrows, and she shook her head. "I know you're not being truthful, but it's okay. I can understand the need to keep something like that private, and I would never dream of telling, but I don't want you to think I don't know. I do. Actually, I find that it's really and truly . . ." She gave a low, sexy hum. "Provocative, tantalizing, and extremely sexy." She leaned close and kissed him, loved the way he groaned into her mouth and wrapped his arms around her. Now that her hands were free, she cupped his head in her hands.

He rolled her to her back and covered her like a warm blanket. Neither of them had gotten around to putting clothes on. He rolled his hips, nestled between her thighs. Studied her.

"I wish . . ." He shook his head and shrugged. "There are some things I can't change."

She smiled at him, loving the weight of his legs covering hers, the way the rough hair on his thighs softly abraded the sensitive skin on hers. She reveled in the warm press of his belly against her middle and the jut of his cock between her thighs. "Sort of a werewolf code of honor?"

He stared at her so intently, she wondered if she'd gone too far.

Finally, he glanced to one side, exhaled noisily, and then focused on her face again. "Yeah," he said. "Sort of."

"That's all I need to know." She wrapped her arms around his neck and pulled herself close enough to kiss him. He nipped at her breasts, the line of her ribs, the taut skin at the juncture between neck and shoulder, each tiny bite a sharp pain he soothed with his tongue.

When he entered her, the hard length of him filled her so exquisitely she felt tears prickling her eyes and trickling from their corners into her hair. She seriously wondered how she would ever let him go. They made such a flawless rhythm together, yet she knew this was nothing more than a vacation fling. That's all it could ever be with a man who wasn't really a man, but she'd never forget him, never get over him, and she was positive she'd never find another man nearly as wonderful as Lawson Jakes.

The tempo of his thrusts changed, short and fast, deep and hard, until she was gasping for air, whispering his name, so close and yet not close enough with that tiny tickle of arousal slowly growing and expanding, curling her toes and sending hot chills across her skin. He changed the angle of his hips, sliding across her clit on every stroke until the shivers all ran together and her muscles tightened, inside and out.

She flew, crying out, weeping with the frightening power of her climax, her fingers digging into the taut muscles of his shoulders, her legs clamped tightly around his waist.

He held his weight off of her, but his arms trembled, and his head hung low to her breasts. They stayed like that for a long moment, both of them sucking air, bodies sated for now, hearts still thundering in the aftermath of what felt like a nuclear explosion—or something really close.

Finally, he grasped the condom around the base of his cock and rolled to one side, slid out of bed, and went into the bathroom to dispose of it. When he got back to the bed, Dar was sitting up, leaning against the headboard. He crawled into bed beside her and pulled her into his arms. She went willingly, feeling unaccountably sad that this couldn't possibly last, but she still snuggled against his damp chest. He'd sweated even more than she had.

She ran her fingers through the happy trail beneath his navel. "I don't remember you even putting that condom on. Thank you for thinking of it, because I sure didn't."

"I had it on when I woke you."

"You woke me? I thought I just woke up."

He grinned at her and kissed her. "You did, after I tickled your nose. Then I sort of tweaked your nipple, like this." He demonstrated.

Laughing, she batted his hand away. "No wonder I woke up. You realize it's only four in the morning."

"I know, but I needed you. Hoped I could convince you what a great idea it was."

"You were right, but damn, I'm so easy."

He laughed. "That you are. It's one of your finer attributes."

Her hand slipped lower; she wrapped her fingers around his penis and stroked him. He was actually flaccid for the first time in a long while, but his shaft reacted to her touch, quickly filling her hand as it grew engorged and erect.

He sighed. "Now look what you've done."

She smiled sweetly and turned him loose. "I was merely proving to you that you're easier than I am."

He didn't say a word, but his fingers slipped between her legs and gently stroked. Her clit was still sensitive from her orgasm, and her inner muscles clenched in reaction to his touch. In what seemed like merely seconds he took her to the edge and held her there, whimpering with need, begging for him to finish, to set her free.

He thrust two fingers deep inside, and her body exploded.

Screaming his name, she flew. His laughter was its own music.

Tuck held Elle in his arms, his lips buried in her burgundy hair, their bodies sweaty and sated from the most amazing sex he'd ever experienced in his life.

She hadn't forced the issue, but it was obvious she'd figured them out. He hadn't had a chance to get together with the other guys and Trak, but they needed to talk. Had to figure out how to deal with this, because it was either the best or worst thing that could happen.

He thought of what she'd asked him, wondered if she'd been serious. He was taking her with him later today when he did his rounds in town, and he'd remind her of what she'd said, that she was interested in working for him as his assistant. Practically speaking, he really did need an assistant. One who could heal broken bones with her touch? Invaluable.

One who made him laugh, who was luscious and so damned sexy she made him ache? Absolutely priceless.

———

Jules awoke to a subtle but unfamiliar buck and sway, the bed doing its own rhythmic dance powered by both Manny and Drew. She lay there with a half smile on her lips, unself-consciously stroking between her legs as she watched the two men making love beside her.

Drew lay on his stomach, his face turned toward hers, his smoky-blue eyes closed, long, light brown hair curling softly around his face, and a smile on his very kissable mouth. Manny covered him, his hair, longer and darker than Drew's shielding his face, the muscles in his arms knotted with tension, his muscular ass and strong thighs driving his rather large cock slowly and surely into and out of his partner.

He was so big, she was secretly relieved they hadn't wanted her to try that kind of sex last night. One baby step at a time, and having Drew sucking her nipples and Manny doing the same to her clit was just about as outrageous as she'd been ready to go. At least today.

She might be a bit more adventurous by tomorrow.

She certainly couldn't have imagined herself lying in a big bed next to two truly stunning men as they had sex with each other. Not only that, but giving herself pleasure—in full view if they chose to look—and doing it without guilt. That hadn't even been on her radar. But last night? That hadn't, either. The two of them had made her come so often and so ingeniously for hours that she was actually sore this morning, but it was a soreness she wouldn't trade for anything. She'd discovered that Drew really, really loved her large breasts. He's spent hours showing her just how much, and with Drew concentrating on all her erogenous zones above the waist and Manny on the ones below, she'd had an experience unlike anything she could possibly imagine.

She'd actually teased Manny, told him his tongue should be licensed. Just thinking of the ecstasy she'd experienced, what he'd managed to wring from her with his lips and teeth and tongue—and some rather ingenious use of his fingers—sent a fresh rush of moisture flowing between her legs. Well, that sensual memory and the current hot visual of two extremely luscious men treating Jules to her very own adult feature film.

These last couple of days had been filled with firsts. She'd never been the adventurous type, at least according to Andrew. But after they were dating and already intimate, he'd dropped the biggest relationship bomb ever, the fact he fully expected to share multiple sex partners and an open relationship with Jules.

That had been the beginning of the end, as far as she was concerned. And when she'd accused him of infidelity during that same conversation and he'd hit her?

She'd quit her job and Andrew the sleazebag dentist the same day.

Oddly, she didn't have a problem at all with Manny and Drew, but they'd merely offered her a fun week at the resort, not teased her with a lifetime commitment that meant absolutely nothing. Though she had to admit, after last night, both Manny and Drew meant something to her.

No woman could spend hours so intimately connected with two hot, fun, intelligent, thoughtful men and walk away

unscathed. She would miss them. Miss the woman she became with them. She didn't even want to think what it would
be like when she and the girls drove away on Saturday, but
she knew it was going to hurt.

That was okay; it would be worth the pain. They were
worth it.

And so was she.

Jules knew, with a clarity that shocked her, that that
was the most important thing that had happened to her,
being loved by two men, laughing with them at silly things,
feeling so comfortable in her own skin. Without doing or
saying anything specific, they'd given Jules back to herself,
the woman she'd lost when Andrew turned on her.

All they had done was treat her with respect—more than
that, they'd openly worshipped her body. To them she wasn't
heavy or "matronly," as one jerk had described her. She was
voluptuous and full-figured in all the right places, and she
knew they meant what they said. When they'd looked at her,
touched her, tasted her, they'd done it with hands trembling
with desire, with lips parted, and hearts pounding.

Because of her, and because of them, all of Andrew's hate-
ful words had turned to so much dust. She pursed her lips
and blew softly, and like that, he was gone, along with the
ugly things he'd said. The pain he'd inflicted. The terrible
words and cruel acts that had begun to define Jules in spite
of her awareness that the man was a jerk, that he should
have no power over her.

Well, obviously he had, because the lightness she felt now
hadn't been part of her for a long, long time, and she gloried
in her newfound freedom to be.

To be Jules again.

Her fingers were slick with her arousal, her heart pounding in her chest as she watched the two men, recognized the tension, their muscles taut with impending climax.

She raised her head. Drew's dreamy blue eyes were open, and he watched her. Without thinking, she moved closer and offered him her breast. He latched on to her nipple, groaning, gently squeezing her full curves with one big hand as he sucked her sensitive nipple tightly against the roof of his mouth with his tongue.

She felt the pressure like an electric shock running from nipple to clit and back again, two powerful erogenous zones connected by hot, wet suction and pure sensation. Drew slipped his hand between her legs and gently moved her fingers aside, thrusting into her moist heat, taking her closer to the climax hovering so close.

Jules arched her back, pushing her hips closer to Drew, and at the same time slipped her hand beneath his belly, found the thick length of his cock trapped against the sheets and circled him with her fingers.

He groaned and turned just a bit so that she had better access. Manny grinned at her as he continued thrusting slow and steadily into his partner. "Good morning, Jules."

So polite. She giggled. "Good morning to you, Manny." She squeezed Drew's cock, and his hips bucked. "And to you as well, Drew."

He turned her nipple free, licked the tip, and said, "Good morning, Jules." He glanced over his shoulder at Manny. "We've created a monster."

"Damn, I certainly hope so, because she's absolutely sensational like this." Manny winked at Jules and grabbed Drew's hips, lifting him to his knees so that his balls hung down between his legs and his cock angled up toward his belly.

Fascinated by Manny's easy strength and the pure carnality of the scene, Jules slipped beneath Drew's flat belly, took his cock in her hands, and angled him down to her mouth. This was something Andrew had insisted she do. She'd hated it. For whatever reason, she couldn't wait to taste Drew. She wrapped her fingers around the thick base and licked the ruddy tip, tasted the salty-sweet drops of fluid coming from the dark slit, and decided it wasn't bad at all. Then she sucked him deep into her mouth. She'd heard of women swallowing a man down, but that was going to have to wait for the next lesson. Instead, she concentrated on the last few inches of his erection and the smooth glans that filled her mouth.

She still had one free hand, and with that she cupped the wrinkled sac between his thighs, rolling the two round testicles carefully between her fingers. He groaned, and his hips jerked forward as Manny picked up the pace. She was glad she had her hand around the base of Drew's erection, because she would have had to swallow a lot more of him than she was ready for.

His balls drew up close to his body, and she stretched her fingers between Drew's legs to reach Manny. The moment her palm cupped his lightly furred sac, he let out a strangled cry and thrust his hips forward. Drew's hips jerked. He tried to pull out of her mouth.

She held on to Drew, held on to Manny's balls, and swallowed Drew's release as fast as she could. And the one thing she wished was that someone, somewhere had thought to get film of this, proof that she was not nearly the prissy female Andrew had called her.

Then she wiped that thought from her mind. He was not going to show up and ruin the most amazing wake-up call she'd ever gotten in her life. Besides, she hadn't done this to show Andrew anything. No, she'd done this entirely for herself.

Breakfast was a little late this morning, though from the satisfied looks on everyone's faces, time obviously wasn't an issue. Meg had slept really well. She'd fallen asleep missing Zach and awakened with him in her thoughts, but the big gray-and-black wolf with soulful brown eyes sleeping beside her had kept her from feeling lonely.

It was the weirdest thing, though, that when she'd wrapped her arms around the wolf and gone back to sleep for a little bit longer, she'd felt as if she were holding on to Trak. She had no idea why the beast reminded her of the man.

Think of the devil . . .

"Good morning, ladies. Do you have everything you need for your breakfast?

Elle slipped into her seat and glanced at everyone's loaded plates. "I have to ask, Trak. Are we eating low-cal fried potatoes and nonfat bacon?" At his stricken look, she laughed. "Didn't think so." She loaded up her fork with part of her omelet. "That's why this all tastes so good."

"C'mon, Trak." Meg was having trouble not laughing at the look of relief on his face once he realized Elle was teasing. "Do any of us look as if we worry about calories?"

"None of you looks as if you need to worry about calories." Laughing at himself, he shook his head. "But before I step in it again, I wanted to let you know that the guys and I have a short business meeting this morning, so you'll be on your own for about half an hour. Are you okay with that?"

"I think we can take care of ourselves for a bit." Meg took a sip of her coffee and glanced at Dar. "You look like you're really trying to get into trouble, Ms. Ahlers. What's going on in that devious mind of yours?"

"Well . . ." Dar dragged out the word. "I wondered if we were allowed to gossip about the help while they're off meeting somewhere."

Trak winked at her. "Good gossip only. We'll be at Growl, the bar you passed on the way in. It's our unofficial clubhouse slash office. We try to meet weekly to go over the upcoming schedule, so if you need us for anything, just pick up the phone in the office and hit the red button. It's a direct link to the bar." He glanced at his wristwatch. "I should be back by ten."

"Sorry I'm late." Trak stepped into Growl and headed for the coffeemaker behind the bar. The guys were all sitting at one of the large poker tables, but cards were the last thing on anyone's mind. "The girls are having breakfast, and I told them how to get hold of us," he said. "So what's the status? Do they all know what we are? And if so, are we screwed, or is it going to be okay?"

He pulled out a chair and sat.

Tuck shrugged his big shoulders. "Elle knows. Yesterday,

when we hiked up to Blackbird? Along the way, she heard a fawn in distress and insisted we stop to check on the sound. I really didn't want to do it, figured if the thing was hurt badly and I had to put it down, it would ruin the week for the women."

"So what'd you do?" Lawz sipped his coffee, and if Trak knew his brother, this was at least his fifth cup of the morning.

"I didn't do a damned thing. Elle healed it. Said she's got the same gift her grandmother had, and she just knelt down by that little fawn and knew by touch that it had a badly cracked left front radius. That's the one in the lower part of the leg, in front of the ulna. Can't leave an animal like that on its own in the wild, but she blew on it, and the critter relaxed, and then she cupped her hands around it, and I swear I could see light glowing between her hands. That's what she was doing when you got there, Lawz. She'd told me she didn't want anyone to see, but after about twenty or so minutes, she sat back and said it was fine."

"Was it?" Trak wasn't quite sure where this was leading, but . . .

"Damned right. Little guy got to his feet with help, but he put weight on it, and the mother came out of the woods to feed him. That's when Elle told me to get back a ways, that the deer could pick up the smell of the wolf on me."

"Shit. What'd you say?"

"I denied it, of course, but later, we talked, and I asked her why she thought I smelled like a wolf. She said that the wolf in her bed had reminded her of me, and when she hugged the wolf while she was falling asleep, she realized he smelled like me. Then she said that all of them are special in one way or another. Lawz, did you know that Dar can always tell when someone is lying?"

Lawz nodded. "Yep. Found that out the hard way. Tuck's right. Dar knows, too, though I haven't confirmed her suspicions."

Trak groaned.

Tuck shot a quick grin his way. "Elle asked me not to say anything about her power and promised not to say anything about me turning into a wolf, though she did give me permission to tell you guys about it. I told her I couldn't say anything about the other until I'd talked to . . ." He paused, sighed, and said, "She interrupted me, said she guessed I meant until I talked to Trak, since she'd already figured you were the pack alpha."

"What the fuck? But how?" Now that was a first.

"She said she felt it, that there was a sense of leadership about you, and that it was obvious the rest of us deferred to you. I made some quip about it being impossible, and she just said that yeah, about as impossible as her healing cracked bones with her hands."

Before Trak could come up with a response, Drew and Manny looked at one another and added, "Jules has us figured out, too. She doesn't act like it's any big deal, just that it's who we are. I don't get it. You'd expect most women to get all freaked out, afraid of the Big Bad Wolf."

"Then they all know. I don't know about Meg, but those girls share everything. She's probably finding out now. Shit." Trak buried his head in his hands. They'd never imagined anyone figuring them out. Not like this. They'd interacted with humans for years, had dated women, gone to school with them, worked with them, and to date, the only one to have guessed their long-kept secret had been Cherry, who had done it based on eye color.

They'd thought she was merely an anomaly, because she was just so damned smart, but obviously, a lot of women were too damned smart nowadays.

"Okay, next step," Trak said. "Are any of you hoping to ask any of these women to be your mates?"

"Elle's mine whether she knows it or not." Tuck laughed at that. "She's absolutely mine. I'm taking her with me on my rounds in town today, see how she likes it. She'd already asked if I needed an assistant, so I know she's ready to move up here if I give the go-ahead."

"What about you, Lawz? Do you think Dar'd be willing to give up her job in Portland?"

"I don't know. I've dropped hints that I'd like for her to move to the area, see where things take us. I can ask her outright."

"Okay. You've got time. Give it a couple of days, get to know her better. Manny? Drew? What about you two? Are either of you thinking long term with Jules?"

Manny glanced at Drew. "I have been. Not sure about Drew, and while we've been lovers off and on for years, not sure if he's interested in a role as a co-husband."

"Actually . . ." Drew blushed.

Blushed? Trak raised an eyebrow. "Drew?"

He glanced shyly toward Manny and then looked away. Manny stood so fast he knocked his chair back. "C'mon, Drew. We need to talk."

Without even acknowledging the other guys in the room, Manny grabbed Drew's hand and dragged him out of the bar.

Trak sat back in his chair while Evan righted the one that Manny had knocked over. "Well," he said. "That was interesting." He glanced toward the closed door. "My gut tells me that you need to come clean with your women, but impress upon them the importance of secrecy. At this point, that's about the best advice I can offer, but if the four of you, and that's including Manny and Drew, work this out, that leaves just Evan and me in search of women, and we've got three more weeks of guests before we shut down for the season."

Lawz leaned back in his chair. "What are we gonna do with the place afterward? We've put in a really nice lodge, and we've made a killing on it in just this one year alone."

"That we have. We'll think of something. It's too nice a facility not to use it."

A car pulled up in front. Evan walked to the door to see who it was. "Hey, it's Cain and Brad and Cherry. They're back!"

"Thank goodness." Trak shoved his chair back and stood. "Maybe Cherry'll have some kind of idea on how to get us out of this mess."

"Or maybe Cain will."

Tuck winked at Trak, a not-so-subtle reminder to cut Cain some slack.

Trak smiled and nodded. "Reminder understood," he said as his longtime nemesis walked into the bar.

CHAPTER 10

Now that the guys were busy at their meeting, Dar took the lead. "First of all, whatever we discuss here does not go beyond the four of us. Okay?" Once everyone nodded in agreement, she said, "Anyone here not believe in werewolves?"

No one raised their hands, but Meg laughed. "That would explain so much. They're just too blasted perfect. I mean, Trak's just a friend, but if I didn't have Zach, it would be hard to pick which guy I wanted."

Jules merely shrugged. "Which is probably why I have two."

"Jules!" Elle had a huge grin on her face. "Okay. So maybe I'm just a bit jealous, though I wouldn't trade Tuck for anyone."

Dar nodded emphatically. "I called Lawz on the werewolf bit last night, and he didn't deny, but said he had to talk to the guys."

"Tuck said the same thing. When I asked if that meant he had to talk it over with Trak, he got flustered. He's so cute when he's flustered, big guy like that."

"'Cause Trak's their alpha, right?" Dar shot a glance at Meg. "Did you know?"

"Not entirely, though I've sensed all along that the wolf sleeping next to me reminded me of Trak. Not sure why. And I've always just assumed he was their boss. No reason. He's not bossy, but . . ." She grinned. "Guess he just walks the boss walk."

"They smell the same," Elle said. "Tuck and his wolf— they both have that fresh forest-cedar scent that I love, like fresh air and mountain breezes."

Meg turned to Jules. "Why so quiet, Jules?"

Laughing, Jules spread her hands. "Just paying attention. I've got two of them to deal with, remember?"

"Rough job, right?" Dar's dry comment had all of them laughing.

"Have any of you seen them shift?" Meg glanced at each of them.

"No, but I imagine we will." Dar planted her hands on the table. "Think about the position they're in—they've kept this secret for as long as their kind has existed, and that secret has kept them safe. They've got to be terrified we'll give them away. Can you imagine the nightmare that would cause? News crews and nuts, coming here to the preserve and creating trouble for everyone. Whether they come clean or not, none of us are ever to speak about this to anyone else."

"You can tell me."

Meg whipped around in her seat so fast she almost fell out of it. An attractive dark-haired woman in faded cargo pants and an old Stanford sweatshirt stood in the doorway to the dining hall.

"Hi." She gave them a little wave. "I'm Cherry Dubois. I live here. I just left the guys at Growl." She laughed. "They're all aflutter, discussing what you know. I told them I'd rather meet you than worry about you."

"Can you shift, too?" Dar focused on Cherry, and Meg held her breath, waiting to see if Cherry would lie to Dar or tell the truth.

"I can now. But I couldn't when I first got here. May I join you?"

"Please," Meg said. "We are dying to know what's going on, but we don't want the guys to be afraid we'll tell their secret, and they're not talkin'."

"Good." She walked to the bar, poured a cup of coffee, and took the empty chair next to Elle. "Because that would be bad. For all of us. First of all, I started here as a guest of Feral Passions, just the way you have. My sister and her friend and I came here together, and we all met guys. My sister and her girlfriend are bi, and I was just flat-out repressed." She laughed and took a swallow of her coffee. "By the end of the week, I'd figured out that the two guys I'd fallen for were the same wolves that were sleeping in my bed most nights."

"How'd you know?" Meg hadn't been all that sure about Trak, though she'd suspected, but she didn't know why.

"I'm a computer nerd. My life is all about algorithms and statistics, and statistically speaking, there were an equal number of green-eyed wolves to men with green eyes, same with brown, and with blue. And one guy has absolutely sparkling, almost turquoise eyes, and so does one of the wolves. But the wolves and guys with matching eyes were never together."

"That's part of what gave it away for me. I'm Jules, by the way, and I've got two guys sharing my bed, one with blue eyes and one with brown, but the weird part of it is that I knew the first time I saw the wolves that they were the guys, and I didn't even know one of them very well in his human form. Two wolves came to my cabin at bedtime, and I just automatically called them Manny and Drew. I knew they were men, but I don't know how I knew. It was just bizarre."

"That explains their behavior." Cherry laughed, but she shook her head when Jules questioned her. "Their tale to tell."

"I'm Elle, Cherry. How do you handle it? Your guy shifts and races off into the woods to do his wolf thing. How do you deal with waiting for him, knowing what an amazing experience he's having?"

"I go with them." At least she waited until the collective gasp died down. Smiling, she said, "Werewolves only have male offspring. They don't make their first shift until they're about thirty. They find their mates among the human population after they shift, but wolf law has forced them to keep their existence secret. It used to be until after they fell in love and mated. Then they'd bite their poor, unsuspecting wife and turn her into a wolf."

"I can only imagine the pillow talk after that little episode." Dar's comment even had Cherry cracking up.

But Meg stared at Cherry, this absolutely beautiful and obviously brilliant young woman who was saying she was a wolf as well. For whatever reason, shifting had absolutely no appeal at all to Meg. "I think I'd freak," she said.

But not Elle, Jules, or Dar. They were grinning at one another as if they'd just discovered all the packages under the Christmas tree were theirs.

"That's the only thing I worried about." Elle grabbed

Cherry's hands. "Girl, that is the best news in the world, because I have fallen hard and fast for that big, sexy veterinarian, but all I could think of was how jealous I'd be whenever he went furry and left me home."

"Won't happen if you and Tuck end up mates." She squeezed Elle's hands. "Look, the guys are a bit shaken up, to put it bluntly. They're so afraid of their story getting out. If you and Dar and Jules end up staying on as mates, that's not an issue, but I know they're worried about any of you who don't, which I would bet is going to be just you, Meg. Is this a secret you can keep? If word ever gets out, it would put all of us in danger."

Meg glanced at Dar, Elle, and Jules. "The four of us have been friends since we were five years old. We've held secrets for one another all our lives. There's no way we'd ever talk about something that could jeopardize any of us, much less the people we've met here who are so wonderful. I don't think that's an issue, but I do think we should let the guys lead the way on when they want to say anything. I hadn't really thought how frightening this must be for them."

"Thank you. Now I'm going to grab my men and my luggage, and we're going to go up to our apartment." She laughed as she stood. "I'm exhausted. We drove all night when the guys realized you'd figured them out. They sort of flipped a bit. Trak asked us to come home early."

She yawned and stretched, but Elle stopped her as she turned to leave.

"Cherry? Is it as cool as it sounds? Shifting and running like a wolf?"

"So much cooler than you can possibly imagine. The pine needles beneath your feet, flying down trails faster than you ever imagined moving under your own power. Standing on a mountain peak and howling at the moon? Ya know, it's something I will never grow tired of."

Smiling, she headed toward the door as two men—equally as good looking as all the others they'd met—walked in loaded down with luggage. Cherry paused and kissed both guys. "Ladies, this bad boy is Cain, and this fella is Brad, and they're mine. You may look but not touch. Boys, meet Meg, Elle, Jules, and Dar. Play nice. I'm going to get my bags."

She turned and left. Meg sighed when she realized both men had barely acknowledged any of them at the table. Instead, they stopped in their tracks to watch Cherry as she went out the door, and Meg was certain that was a communal sigh she heard from her buds.

Did Zach ever look at her like that? She wished she could be sure. She'd give anything to know he felt that way about her.

Once Cain and Brad had settled back into their apartment over the lodge with Cherry, Manny hunted them down.

"Cain, you got some free time this afternoon?"

Cain grinned at him, and Manny could see why he pissed Trak off so badly. Cain always looked like he was looking for trouble.

"Depends. I'm still on my honeymoon."

"Yeah, but you'll like this. Ya know the guys logging that piece just north of the property? They've brought in some new contract labor that's a bit questionable. Trak and I are convinced they're poaching. We've found sign on this side of the fence, blood spatters on leaves, what looks like some chunks out of bark that might be from high-powered rifle shots. None of the wolves are missing, but the deer herd is skittish. We're going to do a bit of reconnoitering this afternoon. Want to come?"

Cain's grin widened. "I'd love it." He caught Cherry for a kiss and planted one on Brad as well. "Back when the big guy turns me loose."

"Knew you'd do it. Figure you're probably looking for some ass to kick after two weeks without any trouble." Laughing, Manny led the way out of the lodge.

"Actually . . ." Cain actually sounded sort of wistful. "Two weeks without trouble worked really well for me. I think I'm getting used to waking up to a mate on either side."

Manny thought about that as they headed toward Growl, where they were meeting Trak. And he thought about Jules. And Drew.

By two or so, Elle and Tuck had made close to a dozen calls in and around the community of Weaverville. There'd been no talk of werewolves or shifting, but there were vaccinations to give and teeth to check and lots of people to stop and chat with.

He'd introduced Elle to everyone they met and said she was thinking of taking on the position as his assistant. She loved hearing that, and everyone had been so nice. Finally, they pulled into a quiet neighborhood, and Tuck parked under a big shady tree.

He didn't immediately get out this time. Instead, he turned to her and smiled, and she melted inside just a little bit more.

"This is the last stop, Elle. Mrs. Yates has a Labrador retriever that tends to have large litters. There were fourteen in this last one. I'm just checking to make sure everyone's getting enough to eat. The owner can't be here with them all the time. She's a nurse at the hospital in town, works some odd shifts."

They got out of the truck, walked around the house, and went through a gate to the yard in back. A dark brown Lab lay in the shade of a large tree. She raised her head and woofed, but it was obvious she recognized Tuck because she lay back down again and stretched out in the grass. Pups tumbled all around, climbing over their mother and chasing each other.

"They look like little chocolate kisses!" Elle got down on her knees. The pups spotted a target and attacked. She was cuddling four of them while two chewed one of her hiking boots.

"Hey, Tuck. I was hoping you'd stop by."

Elle glanced away from the puppies gnawing on her boots and curling in her lap. A tall, dignified-looking woman with her long white hair tied in a braid down her back stepped out of the house.

"Mrs. Yates, this is Elle, my assistant." She nodded hello. "You'll notice she's protecting me from all those sharp little teeth." They both chuckled when the pups suddenly took off and did a waddling run around the perimeter of the back fence. He reached down and pulled Elle to her feet. "These little guys are looking great. I don't think I'll need to make any more visits, at least until they're ready for their shots."

"That's good. Thank you. I've got buyers for all of them. Look, Tuck, I'm glad you stopped by. We have an injured driver who was brought in about an hour ago. His car went off the road north of town, and he was still unconscious last time I checked. Paramedics couldn't find a cell phone or ID, but clipped to a screen on the dashboard were directions to your place. The guy's tall, about your age, with salt-and-pepper hair, average build. Works out, has good muscle tone. Sound familiar?"

"He's not conscious?"

Mrs. Yates shook her head. "No. Might be by now. He was unconscious when he was brought in a little while ago. My shift ended shortly after he arrived, so I'm not sure of his condition, only that they hadn't ID'd him."

"Any idea where he's from?"

"Looks like Portland. The car's registered to SeaSun Integrations, but there's no name on—"

"Oh, shit!" Elle slapped her hand over her mouth. "I'm sorry, but did you say SeaSun?" When the woman nodded, Elle turned to Tuck. "That has to be Zach, Meg's fiancé. He owns SSI. We have to go see him. Find out for sure if it's Zach so we can let Meg know."

"Tuck? When you get to the hospital, tell Jennie at reception that you might know our John Doe." Mrs. Yates followed them to the gate. "Please let me know what you find out, and good luck. I know there must be people somewhere worried sick about him."

"Poor Zach." Elle stood beside his bed. Zach was still unconscious, though the nurse had told them scans hadn't shown any sign of trauma or injury to his brain, and he'd awakened briefly a while ago. "I wonder what happened."

The doctor who'd been in Zach's room when they arrived straightened after checking the monitors. "We think he swerved to miss a critter. Animals cross the road there all the time on the way to water. It looks like he braked and then skidded, overcorrected, and hit the berm beside the asphalt. The car did an end over and then rolled, so stuff got scattered. A couple of guys just went out to see if they can find his wallet and cell phone. We were hoping to ID him, so I'm glad you're here. Good thing he was belted in, because the BMW was trashed."

"I'm going to call Meg," Tuck said. "There should be someone in the office who can take the call and bring her out here."

Trak was out doing something with Manny, so Evan brought Meg into town. The others stayed at Feral Passions, since Elle was waiting with Zach.

Zack here? But why? Meg's head wouldn't quit spinning. When Evan got the call from Tuck and found her out by the pool with Cherry and the girls, she'd been laughing and having the time of her life.

While Zach lay in a hospital bed just a few miles away, unconscious. She felt horribly guilty even though she hadn't done anything, hadn't known he was within a hundred miles of this place, but he was hurting, and she'd not known a thing.

Evan held her left forearm with his left hand, had his right arm around her shoulders, walking her down the long corridor like she was a little old lady, but as fragile as she felt, that was probably a good thing.

What in the world was Zach doing there?

"Here's his room, Meg."

She glanced at Evan and slowly nodded—it didn't feel real, as if she walked through a waking nightmare—as he walked her into the room. Zach lay on the bed, both eyes bruised black and swollen shut. Elle'd been sitting next to the bed, but she leapt up and hugged Meg.

"He's gonna be okay, sweetie. The doctors are terrific. Dr. Mabry said his injuries aren't nearly as serious as they look."

Meg nodded. She didn't seem to have any words, but Elle took over Evan's job and led her across the floor to Zach. Tuck pushed a chair beneath her, and she sat, trusting him to have it there. Hell, trust had nothing to do with it. Her legs wouldn't hold her.

She wrapped her fingers around Zach's hand, careful of the needles and wires anchoring him to way too much equipment all beeping and gurgling and whooshing. "Zach. Sweetheart . . . what happened?"

She'd missed him so much, wished he were here with her, but not like this! This was awful. And scary. She heard a shuffling behind her, soft voices, someone coming into the room. She turned, saw an attractive young woman in a lab coat. A doctor?

"You're Megan Bonner?"

When Meg nodded, the woman held out her hand. "I'm so glad we've found Zachary's people. It's terrible to have someone here who's hurting and not know who they are. It's good to meet you. I'm Dr. Mabry. Angie Mabry. I'm not sure what Elle's told you, but we weren't certain how serious Zach's head injury was when he was first brought in. He was unconscious when paramedics got to him, but we're unsure how long after the accident that was. I doubt it was too long because that road is well traveled. A rancher spotted the wrecked car and said the engine was still steaming."

Meg covered her mouth. What if there'd been a fire? What if he'd been dying, what if . . .

"Stop." Dr. Mabry rubbed Meg's shoulder. "I can tell you're doing the what-ifs. And I know that because I do them, too, but remember this: whatever you're thinking, it didn't happen. He's going to be fine. He was awake a bit ago, confused and not sure what happened, but he'll come around. He's got a concussion, but scans are clear, and there's no bleeding. It still might take him a few days to get his bearings."

She felt sort of silly, sitting there with Zach's hand in hers, doing exactly what the doctor had accused her of. She wished he'd wake up. She really had to tell him how much she loved him, how much she'd missed him since Sunday, which was silly, considering it was only Tuesday.

Sighing, she thought about that. She'd wait and tell him after she found out what had brought him here in the first place. What if he'd come all this way merely to tell her it was over?

Tuck had gone outside about fifteen minutes earlier when Evan left to return to the resort. Meg hadn't let go of Zach's hand, though she'd asked Elle if her healing worked on people. No way was Elle going to experiment on Zach, and she said as much, though in a nicer way. Meg looked horribly sad, even though the doctor's last visit to the room had been really positive. Zach was coming around, he had sensation in his extremities, and other than a couple of broken fingers, he essentially appeared to be okay.

"Elle?"

She turned. Tuck was there, obviously concerned. "What happened?" Whispering. Meg didn't even notice them, she was so tuned in to Zach.

"Trak's been hurt. I need to go back to the resort, but I want you with me. Do you think Meg will be okay by herself?"

Elle nodded. "She's not alone. She's with Zach, and we can make sure someone's there to hear the phone if she calls. Let me tell her."

She did, and minutes later they were in Tuck's big truck, heading out to the resort as if the dogs of hell chased them. Elle waited until they'd hit the main road to ask.

"What happened?"

"I'm not sure. Manny, Cain, and Trak were checking the perimeter of the northern fence line. There's been sign of poaching up there near a logging operation. Manny said they came across a couple of guys gutting a doe who ran them off, but not before one of them fired at Trak. I'm not sure how badly he's hurt. Cain's with him. Manny's waiting at the lodge until we get there so he can lead us to them."

"Were they running as wolves or human? Because I don't think I like the idea of you facing guys with guns willing to shoot someone who gets in their way."

Tuck shook his head. "Me, either." He paused a moment, and she knew it had to hurt him to speak words he'd been forbidden to say to anyone not of their pack.

"It's okay," she said. "I know. Look, you need to go to him

as soon as we reach the resort, because you can get there a lot faster as a wolf. Is there someone who knows where you'll be? I'm fast, but not that fast."

"You sure?"

"I'm sure. Trak needs a doctor now. You can get to him faster on four legs. Can you carry your medical bag?"

He smiled, and she knew he'd finally given in. "I've got a harness just for things like this. I rarely have to use it." Quietly, he added, "Trak was a wolf when they shot him."

She reached across the center console and squeezed his thigh. He covered her hand with his, only for a moment, but she had a feeling she'd just passed some sort of test.

They went through the gate to the preserve, and he punched it. The road that had taken the women at least fifteen minutes to cover on their first trip in to Feral Passions was a quick five-minute, white-knuckle ride. Tuck skidded to a stop in front of the lodge. Manny ran out to meet them with Evan on his heels, holding an odd-looking harness in his hands. Tuck explained their plan. Elle grabbed his medical bag out of the truck, and when she turned around, Tuck was ripping off his clothes and going to his hands and knees with the pickup as a shield.

She had no idea where the other women were, but Elle knew she witnessed magic. This wasn't at all like the movies. No cracking of joints or snapping bones, merely a smooth, almost poetic process of sleek skin rippling in shimmering waves as fur appeared and his body changed. It happened quickly, magically, and where a large man had knelt, a dark gray wolf now stood in his place. Manny had shifted as well, so Evan clamped the medical bag into the harness and fastened it quickly to Tuck.

"Go," he said. "Manny told me exactly where they are. Elle and I are right behind you. We'll bring the stretcher, clothes, and shoes."

The wolf nodded and took off.

Elle glanced at Evan. "We good to go?"

"Yep," he said. She reached for one of the tote bags loaded with clothes for Tuck, Cain, and Manny and hoisted it over her shoulder.

Evan slipped a folded stretcher over one shoulder and grabbed the other bag. "You ready?"

When Elle nodded, Evan took off at a slow jog along a narrow trail. They headed due north to the place where Trak lay wounded.

Cain had shifted to his human form to do what he could to stop the bleeding. The bullet was somewhere inside Trak's chest, most likely one of his lungs. There was bloody froth at his nostrils, his breathing was labored, and he'd started shivering. Cain knew Tuck had gone into town, but he didn't know how much longer Trak could hang on without medical care.

Bastards. He'd spotted the hunters gutting a doe they'd shot, and he and Trak had tried to get closer for a better look. They'd gone in as wolves, but they hadn't counted on a lookout who was quite willing to shoot wolves on a preserve. The guy got off one shot, but it was enough. At least he was far enough away that Cain had been able to hide Trak in heavy undergrowth.

Manny had stayed hidden until the men gave up searching for the wolf and went back to their deer carcass, but then he'd found Cain and Trak and stayed long enough to assess Trak's condition.

It wasn't good. They'd been out here in the brush with Trak bleeding for at least a couple of hours. He'd been conscious at first, but obviously in considerable pain. Now his breathing was shallow, his eyes closed, and Cain was terrified.

He knew he wasn't alone. There were at least a couple of wild wolves nearby, keeping watch. It helped, knowing they worried about Trak as much as he did. It was a strange sort of relationship between the werewolf pack and their wild brothers. They didn't compete, didn't really interact, but there was definitely a sense of community among them.

When he'd left Trak in search of something for a compress to put pressure on the wound, the wolves had stood watch. He'd found as much damp moss as he could scavenge off nearby rocks and trees and used that to keep pressure on the wound. Once he had things under control, the wild wolves faded into the forest, but he sensed they were still close.

Holding the compress in place, he sat beside Trak and stroked his thick coat. The man had hated him since the very beginning. Cain was never quite sure why—he'd tried to be a good pack member, but no matter what he did, Trak found fault. He'd often wondered if it had anything to do with his basic nature. He'd been born an alpha, a very strong alpha in a pack ruled by one even stronger than Cain.

He'd learned that the hard way, challenging the man when he was still too young and too stupid to know how to run a pack if he'd actually won the fight. Instead, he'd had his ass handed to him on a platter, and then he'd been exiled. That was actually a good thing—most alphas would have killed the usurper. Trak was still trying to build his pack and had been the only one willing to take him in. Cain would always owe him a debt of gratitude for that, though there were times he resented his own strong sense of obligation.

That was another part of his nature he couldn't control.

He really didn't want Trak to die, though he'd sensed Manny's misgivings at leaving him here to guard their alpha. Everyone knew that Cain and Trak had issues, but Cain was the better fighter, Manny the faster runner. It was the logical choice that Cain be the one to stay.

But the truth was, Cain admired Trak. Wished he could be more like him.

Maybe he needed to tell him that sometime. Before it was too late. He studied the wounded wolf, knew he was slipping away even as Cain sat there with Trak's lifeblood seeping around his fingers, feeling so damned useless. He wanted to make that poacher pay. Even more, he needed Trak to know how he felt.

Sighing, Cain buried his fingers in his alpha's thick fur, but he spoke from his heart—the one Trak didn't think he had. "You're a strong bastard, Traker. Don't give up. You've got to come through this. The pack needs you. Whether you know it or not, I need you. You're the alpha I will never be, a man I've always admired. You're not a hothead like I am. You don't get pissy." He smiled at that, because . . . "Well, not too much, but damn it, you're important to this pack, so you've got to keep fighting. If you're not here, who's going to ride my ass over every little thing?"

The wolf whined and shivered. He was going into shock,

and the ground was cold beneath the trees. "Well, fuck." Cain shifted. His wolf was warmer than his human, and once the shift was complete, he wrapped himself around Trak with his chin holding the compress against the wound. He would do whatever it took to keep his alpha warm—and alive.

Elle was glad she'd dressed comfortably to go into town with Tuck today, wearing a short-sleeved top, jeans, and her hiking boots, because she and Evan covered the two miles of rough trail to a thick copse of trees at the edge of the property in less than twenty minutes. Tuck was human again, naked as he worked over the injured wolf. He looked up with relief when Elle and Evan arrived.

"Elle? Have you ever worked with bullet wounds? Removed a bullet from a patient?"

"No, but I can try. Let me take a look." She nodded, acknowledging the big silver wolf with forest-green eyes—Cain—guarding his alpha, and then knelt beside Trak's wolf. There was a bloody pad of gauze pressed against the entrance wound, more blood-soaked moss on the ground beside Trak. She moved the pad aside and held her hands to the injury until she sensed the bullet in Trak's lung. Tracing the trajectory of the bullet meant following a trail that felt wrong. The trick would be pulling it out without causing more damage while keeping his lungs working. Her gift snapped fully into place as she slipped into the strange fugue state that allowed her to heal. The soft whispers of Trak's worried pack faded into the background.

"What's she doing?" Manny's question probably echoed all their thoughts. Cain knew he was damned curious, but Tuck seemed to trust her.

"I wish I knew," Tuck said, "but I saw her heal a fawn's cracked leg with the touch of her hands. She said it's a gift, that her grandmother could do it, too. Quiet, now. We don't want to pull her out of whatever she's doing."

About twenty minutes after Elle began her healing, Tuck remembered food. "She's going to need to eat when she finishes. She's burning a lot of energy, and she'll come out of this totally depleted. Can one of you guys get a sandwich or something and bring it out here?"

Cain stood, raised a paw, and scraped Tuck's knee. "Good. Go, Cain. Whatever you can find for her."

The wolf spun away from the group and was gone.

"When Trak is all healed up," Manny said, smiling for the first time in hours, "someone had better tell him how hard that man's worked to keep him alive."

Dar, Jules, and Cherry hung out by the pool. The place had been unusually quiet today. Drew was bartending at Growl, and Cherry's mate Brad was in the kitchen working on dinner. Lawz had driven over to Eureka on business. Dar didn't expect him back until tonight. As far as she knew, Elle was still in town with Tuck, and Meg was with Zach, though she'd expected to have heard something by now.

She said as much, but Cherry suddenly raised her head. "What's going on?"

They all turned just as a huge silver-and-gray wolf raced

up the front steps to the lodge and shoved the door open with his shoulder.

"Something's wrong." Cherry was up in a flash and running across the grass to the lodge. The others followed. They raced into the lodge just as the wolf rippled and shimmered and Cain quickly rose to his feet, naked and obviously distraught.

He glanced over his shoulder, said, "Sorry, ladies," and turned to Brad. "I need food now. A sandwich, something with protein to take back for Elle. Trak's been shot. Tuck was working on him, but Elle's there now doing some kind of mojo to heal him. She needs to eat as soon as she's done. She's burning a lot of energy."

"Gotcha." Brad reached into the refrigerator and grabbed a couple of big sandwiches left over from lunch. Cherry went to the pantry for a bag of cookies and a couple of sports drinks. Between the two of them, they had a meal ready to go in about a minute. Brad stuck everything in a bag with a harness while Cain shifted. Cherry strapped it on him.

Brad touched his shoulder. "Be careful, Cain. You know we love you."

The wolf nodded, a very human response.

Jules walked across the room and held the door open. Cain turned away from Brad and Cherry, raced past Jules, and disappeared into the forest.

CHAPTER 11

Dar shoved her fingers through her hair. "Crap. I have no idea what's going on, though it must be serious because they're not even trying to hide what they are. I just realized that if Elle's healing Trak, Meg's alone at the hospital with Zach."

"I would go, but I don't want to be gone that long," Cherry said. "Cain will need me when this is over. He looked really upset."

"I'll go. Is there a vehicle I can borrow?" Dar said. "Meg shouldn't be alone."

"I can take you in, but I'll need to come back," Cherry said. "Call when you want someone to pick you up. Meg might be ready to return and get some rest at some point."

"Give me ten minutes." Dar took off to change clothes. She was back in five, and Cherry was standing on the deck at the lodge waiting. Brad walked out with a covered basket and handed it to Dar. "Brownies. I made a batch to restock the freezer. Take these for the staff." He winked. "They're terrific people. They deserve every cookie we can send."

Dar took the basket and glanced at Cherry. "He's good," she said, teasing.

"The very best." Cherry grabbed Brad's arm and hugged him close.

Obviously, she was dead serious. He kissed her, and she turned him loose. "C'mon. It'll take us at least twenty minutes to get there."

Meg lost track of time. She'd been with Zach for hours, but wasn't certain what time it was. She didn't wear a watch and hadn't brought her cell phone, but there'd been a shift change and a new nurse was on duty. Zach was restless; he'd awakened briefly a couple of times, though he hadn't said anything she could understand. Dr. Mabry continued telling her not to worry, that concussions were weird and they were monitoring him carefully.

She wished she knew why Zach was here in Weaverville at all, even though she'd missed him horribly and had wanted to invite him. He'd come on his own. But why? She ran her fingers through his hair, touched the sharp jut of his collarbone, rested her palm against his heart. It beat steadily, so strong and warm, and it was killing her to sit beside him when she wanted to crawl into bed next to him and hug him so hard. Hug him until he couldn't ever get free, even if he wanted to.

His eyelids fluttered, but he didn't awaken. She thought about kissing him, but she was afraid. If he didn't love her anymore, that wouldn't be right, kissing him when he couldn't tell her to leave him alone. She took hold of his hand, the one that had been resting on his chest. Two of his fingers were taped together. The doctor said those were the only broken bones he had. Probably from the air bag, she'd said. His car was trashed.

He could so easily have died. Meg blinked back tears. She'd been doing that a lot today. "Oh, Zach." She sniffed. "Please wake up. I love you so much, and I hate to see you hurting."

"Meggie?"

"Zach!" She leaned close, still carefully holding his broken hand. His eyes were closed, but they were so bruised and swollen and . . . "Are you okay? You've been out for so long."

"Where? Thirsty."

"Let me call the doctor. I don't know if I can give you anything."

But someone must have been watching the monitor, because two new nurses and Dr. Mabry were coming into the room, and she had to let go of his hand and move out of their way.

"Meg?"

She turned, and Dar stood in the doorway, and that was all it took. Sobbing, she fell into Dar's arms while the doctor and nurses checked on Zach.

Racing through the woods toward Tuck and Elle, Cain was relieved to see Manny and Evan carrying the stretcher with Trak in his human form carefully strapped in. He didn't stop to see if his alpha was conscious or not—the fact he'd been able to shift and the smiles on the guys' faces told him all he needed to know.

They waved him on, and he reached Elle and Tuck a couple of minutes later. Tuck unfastened the harness and grabbed a sandwich and a sports drink for Elle. She looked totally wasted, her normally sleek, dark skin a sickly gray. Since she obviously knew they were werewolves, he went ahead and shifted. Tuck tossed him a pair of sweatpants.

"Hide the jewels, big guy. Evan threw in an extra pair of pants for you."

"Thanks." He pulled the sweats on and slipped his feet into the moccasins Tuck handed him. "You okay, Elle?"

She nodded and kept chewing, but she gestured toward Tuck. "Yes, dear." He patted her leg and glanced at Cain. "And if I sound a bit pussy whipped, guilty as charged. But what an amazing pu—"

"Kentucky Jones!" Slapping her hand over his mouth, she swallowed and then laughed. "I just wanted you to tell the man how Trak's doing so I can recharge the machine. No reviews and no editorializing." She took another bite.

Grinning like a fool, Tuck sat back with an arm around her waist. "You're no fun, Elle. Cain, Trak's doing great. You keeping pressure on the wound probably saved him. Using moss was an excellent idea—sphagnum moss, the stuff you grabbed—has been used as a surgical dressing for eons, so it was a good call. Elle got the bullet out without further damage, as far as we can tell, and she stopped the bleeding, but he's lost a lot of blood, and he'll be weaker for a few days while he rebuilds the supply."

"Good." He sighed. "I'm glad to hear that. I was so damned scared out here, and I wasn't sure if the moss was a good thing, but it was all I could think of. I'm glad I didn't kill the bastard."

Tuck laughed. "How do you think Trak's going to take it when he finds out you're the one who saved his life?"

Cain just shook his head. "I think he'll be pissed and in no position to show it. I figure I might as well enjoy his discomfort while I can." He reached in the bag and handed Elle a sports drink. "Here. Have another one. It'll help."

"Thanks. Change of topic, but I'm curious. Cherry said she was a guest here. Now she's with you and Brad?"

"That she is. Brad and I have been together for a long time, but we always felt like something was missing. Turns out Cherry was the something. Her sister and her sister's girlfriend are residents now as well. Christa and Steph were a couple, though they didn't figure it out until they stayed here, and they happened to meet up with a couple of guys who were a pair as well. I think a lot of us who are shifters are bisexual, so it's nice when we can find a match. Cherry just likes men. Brad and I already loved each other, but we both love Cherry. It works."

Elle turned her gaze on Tuck. "What about you, Tuck? Is there a man in your life?"

He grinned and didn't hesitate. "I've always preferred women, but it gets lonely out here. On occasion I've found comfort in the arms of another guy. Doubt that will be happening anymore, now that I've found you."

She rolled her eyes. "I've known you for three days. Don't I have until Saturday to figure this out?"

Tuck grabbed her hand, and at that moment, Cain knew that, as far as the good doctor was concerned, he and Elle were the only two in the forest.

"Elle, I hope to give you a lifetime to figure it out. Okay by you?"

She leaned close and kissed him. "I think so. That works for me."

Tuck broke the kiss, jerked his entire body to his left, and held up a hand for silence. Elle didn't move. Cain quietly slipped out of his clothes and shifted. Tuck tapped Cain's shoulder when the shift was complete and pointed toward the fence. Soundlessly, Cain glided into the thick undergrowth.

Elle was afraid to move. She heard men's voices, but couldn't tell where they were. Tuck leaned close to her, whispering. "I'm not sure if it's the same guys, but I think our poachers are back. I'm going to let them know I'm here and step out so I'm visible. I want you behind a tree, where you're safe. Yell at me. Tell me the sheriff's deputies are almost here. With luck, they'll get the hell out of here without shooting any of us."

Elle hugged herself. "That would be a very good thing."

"Be careful," he said. Then he kissed her and stepped out onto a trail that led in the general direction of the fence line. Elle quietly took her place behind a huge pine tree and waited where she felt safe and yet still had a good view of Tuck's back.

"Hey!"

Her guy stepped out into an open area. She couldn't see anyone but Tuck. The voices were closer.

"Who the hell are you?"

"Dr. Kentucky Jones. I'm the vet for this wolf preserve, and you're trespassing. This is private property. No hunting allowed."

"Think you can stop us, big guy?"

Elle cupped her hands around her mouth and called out.

"Hey, Tuck. Sheriff's office just called, said deputies should be here in a couple of minutes." She heard some mumbling among the ones she couldn't see.

"I agree," Tuck said, obviously responding to something one of them had said. "You gentlemen need to leave."

Elle moved quietly along the trail, glad her clothes were all shades of green and brown. Should make it harder for anyone to see her. She didn't have to go far to get a good view of Tuck. Three rough-looking men, all armed, stood in a semicircle in front of him. Two had rifles slung over their shoulders, the one in the middle had a large revolver in a western-style holster carried low on his hip.

"I don't think so." The middle guy, almost as large as Tuck, crossed his arms over his broad chest. "Looks like there's only one of you and a bitch afraid to show herself."

Elle pulled her cell phone out of her pocket. This bitch was smarter than that. She'd kept her cell phone on her in spite of the lack of signal. Didn't matter, when all she needed was the camera. Muting the sound, she first took a couple of photos of the men. Then she turned on the video.

"Not necessarily. You're on a wolf preserve. The animals here trust us to protect them. Now that they know you're a threat, they won't stay hidden when you come on the property."

A low growl rumbled out of the brush. Had to be Cain. But then she heard another growl on the opposite side of the clearing. And another behind the men. Two of them were looking in all directions when the one in the middle threw a punch, going straight for Tuck's face. Tuck spun to one side, grabbed the idiot's arm, and threw him. There was an audible snap before Tuck turned him loose.

The man screamed. His partners turned and ran, but Elle managed to get film of everything. The guy rolling on the ground, hugging his broken arm, was easy to film, especially when she walked closer and got him full frame.

"Good, Elle." Tuck wrapped his arm around her. "I was wishing we had a way to get these bastards on film."

"Where are all the wolves? I heard at least three."

Cain walked out of the woods, in his human form again, wearing the sweats and moccasins. "Our wild brothers stepped up to help. They've stayed close, worried about Trak and these jerks and their guns."

He slung an arm around Elle and planted a big kiss on her cheek. "You, my dear, are a keeper. Tuck? Don't blow it."

"Gotcha. Don't plan to." Tuck glanced at the man lying on the ground, still clutching his arm and moaning. Blood seeped through the upper sleeve of his shirt. "Looks like we're going to have to get someone in here to take him to the hospital." He hunkered down next to the man and slipped the revolver out of the guy's holster. "Compound fracture. That's gotta hurt. Don't you know you never swing at a guy bigger than you with your feet planted like that? Gave me the right leverage to break that sucker."

The man was obviously in too much agony to say much, but Elle figured he deserved it. Healing Trak had been an exhausting, emotional experience. She'd known he was in horrible pain, possibly caused by this man. She had no sympathy. None.

"So." Elle glanced at Cain, then turned her focus on Tuck. "What now?"

Cain answered. "We wait for the sheriff. Manny planned to call as soon as they got Trak back to the lodge, said he'd send them out here, just in case. We need to report the poached deer. I found a couple of other stripped carcasses not far from the first one."

"Will Trak go to the hospital?"

Tuck shook his head. "I doubt it. The bullet's out, and he'll turn it over to the sheriff. I imagine it will match one of the guns these idiots were carrying."

"What are you talking about?"

It appeared their poacher could talk after all.

Tuck's hands curled into fists. "The man you shot, you jerk. It's one thing to poach wildlife. Shooting at a man trying to protect his property is something else altogether."

"No one shot anyone. Ralph fired at a fucking wolf that was after the kill."

"Doesn't matter who Ralph says he fired at." Tuck glared at him. "The one with the bullet in his lung is a hundred percent human. I think that's attempted murder."

It was almost dark by the time the deputies showed up, collected their guy, and took statements from Tuck, Cain, and Elle, before they were finally free to go back to the lodge. Elle was ready to drop, but she wanted to check on Trak first.

"No." Tuck planted his big hands on her shoulders. "You get a shower, have a glass of wine, relax, and come back here so I can feed you. I'll meet you in the dining room. Then we will go check on Trak. He's not going anywhere."

Tuesday night
Tuck had leftovers all warmed up for her, and he and Elle ate together. "Where is everyone?"

He grinned at her. "I'm here. Does anyone else really matter?"

"Of course they do. But you're the most important," she added, soothing the male ego.

Tuck just laughed. "Dar and Meg are still in town, but they're due back in about an hour. Evan's driving in to pick them up. The fiancé is doing better, though he's got a concussion and might have to stay in the hospital for a few more days. Jules is down at Growl, hanging out with Manny and Drew. Lawz isn't back yet from Eureka, though I expect him any minute. I finally got hold of him and let him know about Trak. They're brothers."

"You're good." She laughed at his flawless accounting of all the pertinent names. "I've never been to the bar. Is it all that busy? I mean, this is a gated preserve. Who are the customers?"

"There are a lot of folks who live back in the woods, and we cater to that crowd. The ones who don't really want any part of society but occasionally want a drink or a sandwich, a chance to catch up on stuff. Not everyone lives in a city or even a community. A lot of guys are veterans, a few going back to the Korean War and Vietnam. Guys who came back from the Middle East totally fed up with man's inhumanity to man. They've got their own society in a way, and Growl has become a meeting point for them. No guns are allowed, and if they get rowdy, they know they'll get tossed and not be allowed back. Keeps them in line."

"Guess you have to do that if you've got guests from the resort visiting the place."

He laughed. "That's when the rules changed. Acting rowdy didn't used to be an issue."

Elle set her fork down and wiped her lips with her napkin. "Okay. I've eaten. Let's go check on Trak. Where's he staying?"

"He's in the apartment upstairs. We put him in Cherry, Cain, and Brad's spare room. We didn't want to leave him alone until the wound had completely closed and he was feeling better. He's still really wiped out, but I know he wants to see you." Tuck gave her an assessing glance and then looked away. "He said it was a very intimate experience, your healing."

She'd wondered about that. "I only know what I experience from my point of view. When I touch an animal, I feel its fear, know where it's hurt because in some ways I feel its pain, though it's not truly painful for me. More a sensation that I recognize as pain without actually hurting, if that makes sense."

"It does, actually. I'm curious to see what Trak felt. I wondered at the time if he felt pain when you pulled the bullet out."

"I was afraid of that, too. I'll ask him. I tried to be careful." Elle turned toward the big window in front. "Someone's pulling up outside."

"That's Evan's truck. He's supposed to have Dar and Meg with him."

They reached the front deck just as Evan and the women got out of the truck. Brad had been in the kitchen, but he was right behind them. Meg looked exhausted. Dar wasn't much better.

Elle leaned over the railing. "Meg? Hon, how's he doing?"

She nodded. "Okay, I guess. Still out of it, but it was a serious concussion. He woke up a couple of times, finally recognized me, remembers a bear running in front of his car, but he doesn't remember the wreck. They're going to keep him at least through tomorrow."

"You know you're welcome to bring him back here as soon as he's able." Tuck glanced at Elle. "Do you do brain injuries?"

She shook her head. "I don't know. I told Meg I'm afraid to experiment on her fiancé. Trak's the closest I've come to working on a human, and he was a wolf when I did it."

Frowning, Meg asked, "What happened to Trak?"

"Brad?" Elle had liked Cherry's guy the first moment she met him. "Will you fill them in? Tuck and I were just going to check on him. Meg? I'll give you the rest of the info later, okay? I'm really glad Zach's doing okay. It's been a crazy day."

"That's an understatement." With his hand lightly grasping her shoulder, Tuck guided Elle back inside the lodge and up the stairs to the apartment. He knocked quietly on the door.

Cain opened it. "Hi, Elle. I'm glad you're here. Trak was just asking if you were going to make it up to see him."

"Tuck made me eat dinner first. Good thing. I was starving. Where's Trak?"

He was sitting up in a big bed in the spare room, supported by mounds of pillows. There was a fresh bandage around his rib cage, and his face looked drawn, but he was in a lot better shape than when they'd placed him on the stretcher. He'd shifted while still lying on the ground because the shift helped the healing process, but it had been painful and obviously not easy, as badly as he'd been hurt.

"Elle." He held his hand out and took hers. "Thank you. Cain told me what you did. I remember it like a dream. Wasn't sure you'd really been there helping me."

"That was me." She sat on the edge of the bed. "You're the first patient I've ever had who can tell me what I did." She held up her hands. "I can feel heat, and I know what I need to do, but I have no idea how I do it or how my patient perceives it."

"As warmth. A very comforting warmth that takes away the fear. When you're hurting and, in my case, having trouble breathing, you're terrified. Heart pounding, adrenaline rushing through your system, and that fight-or-flight instinct in full 'get it done' mode, but you can't do a damned thing because you're dying. The body wants to shut down, and the fear keeps it revved up, and then you touched me, and everything went still. I could breathe easier, could think past the fear."

She nodded, remembering. "That explains so much. Animals that are afraid and struggling go still when I touch them. I never knew why. That's good. That's a good thing. When I moved the bullet out, did I hurt you?"

"No. I could feel it moving, which was weird, but there was no pain. Nothing you did hurt me at all. It all made the pain go away. But what did you do?"

"I have no idea." She felt so stupid admitting that, but it was the truth. "My grandma Memaw said it was a gift. I've accepted it as that. No questions."

"Probably a very smart decision. Thank you. Cain said you were wasted when you were done. I hope you're better now."

She laughed. "'Wasted' is a good way to describe it. I think healing sucks every bit of energy I've got, but a little bit to eat and I'm good to go. I'm really glad I could help you, Trak. I hope those bastards go to jail."

He nodded. "So do I, Elle. We're telling the authorities

that the guy shot me, not a wolf, and Tuck removed the bullet. He's not supposed to operate on humans, but it was an emergency situation done as a field surgery. I hope you're okay with that. We really didn't want to involve you in what's essentially a pack problem."

"I'm fine with that. Thank you. And Cain? Thank you for bringing me the sandwiches and sports drink. I might have saved Trak, but you saved me, and Tuck, too." She leaned into his embrace. "I not only feel really weak after healing, I'm super grumpy. You don't want me grumpy."

Trak turned and focused on Cain. "I understand you weren't the only one who saved my life today, Elle. Thank you, Cain. You were there for me like I've never been there for you. I'm having to rethink a hell of a lot about the way I've treated you for all these years."

Cain's lips quirked up on one side. "Well, I imagine I deserved most of it. Not all, mind you, but enough."

"You notice I'm not arguing that point?"

Cain's laughter burst out of him, and then he held his side and groaned. "Well, a little arguing might have been appropriate."

Tuck reached over and grabbed Trak's hand. Squeezed his fingers. "On that note, Elle and I are going to bail for now. It's been a long day."

"You're not kidding." She wrapped her arm around his waist and hugged him close. "It's only Tuesday. Trak? Are your vacation packages always this full of excitement? Because if they are, I don't know if I'll survive the entire week!"

———

Trak watched as Elle and Tuck left. Cain was still with him, but as he turned to go, Trak grabbed his hand. "Cain." He looked at their clasped fingers, tried to make his voice sound like he wasn't talking around that huge lump in his throat. "I was aware that whole time, when you sat beside me and kept me alive. When you found the moss and packed the wound. Hurt like hell, but I knew it needed to be done. I heard what you said, how you didn't understand why I'm always ridin' your ass. I've been wrong, but I've been too big a coward to admit it."

"The fact I'm an alpha?" Cain focused on their clasped hands for a moment and then raised his head and looked Trak in the eye. No hesitation, no subservience, either. "Trak, that's foolish. I don't want your pack. I never have. You have my word. I will never challenge you. All I've ever wanted is a place to call home. I challenged my first alpha because I was a dumb shit with more balls than brains. I lost. Badly. I'm lucky to be alive.

"He taught me a couple of good lessons, though. One, that I wasn't nearly as strong as I thought I was, and two, that if I'd beaten him, the pack would have fallen apart because I'm not a leader. By allowing me to live but publicly exiling me, he set an example that will keep him in charge until he voluntarily gives it up. I'm strong enough and smart enough to be a good enforcer, which is the job you gave me, but not to lead this or any other pack. You're a good leader, Trak. A strong leader. Please don't ever see me as a threat."

Trak nodded. Damn, he was so tired, and not feeling at all like a leader.

"Look, man, you're toast. Do you need help getting to the bathroom? Anything to eat or drink?"

"No. I'm fine. Go hang out with your mates. I'm sure they're curious, probably want to know how we can be in the same room and not be trying to kill each other."

Cain snorted. "Shit, Trak. I hadn't thought of that. If you want to keep bitching at me for everything, it's okay. Otherwise we might really mess with their heads."

He didn't even try to hide his smile. "Get outta here. I need my rest."

"That's better. You sound a lot more like the bastard we all know and love."

Trak flipped him off, middle finger high.

Cain flipped him back. Still, when he left the room, he left the door partly open in case his alpha needed help during the night.

CHAPTER 12

Wednesday morning

Elle rolled over and came nose to nose with Tuck—Tuck the man, not the wolf. "Good morning. Are you serious?"

"'Bout what?" He nuzzled her throat.

"Oh, about waking up like this for many years to come?" He'd said it again last night, that she was his and he wasn't letting her go. She had news for him—she wasn't letting him go, either.

"Hell, yes." He gave her that sexy grin she loved. "Good assistants are hard to find."

"And that's all I am to you?" She tried sending a look that should have told him how mortally offended she was, but she couldn't pull it off. She loved him way too much.

"You are so much more, Elle Marcel of the burgundy hair. You have become the air I breathe and the sustenance I need. I love you. I don't need you to leave me for a week to prove that. I don't want to spend another night without you for as long as we both shall live."

"Works for me, Tuck. You're the one I've been hoping for all my life. I'm not going anywhere."

Thursday morning

Meg was so nervous Thursday morning she could barely button her blouse. She was bringing Zach home today. Well, not *home* home, but home to Feral Passions. His mind had begun to clear up yesterday, and he'd been mostly back to normal by last night. He wasn't hurting too badly, and he was anxious to get out of the hospital.

Trak had teased her, said he was putting a couple of chairs on the deck at the lodge so he and Zach could oversee the activities. For whatever reason, she was nervous about Zachary and Traker Jakes getting to know each other. In the back of her mind was the memory of that kiss.

The one that hadn't done a thing for her. But she was bringing Zach to her little cabin, and he hadn't kissed her since he'd awakened. Not once. Which meant she'd probably been right and the reason he'd driven all that way was to tell her it was over.

She needed to hear him say it before she'd really believe it, but she figured she wouldn't be at all surprised when he did. She'd play it cool, and she'd survive. Of course, that meant she'd have to find a new job, and she loved that office.

She loved her boss a whole lot more. She looked at the sparkling diamond on her left hand and wondered if she should just take it off now, except she couldn't. She really, really wanted to be wrong.

She heard a light tap on her door. "Come in. I'm decent."

Brad opened the door. "Well, damn. You're no fun." He gave her a quick appraisal. "You look really nice. Do you mind going a little early so I can pick up some groceries? I'm out of a couple of things, and with an extra mouth to feed, I need to make sure I impress your guy with the amazing food here."

"The food is amazing. It's been the best part of our visit. Well, for me, at least. This has been a really odd week." She grabbed her handbag and a light sweater. "Are we taking the truck?"

"No, the van's a lot more comfortable. And Cherry's going with us."

"Good. I'm glad." Actually, she was relieved. Cherry already felt like a good friend. She might be able to figure out what was going on with Zach.

It felt weird to have regular clothes on, after three days in a hospital gown, but Zach was more than ready to get out of this place. One of the paramedics had gone over to the wrecking yard and recovered his backpack from his trashed car, so at least he had his own clothes, though not many extras.

He really hadn't thought this trip out very well, and he still felt out of sync, as if he couldn't connect with Meggie at all. She seemed so sad when she was here with him, and he wasn't sure why. She hadn't kissed him, or hugged him, or acted like she was glad he was here, but the hospital wasn't a good place to figure that out. He wanted to be sure he was thinking clearly if they had stuff to work through.

"Zach! You're dressed!"

"Hey, Meggie." Damn but he loved her. She was incredible, an island of calm in the storm that was his life. He took a deep breath, forced himself to settle down. "Yeah, they found my backpack with a change of clothes. I was worried

I might have to run around town in a hospital gown." She stood there, looking so awkward, his Meggie who was always so self-assured. What the fuck was wrong? He held his arms out. "I'm not broken. Don't I get a kiss?"

She wrapped her arms around him and held on as if she wasn't ever going to let go. "Meggie? You're trembling. What's wrong?" He kissed her and then leaned back and looked into her expressive gray eyes. Right now, he saw more confusion than anything.

"I've been so worried, Zach. Look, let's get out of here. Brad and Cherry, a couple from the lodge, are waiting out in the parking lot for us. Is there anything you need to do or sign or anything like that?"

"All taken care of. I'll just let them know you're here." He turned carefully and grabbed his beat-up old backpack, one he'd had since college. "I feel kind of silly now, but I packed at three in the morning and left before four. Didn't even throw in a razor." He rubbed his jaw. "The nurse shaved my face yesterday." He raised an eyebrow. "It was actually kind of nice. Think that's something you'd be interested in doing once we're married?"

She laughed and gave him a flirty, dirty look. "Depends. What do I get in return?"

"I'm sure you'll think of something appropriate." He was afraid if he got started with suggestions, he'd scare her off. She'd been way too careful around him since his wreck.

They stopped by the reception desk, and he made sure they had all his contact info, and then he met Brad and Cherry in the parking lot. Good-looking guy, a really awesome woman, both of them friendly and outgoing.

They were on the road and headed out within a couple of minutes.

"Zach?" Brad glanced over his shoulder. "Anything we can do about your car? Can it be fixed?"

He laughed at that one. "God, I hope not. It's trashed. One of the paramedics stopped by this morning with pictures that he transferred to my phone. Said he was impressed I'm still alive, but the airbags and seat belt did their jobs."

Meggie grabbed his hand. She held on to it all the way out to the resort.

Manny hunted Jules down right after breakfast. He'd told her to wear her hiking clothes, and she looked great in olive-green rip-stop cargo pants and a black fitted tank top. She'd stuck a safari hat on her head, had a lightweight jacket tied around her waist, and wore sturdy hiking boots.

She looked stunning, and he told her so.

"So. What's your nefarious plan, Mr. Vicario? Why am I dressed like someone out of an REI catalogue?"

She gave him a slant-eyed look, and he laughed. In less than five days, he'd learned her moods, her looks, her wicked sense of humor. The places she liked for him to touch. The places she wanted to touch, and thinking of her touch on those places had him uncomfortably straining the faded jeans he'd decided to wear. "Today, my dear, Drew and I are taking you on a hike. We're showing you some of our favorite places, ones not on the guest map. More private."

He waggled his eyebrows and leered. She punched his shoulder. "Where's Drew? I'm not going anywhere private unless he's along, too."

"I'm right here. Sorry." Drew leaned close and kissed Jules. "Thanks for standing up for me. Trak asked me to move a couple of chairs for him."

Manny cocked an eyebrow. "What's going on? Trak's supposed to be recuperating."

"He is. He's doing great, but Meg's on her way back from the hospital with her guy, and Trak's now got a couple of Adirondack chairs positioned on the deck so he and Zach can oversee the guests while the two of them recuperate in comfort close to the bar. His words, not mine."

Jules laughed at that. "I'm almost sorry to miss that, but I'd rather go with you two."

Manny wrapped an arm around her shoulders like she was one of the guys. "And why is that?"

"Because I'm on vacation, and you two are the entertainment. Now, where are we going?"

Drew slapped a hand over his heart. "She wounds me."

Frowning, Jules looped her arm through his. "How so?"

"You're treating us like sex toys. I'm insulted."

Jules rolled her eyes. "C'mon, big guy. Get over it. Manny, let's move it."

"Yes, ma'am." He glanced at Drew. "Remember, my friend. Boyfriends come and go, but a good dildo lasts forever."

"As long as you don't forget to replace the batteries." Grumbling dramatically, Drew took Jules's other arm, and they were off.

This had been a strange, magical, sometimes heartrending crazy week, and Jules had never been happier in her life. Tomorrow would be their last day, since they had to leave early Saturday to get all the way back home to Portland. She refused to see this brief romance with creatures who shouldn't even exist as anything beyond a chance to experience a fantasy out of time, a utopian interlude that would have to carry her through the rest of her life. She knew she would never find anyone like Manny and Drew again—two men she'd discovered were beautiful both inside and out.

Manny was a forester who kept the animals on the preserve safe. That's why he'd been out patrolling with Trak when the alpha was shot, but it was an important job, a dangerous one as well, that he said he absolutely loved. He was funny and sweet and sometimes so charming he took her breath. She could love him so easily.

Drew was a bartender at Growl and a lot of the time acted as Manny's foil. They played off each other with the ease of longtime friends—and, as she'd discovered, lovers.

Elle was serious about staying on with her veterinarian. All the girls knew she'd always wanted to be a vet, that she had that amazing affinity with animals and her own magical ability to heal them. For whatever reason, it was way too easy to see Elle as a fierce and powerful female wolf. She'd had them all laughing at breakfast, joking about finally deserving the name way too many men had pinned on her: bitch.

"How ya doin', Jules?" Manny draped his arm over her shoulders. They'd been walking single file along a narrow section of trail that skirted a rushing creek, but they'd hit a wide spot. Manny was quick to take advantage of it.

"Doing great. It's amazing out here." It was, with the craggy mountains and thick stands of evergreens crawling up the steep slopes, the creek they followed through small meadows filled with wildflowers even this late in the summer. The afternoon had turned warm, and the air was filled with birdsong. "I've never been in country like this, though I see the mountains from Portland all the time. I've just never gone to see them up close. I envy you, living here."

"Do you?" Drew wrapped his arms around her from behind and rested his chin on top of her head. "Wouldn't you get bored?"

"You're kidding, right?" She turned and kissed his chin, something she would never have done to a man just a week ago. "I've always wanted to write, but could never afford the time off to do it. I quit my job when I realized what a scumbag my boss was—he's the one I was dating until I discovered I was exclusive but he wasn't—and I actually started a book, knowing I couldn't start job hunting until after this trip. It's been planned for months. Luckily I had some savings, but I realized I liked staying home and writing."

"What do you write?" Manny slipped an arm around her.

She loved being sandwiched between two killer men. She was positive she could use it in a story at some point. "Don't laugh. I'm writing a romance."

"Why would I laugh?" Manny leaned away from her, frowning.

"People who haven't read them make fun of the books, call them bodice rippers. They forget the main tenet of a romance other than the romance is that it has to have a happy ending. Yes, they can have graphic sex and sometimes silly stories, but I dare you to read a good romance and walk away from it feeling sad."

Manny took her hand and led her away from the trail, over to a grassy spot beside a huge incense cedar. Drew pulled a blanket out of his backpack and spread it on the ground. "Time for a break. Sit."

She sat with a guy on either side. It wasn't awkward at all. It felt right.

"So, any chance Manny and I might turn up in one of your books?" Drew tapped the end of her nose and made her laugh.

"Believe me, gentlemen, whenever I have to write about a sexy hero, you two will be foremost in my mind. I'm going to miss you so much when I leave here. I'm hoping that writing about you will be a way to keep you close."

"Ya know," Manny said, "when we first built Feral Passions and opened the doors last spring, we had a rule that if any of the guys met a woman he loved enough to keep, he had to wait until at least a week after she'd gone home to find her and see if she still felt the same about him as he did about her. But that was with women who didn't know what we were, what we were offering. So far, only Brad and Cain and Wils and Ronan have met women they could see themselves spending a lifetime with. Of course, after they followed the girls to San Francisco, they discovered that Cherry had figured out our secret."

"She said it was eye color that tipped her off."

"That's right," Drew said. "That night, when Manny and I came to your room, you called us by name. You were right. How?"

"I don't know. I was asleep. I'd been dreaming about Manny." She glanced at him and smiled. "Very good dreams, by the way. In my dream, he was a wolf, and when you both showed up as wolves, I knew who you were. No reason. I just recognized you in the wolves, somehow."

Drew took her hand, played with her fingers. "Freaked us out. We had no idea how you knew."

"Sorry. Neither did I. I still don't."

"Jules, Drew and I wondered how you felt about us. Could you see a future with a couple of guys who tend to go furry on occasion? Maybe spend some time on the furry side yourself? Occasionally howling at the moon?"

"What?" She looked from Manny to Drew and back at Manny.

Manny ran his fingers through her hair. Pulled her close for a kiss. "I can see a lifetime of kissing you, making love to you. I can't imagine growing tired of you." He raised his head. "Or this guy. You see how it works with Cherry and the guys. That's what we're asking for. With you."

"But you need to know everything," Drew said. "We finally convinced Trak that you should know the truth before you really think about it. If you agree, we'd both need to bite you. Not bad, just enough to break the skin, but you'd go to sleep, and when you woke, you'd be able to shift."

"If you agree," Manny added, "you will only have sons, not daughters. Werewolf males are born, the females are made, but you'll live far beyond your normal life span."

This was amazing. Crazy. She'd have to be nuts . . . not to. "How far beyond?"

"Well, how old do Drew and I look?"

She shrugged. "Low to midthirties."

Drew grinned. "I'm the kid here. I was born in 1911. This old fart was born in 1897."

"Holy. Shit." She stared at the two of them. Manny was born in the nineteenth century! "Manny, you're almost a hundred and twenty years old!"

"And he doesn't look a day past a hundred." Drew snickered.

Manny mussed his hair and in a shaking voice said, "Be kind to your elders, sonny."

"I've been thinking of this week as an impossible slice out of time I never want to give up. You're offering me the fantasy for the rest of my life. I'd be crazy to say no."

Drew took one hand, Manny the other.

"We still have to give you a week away," Drew said.

"Time to think it through," Manny added. "Time to think us through. Drew and I have been off-and-on partners for years, never as committed as Cain and Brad. I asked him this week if he loved me enough to be my partner, even if you weren't part of it."

"And I said yes, because I've loved Manny for years, but I told him it would be a lot more fun if you were part of the mix."

"I want that," Jules said. She meant it with all her heart. "I want both of you."

Dar was the only one by the pool Thursday afternoon. Everyone had found someplace to be—Jules with her guys, Elle and Tuck checking on a mare near town having a tough labor, and Meg with Trak and Zachary.

Lawz had gone into town to check on the sheriff's case against the poachers. They'd arrested all three guys Tuesday night and found a huge freezer filled with frozen game on Wednesday, most likely from the preserve, though at this point there was no way to prove it. No matter, it had been taken out of season, and Trak was paying to have DNA tests done against the carcasses found within the fence line to see if they could make a match. No wolves had been killed, but the men had been charged with attempted murder, poaching, trespassing, and because they all had prior prison records, felons in possession of firearms.

The sheriff assured Lawz they'd be spending a long time behind bars.

Dar picked up the book she'd been reading. Brad had come out and refreshed her margarita, and she honestly couldn't remember feeling this relaxed. She realized that this was the first time she'd actually been alone since the drive down last Sunday. The weird thing was, she didn't miss the girls, her closest friends ever. She missed Lawz. He'd spent the night in her bed, just as he had every night since she'd arrived. He'd been a wolf that first night, but the man was addictive. More than addictive—she wasn't sure she could walk away without a broken heart.

He hadn't made any declaration like Tuck had to Elle, essentially telling her she was his and talking about a future. It felt as if Lawz was hedging his bets, but she wasn't sure why. The attraction between them was off the charts, and they truly enjoyed each other's company, but for whatever reason, while he'd talked about not wanting to let her go, he hadn't asked her to stay.

Maybe she needed to ask him. Men could be so obtuse sometimes.

With that plan simmering in the back of her mind, she went back to her book. She shouldn't have been surprised when Cherry offered the loan of a terrific werewolf romance. So far, though, Dar thought Lawz was a lot sexier than the hero in the story.

———

Meg stretched and yawned. They'd been out on the deck for the past couple of hours while Traker talked about the pack history. He'd told Zach that he had to trust him to keep their secret, but he didn't want Meg's friends to feel they couldn't talk openly with him and Meg. Trak didn't think that was fair to their friendship. At first, Zach thought they were making fun of him, but then Cain had dropped his pants and turned into a wolf right there in front of them.

He'd never seen anything so astounding, so flat-out mystical, in his life. He'd held on to Meg's hand and realized what had to be impossible was happening right in front of him, and somehow, that made just about anything possible.

Even Meggie loving him. Damn, but he wished he knew what was wrong.

"Zach, honey? I'm going back to the cabin to take a nap. If I don't show up for dinner, will you come wake me?"

"Of course I will."

She leaned over and kissed him. Her lips felt warm and soft, but her eyes were sad. She'd been sad since he'd gotten here. At first, he thought she was worried about him, but then he began to suspect it was something more. He honestly didn't know what it might be, and if it was that she didn't love him anymore, he didn't want to know.

He watched her follow the trail until she disappeared into the woods. He'd gotten to be friends with Traker, both of them stuck on the deck healing. The man was the pack alpha, a leader, and he definitely had the pulse of his pack. Nothing got by him.

"Trak? I need some advice. What the fuck is wrong? Meggie's just . . ."

"Do you love her?"

"What?" Frowning, he stared at Trak. Maybe the guy wasn't all that smart. "Good lord, man. Of course I do. Why do you think I was driving down here when I wrecked my car? I missed Meggie so much I couldn't stand it. I'd been awake all night and finally got up at three because all I wanted was to be with her. Why would you ask me that?"

Trak smiled, sort of a big Cheshire cat grin. "Then maybe you need to tell her."

"I tell her I love her all the time. I asked her to marry me. I've never asked any woman to marry me, figured it wouldn't happen, but when she came along, I knew she was the one."

"Zach, I knew Meg was troubled as soon as she got here. The others were laughing and teasing the guys, having a great time, and she was keeping to herself, sort of quiet. Even her friends knew something was wrong."

"Do you have any idea what?"

"I do. Some I got from her friends, some from Meg when I asked her, and she told me the whole convoluted story. What it comes down to is that Meg doesn't think she's good enough for you. She's afraid you're going to wake up about a week after you're married and realize you made a mistake."

"I don't understand." He shook his head. Trak couldn't be right. Could he?

"Another thing. Jules once had an abusive boyfriend. Dar asked Meg if you were abusive."

"Me?" Zach shook his head. "Hell, no. My father treated my mother like shit. Her spirit was totally broken by the time I came along. I would never treat a woman like that."

"Meg denied it, and then she went on to list enough qualities to make you sound like a fucking saint."

He laughed then, but Zach still didn't get it. "At least it's not just me thinking she's unhappy. Do you have any idea why?"

"Yeah. It's simple. She said you're so wonderful, she can't believe you really love her because she's nothing." He held up his hand when Zach interrupted. "I'm just repeating what I heard the others talking about after a hike they took together. That's when they confronted her. I guess Meg's family life wasn't very supportive. Her mother and father were way too open about the fact they hadn't wanted her, that if not for a broken condom she'd never have been born and they wouldn't have married. That's a horrible thing to tell your child, and Meg's self-esteem is in the gutter. Not professionally. I get the feeling she's afraid that she's such a good personal assistant that you're marrying her to make sure she stays on."

He stared at Trak for the longest time, going over conversations with Meggie since he'd arrived. Nothing. "I can't believe that. Shit." He sat there on the deck with his head in his hands and tried to recall if he'd ever told Meggie why he loved her as much as he did. He'd tried to show her. Their sex life was amazing—shouldn't that convince her? He said as much to Trak.

Who laughed way too much for Zach's peace of mind.

"Zachary my friend, that is such an egotistical, totally misogynistic statement that it's one for the records. That good sex is Meg's gift to you. Don't ever think otherwise. In the pack, we treasure our women. They're a powerful part of our world, the stability that keeps a pack healthy. That's why we're so desperate to find mates. I would suggest you go back to your cabin right now and tell Meg exactly why you made that long trip from Portland. Let her know you would follow her anywhere, do anything for her. She makes you whole, Zachary Trenton. But she doesn't know that because you've never told her how you really feel."

"You're right." He felt like such an ass. "I need her more than I like to admit. I didn't want her to think I was a neurotic weakling."

Trak grinned at him and shook his head, laughing. "Idiot. You were afraid to tell her the truth. You are a weakling. Not so sure about the neurotic part, but man up, Zachary."

Zach didn't get pissed, but he didn't laugh, either. Inside he was laughing at himself, and it wasn't a pleasant feeling. Trak was right on all counts. He stood, reached out, and shook the man's hand. "Thank you. It appears I have some groveling to do."

"It appears you do."

Trak was still chuckling as Zach took the trail to Meg's cabin.

Dar glanced up as Lawz pulled into the parking lot in his shiny red pickup truck. It was flashy, like something you'd see a good old boy driving down the freeway with an American flag flapping from the back, except he wasn't a flashy guy. One day, if they ended up together, she'd have to ask him about it.

She thought he'd go straight to the lodge to check in with Trak, but instead, he cut across the lawn and walked over to her and her spot under an umbrella by the pool. "Hey!"

She pulled off her dark glasses and smiled at him. "I wondered when you'd get back."

He shrugged. "Had some things to take care of."

"Did you get them done?"

"I did." He grabbed a chair at another table, dragged it over to a spot directly across her small table, and sat facing her. He took both her hands in his and looked at her so directly she felt as if he could read the small print inside her. "Darian, I've been doing some checking with a TV station in Eureka. It's a network affiliate and covers a lot of the North Coast. I mean, it's not huge, not Portland huge, anyway, but I asked if they might have a spot for a talented newscaster from the Portland area. I told them who you were, and the station manager jumped on the idea as soon as I mentioned your name. Said he's heard only good things about you."

She didn't say anything, but there had to be a damned good reason why he'd been checking on something like that behind her back. Maybe she wouldn't have to ask him that commitment question after all.

"The thing is, Dar, I want you to stay with me. I mean, I know I have to let you go for a week—that dumb rule we all agreed to—but I want you to want to come back here with me. To live with me as my mate. I spend most of my time in Eureka and parts north, and I've got a nice house over there, but this will always be my home." He shrugged, but because he knew structure was important to women, he added, "I've got a sturdy little place here, too, though I don't live here much. Do you think you could love me, Dar? Because I'm already almost there with you. I just want to know you better, but we'd have all the time in the world ahead of us."

She stood, leaned over the table, and kissed him. "I am

so glad you asked, silly. I've been sitting here wondering if I needed to ask you, because there's no way in hell I'm letting you go. I can easily see spending the next sixty or so years beside you."

She did like that smile of his, though she wasn't quite sure what he meant when he chuckled softly, glanced away, and then focused those sparkling brown eyes on hers.

"Well, Dar." He actually laughed harder. "That sixty years? That's something else we probably need to discuss . . ."

Zach opened the door to Meg's cabin quietly, in case she'd fallen asleep. She was lying on the bed, still dressed in the long skirt and tank top she'd had on, but she wasn't sleeping. No, even though her back was to him, it appeared she was crying.

Traker must have nailed it, and Zach was an absolute ass.

He walked around the bed and sat on the edge beside her. He didn't look at her. He couldn't, because Trak was right about something else. Call it a hangover from his father's brand of parenting or pure cowardice on his part, but he couldn't face Meggie while he confessed what a jerk he was. How afraid he was to tell her the truth.

Instead, he reached for the box of tissues beside the bed and handed it to her. She blew her nose and got herself under control. He only knew it from the sounds, because he still couldn't look at her. Didn't want to see how miserable he'd made her because he was such a fucking coward. Finally, he heard her draw a shaky breath, and knew he'd run out of time.

"Meggie, do you have any idea how much you mean to me? No." He shook his head. "Don't answer that, because it's obvious you don't, and that's my fault. You probably don't even know why I had that stupid accident."

"Because a bear ran in front of your car?"

He laughed, but the sound was torn out of him. "Well, that and the reason why I was headed down here, driving like a bat out of hell. See, I'd slept okay the first night you were gone, but Monday night slid into Tuesday morning, and when I was still awake at three and missing you so much it was like an amputation because part of me was just gone, I threw some stuff in my backpack and hit the road. I even turned my phone off so, on the off chance you called me, I couldn't answer, because I can't lie to you, Meggie."

He turned then and took her hands in his. "I can't lie to you, and I was scared to death if you called and I told you I was coming to see you, you'd tell me to go home. That you didn't want me here. And you shouldn't have, because it's your fucking bachelorette party, which means no men, but I kept thinking you were using this time to convince yourself I didn't love you when I love you so much it scares me. You have so much power over me. You could destroy me so easily. You're my anchor, Meggie. The one person in the whole world I know will love me no matter what. I've never had that before, not from my parents, not from friends, and never from a girlfriend. I've never had anyone like you in my life, but you're the one person I've hoped for all along. If I ever lose you, I lose everything that's important."

"Zach? I don't understand. You're everything I've ever wanted in a man. You're absolutely perfect, but . . ." She turned her face away, wouldn't look at him.

The truth hit him, then. So damned simple he'd been an idiot not to see it. "No, Meggie. I'm not perfect. I'm so far from it, but maybe I'm perfect for you. And no matter what you think of yourself, I know you're exactly the woman I want. The one I need. The one I love beyond measure. Can we let it go at that, accept the fact we're both probably neurotic as hell but lucky enough that each of us has found exactly the right person to love?"

"Yes," she said, covering her mouth with one hand, blinking away tears. "I can do that." She was laughing and crying at the same time, so that it was hard to understand her, except he knew exactly what she meant.

"Good," he said, nuzzling that sweet spot behind her ear. Breathing a deep sigh of relief. "Me, too."

CHAPTER 13

Friday

The guys were down at Growl for a morning meeting. In spite of all the drama this past week, they had guests showing up on Sunday. Cherry was upstairs in her home office, catching up on work she'd missed while on her honeymoon.

Elle and the rest of the gang of four, along with Zach, huddled around a small table in the dining room. "So, ladies." She smiled at Zach. "And token gentleman." He saluted with his cup of coffee. "This is our last full day here, but I wanted to let you know that I'm not leaving."

"What? You're shittin' me!" Dar's bark of laughter had everyone cracking wise.

"Nope. I'm not a child, and until Tuck bites me, I'm not subject to Trak's rule as alpha. I talked to Tuck about it last night. That stupid one-week rule was set up for women who didn't know what they were getting into. I know. So do you, Jules, and you, too, Darian. Tuck likes having me as his assistant almost as much as he loves me in his bed. And that works both ways. I'm staying with Tuck, and I suggest that if you're sure about your feelings for your guys, you two do the same."

Dar nodded agreement. "Lawz and I talked about this last night, too. I need to go back to give notice at the station and clean out my apartment, but I don't want to stay away. My contract is actually up for renewal this month, but I wanted to do it after this trip."

"Good plan!" Meg high-fived her.

"Yeah, by accident. I sure didn't plan on Lawz! I was thinking of holding out for more money. Never dreamed it would leave me free to quit. Lawz wants to make the trip with me so we can go to the station in Eureka first and get me locked in there for the job before I give notice in Portland, then figure out what stuff I need to keep and what I can dump. What about you, Jules?"

She merely shrugged. "I don't have a job to quit, and my apartment lease is up next month. That'll give me time to move, but I don't want to leave here at all. I'm ready to start life with two men I'm definitely falling for, and fast. It's almost scary how much they mean to me."

Elle stood. "I say we make a short walk to Growl and present our case to the gentlemen in question. Trak's still not entirely recovered—Cain took him down to Growl in the truck. Maybe he won't have the energy to argue."

"One can hope." Jules stood and glanced at the others. "Meg? You don't have to come, but I wish you would. You too, Zach, though I don't want to interfere with your man standing with the guys."

Zach stood and held out a hand to Meg. "My man standing is with the ladies, because I agree with you. Strength in solidarity, right?"

They all clasped hands in the center of their impromptu

circle. Elle felt like part of an uprising. It was a heady experience. Then the phone in the office rang.

Meg raised her hand. "Business calls. I told Brad I'd take any calls that came through. Back in a flash."

"I don't want Elle to leave, Trak. She's slipped into place as my assistant, and she already feels like my mate. I love her. The week apart doesn't make sense when she already knows what she's getting into."

"Same here." Lawz glanced at the guys before speaking directly to Trak. "And we're dealing with a time issue. Dar's contract is up at the station in Portland, but she doesn't want to step away until she's legally locked into the job in Eureka. It's a huge switch for her, going from weathergirl to news desk with a path to anchor. It needs to be done as soon as possible."

Manny and Drew looked at each other and laughed. "We just don't want Jules to leave, period." Manny grabbed Drew's hand. "Once we got together and included Jules, hell, it's like our lives have opened up. Lots of possibilities ahead."

"And laughter." Drew shook his head. "She's brought an element of laughter to our lives that's been missing way too long."

Trak had sort of expected this, but he still didn't know how to deal with it. Sometimes it felt as if this whole resort idea had been a fiasco, until he looked at Cain and Brad and the love they had for Cherry, at Wils and Ronan, two guys he never thought would find women willing to fit their four-way dynamic. But they had six new women showing up on

Sunday and four guys who wanted to take off with their women.

So he said as much. "I have to agree with you on the issue of the week apart. This is, I hope, a unique set of cases, but the fact is, we have six women arriving Sunday afternoon, and I'm still not able to do much. Wils and Ronan won't be back until Wednesday, but that leaves just Brad, Cain, Evan, and me to man the fort." He laughed. "And it appears Evan's the only one capable of offering extracurricular activities."

"The rest of us are out of the loop as well." Manny shrugged. "I know I'm not interested in spending time with another woman."

Drew punched him in the shoulder. "You're not interested in Jules coming after you with a meat cleaver, you mean. I don't think she's willing to share."

"You're right. I'm not." Laughing, Jules led the women through the door to Growl, with Zach bringing up the rear.

Trak focused on Meg. "What's up?"

"Well, a couple of things. On behalf of Dar, Jules, and Elle, we're here to discuss abolishing your one-week rule for this particular group of candidates. They know what they're getting into, and going in with hearts and eyes wide open." She took a small bow to the men's cheers and applause. "And on behalf of the Feral Passions Resort, I need to report that your group scheduled to arrive on Sunday has canceled due to a shared gastrointestinal illness from their cruise ship adventure last week. I told them you would follow up regarding rescheduling or refunding as per your contract with them."

Trak grinned at Zach, standing behind Meg with his

hands planted possessively on her shoulders. It appeared he'd made his case last night. "They'll get a full refund, because it solves the other problem. As far as the one-week rule, you're all adults, and I'm not about to stand in your way."

He made eye contact with each of his men, all trustworthy guys he was proud to lead. They were men smart enough to know when to tell him he was wrong and brave enough to stand by him. "The thing is, we'll still need to figure out a work schedule to get us through the end of the season. Hopefully, Evan and I will meet someone, and if that's the case, we'll find another way to use what we've built."

"We're planning our wedding here October 2," Zach said. Standing behind her, hands still locked to her shoulders, he kissed Meg.

She covered his hands with hers. "Might be a good way to retool things, Trak. There's a huge demand for unique wedding venues."

"Something to think about." He glanced around the small bar.

Elle had grabbed Tuck, and the two were already off in a corner, making plans. Lawz had his arms around Dar, and if he didn't love his big brother so much, Trak might have been jealous, because she was certainly a fine-looking woman. Manny and Drew were the surprise of this bunch, but it was really special, seeing their longtime friendship blossom this way. Jules had brought them together, and she fit in like their own personal puzzle piece.

So far, each of the new pairings had brought strong, vital members into the pack. He caught Evan's eye, and his buddy merely shrugged. They hadn't met their mates yet, but the season wasn't over.

Standing, still a bit shaky, Trak slapped his hand down on the table. "Meeting adjourned, gentlemen, ladies. We're lucky we have next week off to get our acts together. I think there's a group of circus performers week after next." He turned to Evan and, behind his hand, whispered, "Ever fancy a trapeze artist?"

They were both laughing as the meeting broke up.

HER
PERFECT
MATES

A. C. Arthur

CHAPTER 1

"Put your hand right here," she directed, her voice smooth and just a touch husky.

Malec Zenta did as he was told.

"Feel that?" she asked.

He felt something, that was for damned sure.

"It's supposed to be hard," she continued, moving her hands up and down and sighing heavily.

Malec's hand followed hers, his heart thumping wildly in his chest, dick pressing hard against the zipper of his jeans.

"Somebody broke his leg. Both of them," the veterinarian continued, moving from one leg on the buck Malec had brought into the office for her to examine to the other.

Her hands were small, moving with practiced precision, gripping and touching the animal with careful diligence. Instinctively Malec shifted his hand until it was beside hers, waiting a beat, and felt the wave of heat flush quickly through his body as she moved her hand and brushed over his.

"Something very powerful did this," she continued, succulent lips pursing as she focused on the wounded buck.

"A hunter?" he asked, chafing momentarily at the thought.

They lived in Blackbriar, Montana, a small town located along the Blackfoot River and backed against Blackbriar National Park, where hunting certain species during restricted time frames was prohibited. Deer and elk season began in September. It was the middle of the summer.

The doctor shook her head. "A hunter would have killed it and taken it with him. Then you and I wouldn't be standing here trying to figure out what happened to this poor animal."

Malec nodded. "Right," he said tightly, noting that a lot of things had come into play this morning to bring him to this moment where he stood across the table from a most delectable human female.

"There's another scar up here that's a bit strange as well," she continued, and Malec tried to keep his focus.

He was here, in town, at the office of the new veterinarian in Blackbriar—Dr. Caroline Douglas, he recalled from the bright pink paper signs on the front door, because he'd found this wounded deer in the middle of the path he ran every morning before the sun rose. For that reason alone, Channing and the others thought it was Malec's duty to bring the animal in to see if it could be saved. Malec had disagreed mostly because he hated coming into town and having to deal with the people here looking at him like he was some type of pariah—when they really had no idea what he actually was.

He looked toward the deer's neck where there were scratches, four of them. He moved to the top of the table, lifting the animal's head so that he could see the other side of its neck. Four more jagged breaks of the animal's skin.

"Its head should have been severed," he said.

She nodded. "Should have been. With just a little more pressure I'm guessing it would have. Each of those cuts will need to be stitched. He's lost a tremendous amount of blood. But the real question is, what type of animal would have grabbed this deer around the neck and then tossed it onto the trail where you found it?"

The animal had been sedated ten minutes after Malec had carried it in and put it on the examination table, so it was still and bleeding onto the stainless steel. And she was right; that was the real question. What the hell had happened out in that forest? Instead of answering, he asked, "Can you save it?"

To his question Malec expected a simple reply, yes or no. Possibly—even though he really wasn't in the mood for it—some bogus doctor jargon about seeing what she could do, or doing her best. All of which really equated to "The animal's going to die, so I don't know why you wasted your time bringing it in here."

Instead, what he received was a jolt of lust so intense he had to take a step back from the table. She was staring at him, her bright eyes wide, blinking as if she wasn't quite sure what she was seeing. Her lips, of medium thickness and glossed a blushing shade of pink, parted slightly. She had a round face, her complexion mocha, no cream and no sugar. Just passion and an edge of something more. His gaze lowered instinctively as if she'd willed him to keep looking, to explore, to find, to conquer. Malec's dick jumped, thrusting as it grew harder, pressing almost painfully against the zipper of his jeans. She wore a sweater, pale blue and thin, that did nothing to cover the voluptuous breasts pressing beautifully against the material of the white shirt she wore beneath it. And there, right there like a beacon, were the piercings. He could see them as clearly as if she were standing before him naked, her nipples hard, puckered, and visible even though he was certain she wore a bra. On the side of each thick nipple were smaller beads—nipple piercings that made Malec want to growl with primal hunger.

"I will do it," she said, her voice cutting through the haze of desire that had clouded his thoughts.

"You will do what?" Malec asked her.

Let me suck your nipples until you come?

Sit on my face while I look up to see your heavy breasts with those big pretty nipples smiling down at me?

Let me fuck you until there are no other thoughts in my mind, in this world?

The burn of his nails elongating, the beast within threatening to make its horny presence known, pricked the inside of his palm as he clenched his fists.

She licked her lips, her tongue—wet and no doubt warm, like her mouth—darting out quickly, and he imagined that lick tracing the tip of his dick.

"I will get started immediately," she said as if coming out of her own trance and definitely snapping Malec out of his as she turned away from him. "There's some paperwork you will need to fill out with the receptionist. Leave your contact information with her, and I'll give you a call if you'd like. Or, if this was your Good Samaritan job for the day, I'll simply call the park vets and have them arrange for the buck to be moved when it's stable enough."

She continued to talk with her back to him, moving about as if whatever she was doing—gathering supplies from a cabinet below, opening packages, preparing, he figured—was more appealing than looking at him.

Malec didn't know why that irritated him. He shouldn't give a damn whether or not this human female looked at him or not. Correction, he didn't give a damn how she or anybody else looked at him; he wasn't ashamed of who and what he was. Besides, he wasn't here for her to judge him—he'd brought a buck to the doctor to see if it could be saved. That was all.

And yet, he felt like there was something here he needed to prove. To her or to himself he wasn't certain. Malec moved without speaking, walking until he stood directly behind her. He reached into his back pocket, pulled out his wallet, and took out a business card. She'd stiffened the second she felt him so close. Malec both liked and despised that action. Still, he moved in even closer, until he knew his thick length rubbed against the round curve of her ass. Reaching around her with one arm, being sure to scrape over one of those mouthwatering nipples, feeling the hard brush of the piercing against his sensitized skin, he put the card down on the counter in front of her.

"Call me," he said after he'd leaned forward, his mouth directly against her ear. "Not the park doctors or anyone else. Call. Me."

She nodded at first, then gulped, a sound he heard with his sharp lycan hearing, loud and clear.

"I will," she whispered.

Malec walked away then, using every bit of restraint he'd learned to possess during his years in the corps. He walked out of that office, not bothering to speak to the receptionist—who he knew was staring at him with questions in her eyes—and not taking a breath until he was out in the morning air. He gulped, taking in deep breaths in an attempt to calm the throbbing ache in his dick and his temples.

This was bullshit! His mind roared with that statement over and over again as he stood on the sidewalk, citizens and tourists just beginning to make their way along the small-town streets.

She was a human. Which meant she was off limits to him and the dark sexual desires that pulsed through his blood like a fatal disease.

Malec did not do humans. And he did not do women by himself. Yet he'd envisioned so clearly, sucking the good doctor's big breasts and thrusting his cock into what he knew would be a juicy, sweet pussy. He wasn't an emotionally stable man. He was a damaged lycan who had decided a long time ago, based on his past experiences, that this was the life choice for him. He was a member of a pack that had a mission much larger than this little town of Blackbriar.

And he did not fuck humans. Ever.

Reaching into the inside pocket of his black jacket he pulled out his Gucci aviator sunglasses, slipping them onto his face with one smooth motion. In the next instant he was walking toward his black Ford F-150, where just about an hour ago the buck had lain in the cab, writhing in pain. People stared at him as he moved, watched him climb into the truck and start the engine. They wondered about the man that lived miles away toward the lake and the mountain base in that big remodeled log cabin with those other men that nobody knew a damned thing about. They formed opinions, made judgments, and were probably as wrong as two left feet in all of them. Malec told himself that he didn't care. That the thoughts and misconceptions could never touch him, or guide his actions in any way. Not like they had with Mason.

He pulled away from the curb without looking back, trying to center his thoughts on his one and only mission in this life—to protect his alpha at all costs.

It definitely wasn't to slip his hard dick inside the hot, honey-coated walls of Dr. Caroline Douglas, that was for certain.

"Dammit," Caroline swore. "You have got to get it together, CeeCee."

Using the nickname her mother had given her was supposed to strip her of the totally carnal thoughts she was having at this moment. It was supposed to bring her back to earth, where she had a very badly wounded buck to tend to. But that was a laugh, considering Maxine Douglas had been a prostitute since she was ten years old.

Instead, Caroline remained standing at the window in her office where she'd sought refuge the moment Malec Zenta left.

Malec Zenta.

That was his name. A strange and masculine name for someone who was all man, all sex, all the time. She had no clue how she knew that for certain, but from the looks of him—probably a little over six feet tall, possibly 220 or 230 pounds considering all those bulging muscles, skin the color of churned butter, eyes dark, simmering, alluring—he was a woman's fantasy.

Only she was definitely not that woman.

Blackbriar was Caroline's fresh start. It was the small town where no one knew who she was or what she'd come from. A place that needed a veterinarian and that Caroline needed to hopefully, finally, fit in.

As for the guy, Malec Zenta, he was the last thing she needed right now.

That thought circled in her mind as Caroline held the business card he'd given her in one hand, letting its edges pinch into the skin of her palm. She stood right there, staring out that window, watching as he climbed into the big SUV with its shined-to-a-sparkle rims that only made its black color seem darker and its owner sexier.

It was in times like these that Caroline was glad for her thick thighs, because as she saw that truck disappearing down the street she remembered how close Malec had stood to her and how wet her pussy had become from that proximity. It was startling, this quick and fast punch of desire sparked by a stranger. She'd never had that happen before, never thought that type of desire existed. No, Caroline knew it existed, she just never thought she'd experience it again. Truth be told she'd never wanted to experience that immediate and insistent need for sex again. It never ended well, she knew that with brutal certainty. Part of the reason she'd gotten her nipples pierced was to promote her own stimulation. The other reason was that she liked how it looked, how feminine and in control it made her feel each time she stared at herself in the mirror. Funny how the memory of the man who had given her the piercings didn't spark the same positive feelings.

Caroline squeezed her thighs together so tightly, trying

to gather just enough pressure to ease that burn that had developed deep in her center, but not quite reaching it. With an exasperated sigh she went to her chair and sat down, still holding her legs together tightly and closing her eyes to resist the urge. It was there, singing a silent melody throughout the privacy of her office.

"Touch it. Just this once. Real quick, to ease the ache," she whispered to herself, as she'd done so many times before. "Just one more time."

But it wasn't just one. It would be another and another, because that's what she did; it's how she found the pleasure that she often feared she was addicted to. The pleasure that she still somehow thought wasn't enough.

A brisk knock on her door, and then it was opening, Olivia, her receptionist coming in.

"Did you smell him?" Olivia asked.

Caroline frowned, bringing her elbows to the desk, moving her hands quickly away from her inner thighs where she desperately wanted to place them. "What? Who? The buck?"

Olivia's sharply arched brows drew inward, ruby-red painted lips twisting. "Ewww, no. But Martin said to tell you the sedative's going to wear off soon, so if you're operating you'd better get to it."

Martin Wood's official title at the clinic was assistant veterinarian even though he was older and had been there much longer than she. Caroline had inherited him when she'd taken the job at the River Vet Clinic. Olivia had come with the package as well, but she was much more amenable to the shift in power than Martin even tried to be.

"Yes," Caroline said. "I'm coming."

"Girl, I would be too if that fine-ass Malec Zenta would

put his strong hands on me," Olivia added, her face now alight with her imagined pleasure.

With a shake of her head Caroline stood from her chair, pulling her sweater closer around her breasts. "I wouldn't know all that. All I know is that something happened to that buck, and I have to go in there and see if I can save it."

"Mmm-hmm," Olivia continued with a nod. "And then you can call Mr. Sexy and ask him can you come see him. Because nobody in town has been out to that log fortress they've built in the wilderness. You go out there to report on Bambi and get a look at all those other fine specimens walking around that place. Four of them, tall, dark, and oozing sex and money in equal parts. There's enough for you, me, and two other lucky women in this backward town to hit it big."

Caroline had left her office with Olivia still chatting and following her toward the operating room, where she presumed Martin had moved the buck. She stopped to stare at the recent college grad who talked much more and even faster than she did anything else in the office.

"You've got that all planned out, huh?" she asked.

"Hell yeah!" Olivia nodded.

Caroline couldn't help but smile.

"Get your mind on business. Fill out an incident report based on the notes I left in the exam room. I like to record my surgical procedures. You can transcribe it later," she instructed Olivia, who had gone back to frowning.

"So you aren't going to call Mr. So Fine I Almost Went Blind?" Olivia asked with a look of pure disbelief.

With a shake of her head, Caroline opened the operating

room door and headed inside. "When I save the buck I'll call him to let him know."

"And to tell him you'll take one night of hot passionate sex as payment," Olivia continued as she walked in the opposite direction toward the front of the office.

Not if the devil himself offered to raise her mother from the dead, Caroline thought and proceeded into the room.

CHAPTER 2

She was there again.

In his dreams, traipsing her sweet, plump ass around his bedroom as if she owned him and everything in the vicinity. She was naked, of course, just the way he liked her. Pussy waxed, nipples hard, and mouth ready to take his engorged length deep and long.

Malec lay back against the pillows and sheets, now damp with sweat, his heart thumping, chest heaving with the effort of pulling himself out of the seductive clutches of that dream. Why? Because not only had Caroline been there in his mind, teasing and tempting him until he'd had no other recourse but to crook a finger, beckoning her to come closer, but she'd obeyed his every command as if it were what she was born to do.

Crawling on her hands and knees across the mattress until she was between his outstretched legs, pushing his hand away from where he gripped the base of his thick cock. She'd dipped her head, immediately catching the tip of his erection, holding it still right there while her tongue eased in and out of his slit.

Malec had looked around at that moment. He'd watched

for the second when Channing usually appeared, standing at the end of the bed, stroking his length while staring at the female's ass, waiting for the moment he could slip seamlessly inside her. That's what Malec's sex life entailed—sharing his females with Channing. It hadn't been that way from the start, but eventually, after life had dealt both of them a raw deal and then thrust them together on the battlefield, the two lycans had found a common link to releasing the darkness that lived inside of them, and they'd held on to it for dear life.

Malec always chose the women, and Channing always agreed. They had a rhythm together—who would touch her first, kiss her, make her moan, and then who would come in second and seal the deal. Channing assured the women were emotionally stable enough for the thought of taking two virile lycans inside of her at one time, while Malec only promised the pleasure. And when he was done seeing to her pleasure, and achieving a modicum of relief for himself, he left. Channing took care of the rest.

But not this time.

This time, with this woman, Malec was alone.

He tried to wake up at that point, but had not succeeded. Caroline continued her assault on his cock, taking him deep, then pulling out until there was a loud popping sound as the head of his erection slipped free of her lips. Not too thick, but just succulent enough, her lips looked absolutely perfect coated in that pink gloss gliding once more over his veined length. Malec had wanted to come at that very moment, to see if she would take every drop of his essence into her hot little mouth.

But that never happened because something was wrong

with this scene. There was no denying that fact and no continuing in his mind. This simply was not how it happened for him, ever.

So he'd finally bolted up in the bed, breathing as if he'd just run a marathon in double the time of his normal lightning-fast lycan speed.

For he didn't know how long Malec simply sat in the center of his king-sized bed, staring out to the dark room, listening to the quiet and wondering what the hell was going on in his mind. Eventually he lay back, folding his arms behind his head, unable—or quite possibly unwilling—to ignore the daunting question of what the hell Caroline Douglas was doing in his dreams in the first place.

Not only did Malec not do women alone, he did not do attachments of any kind, especially with humans. Becoming attached to a woman intimately and emotionally was like a death sentence to Malec, the amount of responsibility he would incur in making such a foolish mistake like a noose around his neck. Being intimate with a human might even be a fate worse than death since humans held themselves to what Malec thought was an absurd moral standard where relationships and sex were concerned. There were humans who disapproved of an official ménage relationship, even though they ran around behind their spouses' back, sleeping with whoever they pleased on a daily basis. Taking a ménage to other limits, such as the group sex some of the lycans were accustomed to, would definitely gain more recriminations from the humans.

No, thank you, very much, Malec had made his decision of what type of sexual life he would lead a long time ago. The emotional aspect becoming clear as a direct result of his twin brother's death. Mason had been the other part of Malec, and the void his twin had left had never been filled, not even by Channing or the other lycans in the pack. That part of Malec remained missing, and although the pain had been almost unbearable in the beginning, Malec believed in things happening for a greater purpose. He believed that Mason's death was an act that needed to take place in order to bring Malec to the point where he was today. A member of the Trekas pack and a part in protecting Blaez Trekas, the half-demigod, half-lycan alpha, from the forces that would conspire to take his life.

So rubbing his eyes Malec climbed out of bed and told himself once again to stop thinking about that doctor because they had bigger obstacles to overcome. Besides, it had been two days since he'd dropped the buck off to be treated, and she hadn't called him at all. He supposed that meant the buck had died. That was a shame.

It was still dark, sunrise about an hour or so away, when Malec pulled on sweatpants and a T-shirt. Bending over to tie the tennis shoes he'd also put on he wondered briefly about what could have caused the deer's injuries. As he and the vet had discussed, if it were another animal, why would it not have simply killed its prey and eaten it? Why leave it there, on the trail so that anyone running or walking by could find it?

Malec moved through the house silently as usual. Blaez and his mate, Kira, would be asleep in their wing of the dwelling the pack had redesigned and rebuilt in the last year since they'd come here to Blackbriar. The alpha and his alpha female had their own wing on one side of the residence while Channing and Malec shared the other side—Malec upstairs and Channing down. Phelan had built his own rooms as an addition to the house toward the back side on the first floor, his way of being separate, but still a part of the pack. Punching the code into the keypad at the front door disengaged the inside locks that had been installed, and Malec walked out into the early morning air.

His shoes were quiet as he crossed the wide wood-planked porch and stopped. At the top of the stairs leading down to the walkway Malec looked around. It was still dark, treetops stretching like shadowy arms up toward the sky. In the distance was the mountaintop, its majestic peak a reminder of the powerful forces of nature that surrounded them. Beyond that peak was more power and legend than anyone walking on this earth could ever imagine. The power of the gods that still ruled and wreaked havoc, still manipulated and controlled, blew as blustery as the strongest storms.

That storm was coming, Malec knew. Blaez could not hide forever. They all knew that even though they rarely spoke of it. There were two groups of lycans, the Hunters and the Devoteds. The Hunters believed and craved total dominance, but to gain that they had to be rid of the Devoteds, who would undoubtedly continue to preach their simplistic coexistence with the humans. It was the Hunters' goal to wipe out all the Devoteds so they could become the reigning lycan breed on earth. But to kill a Trekas—a direct full-blood descendent of Nyktimos, their creator—would hit the Devoteds in the very heart of their breed and would certainly be a coup any Hunter would love to brag about.

If that was their only worry Malec knew they could handle it. The Hunters were deadly in their own right, but they were no match for the elite pack that Blaez had assembled. Each of them—Malec, Channing, Phelan, and Blaez—had served in the US Marine Corps, all of them excelling to the point where their team had been called on more times than they could count to perform special covert missions. Even after they'd retired from the corps, contracted missions were being presented to them. Only in the last three years did Blaez take them off the grid.

"They're getting closer," Blaez told them one night. "Closer to finding out the truth about me and the danger I present to Zeus."

"We're trained and experienced now," Channing had spoken up. "We can take them."

Blaez shook his head. "We're talking about Zeus, *the* god of the gods. If it were not for the power of his vengeance, our breed would not exist at all."

He was right, Malec recalled thinking. It was Zeus's feud with Lykaon, ruler of Arcadia, that led to Zeus turning Lykaon into a wolf and killing all his sons. Only Nyktimos, Lykaon's youngest son, had managed to escape with Gaia's help. Lykaon, angry and bitter about his fate as a four-legged creature, eventually found his son and bit him. Not possessing the power of a god, Lykaon's bite only turned Nyktimos into a werewolf—a man who would change into a wolf only for the duration of the full moon. It was Nyktimos who fell in love with a human female, biting her and turning her into a lycan—a human breed that could not shift into a full wolf, but could take on a wolf's features—teeth, nails, facial features—and possessed the abilities of a wolf at all times, drawing more power and strength on the night of the full moon. Nyktimos's mate, Aleya, hated the change and despised him for changing her. She eventually took her own life, but only after she'd given him three children. Alex Trekas, Blaez's father, was one of them. Blaez's mother was Kharis, the daughter of Artemis. When Zeus finally learned that Nyktimos was still alive he vowed to track him and any of his descendants down and kill them. Only, just like Nyktimos, Blaez had not been there when Zeus killed his family. Thus leaving Blaez the only pure-blood lycan and demigod in all the world. And number one on Zeus's kill list.

"How long do you think we can hide?" Malec had asked Blaez that night.

"As long as we have to," had been the alpha's response. "Because I will not let Zeus take me without a fight, and I'm not certain that an all-out battle with him won't destroy this world and the one from which we originated."

That night, the three lycans had pledged their lives to Blaez and his purpose to live in harmony with the humans just like the other Devoteds. They followed Blaez to this small mountain town without anyone knowing who or what they were and vowed to protect him with everything that they possessed. Initially, their plan was to stay forever, but Malec wasn't sure that was possible, especially not now since Blaez's mate had come from a Hunter pack. Someone was bound to realize who Kira was and wonder about her father's pack that Malec, Channing, and Phelan had killed. And when the other Hunters figured that out, they'd come for them.

Clenching his fists at his sides, Malec relished the moment when that would happen.

But even that wasn't the storm he'd referred to as coming. No, this was something stronger that Malec sensed as he inhaled deeply of the fresh mountain air. This was more powerful than any Hunter could ever be.

With that thought Malec figured he'd best be prepared. To his way of thinking that meant being as physically fit as possible, and so he hurried down the steps, breaking out into a full-speed run the moment his feet hit the walkway. He was heading into the forest, where he ran each morning, and where he'd found that wounded deer two days earlier.

Malec was the fitness buff of the pack, purchasing all the equipment they had in their home gym and giving Channing tips on the healthiest foods to prepare for them—even though Channing rarely listened. And since Kira had stepped in as the alpha female of the house, Malec's healthy obsession had fallen even further, as Kira preferred to come up with her own menus, without any suggestions from health fanatics, as she liked to call him.

Long and hard, that's how he liked to run when he was alone, mastering the rough terrain with the help of his inner beast. He dodged fallen branches, moved through the trees, took steep inclines, and rounded sharp curves with prac-ticed ease, and was barely out of breath. It felt good to push himself harder and harder each day, going farther, running for longer stretches of time. It was refreshing and usually made the rest of his day much easier to cope with. What it did not do, unfortunately, was ease the sexual urges that beat at him this morning with unfettered insistency.

There were three weeks until the full moon. Twenty-one days until the night lycans were the horniest and the only night on which they could claim a mate. Five hundred and four hours of complete torture, Malec thought, if he didn't find some way to relieve this excess energy very soon. If none of them had other plans, Channing, Malec, and Phelan visited the same bar just outside of Blackbriar on the night of the full moon. It was owned by a lycan and frequented by other shape-shifters and mythological beings that walked the earth in human forms. While the moon didn't affect the other beings in the same way that it did the lycans, Selene, the moon goddess, had long ago made sure her night of crowning glory was recognized in some way by them all.

Running even faster Malec told himself that was Blaez's concern because he was the one who had claimed a mate. Fool that he was. Malec had never disrespected the alpha, but he disagreed with any lycans tying themselves emotionally and physically to another. All his other rules and beliefs aside, it was a weakness, he thought, even as Caroline's face appeared in his mind once more.

Malec despised weakness. He despised any chinks in the armor he'd built around himself, anything that another— an enemy—could use against him. Still, she not only appeared in his vision, but as he closed his eyes and tried to focus on anything else she was there.

Her voluptuous body, curving in all the right places, those tempting lips, and he couldn't forget about the piercings. His dick pulsed hard and hot against his thigh as he recollected the two beads on either side of her puckered nipple.

Malec came to a quick stop at that moment, leaning over, hands on his knees, chest pounding, but not because he was out of breath from running. No, he hadn't pushed himself that hard just yet. This time he was out of breath because the need was so strong and so urgent he couldn't take another step. Instead, he felt his body tightening, felt the need rising in his throat until he opened his mouth and howled.

The sound was loud and long and reverberated through the forest. Seconds later Malec's hand thrust quickly down the band of his sweatpants, freeing his erection. With fast motions—up and down—from base to tip, jerking so hard to a passerby it might seem painful, he gave in to the heat that had been burning in him since that day in town. Since the day he'd seen her.

Tilting his head back and closing his eyes once more Malec let the visual take shape, let it form until it filled his mind and guided his hand.

She was lying there, on that exam table where the deer had been, her hands gripping the full mounds of her breasts, the silver glint of her piercings a direct contrast to the dark tone of her skin. She played with them, lifting them until her tongue extended to stroke along the smooth skin. Malec grunted as his gaze skimmed lower to the soft span of her hips, watching as her legs spread wide and dropped to the side for him. Her pussy opened like a precious flower, her vulva lips glistening with arousal, clit hard and puckered, aching for his touch.

Malec moaned this time, moving until his back flattened against a tree, the motion of his hand on his dick never ceasing. His mouth opened as he heaved, sharp teeth elongating and pressing painfully against his lip. The beast was awake, and it was hungry, as hungry to be inside this particular female as it had ever been for another.

Oh, how he wanted to climb up on that exam table and to thrust his thick length deep inside of her, imagining her tightness clench around him until he struggled for breath.

Because that's how it would feel, he knew without a doubt. She would strangle him with her perfection, smother everything he thought he knew and wanted in this life. She was a threat—a delicious and enticing threat—that had his balls tightening and his come spewing in thick white streams in a wide arch before falling onto the forest floor.

He wasn't even finished, his dick was still hard, the need still raw and burning in his chest, as Malec threw back his head once more and howled louder and longer than he had before.

Then his head fell forward, his body caving to the exertion of running, coming, and howling in quick succession. He stood for seconds attempting to regulate his breathing and to will the hard cock away, stuffing it into his pants with an angry motion that disgusted him. He was shaking his head, trying to clear the traitorous thoughts when he heard it.

Another howl.

One in answer to his own.

Another lycan was in the forest.

No, Malec thought, standing up straight and looking all around him. He could see just as clearly in the dark as he could during the day. However, in the time he'd been out, the sun had begun to rise, creating a dusky haze that weaved its way throughout the tall lodgepole and ponderosa pine trees, falling in bright slashes along the ground.

Nothing was there.

He inhaled deeply, letting everything from the scent of the dew on the leaves to the scat of a bear miles north toward the mountain filter throughout him.

Malec shook his head again, convincing himself that he'd been hearing things because he hadn't picked up the scent of another lycan. None at all. Which meant there were no wolf hybrids in this forest. Only the true animals that belonged there. So it was quite simple, Malec thought; he was losing his mind and hearing things.

Breaking into a slow and steady jog he headed home, keeping thoughts of what he'd just done and the reason why tucked securely in the back of his mind. He'd just made it into the house when the vibrating at his hip reminded him that he'd clipped his cell phone to the band of his pants earlier.

"Zenta," he answered.

"There's another one," Caroline said, her voice husky, words coming quickly.

"Another what?"

"Another buck. It was here, wrapped in a tarp in front of the office when I arrived. And it wasn't alone. There's a lynx wrapped with it. Both of them are injured, but not dead."

Malec's teeth clenched, his hand tightening on the phone.

"I'll be right there," he said without hesitation.

He pulled up in a black Lamborghini Aventador, sliding the half-million-dollar car into the spot alongside the curb of the animal clinic as if he were parking in Manhattan instead of the small mountain town. So he was rich as well as drop-dead gorgeous, Caroline thought as she moved away from the window and headed to the front door.

There were a couple of things in this life Caroline knew without a second thought, and one of them was cars. Natalie, the foster mother that had taken her in when Max died, dated a mechanic. His name was Joey. And Joey liked

Caroline, a lot. So much that he'd been the one to take her virginity about ten minutes after she'd turned eighteen and twenty-four hours, give or take, before Natalie had put Caroline and all her stuff out on the streets. She'd stayed with Joey in his apartment above the garage for the next four months—in which time she'd learned things about herself and him that would change the rest of her life.

So Malec Zenta had to have money to own a car like that, or he was into something illegal, which she had a hard time believing considering how he cared about these animals. In her world, that type of compassion couldn't possibly come from someone who facilitated the sale of drugs to anybody who could pay, thus killing more people than he could with a loaded pistol. And again, he was fine as hell.

As she opened the door to see him standing there wearing a T-shirt and sweatpants, shades covering his eyes and that come-and-get-it-if-you-want-it look he possessed, Caroline had to take another breath. She was aroused already, she thought, moving to the side and letting him walk past her. Aroused and ready to be fucked. To some it would probably seem strange the way she could admit that to herself and not feel one ounce of recrimination. She owed that to Joey as well. He'd opened her eyes to her sexual appetite, piercing her nipples and showing her how to get the most out of her own self-pleasure. He'd been one hell of a first boyfriend, even if the word *loyalty* was like a foreign language to him. She supposed she should have known, but she was grateful for all that she'd learned in the process and thankful for the day she'd finally gotten him out of her life.

She was so grateful that she watched Malec's ass as he walked down the hallway toward the same exam room they were in before with unadulterated pleasure. He was in front of her, so he didn't see her reach a hand up to pinch her nipple and the piercing, sending a bolt of pleasure/pain shooting straight to her clit. It was a brief and mild reprieve to what felt like a building storm inside of her.

"Was there a note with them?" he asked.

Caroline shook her head as she came to a stop on the other side of the exam table, licking her lips and taking another deep breath before replying, "Not one that I saw."

He looked up at her, glasses still in place. "Where's the lynx?"

"It didn't make it," she said, her voice just a touch sadder than before. "These cuts are deeper than the ones on the other buck. That one lived after surgery, and I was able to call someone from the national park to come and retrieve it. He'll convalesce there and then be returned to the forest when he's completely healed."

He was quiet, and so she looked up from the animal to find him staring at her. No, she couldn't see his eyes through the dark lenses, but she knew he was looking at her. The heat circulating throughout the pit of her stomach rose steadily until her breasts felt full and her mouth watered. Damn, she wanted this guy, more than she thought she'd ever wanted anyone before.

"Why didn't you call me?"

She swallowed at his words, trying to assure herself that he wasn't asking on a personal level.

"For one, you weren't a paying patient. And for two, I had other paying patients in the clinic that day. I called the national park and had the buck taken care of," she replied, her words and breath coming a little too fast.

"I asked you to call me with the results of the surgery," he continued.

His tone was scolding, and from his stance and the way his head was slightly tilted toward her, Caroline got the impression that he might actually be considering spanking her too. That was ridiculous, she admonished herself. No way did this guy, with that car and that supercut body, want her, a twenty-seven-year-old stranger to this town with big hips, tits, and ass. She was certain she wasn't his type—no matter how hot he made her. Yet he had pushed up on her two days ago. She remembered that moment and the feel of his long, thick cock pressing against her ass as if it were just yesterday. She both recalled and relished it.

"Look, if I'm going to attempt to save this one, I have to get to it. And since it's still too early for my staff to be here, you're going to have to help me," she told him and then stepped away from the table to gather the tools and supplies she would need.

"This one won't live," she heard him say, and she turned around in time to see his hand splayed across the buck's stomach.

"Do you have a degree in veterinary medicine?" she asked him as she moved back to the table and put the supplies down.

"No," he told her simply. "But I know animals. His heart rate is dropping because he's lost too much blood. Like you said, the cuts were much deeper this time, almost as if it was meant for him to die."

Caroline looked down at the buck, whose breaths had gone noticeably shallower. Pulling the penlight from her jacket pocket, she looked closer into the buck's eyes, saw the

waning of life there. She lifted the earpieces of her stethoscope to her ears and leaned forward, placing the diaphragm
over the buck's stomach, just a few inches from where
Malec's hand still lay. When he didn't move, she did, going
around his hand to listen in several different locations, until,
with a heavy sigh, she pulled the stethoscope free, dropping
it onto the table.

"Why not just kill it in the forest and eat it? I don't understand," she said with a shake of her head.

Malec's hand slid off the animal slowly, his words coming
out in a measured way that had Caroline looking up at him.

"I think I do," he said.

"Really? You want to clue me in on why you think that?"
she asked.

"No," he replied quickly.

A simple, curt response that had Caroline frowning.

"Where's the tarp?" he asked, flipping gears so fast Caroline blinked in confusion.

"What?" she asked in reply.

"You said the animals were wrapped in a tarp. Someone
wrapped them up and brought them here to you. I want to
see the tarp."

She was already shaking her head. "I put it out back."

"I'll get it," he said before she could ask him another
question.

Alone with the buck, the second dead animal she'd had
the liberty of seeing before it was even eight o'clock this
morning, Caroline sighed, her heart heavy with the loss. The
one constant in her life had always been her love of animals.
From the time she was five when her mother had purchased
a hamster for her and Henny—that's what she'd named

him—had gotten sick and died, she'd known what she wanted to do with her life. She would heal the sick animals of the world and try to keep other owners from going through the agonizing pain of losing them the way she had. Of course, as she'd grown up and watched her mother die after suffering for years with cirrhosis of the liver, Caroline had understood that loss was a necessary part of life. Without it, one never learned to be grateful for what one had and to not take anything—not time, people, or circumstances—for granted.

Still, something bothered her about these two deaths and about the man that also seemed concerned. There was an element that she was missing, and that wasn't like her. Growing up with a mother who worked long hours and stayed drunk for even more, Caroline had learned early on how to take care of herself, and part of that meant being observant, meeting people, and assessing their roles in her life before they even had a chance to put their plans in motion. She'd been good at it all these years. Hell, she'd even known that Joey had wanted to have sex with her from the moment she'd walked into Natalie's house. But right now, she couldn't figure this out.

"Come here."

His voice was deep and commanding. It had been since the very first time he'd spoken to her, and Caroline was still trying to decide if that were a good or bad thing.

"Why?" she asked as she turned around to see he'd come to stand in the doorway.

"Show me where you put the tarp," he told her, his tone of voice still staying the same.

"I told you I put it outside with the rest of the trash," Caroline was saying as she walked through the door.

She'd turned to the side, sucking in every part of her body that she could so that she wouldn't touch him. She headed toward the back of the clinic. He'd left the back door open, so she pushed through the screened door and stepped outside. The words she'd been about to say died in her throat as she looked toward the big green Dumpster and then around it where she knew she'd tossed that blue tarp.

"I threw it out here," she said.

Malec had come to stand beside her, and he was sniffing. With a jerk of her head she looked at him to see what he was doing and wasn't totally shocked to see that he was indeed inhaling the air.

"It smells like trash," she told him. "And the tarp smelled like blood. The animal's blood. Only I have no idea where it could have gone. It's so early, nobody would even be back here."

"But someone was," he said, taking her by the elbow and moving her hurriedly toward the door.

"What? Wait a minute," she was saying as he pushed her through the door and shut it behind her.

"Wait just a minute," she repeated with much more authority this time. "This is my clinic. Those animals were my responsibility. I don't know what's going on around here," she said, lifting her arms to drag her fingers through her hair.

This time Malec did not speak. But he did take off his shades. He tucked them into the neckline of his shirt and took a step closer to her.

"You know something," she stated. "Are you going to tell me what's going on?"

He was moving toward her, and Caroline felt a spurt of

fear at the base of her throat. She swallowed hard, telling herself to remain calm. Malec had brought that buck to her to save, and he'd come running when she'd told him of the other wounded animals. So he obviously cared about animals. Surely that meant he wouldn't harm a human being either. She hoped.

When his hands came up, palms facing her and landing solidly on her breasts, she gasped, not sure what else to do.

"You pierced your nipples," he said through clenched teeth. "Why?"

"What?" she asked, slightly confused at his abrupt change of subject and more than a little aroused at the gruff way in which his words had been spoken.

Caroline couldn't breathe.

She couldn't speak.

All she could do was feel.

Ripples of pleasure moved like lightning bolts from the spot his hands occupied on her breasts throughout the rest of her body so fast her knees went weak.

"You—" he started to say, his fingers clenching over her breasts.

She should have pushed him away. Should have screamed how inappropriate this was. He shouldn't be touching her. And he shouldn't be enjoying it. But he was, and dammit, so was she. With every squeeze sharp bolts of pleasure soared through her, resting warmly at her clit, that pulsated and hardened as if on command. She inhaled deeply, reminding herself that this was her office and that her staff would be coming in at any moment and that . . . damn, his hands felt so good.

He watched her. His eyes like dark lasers shooting

straight into her soul as he stared without blinking, squeezed without any visible reaction to what he was doing. But that was okay, because Caroline was reacting enough for the both of them when his fingers came to squeeze her nipples, lightly at first because he knew the piercings were there. She realized that when his gaze lowered, his lips parted slightly. How had he seen them? How had he known to tweak them just the way he was, sending quick bolts of pain to her pussy that clenched and creamed in reaction?

She hissed, closing her eyes as he repeated that delightful little action again and then again.

"You tempt me," he said, his voice husky, strained.

"I—" She paused because she had no idea what she was about to say or what the hell else was going on around her, except for the quaking of her thighs and the heat washing over her.

"Don't. Tempt. Me."

His fingers left her abruptly, and she missed them instantly. He stepped back as she gaped at him.

"Call me if there are more animals," he told her before turning and walking away.

Minutes later Caroline still stood in the same spot, staring down the hallway as if she thought he might magically appear again. But he was gone, and she was still aroused.

Dammit, she was very aroused.

CHAPTER 3

"There might be something in the forest," Malec said to the rest of the pack later that evening. "Something that's attacking these animals, but not killing them."

"What makes you think that?" Blaez asked.

The alpha sat at the head of the dining room table. The nine-foot cherry oak table they'd all helped to build. In chairs made of the same oak, with sturdy high backs and the bright red cushions that Kira had purchased online because she said the wood hurt her butt after a while of sitting, each member of the Trekas pack sat after Malec had called for a meeting.

"A hunter stalks its prey. Then it goes in for the kill. A wolf, for example, hunts with its pack. They collaborate and coordinate to test their prey and sense any weaknesses it may have. They use visual clues, hearing, and scent. They don't ambush, but instead will chase their prey for long distances. Each member of the pack has a duty, a part in the overall victory. And then they act. They attack and they kill, because that's the sole purpose of the hunt."

"But these animals weren't killed," Kira said, folding her arms across her chest. "That's the key factor here."

She was thinking. For as pretty and sexy as their alpha female was, she was just as smart and cunning as her position required she be. An alpha female took care of the pack by cooking, cleaning, and organizing. She organized their attacks, working through the pros and cons before presenting the plan to the pack. She had to be cunning and deadly and still handle the insatiable sexual appetite of her alpha. In short, she was one bad bitch!

Channing smiled to himself as he thought that on an almost daily basis about Kira in the months that she'd been with the pack. In fact, he'd been the first of them to actually realize just how valuable Kira was eventually going to be to their pack. This was because she was a Selected, an alpha female that Selene had paired with a specific alpha male. These were matches that would enhance them both, creating a mighty force that could hopefully keep the peace between the warring breed.

"What type of wounds are they sustaining?" Phelan asked, his voice laced with that deadly edge that the lycan couldn't shed even on a good day.

"Slashes at the throat, wounds to the legs so they cannot get away," Malec informed them.

Channing drummed his fingers on the table, watching his closest friend and fellow pack mate, hearing what he was saying and sensing something more.

"So they've been slashed and immobilized and then left to die," he said, keeping his gaze focused on Malec.

Channing knew this lycan as well as he knew himself, if not better. He was a six-foot-one-inch, 211-pound lycan of pure muscle with pain in his soul and a darkness living inside him that manifested in his need to share his women.

For Channing, the almost polar opposite of Malec, that dark need had served a purpose for him as well. Malec had served a purpose. He'd given Channing something that Channing had never thought he would ever have—a place where he belonged. He was Malec's third, since the very first time. He was also his pack mate, the one who'd fought beside him as they'd carried out covert operations for the government and planned attacks as lycans. They were as close as any blood relatives. Which was why Channing was the only one to see that these animal deaths were only a fraction of what was eating at Malec tonight.

"Left to die on the trail where anyone could have found it. That was the first buck, the one that lived after the vet operated and shipped it off to the national park. The lynx and the buck from today, they were wrapped in a tarp and dropped off at the vet's door."

"Why were these dropped off instead of left on the trail like the other one?" Phelan asked.

"Because somebody wanted to save the animals," Blaez added.

"Or someone knew that's where Malec had taken the first animal and thought they'd do the honors this time," Kira added.

Phelan shook his head. "But why not stay there until the vet came in? Why not tell her what they'd found the same way Malec did?"

"There's something else," Malec told them, leaning forward to rest his elbows on the table. "When I was in the forest this morning I howled."

Blaez grimaced. "Was that your first time?" the alpha

asked with humor that wasn't always present in his tone. Another testament to the alpha female sitting to his right.

"There was a return call."

Malec looked at each member of the pack, knowing they would immediately connect the dots. Channing did. All of them.

"You mean there was another lycan in the forest?" Kira asked. "A lycan that answered your call even though it's not a member of our pack?"

Malec nodded.

Phelan swore.

Blaez's expression migrated to a heated glare.

Channing raised a brow. "Did you find it?"

Malec turned to him. "No. I thought I was hearing things."

"But you never hear things that aren't there," Channing said. "You're always on alert when you run, especially after our brush with the last pack of Hunters. You would have heard the reply call and hunted it down. But you didn't."

"That doesn't matter," Malec said and then frowned. "I should have hunted it down, but I didn't. I tried to scent it, but there was nothing there. Or at least I didn't pick up on it. I've been at the national park all day, visiting the first buck and going into the forest there to see if I could pick up a scent. Now, I'm going back out in our direction, and I'm not coming back until I find it."

"No, you're not," Blaez said immediately.

Everyone was silent, except for Malec.

"What the hell, Blaez? I just told you that another lycan is in the forest. Do we really want to sit here and wait until it knocks on our door, like she—"

Malec stopped, his gaze breezing past Kira before returning to the alpha's.

"Kira did not knock on our door. I found her. I was supposed to find her," Blaez said slowly, the way he always did when he didn't expect any argument from his betas. "And yes, she was a member of a Hunter pack that eventually came for her. We all know that story. What we don't know is what or who is out there now."

Malec sighed, an action that was out of the ordinary for the normally respectful beta. Phelan was the one that tended to verbally spar with Blaez the most. He was also the one that had known Blaez the longest and had been closer to the alpha, which Channing knew gave Phelan the leeway Blaez afforded him.

Blaez continued as if he hadn't heard Malec's response.

"That is why we will not go running blind into a situation we may not be able to control."

"It's one lycan," Malec countered. "I can take one damned lycan."

"Did you see it?" Blaez asked. "Did you scent it?"

Malec did not reply.

"That's what I thought, and that's why we're not running out there at this time of night. We're going to think about this and plan and go out tomorrow, prepared for whatever we may find," Blaez told him.

Kira cleared her throat, sitting up in her chair and looking over to Malec. "Let's go over everything that's happened again, and we'll start from there. You found the first buck, took it to the vet."

Malec nodded. "Her name's Caroline Douglas. She's new

in town. She said she would operate and that she would call me with the results."

Kira nodded slowly. "That was two days ago, right?"

Malec nodded also, in response.

"And she . . . Caroline . . . didn't call until this morning?" Channing asked pointedly.

A muscle in Malec's jaw twitched.

"She had two new animals this morning, the second buck and the lynx. I'd been out for my run, and that's when I'd heard the returning howl. Caroline called afterward, and I went directly into town."

"Why did you howl in the woods?" Channing asked, already knowing the answer.

Malec was extremely tense. His broad shoulders were rigid, his words coming in a clipped and testy tone. His thick eyebrows were drawn together, and that muscle twitched in his jaw each time he looked at Channing. He was horny, Channing thought instantly. Very fucking horny.

"It doesn't matter. I did and there was a return howl. I know there's a lycan out there, and I'm betting it's the one that's hurting these animals," Malec said adamantly.

Kira shook her head. "We don't hunt animals. There's no need. We don't eat them, and we can easily overpower them if they attack us. If it were one of us and the animal attacked, a Hunter or a Devoted would have simply killed it."

"But this one was left on the trail so that someone would find it, and then the others were dropped off at the vet's. Someone wants it known what they are doing, but they're not ready to reveal themselves as the culprit," Phelan offered.

"And that is why we need to get it before it does this again," Malec replied, almost vehemently this time.

Blaez nodded. "And we will. Just before dawn was when you heard it, so we'll head out tomorrow at the same time. We'll see what we can scent and, if need be, send out another call. We'll find whatever is out there to be found, and we'll deal with it. Understand?" Blaez asked Malec.

Malec nodded tightly. "Understand."

He stood from the table and walked out of the room. Channing waited only a moment before standing and following him.

"You wanna tell me the rest?" Channing said from the doorway of Malec's room.

It was always dark in there, despite the two large windows on the one wall. Custom-fit room-darkening blinds were to blame for that. Malec had insisted upon them, causing the others to tease that maybe he was actually a vampire instead of a lycan. In contrast to Channing's room, all of Malec's furniture was heavy, dark wood polished until it gleamed. His king-sized bed sat in the middle of the bedroom floor, dominating the rest of the space. Two chairs situated near the window held black leather cushions and on the small table in between, a lamp and Malec's tablet. The top of the dresser was clear but for another lamp and was where Malec had stopped to place the cell phone he removed from his sweatpants pocket and his car keys.

"There's nothing more to tell," he answered, his voice clipped and notably irritated.

Channing slipped his hands into the back pockets of his jeans. "You don't usually howl when you're running."

"I don't usually find half-dead deer when I'm running

either," Malec snapped before pulling his T-shirt up and over his head.

With a nod Channing allowed the snap and entered the room when he knew that was the last thing Malec wanted him to do. Malec Zenta liked his space. He liked to brood alone, to think about his past, and to contemplate his future. He would probably have been a loner if he had not found their pack, since he'd walked away from his family after his twin brother's death. That had been Malec's way of walking away from the breed and the "curse" as his brother, Mason, had put it, once and for all. And then he'd joined the Marines and met Blaez.

Channing had already met Blaez at an assembly in his senior year of high school. Blaez had been there speaking on behalf of the armed forces, telling the students that hadn't already decided to attend college that there was a place for them in the Marines or any of the other branches of the military. Channing had no idea what he wanted to do once he graduated, and after listening to Blaez speak he still didn't know. What Channing had known for sure was that he was going to follow that man and ask him about being a lycan because, after the strange thing had happened to him when he turned fifteen and all the research he'd done in the two years since then, Channing was certain that's exactly what Blaez Trekas was.

He hadn't had to ask Blaez a damned thing or follow him for that matter. The alpha had been standing right beside the beat-up old Toyota that Channing had saved all summer to buy. Out of twenty-two hundred students in that auditorium Blaez had recognized Channing as a beta, and that day in the parking lot he'd brought him into his pack.

As for Malec, he'd come along about six months later, after Channing was halfway through basic training. Malec had just been transferred to their barracks, and before he could change out of his street clothes Blaez had called Malec to meet with him, Phelan, and Channing. And from that moment the Trekas pack was complete.

The bond between Malec and Channing had grown steadily, if not begrudgingly, from that moment on. Malec was a constant storm while Channing considered himself the calm aftermath. There could not be one without the other.

"You need to relax," Channing told him. "Why don't we go out?"

Malec paused. He'd been on his way into his bathroom when he turned to look at Channing.

"You've been going out without me. Why ask now?"

"I know when to leave you alone," Channing replied. "And when you need to find release before you really hurt someone or yourself."

Malec shook his head. "You know that's not me."

No, it wasn't, Channing thought. Malec's twin had committed suicide because he couldn't handle a life of being a lycan, being different from the majority of the world and the burden of keeping that secret. On the other hand, Malec owned who and what he was, and while he didn't wear it as a medal of honor the way Channing had come to look at it, he accepted his responsibilities, and he'd made a commitment to Blaez. There was no way he would ever do any intentional harm to himself.

But he had been denying himself release for weeks now, ever since they'd battled Kira's father's pack. Two full moons had passed in that time, two cycles of power and lust that would drive a normal lycan insane. *Repressed* was not an accurate enough word for what his friend was going through right now. Which was probably the real reason for his howling in the forest this morning. Malec was horny. He needed to get laid like yesterday, and if there was another of their kind in the forest, it was a dead lycan walking if Malec didn't get ahold of his frustrations before tomorrow when they all went out into the forest to find it.

"Be ready in twenty," Malec finally answered, turning away from Channing again and slamming the bathroom door closed behind him.

Channing would be ready, he thought as he walked out of Malec's room. He just hoped whichever female they hooked up with tonight was ready as well. He had a feeling this was going to be a very long night.

CHAPTER 4

Malec saw her the moment he walked into the bar.

Or rather, his dick recognized the plump curve of her ass in the tight skirt that barely scraped along her knees. He was hard instantly, his body reacting to the sight of her standing at the bar, one hand propped on her hip as she talked to the bartender and the female standing in front of her. Her waist curved in, giving her one hell of an hourglass silhouette. He already knew that a frontal view would show her generous breasts, and if her top was as tight as her skirt he would surely see the imprint of her nipple piercings once more.

He licked his lips and began to walk, even more confident than usual, because tonight, he knew he wasn't alone.

The bar was crowded tonight, probably because of the hot new band Channing told him was playing this week. Malec didn't keep up with music or who was hot and who was not. The only reason he paid any attention to the news at all was because they needed to stay abreast of what was going on in the world now that the Shadow Shifters had been unveiled. The humans knew there were shape-shifters living among them, men and women who looked like them at first glance but could change in the blink of an eye to a big, ferocious, and deadly cat. This knowledge had been out for a year now, the Shadow Shifters scattering all over the world, some in hiding and others braving the world in the hopes that no one would ever see them shift. But the delicate balance between humans and the otherworldly had been tipped, which meant it was only a matter of time before all the shit hit the fan.

For tonight, however, the only thing Malec wanted to think about was how enticing Dr. Caroline Douglas would look naked and oiled from head to toe, lying dead center in his bed, ready to be fucked by both him and Channing.

"Let's dance," he said, coming to a stop directly behind her.

She turned quickly, as if he'd startled her, and Malec frowned.

"Oh, hello," she replied, the smile she'd had slipping as she licked her lips nervously. "I was going to call you in the morning. I found something else on the buck after you left."

He wanted to hear what she had to say about the animal, but not as much as he wanted to feel his body up against hers, immediately. There was a war going on inside him right now. The one where he had a duty, a greater concern going on than the throbbing in his pants. Yet that throbbing was diluting all his thoughts and actions, pushing him to do whatever was necessary to seek relief.

"Tell me while we dance," he said through clenched teeth, feeling as if he'd come to a great compromise.

Malec took her hand then, lacing his fingers through hers, jolting only slightly at the oddly intimate response to that touch. He began walking across the dance floor, totally ignoring the girl that had been with Caroline as she gaped at him. It was the receptionist, Olivia, from the clinic; he knew that much because she'd looked at him pretty much the same way when she'd seen him two days ago. They all looked at him like that, Malec thought. The females in Blackbriar, whenever he ventured into town, stared at him like they wanted to say something but couldn't. He wondered briefly if they thought he might be a Shadow Shifter. The thought made him chuckle inside because he was so much more.

A song was playing, something slow and sexy, instrumental. The dance floor area was dim, patrons sitting at their tables ordering drinks while they waited for the entertainment. But Malec walked them to the middle of the floor, turning and grabbing Caroline around the waist immediately. He pulled her close, his arms tightening around her, blood pumping quickly through his body, landing in all the important places. His hips thrusting against her body was proof of that.

She looked up in surprise, her lips forming a small o before she sighed.

"So," she said slowly as Malec began swaying to the seductive rhythm. "As we discussed before, the cuts in this deer's neck were deeper than the other one. It was a wonder its head remained connected at all. Each one of the cuts was deeper—that's why there was so much blood. After that I thought I should check the lynx again, and it was the same— much deeper cuts this time. It looked almost violent."

Malec's hands were at the small of her back, his fingers itching to go lower, to splay wide and possessively over the curve of her ass. He heard every word she spoke in the husky tone of her voice. He watched her lips moving, glossed with a red hue this evening that matched her blouse. Her hair was an array of curls, falling down past her shoulders, lying seductively over her luscious breasts.

"He meant for them to die this time," he stated, once again his thoughts—lustful and contemplative—comingling until he did not bother to monitor his words.

"'He'? You think a man did this?" she asked.

Malec stared at her then. He let himself focus on how close she was to him, breasts and pussy pressed up against him as if she wanted him as much as he wanted her.

On impulse, he jutted his hips forward. "Do you feel that?" he asked her, completely changing the subject.

She licked her lips. "I do."

"Do you want it?"

She hesitated.

"Don't lie to me," he whispered. "I'll know if you're lying."

"What is it you think I'm going to say?" was her next question.

"You're going to deny it," Malec told her. "But it will be a lie."

His hands did flatten on her ass then, moving down to press her even closer to him. He just barely resisted the urge to moan when he saw the lycan over her shoulder.

A part of Malec settled into familiar territory as he'd known Channing would appear. This was how they worked, what they were used to. Now, it was time for Caroline to see, to experience the pleasure they had in store for her.

"You think you know everything, don't you?" she asked. "You think because I'm not arguing about you rubbing your hard dick against me that I must want you in my bed."

Passion and fire, confidence and strength. He'd sensed it all in her from the moment he first stepped into the room with her at her office. She'd drawn him in, Malec would not deny, and now, he would have her.

"It doesn't have to be in a bed," he quipped.

She swallowed hard but did not break eye contact with him. Nor did she try to pull away.

"If I wanted you, Malec Zenta, I wouldn't lie about it," she said, her words sending bolts of desire cutting straight through to Malec's skull.

"Is that so?" he asked.

She nodded. "That is so. I have no problem stating what I want, when I want it. None at all."

Channing stepped up to her at that moment. Malec moved his hands to her hips, as he knew that Channing's groin would now press into the delicious curve of her ass. They surrounded her, giving her no room to run or to deny their intentions.

"Tell me what you want right now," Malec prompted.

She gasped then, as Channing reached around her, touching a heavy curl of her hair before letting it fall again, slowly moving his hand away from her breast.

"We're here to give you whatever you need," Malec continued. "Pleasure like you've never imagined."

The music had stopped, or at least Malec no longer heard it. All he could hear now was the rapid beating of her heart, the hitch in her breath. He could sense the hardness in Channing's body, the heat forming between him and Caroline, circling around the three of them as they stood in the middle of the dance floor. It was immediately intense and damned intoxicating, spurring the hunger inside him.

This was exactly what he needed. Having her between them right at this moment was proof of that fact. He'd been denying it for weeks, withholding the pleasure he needed to keep himself steady. It was a careful balance Malec kept, walking slowly along the tightrope of his life and his duties. They warred with everything he knew and all he'd experienced, until only this—the threesome—could bring him any type of solace. His body vibrated with need as he watched her, inhaled her scent, and craved like he never had before.

"This dance is over," she said abruptly, slipping from between them and making her way across the room.

For a moment Malec stood staring after her, watching as she headed toward the ladies' room. She couldn't walk away. She could not deny him. Not this, not when he knew damned well that she wanted it. But when he took a step to go after her Channing grabbed his arm.

"Let me guess," Channing said with an arch of his brow. "That's Caroline."

Malec looked at him, saw everything the beta was thinking in his eyes, and continued.

"That's the one I want for tonight," he told Channing.

Channing nodded, certain he'd already known those words were coming. "Then I'll go talk to her. See if she's game."

"No," Malec replied adamantly. "I'll do it."

For a second Channing looked confused. Malec understood why. Channing was the talker, the charmer. He got their permission, and he handled the aftercare. It was his personality to take care of people, and he did it so well. When they'd begun sharing women, it was a given that this was what he'd do.

Yet this time Malec wanted to try.

"That's not how we work," Channing reminded him. "What if you frighten her?"

"I won't frighten her, dammit! I'm not a monster, and I know how to talk to a woman," Malec replied emphatically through gritted teeth. Channing continued to stare in question, a look that was really beginning to piss Malec off.

"You sure about that, buddy?" Channing asked with a knowing smirk, his grip still on Malec's arm.

Malec inhaled deeply, releasing the breath slowly. The tension was real, the need pressing against him like hundreds of boulders, until every part of him ached. "I've got this," he told Channing. "Just be ready."

Channing hesitated only a moment longer before giving a shrug of his shoulders and stepping to the side. Malec crossed the room not giving a damn about the people who stared at him now. With long, purposeful strides he entered that dark hallway, stopping just short of the ladies' room door where she was about to enter. She stopped as well, as if she'd known he would follow her, and then turned around to face him.

There was no hesitation and no invitation, but Malec stepped forward, wrapping an arm around her waist and pulling her close once more. He cupped a hand over her breast and lowered his head.

And then he kissed her.

Mouth open, tongue delving deep to tangle with hers. He fell into the kiss instantly, ignoring that warning bell that sounded resolutely through his mind, screaming at him to remember one of his golden rules where women were concerned: absolutely no kissing.

Caroline felt like she'd boarded a roller coaster, expecting a fast and exhilarating ride, but was experiencing quick twists and turns and finally a steep downward drop that left her breathless and aroused as hell.

Malec was kissing her as if she were the next-best thing to breathing. He was palming her breasts similar to the way he had at the clinic, and he was holding her tightly against him, silently telling her she had no chance of getting away.

Strange thing was, she did not want to get away from him. That was the first thing Caroline thought as she opened herself to his kiss, wrapping her arms around his neck to pull him down closer. He smelled like fine wine tasted, delectable. He felt like every erotic dream she'd ever had all rolled into one. There was no doubt he would know how to stroke her, to touch her, taste her until she came strong and hard enough to last for a thousand years. He was that type of guy.

But he hadn't been alone.

He'd said "we," and there had been another guy's dick pressed up against her ass. Forget the arousal she'd felt at that moment, and now, for that matter. What mattered most was the realization that came barreling into her mind like a ferocious storm.

This man was going to make her lose everything she'd worked so hard to this point to get.

Blackbriar was Caroline's second chance. It was the place where no one knew about her or the affair she'd had with Brent, the very married and eventually confessed gay doctor at the previous animal hospital she'd worked at. That scandal had erupted and exploded with a devastating ferocity back in Portland. She'd not only lost her job, but her friends and a good chunk of her savings that she'd had to spend paying the attorney. Brent's wife had filed a lawsuit against her for the pain and suffering her sordid affair—coupled with the illicit pictures of her and Brent that were revealed—had caused. It was a nightmare, and Caroline had spent the last year of her life figuring out where to go and how best to move on and to find another place to belong and to fit in.

This was all too familiar for Caroline.

So regardless of how good he felt and how much she wanted to continue this little tryst, she would not . . . unless it was on her terms.

A quick glimpse at the second guy as she'd turned to leave gave her a snapshot of a tall, slimly built man with his own measure of muscles and eyes that for just an instant had beckoned to her. His gaze had been intense and, as she recalled the feel of his hard length against her backside, hers had faltered.

Caroline pulled back from Malec at that moment, letting her hands fall to her sides as she looked away. He was still holding her, still rubbing his finger over her hardened nipple, which was damned distracting as she tried to get her thoughts together. This wasn't what she wanted—even though her body was definitely sending other more agreeable messages. Giving into these urges was dangerous. It could destroy her in the end; she knew that without any doubt and had sworn to be smarter the next time—*this* time.

"I'm not into that," she said with finality.

"Into what?" he asked. "Pleasure?"

Her head snapped up as she met his gaze.

"Kinky and socially unacceptable acquaintances that could cost me my job. Been there and done that," she quipped. "Don't care to do it again."

"But you want to," Malec said as if he heard her, but

heard something else as well. "You want every bit of plea-sure we can give you."

"What can *you* give me, Mr. Zenta?" she asked in re-sponse, shocking even herself when she reached forward and cupped his thick erection. He obviously wanted her, and he was right, she did want him. So why couldn't it just go that way? Why did it have to involve more? A quick and po-tent bolt of desire shot straight to her clit at that thought, and Caroline bit her bottom lip to keep from crying out.

Warmth immediately spread through her palm, her pussy creaming as if she'd pressed some magic button granting permission.

"That and then some," was his confident response.

"Then let's go," Caroline offered. "You and me. My place is just a few minutes from here."

"Great," said the smooth and sexy-as-hell voice from behind. "The sooner we get there, the sooner I can make you scream."

She didn't feel him pressing against her this time, but he was still close. His hands rubbed up her thighs, lifting her skirt with the motion. The skirt was tight, a very thick Ly-cra material that smoothed all her curves and gave her a neat and voluptuous look. And her ass was round enough to make lifting that skirt all the way up just a little more difficult than anyone could anticipate.

Caroline was very thankful for that at the moment.

Or was she?

His hands felt just as good as Malec's had. Even if she wanted to ignore that thought, the quick shake of her thighs was a dead giveaway. And he smelled good. His cologne mix-ing with the very masculine scent that permeated from Malec.

Yes, Malec.

She looked up at him then, saw that his eyes had grown even darker, his fingers toying with her nipple piercings.

"You like his hands on you too," he said to her, his voice going lower, deeper. "His hands and my hands equal nothing but pleasure, Caroline. Exquisite and undeniable pleasure. That's what you deserve. It's what you want."

"No," she said in what sounded like the weakest voice she'd ever heard in her life. "It's not."

She was shaking her head, even as the one behind her slipped his hands around to touch the inside of her thighs. Either she'd backed up or he'd stepped forward, but she could feel his arousal once again. Hard and long, rubbing against the slit of her bottom, giving her the urge to bend over and let him inside. Caroline shook her head again, harder this time.

She swallowed, closed her eyes, and opened them again. "Malec."

Hell, even whispering his name was arousing her, as she imagined saying it while he was deep inside of her, riding her until all she could think about was that pleasure he'd promised. Her hand had slipped away from his dick, but her palms were warm as she recalled feeling the hardness there.

"I can't," she said. "Please."

Malec paused, his features freezing, passion locked in his gaze even as a muscle twitched in his jaw.

It occurred to Caroline at this very moment that no matter how hard she tried, she always seemed to end up in the same predicament. It was the one where she needed to decide whether or not to follow the desires and urges she'd felt since she was too young to really know what they were.

Or to take the education she was still paying for and finally create some semblance of a "normal" life for herself.

Max had been faced with that same decision, and she'd seemed perfectly fine with it. Unfortunately, her mother's choice had led to a life of chastisement, judgment, and embarrassment for Caroline. And after Max's death, getting involved with Joey, the older and more experienced man who had taken her virginity and broken her heart, hadn't done anything to garner a better reputation for Caroline.

There was no way she ever wanted to make those mistakes again. Absolutely no way.

So with every bit of strength she could muster Caroline moved to the side, severing the grip Malec's friend had on her.

"Good night, Mr. Zenta," she said finally, and when he still hadn't found his words, the arousal vibrating like a thousand pinpricks throughout her body threatened her resolve.

It was she who turned away from him, looking this time into stunning blue eyes that had also grown darker with desire, his lips twisting slightly in what she thought may have been an apologetic gesture.

"And good night to you too," she said to him, before clearing her throat and pulling her skirt down.

"He takes some getting used to," the friend said after Caroline had taken a few steps away from the twosome.

Oh god, why couldn't they just go away! Why couldn't they both simply walk away and let her get into this bathroom to do whatever she could to relieve the ache he—no, they'd—caused. With a sigh, Caroline stopped and turned, expecting to see them both and already willing herself to turn them down again.

She noticed his eyes once again. What was it about them that always drew her in? They were softer now, cornflower blue, she would call them. Wise beyond the thirtysomething years of age she pegged him at. And just one facet of a very handsome face. He wore a beard, neatly cut and not too thick, his hair was short also, almost shaved on the sides, longer at the top. He was Malec's friend, and he'd aroused her too. Damn.

"If you say so," she replied with a shrug as if she didn't care. When the truth was, Caroline thought she just might care a little too much.

"I've known him for a long time, and he's really a good guy," he continued. "And he wasn't lying. We could bring you pleasure you've never experienced before. But only if you're open to it."

He was about the same height as Malec, his body more on the slim, athletic-build side in comparison to Malec's blatantly muscular physique. Where Malec appeared darker in complexion and personality, this guy was lighter, with his olive-hued skin and dusky brown hair. He wore jeans that fit as if custom made for him and a shirt, long-sleeved, white, gripping him like a second skin. Yeah, he was definitely attractive in that breath-stealing superhero type of way.

"What makes you so sure I'm a stranger to pleasuring myself?" she asked, but then held up a hand before he could reply. "Look, Mr.—"

"Verdi," he offered with a quirk of his lips. "I'm Channing Verdi."

Channing Verdi and Malec Zenta. Even their names piqued her interest.

"Mr. Verdi, I am well versed in pleasure and in kink, so

please don't think I'm a prude. I'm simply not up for what you and your friend are offering. I hope you take no for an answer better than he does."

"Actually," Channing said, stepping closer, but stopping before she would consider him too close. "We're not in the business of forcing anyone to do anything. But if you're telling the truth about your experience with pleasure, you won't be able to hold out for long. So I'll bid you a good night and tell you that when you're ready, you know where to find us."

This one didn't just turn his back and walk away. No, he moved at a much slower pace, taking backward steps while keeping his heated gaze on her, until it was necessary for him to turn and walk through the doorway leading back to the bar.

When he did, all Caroline could do was sigh and lean against the wall.

Malec Zenta had left her nipples tingling, her lips and tongue still tasting his mouth. While Channing Verdi and the memory of his hands on her had left her wet and achy and damned intrigued. They were a very dynamic duo, she thought moments later when she'd finally steadied her breathing. Dynamic and sexy as hell.

What had Malec told her earlier today? Don't tempt him. Hell, he and his friend were doing a damned fine job of tempting the hell out of her.

CHAPTER 5

"We've been waiting for you, pretty boy," Phelan snapped the moment Malec finally emerged from his room. "You finished getting all dolled up?"

They were all sitting in the living room, across from the huge stone fireplace. Waiting, as Phelan had just stated, for him. And not pleased by that fact, he surmised from all the eyes that were now on him.

"Bite me," was Malec's quick reply as he kept moving toward the front door. "Let's get going before the sun comes up."

"And now he rushes us," Phelan was saying, but Malec didn't turn to address him again.

He was cranky as hell, his body rigid with the release he'd been denied last night. It was the first time Malec had ever been turned down. The first time he and Channing had been turned down for a threesome. To be fair, it was the first time they'd approached a human, which could have had a lot to do with the response they'd received. But Malec wasn't in the mood to be fair.

His balls were so tight and sore, his dick remaining hard no matter how many times he cursed Caroline's name and her succulent lips. He'd wanted those lips on his cock last night. After he'd kissed her in that dark hallway, that fact had only been further cemented into his mind. But when Channing had come back to the truck alone, Malec had known that wasn't meant to be. He thrust the key into the ignition with all the pent-up energy that woman and her denial of them had caused and was cursing when Channing climbed into the passenger side.

"Should have known better," Malec had said as he pulled out of the parking lot. "Should have known not to fuck with a human."

A few moments later Channing had replied, "You should have known better than to approach her on your own. That's not how we normally work."

"She's not our normal target," Malec had snapped, his temples throbbing with the headache he knew would stay with him throughout the night.

"I agree with that part," Channing said. "She's a human, and that makes her totally different from the others. But she's sexy as hell. Her ass was so soft and pliant. I wanted to pull up her skirt up and fuck her right there in that hallway."

Malec groaned at the thought. He would have loved to watch Channing taking Caroline from behind, watching the pleasure on her face as Channing moved slowly in and out of her, stretching her wider and wider. That was one of his favorite things about a ménage: he could watch the woman receive pleasure. When he was the one giving it to her, it was sometimes hard to see it firsthand, but watching, hell, that made him even hotter than participating.

Even with that thought, Malec knew without a doubt that he wanted to be inside of Caroline Douglas. He wanted her mouth on him and his on her. He wanted her much more than he should have, and that caused him even more worry than the matter at hand.

"You good?" Channing asked, coming up beside him as they walked into the forest.

"I'm fine," Malec replied.

"You're a horrible liar," Channing continued. "But if it makes you feel any better, I think she's going to come around. I could see it in her eyes last night. She wants us."

Malec was on the verge of groaning out loud at that thought when a scent hit him, and he went completely still. His head lifted to the early morning air, nose twitching as he inhaled deeply.

"He's here," Malec announced seconds before his teeth elongated, forehead stretched, and sideburns grew thick.

A low, deadly growl came next as sharp nails extracted from his fingers. Beside him, Channing must have picked up the same scent because his lycan also appeared, eyes glowing a vivid light blue in the dark of the forest.

"This way," Blaez said, stepping before Malec and Channing, taking his place at the front of the pack.

His dark hair had grown longer with his shift, body even broader than usual as he stood staring into the depths of the forest, looking for the one that carried the scent.

"Another lycan," Phelan added with a growl, his lycan the most menacing looking of them all, with his bushy brows, bright eyes, and perpetual scowl.

The lycans moved together this time, each of them looking in a different direction, spreading out so that they formed a circle with Blaez front and center.

The forest had gone totally quiet. They were at a higher

elevation here, near tree lines, so there were various animals that occupied this space. But in the last seconds there had been no nutcrackers squawking loudly or thumping their wings audibly, no rubber boas slinking along still attempting their nocturnal hunting habits before the sun made its appearance. There was also no movement from the bigger mammals in the area, the deer, elk, or lynx, likely because they all knew the lycan stranger was there too. And they knew what he was capable of.

His scent was strong, filtering through the moist air. Malec inhaled deeply, closing his eyes and opening all his senses to this task. The lycan was here. Malec could not only smell him, he could hear the insistent pounding of its heart. His eyes opened with that thought, head turning quickly in one direction, where he immediately caught sight of another pair of glowing eyes. Malec took off running. "Over here!" he yelled to the others.

They all moved through the lines of trees, standing tall and proud in this majestic setting. Their feet might have made a sound over the leaves and dirt-lined forest floor, but for the speed in which lycans moved when running. If someone were watching they'd barely see a blur of movement, not the human bodies with wolf features traveling quickly through the early morning.

He'd only seen eyes at first, and then they were gone. It was running, Malec thought, and he was damned sure going to catch it this time.

Cutting through the closely lined trees, jumping over downed branches, teeth bared and chest pumping with adrenaline, he moved with only one thought in mind—catch this sonofabitch!

Channing howled, the sound cutting through the haze of fury and determination in Malec's mind. The howl came again, and Malec turned in that direction. He moved toward his pack mate, at the signal that beckoned to each of them. Coming to an abrupt stop in a clearing near a grass-covered ledge that dropped down to a waterfall and the rolling creek that dumped into Blackfoot River.

"It was here," Channing said, pointing down to a large rock near the edge of the cliff.

The others closed in, each looking down at the huge slab of rock that protruded from the ground. Blaez knelt there, rubbing his clawed fingers over the scratches that cut right through the hardened surface. Malec knelt beside him, glaring down at the markings that looked just like the ones he'd seen on the deer and the lynx.

"It's him. He's the one attacking the animals," Malec said.

Blaez nodded. "He's a Solo."

The admission had Malec's head turning sharply to the alpha. "Are you sure?"

Another slow nod and a low growl from Blaez. "I'm positive. These are the only markings. There's only one scent. He's acting alone, without an alpha's direction. Without a pack."

"Dammit!" Phelan roared from behind them. "First Hunters and now a fucking Solo. What next?"

As if in answer to his loudly spoken question, there was an awful screeching sound that echoed throughout the air. Above, the still-dark sky crackled with deep, booming thunder before a bright stream of green shone down like a pathway. From the brightness the screeching came again, and then the huge black-and-gold wings that flapped in the air as the bird made its quick and loud descent to where the lycans stood.

"Shit!" Phelan cursed, stepping in front of Blaez.

Malec came to his feet, turning his back to Blaez and blocking him just as Phelan had. Channing stood to the other side so that Blaez was out of view.

The bird, larger than anything he'd ever seen before, swooped down, landing its taloned feet on the ground with a thud that shook them like an earthquake. Its head was that of a human, turning back and forth, beady black eyes glaring, and long golden hair flowing down its back. It opened its mouth and screeched again. Phelan lunged forward first, and the harpy extended a huge wing, knocking him back on his ass. Both Channing and Malec roared at that point, snapping their hands down at their sides so that the sound of their sharp claws releasing was a warning for the bird.

Phelan was hurrying to his feet as Malec felt a nudge behind his legs. A glance down showed that Blaez had shifted into his wolf form. He was large and black with eyes like bright blue jewels.

The bird screeched once more before lifting off its feet, landing right next to Phelan. The lycan swung at the bird's human face, only to receive another swat by the harpy's wing, and this time the attack of its talons scraped over his chest as he fell back to the ground. Channing and Malec ran toward the bird with the thought of assisting Phelan, but the lycan jumped to its feet once more.

"Tell Eureka I said to kiss my ass!" Phelan spat at the bird, this time using his claws when he swiped at the wing that had twice knocked him down.

The sharp nails nicked the bird, sending feathers flying

and the bird howling in pain before lifting from the ground and flying back into that eerie green abyss. In the next seconds they were ensconced in darkness once more, the quiet of the forest surrounding them.

"What the hell was that?" Channing asked.

Phelan was clearly not pleased as he stared down at his ripped shirt before looking back at them. "A freakin' harpy," he replied distastefully.

"Looking for you?" Malec asked.

"No, although I've met this particular one before," Phelan replied. "She's probably looking for Blaez and was most likely sent by Zeus, which means he knows Blaez is close by."

Channing nodded then. "That's why he shifted so that she wouldn't recognize his lycan form. They have no idea he's a demigod and what that means."

"But they know he's in this area now, most likely because of those Hunters we killed. They know they're close to a Devoted pack," Phelan said.

"And so does the Solo," Malec added.

Caroline was having a shitty morning.

Really, from the two pairs of stockings she'd ripped because she'd thought wearing a skirt into the office was a good idea, to the weird and awful sound her car had made during the entire ride to work. And now, to Olivia's incessant commentary on what happened last night and what she believed should happen next.

"You guys totally looked like you were about to strip naked and get it on right in the middle of the dance floor," she was saying, one leg crossed over the other, red polished toenails sparkling through the open-toed sandals she wore.

Caroline continued to act like she wasn't paying attention, while wishing there actually was a button she could push that would totally tune out the woman's voice. Problem was, there wasn't, and so she heard everything Olivia was saying and felt as if someone was dragging several pieces of chalk annoyingly down the chalkboard.

"I mean, I'm not as repressed as some of the folks around here, and I gotta admit that seeing those two hot-ass guys get it on with a woman—even if said woman is my boss—was hella arousing," Olivia continued. "And the way you were standing there, I thought you were totally into it."

"I was into the dance," Caroline tried to rebut.

"Uh-huh," Olivia replied. "I think you were trying to make it seem like that until finally you just had to get away. But I'm telling you that you should go out to that lodge and see them. If not, you should definitely go for the Malec guy, the one that keeps coming in here, because he's got a thing for you. I can see the way he looks at you when he's in here, and believe me that look has nothing to do with the animals.

"The other guy," Olivia continued, uncrossing her legs to turn toward the desk and the phone that was ringing on it, "he's sexy too. Did you see his eyes? Like he's looking right into your soul, and when he smiles, ahhh, swoon." She ended with a sigh before grabbing the phone and rushing through the greeting.

Caroline would have taken this opportunity to escape, but Olivia finished with the call too quickly.

"You know I told you that people are curious about what they're doing out there, right?" Olivia asked her.

Caroline looked up and over to where Olivia's desk was situated in the front part of the office. Caroline had taken refuge off to the side, behind a counter where the file cabinets were housed. She'd made files for each of the animals that had died because she'd wanted to be completely thorough in her documentation. Now she had to file them, but the system that Olivia had instituted was beyond any alphabetical or numerical filing system Caroline had ever encountered.

"Who is curious about what who is doing?" she asked, hoping to maybe confuse Olivia into being quiet. It didn't work.

Olivia sighed in exasperation.

"The hot guys that live out there in that lodge. They're, like, surrounded by the woods too. You can't even see their place until you're right up on it. Ernie, he delivers the mail, and he says whenever he has to go out there, he's totally focusing on his GPS because he'd get lost on those dark back roads, and you have to actually drive through a road they created that goes right into the woods.

"Anyway," she said with a wave of her hand. "That was Nora Bentley from the beauty shop. She was at the bar last night, and she wanted to know if you spent the night with either—or both—of those guys."

Caroline almost groaned. But she'd learned a long time ago to not let the ignorant gossipers know that their words were cutting her like a hot blade. Without even realizing it she'd squared her shoulders and come to a complete stand.

"First of all, who I sleep with or take home is none of Nora's or anyone else's business. And second, it's just rude for her to call here and ask you those types of questions.

This is a place of business, and I will not have gossip running in and out of here like we're . . . well, for lack of a better comparison . . . the beauty parlor."

"Don't get all snippy," Olivia said, raising her hands as if in surrender.

Caroline wished.

"I'm just telling you what she said. And anyway, they're just curious. We all are. Aren't you?"

"No," Caroline snapped quickly. "I don't want to know anything that I shouldn't."

The phone rang again, and this time Caroline did walk out of the reception area. She was heading back to her desk when she heard the knock at the back door and frowned. Their office hours were clearly printed on the front window, and the front door was open. So why was someone knocking at the back door?

With an exasperated sigh of her own now because—despite that she hated what Olivia and now apparently Nora from the beauty shop had been saying—she had tossed and turned all last night thinking about those two guys and how attracted she'd been to both of them. How a part of her, a deep and probably depraved part, had actually entertained thoughts of them together. Those thoughts had come in the late hours of night as she'd lain alone in her bedroom and had eventually moaned with how vivid and exciting the thoughts had actually been.

Shaking her head Caroline told herself not to go there. That nothing good could come of letting down her guard and acting on those dark desires again. She had to be smarter this time and stronger. Yes, she was going to have to be much stronger to resist those two and stand her ground.

Yanking open the back door Caroline silently reminded herself of those facts, just before gasping at what she saw on the steps.

Caroline was a vet, after all, so the sight of a wounded animal should not have rendered her silent, her heart hammering in her chest as if she were waiting for something else. When it whimpered, she immediately went to her knees, scooping it and the blanket it had been lying on up into her arms. She hurried back to an exam room, carrying the animal and calling out to Olivia for assistance. Martin had asked for the day off, and Caroline had quickly given permission since she was already nursing a bad mood, and the guy really was a pain in the ass to be around.

Now, she thought with another sigh as she finally placed the animal onto the examining table, she was chastising herself for letting her mood override her professionalism.

Pulling back the blanket told Caroline a couple of things: one, that the dog—a liver-colored pointer—had been badly cut, so much so that blood was oozing from everywhere and she had yet to see the actual wound; and two, there was a plastic bag, now covered in blood, with a piece of paper inside of it. Reaching over the still-moaning dog, she lifted the bag. Alarmed by the sight of the blood, Caroline began to read the note through the plastic.

It's your turn to make a delivery. Take this to those in the cabin by the forest. They'll know what to do to save it.

Below that was an address and driving directions to the very house that Olivia had been speaking about just moments before. She knew this because Olivia had typed the address into the computer that morning while she'd been talking about Malec and his friends. Caroline ignored the fact that she'd actually remembered it.

"Yuck. What happened to him?" Olivia said, coming into the office.

"I don't know." Caroline's mind was whirling with possibilities, all of which kept circling back to the fact that Malec Zenta was involved. "Get some towels and a bucket of warm water. We're gonna need to clean him up a little first so I can see what's going on."

"He sounds like he's dying," Olivia said in direct contradiction to the slow way in which she moved to do Caroline's bidding.

"He just might if we don't hurry up," Caroline insisted, lifting one and then the other of the dog's eyelids.

What the hell was that note about? Caroline thought as she moved. Who sent it, and what did "those in the cabin by the forest" have to do with killing animals? Or dying animals? Shaking her head, Caroline decided she couldn't think about that note or Malec or any of that stuff right now. She needed to save this dog. Damn, she really needed to save this dog, today of all days. With that in mind she began focusing on stopping the bleeding and preventing any type of infection from ensuing as a result of the very cleanly made cuts that looked as if something or someone had sliced right through this dog's stomach for no other reason besides that it could.

For the next twenty minutes Caroline worked as if her life depended on it, doing everything in her power to save the dog that had its guts just about ripped out by some sick bastard. On the inside she was trembling when she finished the sutures. Knowing the dog had already taken its last breath brought tears to her eyes, and to Olivia's, who had already run from the room, only seconds after the dog had ceased breathing. Her hands remained steady as she tied off that last stitch and dropped the needle into the pan of discarded tools and gauze. Bringing her forearm to her face she swiped the beads of sweat from her forehead and took a not-so-steady step back.

Someone had mortally wounded this dog, and the perpetrator had wanted her to see it die. The perpetrator had also wanted the guys in that cabin to see it. Closing her eyes and taking a deep breath Caroline admitted she might be in over her head. She'd been in this town for only six weeks, and animals were being dropped at her door to die. There was something wrong with that. And soon the rest of the town would be saying the same thing.

She would be talked about and judged, even when she'd done nothing wrong, and that was not acceptable. She had to do something before this situation became out of control.

But what?

Her gaze returned to the books that were stacked against the windowsill. That's where she'd stuck that note that had come with the dog because she hadn't wanted Olivia to see it. Moving slowly, as if still dazed by all that had happened, Caroline retrieved the note, reading the typed words one more time.

It took her a few minutes to wrap the dog in the blanket it had been delivered in and lock it inside a crate. She grabbed that letter and the crate and went back to her office to get her purse. From there she called up to the front desk to tell Olivia to cancel the remaining appointments for the day and to close the clinic because she was about to make a home visit and she didn't know how long she would be gone. She did not tell Olivia where that home visit was for fear of a repeat report on how fine the men out at that house were and how much Olivia wanted one of them.

Caroline left through the back door because she'd wanted to look around back to see if whoever had dropped this dog off—the same person she was guessing had dropped off the buck and lynx yesterday—had left something behind that could identify him or her. She told herself it could also be a woman, but she was really betting on a vicious, sociopathic man for this crime. There was nothing, she thought with growing concern. Not even tire marks from a car. Nothing was on the steps. Nothing was out of place. She looked up and down the back alleyway, which was more like a small street with another building about twenty feet on the other side. She wondered if anyone over there had seen anything. Should she go knock on those doors and ask those business owners? Something told her that would be futile. Besides, a part of her was afraid that those shop owners may have been privy to the beauty parlor gossiping, Ms. Nora's recap of last night.

With a shake of her head, Caroline continued around the side of the building until she came to the small lot where she parked her car every morning. Caroline paused as she walked closer to her car, spotting the paper sticking between her windshield and one of the wipers. She quickly yanked it free.

It was the same note she'd stuck in her purse after wrapping it in paper towels from the clinic. Somebody did not want her to forget. Frowning, she snatched the paper from her window and opened the back passenger-side door, sliding the crate onto the seat. Seconds later she was behind the wheel, starting the ignition. Before pulling off she put the address she'd now memorized into her phone's GPS and then set out to do what, she had absolutely no idea.

All Caroline knew was that the dead animals were somehow connected to Malec and his friends. The note pointed towards that conclusion. Now she wanted to know how and why because she wanted these murdering bastards stopped.

CHAPTER 6

Channing had just finished the energy smoothie Malec had made everyone consume for lunch. After what had happened in the forest earlier that morning, Blaez had come back and gone straight to his room. Kira had followed. The others had stayed in the kitchen discussing what they'd seen and what the presence of the Solo and the harpy possibly meant for them.

"So the harpy was definitely looking for Blaez," Channing had said as he sat at the kitchen table. "Rumor has it Zeus put out some sort of bounty on him."

Just two months ago this kitchen had been an extension of Channing's space in this house. He'd designed everything in this room from the recessed lighting to the redwood porcelain–tiled floors. The seamless blend of country and modern had given him distinct memories of the foster home he'd grown up in with Emma and Ruxton Verdi in Kansas City. A stay-at-home mom, Emma was always cooking, cleaning, redecorating, and being the perfect mother to Channing and wife to her husband. She'd taught Channing everything he knew about cooking and taking care of people. As for Ruxton, he'd given his only son a crash course in every sport there was and cheered him on no matter what in each of the baseball and basketball games that Channing had eventually played in.

When Blaez brought them to this cabin, Channing had instantly seen the potential and began to design the perfect kitchen. In the back of the house, the building that used to contain horse stalls had been partially transformed into a garage for all their vehicles. The other half of the building was transformed into a gymnasium, where Channing often challenged the guys to basketball games. He and Blaez routinely kicked Phelan's and Malec's lycan butts on those occasions.

This place had become Channing's home in the last year, and now he hated that something dark was most likely threatening that serenity.

"I'm not surprised," Phelan said dryly.

The beta was sitting at the head of the kitchen table, where Blaez usually sat, rubbing his fingers over the scar beneath his left eye while staring aimlessly across the table. That meant he was truly pissed off. The memory of the Fury Eureka slashing Phelan's face in a jealous rage years ago always surfaced when Phelan was angered or distressed. Which often seemed like a 24-7 affliction in Phelan's case. But Channing had known this guy for almost ten years now. In that time he'd come to know his moods well. This one he was in right now was not good. Not good at all.

"Zeus didn't send the Solo," Malec chimed in from where he was moving on the other side of the kitchen.

Malec, in contrast to Phelan and any of the other lycans in this house, could not be still when he was angered. He moved constantly, whether working out until his muscles screamed in protest or running until the treadmill belt snapped straight off the machine—which he had done numerous times before. Physical movement seemed to be the only way he could relieve stress. Or take the edge off, as Channing had surmised over the years, because for Malec there would always be a mountain of stress that he would never dare to climb.

"Solos take no direction from anyone," Channing announced. "They have no pack and no allegiance—that's why they remain alone. It's also what makes them more dangerous than any other lycan—they're not restrained by any specific rules or beliefs."

Channing knew more about the lycans and their history, Zeus, and all the mythological beings that lived in another world and sometimes walked the earth than the other betas. Blaez knew more than he did, but that was only because the alpha had experienced more. Once Channing had endured his first shift when he was sixteen years old and spent the week following that locked in his room, struggling to figure out what the hell was wrong with him, he'd decided to never be without knowledge again. He'd searched everything he could online about lycans, and when he felt steady enough to return to school he'd begun hitting the libraries every day until he figured he'd read everything there was to read about the lycans and Greek gods. The thought that something the rest of the world took for only myth could actually be true was a lot to swallow. But for the first time in his life, Channing had felt proud and purposeful. He was a lycan, not just a boy that his birth parents didn't want. There was a bigger role for him to play in this thing called life, he was certain of that fact. He need only be prepared for when it was time to do his part. Those thoughts had encouraged and supported Channing throughout his teen years, until the day he'd been sitting in the auditorium in his high school and had seen Blaez Trekas.

"So Zeus is actively looking for Blaez and getting damned close to finding him," Phelan offered, returning Channing's thoughts to the here and now. "Because if Blaez hadn't shifted into his wolf form, we would have had to rip that harpy's wings from its back and cut off her head to keep her from reporting his location."

Channing nodded soberly, acknowledging the only way to kill a harpy was absolutely correct.

"The Solo is a separate problem," Phelan told them.

"But he definitely wants us to know he's here. He's taunting us with those animals," Malec said, his voice tight as he continued to move, taking veggies from the refrigerator and placing them on the counter near the blender.

"I think you're right," Phelan agreed. "The question is, what are we going to do about him?"

"We find him and kill him," Channing said in a dangerously calm voice.

More often than not Channing was considered the calm one of the pack, the more reserved one who would rather stand in the kitchen and cook all day than go into the gym and work out until he felt like collapsing. He didn't sit and study the news reports and contemplate their next move like Blaez always seemed to do, and he didn't walk around brooding and cursing as Phelan was accustomed to. No, Channing read the celebrity tabloids and autobiographies that he subscribed to. He wrote letters to the Verdis, giving them the impression that he was still in the Marines on top-secret

missions. In short, he'd been content to fulfill what he considered his purpose in this pack. And it made him happy.

But none of that meant he couldn't shift into a deadly
lycan and take the life of whatever entity dared to threaten
him or the members of his pack at the drop of a dime. That
was a simple truth.

"I'll find him and rip his fucking throat out," Malec stated
with the cold, deadly tone that came to him much too easily.

"Well, then," Phelan said. "Sounds like we've got a plan."

Malec had poured the twenty-two-ounce tumblers full of
the green concoction he'd created and set them on the table
in front of Channing and Phelan, saying simply, "Drink."

With a growl Phelan had taken his cup and walked out
of the kitchen. Malec followed, giving Channing a knowing
look, and headed to the gym. Taking his first sip Channing
had tried valiantly not to vomit at the strange-tasting drink.
Malec was a health fanatic, so there was no doubt that whatever was in this glass was good for him. It just tasted like
crap. And besides, Channing thought as he'd taken his cup
into the living room where he planned to sit and read some
of his magazines, they were lycans. What humans needed
to help sustain their bodies wasn't necessarily what fed the
lycans or gave them strength. Their power came solely from
the moon and the rejuvenating sexual encounters that
spiked on the night of the full moon. And for this particular
pack, the military training had given them a specific edge
over their counterparts. But it was important for Malec to
have something to hold on to, something that gave him a
reason to stay connected to the lycan world and this pack.
Channing had recognized that from the beginning, and so
did the others.

422 A. C. Arthur

So it was about an hour later, just after noon, when Channing had finally finished the last of the smoothie and three of the seven new magazines he'd received in the mail, when the piercing, high-pitched screech began to sound.

His head shot up instantly, his body and senses instantly going on alert. It was the sound of the motion sensor going off. Someone was on the property.

Channing's gaze immediately went to the floor-to-ceiling windows that flanked both sides of the stone fireplace. Those windows were tinted so that no one could see in, but Channing could see out and across the yard to the garage and gym. All looked well and fine out there, but the sound continued. It was a high-frequency sound, similar to that of a dog whistle that had been technically amped and wired to sound throughout the house and if the lycans were up to fifty feet from the property. Only the lycans could hear the sound, and possibly a dog or other wolf that may have been close enough to pick up the frequency. At any rate, there was no doubt that someone was there. The others in the house would be on alert as well that they had company.

He should wait for Blaez and Kira; they would decide what to do. Besides, the intel room was closest to Phelan's part of the house, and Phelan was the one that usually did all the monitoring from there. He would already be checking the cameras, rotating them so that he had a view of all angles of their property. But as the sound continued, Channing was pulled to the front door. He'd picked up a scent, his nose twitching with the smell, and he was following it. Every part of him was reacting to this scent now, his body warming, eyes focusing on the huge oak double doors, dick twitching with every step closer to the access.

When Channing touched the doorknob the trancelike feeling that had been pulling at him for the last few seconds intensified, and while he knew he should wait for the others he felt the overwhelming urge to open this door to see who or what was on the other side. He'd never felt this way before, as if he were losing control of his own body and senses, and Channing wanted to know why. He wanted to know what could possibly be having such a strong effect over him.

So without waiting for the others or even knowing precisely what he was letting into their home, Channing opened the door, and like a warm summer's breeze her scent washed over him. Light perfume, something floral, layered with arousal, thick and juicy. His mouth watered at the thought of those juices coating the sweet lips of her pussy. About two seconds later another scent infiltrated his system, and Channing frowned, his gaze going from Caroline's pretty face, down past her heaving breasts, to the cage she held in her hand.

"What happened?" he asked.

"He told me to bring this to you," she replied, thrusting the cage out at him like it was a bouquet of flowers for the house.

The secondary scent he'd picked up was blood. The animal's blood that was also all over the front of Caroline's blouse. He grimaced at the sight.

"Come in," he told her, without immediately taking the cage. "Come in here right now."

She moved past him, and her scent once again took priority over his senses. He clenched his teeth to hold back his anxiousness and wondered how long it would actually take before he finally got his taste of her. After reengaging the locks Channing walked to her and took the cage from her.

"When and who?" he asked while crossing the wood floors and skirting around the couch.

He was placing the crate on the coffee table, being careful to avoid his magazines, but not wasting any time either.

"This morning, and I don't know who," she replied. "I was kind of hoping you and your friends could tell me that."

He'd been glaring down at the dead dog as she spoke. "What makes you think we know?" he asked her.

"This makes me think so."

Channing turned then to see her thrusting a slip of paper out at him.

"This one was on my car window," she said when he took the page from her hands and began to read. "And this one was with the dog."

She dropped the plastic bag with an identical note inside on the table beside the crate.

"So I'll ask you again," she'd started to say before her words abruptly came to a halt.

The room picked up a few degrees, and the muscles in Channing's shoulders tightened. Malec was there.

"You'll ask him what?" he asked, his voice already thick with lust.

Channing came to a stand then, placing himself between Malec and Caroline. He offered the letter to Malec. "Another one. Dog. Dead. This was on her car, and one came with the dog," he said by way of filling him in.

The way he stood between them also confirmed something Channing had been thinking about all night. The attraction between the three of them was extraordinary. The way the air had immediately filled with the sexual tension the moment Malec had entered the room had confirmed it. Channing had already felt his own personal pull toward Caroline last night. It had started innocently enough, as she was the third that Malec had selected for them. Normal, right? No, he'd thought later last night as he lay in his bed. Something more than normal, more than he'd experienced with any of the other females he and Malec had taken together before.

Just a few moments ago when she'd been on the other side of the door, the pull toward her had intensified. She was the reason Channing hadn't waited for any higher authority within the pack to open that door. He'd felt her even before he knew for certain she was here. That was deep. It was serious. And now, standing right here between Malec and Caroline, he knew the three of them being together was inevitable.

"I want to know why these animals are dying," Caroline said, to them both, Channing suspected. "And why are they being delivered to me?"

Neither of the lycans spoke. Malec continued to look down at that piece of paper, and Channing continued to stare at him. Apparently Caroline did not like that.

"Look, I know that you guys live all the way out here because you want your privacy, and really, I don't care about whatever you're doing out here and don't want anyone in town to know. I can respect that. But what I cannot respect, or condone, is the senseless killing of animals. Now either you're going to tell me what the hell is going on or I'm calling the sheriff the minute I get home. And the park rangers," she added as if that were going to be the deciding factor for how they chose to deal with her.

It wasn't.

But the appearance of their alpha was.

"Hello, Dr. Douglas," Blaez said as he made his way into the living room.

Channing turned to face the alpha and his mate. They'd both changed clothes since that morning, Blaez in his signature black jeans and T-shirt, while Kira wore a yellow-and-white maxi dress, her hair pulled back from her face with a yellow band. They were a stunning couple to the human eye and a powerful one in the lycan world. That's what Channing saw when he looked at them, and he couldn't help but wonder what Caroline was thinking at this very moment.

"Hello," Caroline said, extending her hand to shake Blaez's.

"I am Blaez Trekas, and this is my wife, Kira," he told her.

After Kira's official claiming on the night of the full moon, all five of them had gone into the city for a quick civil ceremony to make their union legal in the human world as well.

"I wish we could meet on more pleasant terms," Caroline said as she shook Kira's hand as well.

"Likewise," Kira said, keeping her smile in place although Channing was certain she'd already taken note of the blood on Caroline's clothes.

"This note came this morning with the dog. I did everything I could to save him, but the wounds were just too deep and he'd already lost so much blood," Caroline told Blaez.

"Did you notify anyone else about this?" Malec asked her.

He'd finally passed the note he was holding on to Phelan, who had come quietly into the room.

"Like I said before," Malec said tightly, "he's taunting us."

"I have to agree, Blaez. It does look like he's calling us out," Phelan added.

"Who's calling you out? And why would they use these animals? Should we call the sheriff now?" Caroline's questions came quickly, and every lycan in the room stared at her.

"Why don't we get you cleaned up, Dr. Douglas," Kira suggested.

She was a pretty woman, a thick girl like Caroline, which was always comforting. In a room full of men oozing sexuality like sweat from their pores, it was nice to see that they weren't only focused on the model-thin beauties of the world. Still, Caroline was a bit shocked that there was a woman in the house at all. Olivia hadn't mentioned a woman, and she hadn't stated that one of the hot guys was married.

Not that it mattered because Caroline wasn't concerned about what any of them did. Okay, well, that probably wasn't totally true. She was intrigued, had been on the long ride through those back roads and then into the forest. She'd felt like she was on some type of safari ride as her car bumped and tumbled over the gravel path that had been cleared through the forest. On more than one occasion she'd wondered what type of people would want to live all the way out there, so totally secluded from the town. From the prying eyes of nosy people, like Nora at the beauty salon and Olivia at the clinic. With that thought, Caroline immediately decided that a very smart person would want to live totally secluded from the town.

As she'd finally come through the line of trees onto a cobblestone driveway that winded through some of the lushest green grass she'd ever seen, Caroline admitted to being breathless. The lodge, or log fortress, as she really wanted to call it, was phenomenal. There had to be at least a hundred acres of land, with a two-level log dwelling right in the center of it, like a picture out of a magazine. With its stone chimney stretching up through the center of all the excellently selected wood and numerous large windows, she'd been mesmerized by the time she'd finally pulled her car to a stop.

And when the double-wide door, with frosted glass inlays, had eventually opened, Channing Verdi standing his very sexy self in the doorway, she'd admitted to being stunned into a blissful silence. But then she'd managed to wrap her mind around the problem at hand and found a way to focus on just that—the dead animals. And not the heated way in which Channing had stared at her, or the rush of arousal that dampened the folds of her pussy as she stood in the same room with Malec and Channing together.

"That would be wonderful," Caroline managed to reply to Kira, while her mind was still having conflicting thoughts. "And please, call me Caroline."

"All right, then, Caroline. You can call me Kira," the woman said with a cheerful smile, moving around her husband and linking her arm with Caroline's. "We'll just go upstairs for a few and get you a nice hot shower. You'll feel better in no time," she said as they walked.

Caroline doubted that, but she wasn't going to be ungracious to her hostess. Besides, she wanted to see more of this house. In the living room the gleaming wood floors were only partially covered by plush Persian rugs. The furniture, dark oak leather, against the breathtaking backdrop of floor-to-ceiling windows, a stone fireplace in its center with a mantel that looked as if they'd removed a chunk out of a huge tree and smoothed it to perfection. It was rustic and chic all at the same time with antique sconces on the walls and high-end lacquered lamps that she was sure she'd seen in one of those lifestyle magazines.

The stairs were wide and wood, banisters thick and shined, long hallways lined with wood-planked floors and closed doors on either side. The pictures that hung on the wall caught her attention.

"The phases of the moon," she said, pausing to look at one in particular. Its blue tint was stunning, the brightness of the moon piercing through the darkness.

"Yes," Kira replied. "We have a thing for the moon around here."

"Just the moon, or do you have a thing for astronomy as a whole?" Caroline asked.

With a tilt of her head, Kira looked at her curiously. Caroline stared back at the woman, wondering what she was thinking. There was a moment of silence in which both ladies just stood there, as if communicating on some other level. A level which Caroline did not understand, of course, but still she was certain that she'd felt some type of connection to this Kira Trekas.

"The moon and other things, I would say," Kira told her. "Come on. There's a bathroom just down this way. I'm sure I have something you can put on, so I'll just go in my room and find it. There are fresh towels and cloths in the bathroom. When you're done come right across the hall, in here," she said, pointing toward another closed door. "That's where I'll put the clothes for you."

Caroline nodded. "Thank you so much. I don't mean to impose. I just wanted to know what was going on with the animals."

Kira smiled again. "We all want to know that, Caroline. And don't worry, you're not imposing at all. It's nice to have another female in here with all the testosterone floating around."

She laughed then, and Caroline had followed suit. It was an easy laughter, the kind between sisters, she thought. But Caroline had never had a sister. The last thing Max was going to do, especially in her profession, was have another child.

Caroline went into the bathroom, closed the door behind her, and leaned back against it. She let out a breath. "What are you doing here?" she asked herself. "What the hell are you doing here?"

Her fingers were steady as she undid the buttons of her blouse, stepped out of her shoes, and removed her skirt, stockings, and underwear. When she stepped into the shower beneath the hot spray of water she'd shivered because she hadn't found an answer to her question.

She shouldn't have come. There was no reason why she couldn't have simply called Malec to come into the clinic, the same way she had before. She'd known they would both be here and that the temptation would be great. Irresistible.

"Dammit." She sighed, turning her back so that the warm water cascaded down her back and buttocks.

Caroline closed her eyes this time, leaning until her forehead touched the cool tiles. The scene that flashed before her was as fresh and clear as it had been when she was four-teen years old.

Her stomach had been hurting since the night before when she'd eaten a bowl of cereal for dinner because Max hadn't been home and hadn't gone to the grocery store so that was the only thing left in the house to eat. Caroline hadn't considered that the milk that was left in the refrig-erator may have been bad, but she'd certainly felt the rem-nants of that mistake throughout the night as she ran back and forth to the bathroom. In the morning she'd thought she was better and attempted to go to school, but that had only lasted a couple of hours before she'd had to break down and go to the nurse.

It was almost one o'clock by the time she'd put her key in the door of the two-bedroom apartment where she and Max lived. There was no electrical power in the apartment at the moment because Max hadn't gotten around to paying that bill yet either, but at least she'd paid the rent so that on a cold winter's afternoon Caroline could at least come in and lie in her bed, piling up the thick blankets she'd collected over the years to keep her warm. Only today, there was someone else on that bed.

She'd heard the noises the moment she came in, the groaning and moaning of a couple enjoying sex. Caroline had heard it before—that's how she so easily recognized it. Max didn't have a pimp, didn't need anybody taking her money, she'd told Caroline, so whenever she didn't do her job in the backseat of some guy's car or in some alleyway, she brought her customers home. Max had put a lock on Caro-line's door for just that reason.

So the sounds weren't new, but Caroline just figured they

were in her mother's room and it would be over soon. She always told herself that. Only today, they were in Caroline's room. On her bed. The bed she'd been thinking about collapsing in for the last few hours.

And worse, it wasn't a couple. And it wasn't her mother.

This female was rail thin, her bony back arching, flat chest bared as one guy stood behind her, pounding his thick length into her, and the other guy stood in front of her doing the same, but leaning forward to lick her puckered nipples as well. Caroline had been frozen in that spot, transfixed by what she was seeing.

The lady was so skinny that the guy in front had been able to pick her up without any effort at all. He held her legs up close at his sides, while the other guy stood behind her holding her ass cheeks open wide. Both men were pumping their big cocks into her while she kissed one and wrapped her arm back around the neck of the other. Then she would scream, her face contorted in the strangest type of pleasure, and Caroline had stood right there, watching until they were finished.

She'd watched a lot after that. Staying up late at night when her mother would bring home her clients. That lady she'd seen with the two men before had even come back a few more times, but no more with two guys. Still, the things she'd done with the guys that were there . . . Caroline could never get those images out of her head.

Her body trembled now as she stood in the shower, her clit hard and needy, thighs shaking. She wanted to make herself come, right then and there. The release would be fantastic and then, maybe, just maybe, she'd be able to breathe normally around Malec and Channing. Maybe she'd be able to stand near them and not think of that cold winter's day when she watched two men take that woman and the euphoria that seemed to cover each of them when their release had come. Could that have actually been euphoria? Caroline had never seen that look on another couple's face after that, and so she'd always wondered if that sort of pleasure was unique to a threesome only. Now she wondered if Channing and Malec could make her feel that way. They'd stood in front and behind her the same way those guys had with that woman in her bedroom, and while none of them had been naked last night in that bar, Caroline had to admit that it had felt almost as if they were. The heat had been so intense as they blocked her in, as if their plan had always been to trap her and the desire between them. And earlier, down in their living room, Caroline had felt that same potent desire swirling around the three of them, as if this was the combination that was destined to be.

Caroline took a deep breath and began to wash. She did not stroke herself until she found relief. Instead, she reminded herself for the billionth time that she'd come to find out about the animals, and that was what she planned to do.

Clothes were waiting for her on the queen-sized bed in the room, and she quickly put them on while Kira sat in a high-backed chair near the window.

"I can't believe it fits," Caroline said after pulling the purple tunic down over her heavy breasts. The leggings she'd known would stretch, but she'd been certain she was more top heavy than Kira and had wondered about the shirt.

"There's a great plus-size designer online. Channing turned me on to him, and I've been ordering my clothes from his website since then. I read that he's going to open a shop in LA later this year. I'm already trying to convince Blaez that we should take a trip," Kira said.

"Do you take trips often?" Caroline asked out of curiosity. If no one in town knew that a woman was living with these men, she deduced that could only be because Kira hadn't ventured into town yet herself.

"No," Kira replied, shaking her head. "We don't."

"Why? Do you like staying confined to this house?"

Kira rubbed a finger over her chin before replying, "We do what's necessary."

"Do any of you work? I mean, how can you afford a house like this and cars like that one Malec drives? Plus he has that great SUV with those expensive rims. What do you do to make money?" Caroline asked.

She knew all about women who had other occupations outside a nine-to-five—namely, the business that Max had been in. But she doubted very seriously that Blaez was allowing Kira to do anything along those lines. He'd seemed way too protective of her by the way he'd stood in front of her, keeping her close and almost out of sight.

Again, Kira seemed to contemplate. Trying to figure out how much to tell her, Caroline surmised. Then Caroline wondered if maybe she'd been too blunt. She had a habit of saying whatever came to her mind sometimes.

"They used to be military, and they saved well from the missions they completed," she told Caroline. "And Malec, he's a whiz with investments. You should talk to him sometime about setting you up with something. You'll have a wonderful retirement fund without putting up too much capital."

"Malec is an investment broker?" Caroline would never have figured that.

"Not exactly," Kira said with a chuckle. She leaned an elbow on the arm of the chair and rested her head against her hand. "Malec just has a talent for it. He's invested money for all of us, and he's good at it. He's good at a lot of things."

Caroline wasn't sure, but she thought Kira might be talking about sex. She shook her head, coming to a stand and going to the mirror. Fingering through her hair, attempting to fluff the waning curls she had left, she dismissed that thought totally. There was no way this woman had sex with Malec. And what the hell was that twitch of irritation that came with the thought?

"I'll just bet he is," Caroline said aloud by mistake. She clamped her lips shut, and Kira giggled.

Through the mirror reflection she could see the other woman shaking her head.

"You don't have to try to play it off. I knew you were attracted to him the moment I walked into the room," Kira said. "Him and Channing."

Caroline whirled around so fast she almost tripped over her own feet, an act that would have definitely landed her flat on her face.

"What?" she asked, managing to right herself before taking what would have been an embarrassing tumble.

"Girl, don't even try to deny it," Kira said, coming to a stand. "It's fine. You see, one of the good things about living all the way out here is that nobody knows what goes on behind these walls. And we're all, let's say, sexually liberated here."

Caroline swallowed hard, blinking and then staring at

Mrs. Kira Trekas, trying to make sense of what was going on. "Are you saying you all have sex with each other? Like an orgy or something?"

Kira's head tilted back, and she laughed, loud and long. So long Caroline took a step back, wondering if the woman was losing her mind just a little bit.

"I'm sorry," Kira said between continued guffaws. A hand had gone to her stomach, the other wiping at the tears that formed at her eyes. "That's just so funny. Did you see my mate? The bald one with the look that would scare most every animal in those woods out there?"

Caroline gave a tentative smile. "I didn't mean to offend you," she said, even though she wasn't so sure Kira Trekas was offended at all.

"Please, stop," Kira said with a wave of her hand. "I'm not offended at all. But no, we do not all have sex together. Blaez is not into sharing, and neither am I. But," she added, "Malec and Channing, well, that's what works for them."

Caroline's pussy pulsated at those words, and she licked her lips. "How do you know if you don't participate?"

"Let's just say I know what I've seen. And I'm not bothered by it at all. You shouldn't be either," she told her matter-of-factly.

"I'm not a prude," Caroline added quickly, feeling as if she'd been saying that a lot lately.

"No"—Kira agreed with a nod of her head—"I don't think you are. But this is new to you. Believe me, I know what it's like to walk in here and be surrounded by all of them. The sexual tension can be overwhelming at first. The need that pulses through the air can be suffocating. But once you give in . . ." Her words trailed off as Caroline had already begun shaking her head.

"I won't give in," she said quickly. "I can't."

Kira only stared at her a second longer. "You sure about that?" she asked before touching Caroline on the shoulder and leaving her alone in the room.

The only thing Caroline was sure of at that moment was that she'd walked into a world of trouble the minute she stepped foot in the house. Now, the question was, how the hell did she plan to get out of it?

CHAPTER 7

After her conversation with Kira, Caroline had expected to return downstairs and continue the discussion of who was murdering those animals. Instead, she'd been offered a tour of the lodge and their extensive land. Channing and Kira accompanied her on the tour, providing more answers than she'd anticipated they would about the rebuilding of the house, including the huge garage with its ten vehicles and four motorcycles.

"Why do you all live out here together, instead of getting your own places in town?" she'd asked when they were walking through the grass, heading toward the back entrance of the house.

"We're a family," Channing had replied immediately. "We stick together in our work and home living. It's not so odd. Centuries ago families lived together to save on costs, and in other cultures families still reside in the same home fostering the loyalty and emotional bonds that can never be broken by outside entities."

They sounded like a colony or . . . a pride.

The idea had hit her suddenly, just as they'd taken the brick steps leading to the back porch that wrapped halfway around the structure. There was a railing here, wood planks painted a rustic red color, joined together by rock columns that stretched up to support the porch ceiling. A swing was at one end of the porch, while Adirondack chairs and rockers were aligned along the remaining length.

Caroline had paused at the door before going back into the house, wondering if they were . . . what were the odds . . .

She'd sighed with the question rolling in her mind. Was this a family of the feline Shadow Shifters she'd heard about on the news?

She hadn't had the guts to come right out and ask that question, not just yet. Caroline wanted more time to observe and see if she were thinking in the right direction. So when Kira asked her to help with dinner, she'd immediately agreed.

"Your mother's corn bread looks scrumptious," Kira told her as Caroline took the pan of golden-brown corn bread from the oven.

"She was a great cook, when she had the time," Caroline replied. "And I paid a lot of attention. Because of her work hours I often had to feed myself."

"Oh really? My mom was a stay-at-home mother. I always wondered why she didn't go out and get a job, if only to get away from the people in our house for a while," Kira said in a wistful way. "What did your mom do for a living?"

Caroline hesitated, then resumed rubbing the stick of butter over the hot surface of the corn bread. My mother was a prostitute, she thought about saying. Short and sweet. And very true. Caroline knew all too well how that admission would have been taken by other people. But Kira had just explained how "sexually liberated" they were here. Would she have had the same response—a shocked look or a quick change of subject while she began to pre-judge Maxine Douglas without ever having met the woman? Caroline wasn't sure, so she kept the admission to herself. Her reply instead was, "She was in customer service."

Not totally a lie. According to the repeat business Caroline witnessed, Max was excellent at providing good customer service.

"Do you want me to take this out to the table?" Caroline asked as a way of moving on from a subject she had no intention of discussing.

"Sure. The chili's ready. I'll bring it out in a second, and then we can get the salad and other fixings," Kira replied.

About fifteen minutes later they were all seated at the large dining room table, Caroline sitting—not surprisingly—between Malec and Channing. For the first few moments after she'd showered and changed earlier in the day she'd felt a little strange that Kira knew about Malec and Channing sharing their lovers and that Caroline might be next on their radar. The fact that Kira had continued, throughout the day, to mention how common it would be and how it might just be what Caroline needed in her life at this moment had been more disconcerting. Yet she'd still managed to feel extremely comfortable with all of them.

That was something Caroline had realized while she'd walked with Channing and Kira. For maybe the first time in her life she didn't feel like the outsider. Even knowing that her upbringing was most likely different from everyone else's in this house she still hadn't felt as if they were judging her in any way. She hoped to keep it that way.

So what she was currently thinking, how she was feeling sitting between Malec and Channing, wasn't going to work. Sure, Kira said it was okay, that this particular group . . . or tribe . . . or family was open about their sexuality. Supposedly, if she were to take both of these men as her lovers, no one at this table would blink twice at that reality. But that wasn't something Caroline could do. She couldn't give herself to two men at one time. How could she allow them both to have her body, to touch her, and to "pleasure her" as Malec had said so many times? Even Channing was certain that she would enjoy them together. As for Caroline, while the thought aroused her tremendously, the aftermath still scared the hell out of her. That, regardless of what the only other woman at this table had said, was what mattered most to Caroline. It was what had to matter most.

The "normal" part of her mind continued to rule over the physical, a fact she was proud of at the moment. But what if the people at this table weren't what she would call "normal"? What if they were that other species that had been occupying the news as of late? Would that explain why she was even considering a threesome in the first place? From the first moment she'd watched the men falling to their feet and turning into sleek and powerful cats on the local news Caroline had been intrigued by the entire Shadow Shifter species. Was her lifelong obsession with animals and their care a part of the reason she'd felt immediately drawn to these two men? She wasn't certain, and she hadn't decided if this was the ideal time to consider all these issues. Then Blaez spoke, and Caroline had to quickly decide if it were too soon for other things where this bunch was concerned.

"It might be a good idea if you stay here, at least for tonight, Caroline," Blaez stated a few minutes after he'd

442 A. C. Arthur

complimented his wife's chili and Caroline's addition to the meal as well.

Caroline didn't get a moment to respond before Channing chimed in, "It's a good idea if she stays here *and* gives me the recipe for this corn bread." Channing looked to her with that charming-as-hell smile.

There was something about this guy, she thought as she looked over to him with his soft blue eyes. A peacefulness that Caroline had always sought. He was at home in his skin, she thought, watching him smile and joke with the others in the house earlier. Even now, while Phelan and Blaez had intense looks on their faces and Kira had one of slight concern, Channing smiled. The act lighting his eyes and coercing her to join in. He made her think of happiness and lovemaking, picnics beneath a huge oak tree, and long, sensual nights.

He did not, in any way, remind her of a big, ferocious cat.

"You can have the recipe," she replied to him. "And about staying here—" she began, only to be cut off by Malec's quick statement.

"She can stay in my room."

Everyone at the table continued on with their meal, almost as if they'd expected him to say just that. Caroline, on the other hand, thought it was strange that the first time he'd actually acknowledged her presence since she'd first arrived was to tell her where she would stay for the night.

Again, the "normal" Caroline thought Malec's remark was rude and presumptuous. She should stand up, drop her napkin onto the table—well, that might be a bit too dramatic—and declare that she was leaving right at this moment.

But then Malec looked at her, and the first thing Caroline realized was how different from Channing this guy really was. There was no softness to Malec Zenta, not in his dark eyes or the thick arch of his brows. Not the strong jaw of his chin, covered by a light and tapered goatee. He wore gym shorts and a fitted top, muscles boldly on display.

She didn't feel all warm and fuzzy when he spoke to her or when he smiled—because he never smiled. What she felt instead was just a pinch of sadness draped with a huge helping of lust. There was no doubt she wanted him, wanted to be in his bed for every second that he would have her there. But there was something else where Malec was concerned, and that something else bothered Caroline.

Although it was not enough to change her impulsive response. "If staying will get me the answers I need, then I'll stay."

"What answers do you need?" Malec asked, sitting back in his chair to stare closely at her.

"Why am I not safe now? Just who do you think is hurting these animals and why?" she asked without preamble.

She'd asked earlier when she'd first arrived and had allowed herself to be sidetracked by Kira and Channing and their tour. That was to appease the interest Olivia and the town's gossipers had planted about the people who lived in the house. The theory of them being cat shifters had been put aside in deference to what Caroline thought was the priority—the dead animals and whether or not there would be more to come in that respect. She was not about to let them sweep that under the rug or keep a secret from her.

"You might as well tell me," she continued when no one rushed to speak up. "If this person . . . or . . . whatever is leaving me notes now, sending me out here to you, then we're all connected somehow. I'd like to know why and what can be done to put a stop to the killings."

"We're going to put a stop to the killings," Malec said, his tone brooking no argument from anyone at the table. "And he won't be coming after you again. Not if I have anything to say about it."

His tone was lethal, the look on his face cosigning said tone and sending a slight chill down Caroline's spine. But she, Caroline Marydell Douglas, was no weakling. She'd seen and done things in her lifetime that she knew had made her who and what she was at that moment. Sure, she could cut her losses when circumstances dictated she do so, and she didn't have to be told twice when it was time for a change in her life, but one thing Caroline definitely was not was a quitter. With that said, she gave Malec a nod of acceptance, because she had understood every word he'd said. But then she'd cleared her throat and looked directly at Blaez. "If you know who this person is, I want to know also. I'll agree to stay here for the night if you can tell me it will save another animal's life. But I won't stay under any false pretenses or while you all sit here and lie to my face."

If she thought they'd been silent after Malec's declarations, the sound of the proverbial pin dropping was surely about to ring true at that moment.

Kira was the first one to speak up after using a napkin to wipe her mouth and her hands. Caroline watched as the top and only female of this household sat up straight, squaring her shoulders, and captured Caroline's gaze.

"You're absolutely right, Caroline. There should be no pretenses regarding the matter at hand," she began.

When Malec moved closer to her, Caroline figured he was about to say something to stop Kira from telling Caroline the truth. But one glance from Kira to him kept him silent, even if Caroline could still feel the agitation all but radiating from his body.

"We think this person is trying to send us a message. No, we do not have a name or an exact location of him or her, for that matter. But we're fairly certain these animal attacks are geared toward us. You, unfortunately, have been looped in for reasons we're not quite sure of at this moment," Kira told her.

Blaez nodded at his wife's words before continuing, "And that is why we wish to keep you safe. If you're here with us, we can do that. Going back into town tonight, alone, would be a mistake."

"Because you think he or she will come to the clinic again. That this person will think you didn't get the first message and kill another animal to continue trying to get your attention," Caroline said, trying to make sure she understood exactly what was going on.

"He or she probably won't stop until they know for a fact that they have our attention," Channing offered. "You'll be safer here, Caroline. Trust us."

He'd reached the short distance to rest his hand on hers, and Caroline looked at him immediately with a start. It was there, the instant soothing and calming effect of his touch. But this time it was accompanied by something else—a simmering of desire. Like anticipation brimming just beneath her skin. And when she looked at Channing, his soft blue eyes had darkened slightly, his desire for her evident.

"What does he want you to do? And why is killing the

only way he can achieve it?" she asked after clearing her throat.

Malec stood from the table then, his abrupt movement causing his glass to shake and his silverware to clink against the now-empty plate. "He wants to draw us out, so that we'll come for him and kick his ass for daring to threaten us in any way. You're safer here. Now, I'll show you to my room."

Channing started with, "What he means is—"

Caroline raised a hand to stop him, shaking her head as she removed her napkin from her lap and dropped it onto the table. "I know what he means. I also know that he's rude and domineering, but those are probably traits he was born with."

There was a muffled chuckle from the other end of the table, and she figured it was Kira.

Caroline ignored it and stood, facing Malec, even if they weren't eye to eye. He was much taller than she was, as she only stood five feet six and a half inches tall. And his muscled body could be perceived as intimidating. But Caroline wasn't afraid, not at all. In fact, there was a small part of her, that part that had already been awakened by his tense looks and heated touches, that was reacting to Malec's every word and action.

"You should know that I'd already made up my mind to stay. And," she continued, taking another step closer to him, "before you even think about going out to tackle whoever this person is, you should probably get rid of that tension that has you wound so tight you're threatening to explode."

This Caroline had said while lifting a hand to casually run her fingers down the bare skin of his arm. It was a light touch, but even she had to admit it was full of electricity, desire piercing through her with razor sharpness.

Malec looked as if he wanted to say something, as if the words were right there on the tip of his tongue, but he held them in, his lips going into a thin line before he spoke.

"Let's go," was all he said before he reached down to take her hand and, to her surprise, gently lacing his fingers with hers.

Caroline didn't look back. She didn't wonder about how the others were reacting to what seemed like a strange exchange. No, she simply followed Malec back to his room, to where she hoped and prayed he was going to take her up on her offer of releasing his tension. She had a certain amount of sexual tension of her own going on, and despite all her reservations and proclamations she knew there was no way she would be able to resist this man all night long. Especially not sleeping in his bed beside him. That would be sheer torture.

No, Caroline thought with another punch of lust settling between her legs, she and Malec Zenta were going to have sex. Tonight.

And there was nothing anyone could do or say to prevent it. She was absolutely certain of that fact, or so she thought, but as she continued into Malec's room she knew that Channing's gaze followed her. It was intense and blatantly sexual, adding another strange layer to the arousal she wasn't so certain she could handle at that point.

Malec frowned as he walked. She couldn't see him, he thought. Couldn't see the conflict that was playing a grand game of volleyball inside his mind.

He wanted her.

In his bed.

He wanted her to be safe.

He wanted to take her with Channing.

But he still wanted her in *his* bed, as if this was where she ultimately belonged.

It was a losing battle he'd been fighting all day. He'd watched through the window in his bedroom as she'd walked through the grass with Channing and Kira, listening as they undoubtedly talked about the mountains and the cascading spring just a few miles away. They took her into the garage, showing her the cars and bikes there. She would have had questions. She always seemed to have questions. Channing would have answered her because he believed in being totally honest, especially with the women they planned to sleep with.

Not that Malec was dishonest. He wasn't. In fact, his basic thought was that it was better when people knew the truth because then they had an idea of what they were dealing with and could act accordingly. He didn't like lies or betrayal for that matter.

But this woman was different. She was a human. And he couldn't easily dismiss that fact.

Nor could he readily disregard the danger she might be in because of him.

He and Channing had gone over it earlier today, once the tour had been completed and Caroline had been swept into the kitchen by Kira.

"He took that dog to her because he knew she would either call or come running to you," Channing had said, sitting in one of the matching recliners in the front half of Malec's bedroom.

"I know," Malec had said as he'd paced back and forth from one end of the room to the other.

His fingers had rubbed over his chin, temples throbbing as he'd thought about what to do next.

"If I hadn't taken that first buck to her, she wouldn't be involved," he'd admitted.

"She's a veterinarian," Channing had easily replied. "Where else would you take a wounded animal?"

He was right, Malec had thought, pausing momentarily. "So he's been watching me."

"Probably, but he knows the pack is here. He most likely picked up your scent first since you jog in the forest the most out of any of us. You said you found that first buck along the path where you run?"

"Every morning," Malec had said with a nod of his head, "I take that same trail before I stretch out farther along the terrain. It's not that far from the house."

"So, yeah, he knew you would find it," Channing added.

"I found it, and I took it to Caroline. The next day, he bypasses me totally, then he came back to the forest and howled. Like he was telling me again what he'd done."

"Twice," Channing had said. "He took animals to her twice and then left her a note."

"He wants me to come after him," Malec had stated seriously.

It was Channing's turn to nod. "I think you're right," he'd said. "He wants you to lead the pack after him, to lead him directly to Blaez."

"Or to take us out one by one. I was the last to be added to the pack. The last will go first." Malec had gritted his teeth after those words. His father used to say them to

Malec and Mason, who was the younger twin by eight minutes.

After Channing had left him alone, Malec had searched
every book in Blaez's monumental library, looking for anything he could find on the Solo.

They were lone lycans, either because they were cast
aside by a pack or by choice. At any rate they were more dangerous because they had no rules to follow, none but their
own. And if one was there, hunting him, then that meant it
had a plan for something bigger. A plan that Malec would
relish breaking into tiny pieces, just as he planned to do to
that Solo the moment he found him.

But for now, as he stepped into the dark bedroom, Caroline moving quietly behind him, he had something else to
deal with. He wasn't so certain of how it would end.

Taking women had always been a necessity to Malec. He
was a lycan, with an insatiable appetite for sexual pleasures.
It was like a drug to lycans, coming together and catering
to the body's instinctive pleasure requirements. In the beginning it had been mechanical. His body craved, and so he
lay with a lycan female to feed the hunger.

Then Mason died.

And the cravings became a reminder of the very thing
that had shattered Malec's world. Mason hated being a lycan. He hated knowing that he would never fit in to this
human world and that eventually he would become a killer,
whether by choice or by proxy. He couldn't stand the differences and the quarrels that had been unfairly thrust upon
him, and he'd wasted no time or words telling his parents,
Malec, and their two older sisters how he felt about their fate.

"It is what it is," Oran Zenta had said to Mason one

night after an outburst of emotion from his youngest child. "We are who we are, and we have a place in this world. It may not be the place you want, but it is where we are meant to be."

"We're meant to be outcasts, abominations, and enemies to one another through no fault of our own!" Mason had yelled back.

Lisabeth Zenta sat quietly in a corner, tears streaming down her face. She always cried over Mason's unhappiness, unsure, even as his mother, of what she could do to make it better. Their sisters were out that evening, and Malec had finally stood, beckoning for Mason to come with him. He would take him into the backyard, and they would play basketball the way they always did. The competitive streak that ran deep and long in both of them would provide a provocative game and succeed in washing away the doubts and worries being a lycan could sometimes bring about.

But on that night, Mason hadn't wanted to play.

"I hate it here! I hate this life!" he'd screamed once they were outside.

Malec, with all the knowledge of a seventeen-year-old, had only shaken his head. "Come on, Mason, it's not all that bad. Nobody even knows what we are."

"And they never can know! That's my point exactly," his brother had said, turning so fast that in the next seconds he was in Malec's face. "What if I find a woman and fall in love with her? What if she's a human? I can never tell her who and what I really am. What if I hurt her? What if she hurts herself once she finds out the truth, like Nyktimos's wife did?"

Malec had shaken his head. "Aleya killed herself because

Nyktimos bit her. He forced her into a life she didn't ask for."
Even as he'd spoken the words Malec had known what his
brother would say.

"Just as we were," Mason had mumbled quietly.

Malec had sighed with exasperation. "There's no turning
back, Mason. Like Dad said, we are who we are. We need
only to live the life that was given to us, to fulfill whatever
destiny it is for us to fulfill."

Mason had slowly backed away from Malec then. "What
if I don't want to fulfill someone else's destiny? What if I don't
want to be a pawn in Zeus's petty game? What if none of this
is what I want?"

Malec hadn't been able to come up with an answer that
night. And the next morning when he'd awakened, it was to
his mother's scream and his father's earth-shattering howl.
Mason had hanged himself in the bathroom located in the
basement of their home.

From that moment on everything about who Malec was
and what his role in this life would be irritated him. Sure,
he believed his father's words—they did have a purpose, and
it was up to them to see it through. He was a lycan, and that
could not be changed. But he did not have to like it. And he
would not take the same path as his brother. Even with that
knowledge Malec knew he could not live in that house without Mason. Two days after the funeral he'd enlisted in the
Marines, and he'd walked away from that house in Dayton,
Ohio. He'd never gone back.

After that, when the sexual urges came, as they were
going to do as long as he drew breath, they'd brought with
it a darkness that Malec had never been able to explain. It
was as if everything Mason had hated about being a lycan

had been transferred to Malec so that he abhorred the thought of these sexual urges so much that he'd learned to sate them in the darkest, most depraved ways possible. He'd begun taking lycan females in groups. This way the females didn't need to know him, and he didn't need to know them. They did things, all sorts of things to each other, and then moved on to the next. It was both tiresome and numbing, and when it was over Malec was able to face the world one more time. He was able to do the things that Mason could not.

Channing had called it a stroke of fate that they met while in the service and that both of them had harbored their own dark secrets, allowing them to enjoy the same deviant sexual tastes. It had seemed inevitable that the duo was born, and after the first night that they'd shared a woman Malec had no choice but to agree. The things they did to a woman together, the pleasure that soared through his body, reached down so deep into his soul that it became Malec's lifeline. It became the only way he could continue on without Mason.

"Why do you do that?"

Her voice seemed foreign in the quiet of this space. Maybe it was simply because there'd never been a female voice in there before. Malec never brought a woman into his private rooms. Sure, he and Channing had occasionally, especially since moving out there, brought the lycan of their choice out to the lodge to be with instead of taking her to a hotel as they had when they'd lived in the big city. But on those occasions they used Channing's room, or any other room in the house that was not occupied. Now, they traveled to Entice, a club in Bozeman that was owned and run by lycans.

It was a four-hour drive, but in Malec's McLaren, it usually only took them two and a half.

"Why do I do what?" he replied, immediately releasing her hand because that too had begun to feel foreign.

"You're angry one minute and contemplative the next. You want me and then you act agitated because you want me. Too many contradictions," she said as if she weren't questioning but stating a simple fact.

Malec did not like the statement.

"I know exactly what I want at all times," he replied. It was a lie of monumental proportions.

"Then you may just be the only one in the world that can claim that," she said with a slight chuckle. "Look, I think we both know that there's been a strong attraction between us since that first day at the clinic."

That was a vast understatement, Malec thought. They were still standing in the dark. He hadn't moved to turn on any lights, nor had he turned to face her. Despite his claim of knowing what he wanted at all times, he had no idea what he wanted to do about her at the moment.

"Do you know what I want?" he decided to ask her.

There was something in the level tone of her voice, the way she'd stood toe-to-toe with him just a few minutes ago in front of everyone. She hadn't refused to come with him, but she had made it known that she wasn't coming for any other reason but that she had decided on her own. Confidence and independence. She had both in spades. He didn't know why that intrigued him. He'd never given much thought to the traits of the women he'd been with in the past.

"I know what we both want," she said before touching a hand to his back.

He hadn't heard her move closer, hadn't even sensed it, but now he felt her fingers flattening on his back in a light touch, but one that had his body stiffening and his dick throbbing.

"Right," he said finally. "What we both want."

Malec turned to her then, taking her in his arms. She was soft and warm, all delicious curves and tender arousal. Her hands came up instantly, cupping his face. Her head was tilted, and she tried to stare into his eyes. Because of the darkness she could not see them, could not see how fearful he was at this very moment.

To ensure that was true, Malec closed his eyes. He followed his instincts until their lips met and he kissed her. Thrusting his tongue immediately between her lips, he moaned when she opened for him. A bold and spicy flavor assaulted him instantly. The wine combined with the chili, her arms that reached around his neck to pull him down closer, and the quick thrust of her hips against his growing erection. She had been right—she knew what they both wanted.

As the kiss deepened, so did Malec's thoughts. His hands cupped her generous ass, pressing her full into his raging arousal this time, letting her feel every inch of how much he wanted her.

"Right now," he said, his teeth skimming a heated path along her jaw. "I want to be inside you right now."

She let her head fall back. "Yes!" she whispered. "Yes, Malec, that's what we both want."

He kissed down her neck, stroking his tongue along her bared skin. With his hands still gripping her ass and hers cupping the back of his head, Malec moved even lower.

Without using his hands he pushed at the collar of the loose-fitting shirt as he moved downward, his lips and tongue making their mark along the plump swell of her breasts. Malec groaned as his face sank farther into the cushiony depths, turning his cheek to rub along her nipple.

Cursing, he realized she must wear the thinnest bras ever because he immediately felt the hardness of her nipple and the ball of her piercing. He was growling by this point, reaching up a hand and tearing the shirt and bra from her. He cupped that breast, holding it up to his mouth where his tongue extended, flicking over the pierced nipple and feeling his dick harden with each lick.

Caroline moaned as well, holding the back of his head up to her breast like she was feeding him. When his teeth closed around her nipple and Malec shook his head, Caroline hissed, her nails biting into the skin at his neck. He moved to the other breast, licking and suckling until he was growling with need. The hunger beat at him like a battering ram, and Malec almost buckled under the weight of it. Instead, he pulled away slowly, grasping Caroline's hand once again.

He walked deeper into the room, past the recliners and small table, going straight to his bed. There were small lamps in his room instead of overhead fluorescent lighting because Malec preferred it to be obscure. Actually, his preference was candlelight, as would be evidenced by all the candles he kept in the bottom drawer of his bureau. Candles reminded him of home.

Malec switched on one of the lamps and then led Caroline to his bed.

"Sit down," he told her, but before she could move he touched a fluffy curl of her hair.

It had rubbed along her cheek, and he pushed it aside, tucking it back behind her ear. She had high cheekbones and thick, elegantly arched brows. Her eyes were a dark brown, like almonds, and her lips. Damn, he loved her lips. With the same hand, he rubbed a thumb across her lower lip and gasped when her tongue quickly darted out to lick its pad.

Malec pulled his hand away slowly and watched her stare up at him. In her eyes he could see himself kissing her again, tossing her on that bed and making love to her all through the night.

He turned away quickly.

Caroline moved then. She sat on the bed and leaned forward to take off her shoes. As she was already bare from the waist up, she only had to push the tight pants over her thighs and down her legs before she was totally naked.

"This is me," she said, coming to a stand then.

She turned around slowly while Malec's gaze remained glued to her beautiful body. Those barbell piercings twinkled at each nipple on breasts that hung deliciously and naturally low. Her waist curved inward but remained soft and splayed out entrancingly to her hips and thighs. Thick thighs, Malec corrected himself, just as he liked them. The backside view was just as alluring, with her generous ass wiggling mischievously, causing a painful jerk of his cock.

"Get on the bed," he directed her again.

Her head turned, and she looked at him coyly over her shoulder. "Yes, sir."

Malec almost came in his pants, right then and there. When she crawled up onto the bed, moving slowly, being sure to give him one hell of a show, his fingers clenched at his sides. He'd desperately wanted to tell her to stay just like that, in that position on her hands and knees, ass up in the air so that he could come up behind her and slip his rigid length between the soft globes of her ass.

But he did not.

Instead, Malec went to his nightstand and reached down to the bottom drawer. He pulled out a black velvet bag and then sat on the bed simply holding it in his hand.

"You know, Malec, we can just talk if that's what you would prefer," he heard her say.

Malec almost chuckled. How frequently was it that the woman was the one asking to "just talk" in the bedroom? He was such a freakin' mess.

"Have you ever been prepped?"

"Prepped for what?" she asked in return.

"For pleasure," was his simple reply.

CHAPTER 8

That was the moment Caroline felt her bravado crumble.

She'd been so sure that if she simply stood tall and faced Malec head-on that they'd fall into his bed and make wild, passionate love until neither of them could speak or even think another hostile or restrained word toward each other. And she'd been doing pretty well.

When she'd touched him she'd felt his body go still and knew that he was aroused. As they'd stood in the dark of his room, his mouth on hers, his hands on her ass, she'd figured they were well on their way. It had been over a year since she'd been intimate with anyone, preferring to simply pleasure herself whenever the need became too strong, which it had in these last couple of days since she'd met Malec.

Yes, she was ready to sleep with this guy she'd only known a couple of days. Regardless of all she'd been through in Portland and with Joey, and all she'd watched her mother go through with the men that were in and out of her life. Caroline knew firsthand about promiscuity and the heavy price there was to pay for it, and yet she'd agreed to stay in this house, knowing exactly how things would turn out.

She closed her eyes to those thoughts and to the sound of Malec taking out whatever was in that velvet bag. When he touched her calf, lifting her leg until her foot was flat on the mattress, she forced herself to breathe slowly. If it were truly pleasure he was offering her, she had no reason to be afraid. And there was nothing to make her think he would do otherwise, or was she being too trusting? She wasn't sure, but something instinctual had her remaining still, moaning when his fingers slipped through the damp folds of her pussy.

"Dammit." She sighed as he worked his fingers back and forth from her center up to her clit and back again. It sounded as if he were stirring something liquid and felt like she was on fire as she tried valiantly to remain still.

"Relax," he said. "Open your eyes and just relax."

Caroline did as he said, because his voice was calm, deep, mesmerizing. His jaw was tight when she looked up at him, his eyes darker than they had been before.

"The thing about pleasure is that there's no reason to be tense or reserved. All you need to do is let go and let it take over."

He continued to touch her, circling the tip of his finger around her clit until she bit down on her lower lip, then thrusting two fingers deep inside of her, stretching her until she lifted her hips to pump against him.

"No," he warned. "Just relax."

He pulled his fingers out of her slowly, waiting until her bottom was once again flat on the bed, her breathing still coming in pants but her head was no longer thrashing on the pillow. That's when he leaned forward. She could see his tongue snaking out, long and flat, curling on the tip just before touching her tender vulva lips.

Caroline gripped the sheets and worked like hell to keep from thrusting her pussy up into his face and holding his head right there until she came. It was a fierce urge, and this time she bit down on her bottom lip until she thought she might actually draw blood.

With two fingers he held her lips apart, rubbing his tongue in excruciatingly slow sweeps over the hood of her clit, curling the tip of his tongue again he applied pleasure against the tightened nub, and Caroline couldn't help it— she whispered his name. He seemed to stiffen momentarily, but continued to lick her, up and down, as if he planned to drink every drop of her arousal. When he moved his hands to cradle her bottom, tilting her upward, he speared his tongue inside her center, and this time she did not hesitate. Caroline pumped her hips against his thrusts. She couldn't help it. What he was doing felt so damned good.

As good as it was Caroline wanted to scream when Malec suddenly pulled back. The next time he touched her it was with fingers cool with what she realized was lubricant. He touched them to the rim of her rear, slipping one finger slowly inside, and Caroline's thighs began to shake.

The sound of Malec sighing in pleasure had her creaming so hard she fully expected a gush of her arousal to drip onto his hand.

"So beautiful and so tight," he whispered. "I love how tight you are."

She was going to rip the sheets right off his bed if he didn't soon do something, anything, to make her come, to give her this godforsaken release.

When he pulled that finger out she moaned. Thick with more lube, he pushed two fingers inside her this time, stretched them and her until her legs shook and she gritted her teeth.

"Yes, it's coming, baby. That pleasure is coming very soon."

With his words, Malec's fingers left her once more, only to return with something cool and hard, slipping slowly into that tight hole. She sucked in a breath, knowing exactly what it was and how it would make her feel. Malec inserted the plug slowly, until she'd accepted it, jerking with the tendrils of pleasure filtering throughout her body. After making sure it was positioned securely inside of her, Malec came up on his knees. He touched his moist fingertips to her belly, rubbing over her navel as he stared down at her.

"It's going to be so hot and so fantastic you won't be able to stand it," he told her. "But you won't want to stop it. You'll want more and more. I know you will."

Caroline wasn't entirely sure what he was talking about. Hell, she wasn't certain he was speaking English at all. What she knew was that she was on fire with need right now. She wanted him to fuck her so badly her vision was blurred and no words would come. So when he moved off the bed she wanted to scream, needed to yell out for him to get his ass back here and finish her off, but she couldn't. Her breathing was coming in heavy pants, her body tingling all over, primed for release. She watched him walk through a door, and she panicked.

What if he didn't come back?

What if she was forced to stay like this all night?

What if . . .

The hell with that. As Caroline had often resorted to in the past, she moved a hand between her legs, positioning her finger over her clit and began to rub furiously. She needed to come, there was just no other way around it. Her body was humming with desire, and he'd just walked out on her. Oh hell no!

Channing almost came in his jeans.

The sight of Caroline lying in the center of Malec's bed, her hand working between her spread legs, the sparkle of the rhinestone-tipped butt plug that Malec had no doubt inserted in her twinkling at him.

"Fuck." He sighed, his hand immediately moving to rub his thick erection.

When the knock had sounded on his door just a few minutes ago Channing had known exactly what that meant. He'd watched Malec and Caroline walking out of the dining room, through the living room, and down the hall that led to the rooms on that side of the house. Malec's rooms came before Channing's, and Channing had known without a doubt that was where Malec had taken her. And he'd thought about nothing else from that moment on.

Caroline wasn't like the other women he and Malec had taken together. Channing had realized that the moment he'd seen her at the bar. He'd sensed something in the way that Malec had spoken of the veterinarian when he'd told the pack about what had happened, but once he'd laid eyes on her himself, he'd known. Still, he'd taken the backseat, as he usually did where Malec was concerned. He'd watched Malec go to her and lead her onto the dance floor, all the while Channing's body and mind had been reacting to the sight. Not only did he want to be inside of her, to see and hear her pleasure as he and Malec took her together, oddly enough, Channing found himself wanting something more.

Never in all his life had Channing thought of wanting more with a woman. He'd accepted his place here with his pack and as a second to Malec in all sexual exploits, but he'd never allowed himself to want or need anything else. With Caroline, however, he felt himself faltering, almost instantly.

Walking with her earlier today, watching as she saw the home they'd built for themselves and asked questions about their lifestyle had drawn him even closer to her, made him want to spend more days like that. He could tell her everything. He hadn't, but somehow he knew that he could. There'd been no one besides Malec and Blaez that knew everything. No one he'd ever trusted with those words. And yet, he'd wanted her to know.

It was beyond strange, Channing knew. Malec wanted her with a potency that had Channing second-guessing their arrangement. Caroline did not want them together, or so she had said. The situation was fucked up before it had even really begun. He'd lie on his bed, staring up at the ceiling thinking of all these things and trying desperately not to entertain the thought of Malec having sex with Caroline alone in the other room. Channing had no idea how he would deal with that if it were actually happening because it had never happened before. He and Malec had never competed for a woman, they'd only shared. The question now was, were they sharing the same intense feelings of connection to Caroline, and if not, how would this ultimately play out?

So, after the knock had successfully pulled him from those troubling thoughts, Channing hadn't said a word when he opened the door and saw Malec standing there. Malec didn't say anything either. He didn't have to. Channing followed him back to his room. The second Malec opened the door and they entered, her scent assailed him, and Channing's body reacted instantly. She was going to be sweet and plenty wet, he could already tell and continued to inhale deeply as he moved farther into the room. Malec had already pulled his shirt up and over his head as he moved to the other side of the bed, while Channing stood for a few seconds, mesmerized by the sight.

For all that Malec preferred things darker in his room than Channing did, the satin comforter and sheets on his bed were stark white. Caroline's gorgeous mocha-hued skin glowed in contrast. Her long legs were spread wide, one lifted with her foot planted firmly on the mattress. French-manicured nails were another draw as his gaze moved to watch her fingers circling her clit, slipping farther to dig deep into her center. She sighed when pulling them out, delectable cream from her spot dripping down onto the bed.

His hands moved then, unbuckling his belt and releasing the zipper of his pants. Malec was already naked and now stood watching her as well, gripping his hard cock and moaning. Toeing off his shoes Channing moved until he was now naked, going to stand on the other side of the bed, his hand going to the base of his cock as well.

Caroline's eyes were closed, so he doubted she even knew they'd come into the room. Still, Malec and Channing stood on either side of the bed, jerking their thick erections as they watched her getting closer to her release.

She lifted a hand to grip one of her breasts, squeezing the plump orbs until Channing's mouth watered, a gasp escaping as he moved even closer to the bed. He bit back on a growl when a bead of pre-come surfaced at the tip of his dick. Her mouth was open as she breathed heavily, her tongue scraping along her lower lip where her teeth had just bit down. Channing wanted that tongue on his dick. He wanted her licking every drop that came from his arousal for her.

His body was so tight with need, so hungry to be inside her. He wasn't sure if the need had ever been this powerful, for either of them, Channing thought as he could hear the rapid beating of Malec's heart as they both watched her seeking her own pleasure. It hadn't taken a rocket scientist to see how into this woman Malec was. Channing had never seen him act this way over a woman in all their time together. Malec had never stepped outside of the parameters they'd created together. He always let Channing do his part.

For Malec sex was all about the pleasure. That's all he could afford to allow in his life that otherwise had been filled with such dismal disappointment. For Channing, the ménage held a different meaning entirely.

Sure, he had his own dark history, but nothing that had compared to Malec's. Channing had been blessed with great parents, even if they were only humans. His lycan parents had decided from the start that they didn't want him. And Channing had accepted that. He didn't need to be where he wasn't wanted or with those who didn't want him. The Verdis had wanted and loved him—for that he would be forever grateful. And his life with them had been good, except for the vicious bullying that began during the summer before ninth grade. Channing had stood his ground against Zane

Hendricks, as best as a scrawny fifteen-year-old could against a sixteen-year-old weighing in at no less than 180 at that time. And when that sixteen-year-old brought the three members of his clique along to show "the good boy" as they'd called Channing because he'd rather volunteer at the local rec center than run around town vandalizing old buildings and vehicles, Channing had still stood tall and was ready to face them.

They'd kicked his ass. He'd been in bed for days, including his birthday. The night that changed Channing's life.

He'd experienced his first shift then. He'd become a lycan. And four weeks later he'd slashed Zane Hendricks's throat. Nobody knew but Channing, and the knowledge had served with the same effect as those energy drinks Malec liked to down. Channing wasn't a powerless nobody whose parents didn't want him. He was a lycan, strong and deadly. And he loved it.

Sharing in a ménage gave him that same powerful feeling. To know that a woman was receiving double the pleasure, was taking the wildest sexual ride of her life because he was there helping to give her everything she desired, was a tremendous power trip for him. And no, he didn't show it. He wasn't an alpha, and he wasn't the buff and vicious lycan. He was the quiet and compassionate one, the lycan with power brimming just close enough to the edge to be even more dangerous than the others.

He loved that about himself and instinctively wanted Caroline to see that side of him too.

"Open your eyes, beautiful," he said, because he was the one who talked to the women.

He was the one who took care of them and made sure they were safe and satisfied throughout the entire experience.

Caroline did as he said, slowly, intently, turning her head directly toward him as if she'd expected Channing to be the one standing there all along. Warmth spread throughout his chest in that moment, and he licked his lips.

"Come here," were his next words. "Put your pretty lips right here."

There was a moment of hesitation. A few seconds when Caroline's head turned in the other direction. Looking for Malec, no doubt. He was there too, still stroking his cock, giving her a nod in Channing's direction as if in answer to her unspoken question.

And then she moved. Coming up on her knees she crawled toward him. Channing's cock throbbed in anticipation as he stepped closer, until his knees bumped against the side of the bed. With one last long stroke he offered his cock to her, and Caroline, precious beauty that she was, parted her lips and took him in.

CHAPTER 9

She was divine.

Each stroke inside her hot, wet pussy was like a step closer to heaven, and Malec wanted to run, not walk, to get to the glorious finish line.

As if the sight of her ass—with that pretty little jeweled plug protruding like the welcome surprise inside a delicious piece of candy—weren't enough, watching her lips wrap around Channing's cock was about to make him explode, dripping his come all over the rounded globes of her ass. She'd crawled across that bed like a cat heading for her prey, taking Channing in one slow gulp all the way to the hilt. Channing sucked in a breath, burying his hands in her hair, and held her head perfectly still.

Malec climbed up onto the bed then, his sights now on his own pot of gold. Touching both palms to her ass he let out a low growl. She was soft and pliant, and he pulled back a hand to smack one globe, watching it bounce as his mouth watered. She'd jumped at the contact, then let her back cave so that she was pressing her ass out farther to him, sucking Channing even harder as she moaned over his cock.

Malec smacked her ass in the same spot again, his dick

throbbing as he watched her this time. Then he went to the other side, giving that cheek its own attention, loving the curve of her back and the roundness of her ass. He cupped those cheeks again, spreading them apart and leaned in to kiss the glistening-white gem plug. She pressed back against him, and Malec growled again. Tongue extended he licked down between her legs, lapping up the thick rivulets of cream he'd seen dripping there only moments before.

He'd already had a taste of her, and as he'd walked down the hallway to Channing's room her flavor had stayed on his tongue, keeping his dick hard and his mind focused. Now he pressed two fingers deep inside her, milking her even more. He could hear Channing's moans, hear the slurp and suck motions of her mouth over his cock, and Malec felt even more aroused. She was enjoying Channing's dick as much as she would enjoy his when he slipped his length inside of her. But not just yet because he loved seeing her take pleasure.

She was so beautiful as she did, her hair a wild halo around her face, eyes half-closed. Her body glowed with the desire, every curve and incline of her figure moving in a sensual rhythm. The sight of her masturbating in the center of his bed would never be taken from his mind.

He gorged on her, squeezing her ass cheeks, lifting her slightly so that she was like a meal for him to enjoy. A full-course meal, complete with a dessert that left him completely satisfied. He licked and pumped his fingers in and out of her, and she began pumping back. Malec took those pumps, wanting even more of what he knew she had to give.

It took all the strength he had to pull his fingers from

the warm, tight flesh, but he did, coming up to his knees so he could position his dick at her entrance.

Damn, that plug looked so good, he was tempted to pull it free, to take her there instead, but he knew he needed to wait. She needed to be primed just right for that moment. So he guided his shaft down lower, stroking the tip over her plump and wet vulva lips until she hungrily sucked him inside.

The sound of Channing's dick popping from her mouth and her whispering, "Oh yes," echoed in Malec's mind as his dick was clutched so tight and so sweetly into her pussy. He moved slowly at first, giving her one inch at a time, letting his head fall back, eyes closed with the flush of pleasure moving through his own body.

"Yes!" she yelled again, and Malec gave her more of his thick, long cock.

"Give it all to her," he heard Channing say. "She's hungry for it. She's hungry for it all."

Malec looked up then, saw Channing's gaze had grown darker, his hand stroking along Caroline's cheek as she looked back at Malec. The tip of Channing's dick was still rubbing along her lips, but she was watching Malec, waiting for him to give her more.

He did.

Thrusting fast and hard until he was buried deep inside her, his nails digging into the flesh of her ass.

She screamed, opening her mouth wide, and Channing slipped his dick easily inside once more. Her cheeks hollowed immediately as she began sucking Channing, tossing her ass back at Malec at the same time. Malec moved, pounding in and out of her in an attempt to ease the sudden quickening of his heartbeat. His muscles tensed, his balls so tight he knew he was going to explode any minute now.

Her pussy was so tight and so wet, his dick slipped easily in and out, his groin slapping loudly against the fleshy vibrations of her ass. He held her hips as he worked her faster, harder. Channing held her hair, pumping her mouth the way Malec was pumping her pussy. It was euphoric, he thought for a moment, them together, as they always were. This was what he needed, what he'd craved from the moment he met her. He'd known this second would come, when both he and Channing would enjoy her. In the morning, hell, in a few moments Malec was going to feel exhilarated. He was going to be relaxed and focused and able to get on with his life. He wasn't going to think of her again. Wasn't going to wonder if it was smart to take a human, or to want her, to feel the need to . . .

Channing groaned, and Malec knew he was about to find his release. He watched as Caroline continued to suck him, licking her tongue around the tip of his cock before taking him deep inside again. When the first spurt of his semen broke free, she turned slightly, letting it splash against her cheek. Then she looked back at Malec, her tongue stroking the length of Channing's cock as he continued to come down her face.

Malec held her gaze. Her dark brown eyes boring into him as if she were trying to tell him something. Malec gritted his teeth. He grabbed her ass even tighter, thrusting harder, loving the feel of his own release straining against his balls, stiffening his back.

He should look away. Close his eyes. Enjoy the moment the way he always did. But he could not.

Malec continued to watch her, loved the sight of her tongue on Channing's cock, loved even more that she hadn't taken his come in her mouth. His temples throbbed at that thought, at the way she blinked slowly, pressing her ass back matching the quick rhythm of his pumps.

"Now," she whispered. "Now."

And just like that his come shot into her in thick jets. Her thighs stiffened, and she trembled, her eyes closing slightly as she moaned with her own release. Malec pumped harder, grabbed her ass tighter. He clenched his teeth and resisted the urge to throw his head back and growl as he emptied himself inside her.

It seemed like it lasted forever. And then, not long enough. When his hips finally stopped moving, Malec slipped that pretty plug from her rear, dropping it onto the bed. His dick was still nestled inside her now-dripping warmth, and he desperately wanted to speak. He wanted to say something, to ask her what the hell she'd been thinking. Why had she watched him? Why had she told him when it was okay to come? Why had she held her release until he was inside her?

The questions played like a litany over and over in his mind, until he could do nothing else but pull out of her and turn away. He had to get his hands off her, his dick out of her. The room—his room—where he usually felt solace, was too small. There wasn't enough air, his lungs tightened, breath coming in one painful cough. And then he walked out. He didn't think, and he didn't pause. He just left without looking back.

———

"He hates this," she said as if just realizing that fact.

Caroline moved off the bed, immediately reaching for the clothes she'd been wearing before, when she felt a hand to her shoulder.

"He needs this," Channing said quietly. "We both do."

She stood then, clutching the clothes against her chest, not in a way to cover herself, but just because she didn't know what else to do with her hands, or the thoughts flitting through her mind.

"Let me take care of you," he said after a few more moments of silence. He attempted to take the clothes from her.

She shook her head. "No. I can do it myself."

"You're used to doing everything yourself, aren't you?" he asked.

"Yes," she answered softly.

He was still handsome as hell. Those eyes still caring and warm as he watched her. That was different, she thought. Different from any look she'd ever seen on any of the clients Max had finished with, or the two men Caroline had allowed into her life. Both Channing and Malec were different from anyone she'd ever met.

"Let me guess," she said, her voice holding more edge than she'd intended. "You have to do this. It's your part of the deal. You're the caregiver, and he's . . . he's the what? The dominant?"

Channing smiled. A slow slanting of his lips that had his eyes twinkling. Caroline clenched those clothes against her tighter, resisting the urge to run her fingers through his brown hair that looked so soft. Or to guide her hand along the line of his jaw and the beard that lay there.

"He has a great soaker tub," he said, nodding toward the other side of the room. "It has jets that'll soothe your muscles. You'll like it, and you'll sleep better afterward."

She shook her head, biting her lip against the overwhelming rush of conflicting feelings inside. "I don't know that I'll sleep at all in here . . . after that." She sighed. "Will he come back?"

Channing hesitated only a moment. "Yeah, he will. He just needs a moment to get his thoughts together. He always needs a moment."

"Alone? He needs the ménage, but then he needs to be alone. I don't understand," she admitted.

"I know you don't," Channing told her. "Let's take a bath."

Caroline let him lead her into the bathroom. It was bright with the porcelain tile on the floors and the walls of the shower, and the huge shower stall with glass doors. The tub was in a far corner, and Channing moved quickly to turn the water on. He was still naked, his body long and lean. He had a great ass, but then, she knew that from the way his jeans fit him. There was a confidence in the way he moved, an "I know I look good" that didn't come across as arrogant or conceited. Just a fact.

"Why do you do it?" she asked him. "Why don't you want a woman of your own, to have to yourself?"

He never paused. Coming to a stand he moved to a long, slim closet door. Opening it, he pulled out two plush gray towels and a bottle of bodywash. He set them down on a metal bench on the side wall near the tub, then went to the vanity, reached into the bottom drawer, and pulled out two loofa sponges. He put those on the lip of the tub and then came to stand in front of her.

"It gives me great pleasure and power. I like the feeling of knowing that I was a part of a woman's pleasure. A half of the most intense orgasm she's ever received. It sounds vainer than it is," he said.

"No," she told him, "it sounds like the explanation you've rehearsed."

They stood there for a few silent seconds, naked.

"Why did you do it?" he asked her. "Why didn't you continue to tell him you wanted him alone?"

It was Caroline's turn to move. She went to the tub, taking a deep breath as she lifted her leg and stepped inside. The water was hot, and she moved slowly, sinking down and letting the stinging temperature begin to work on her tired muscles. She'd been just about to lie back when she looked up to see Channing stepping into the tub with her, leaning forward to turn the water off, then positioning himself right behind her.

Caroline moved up farther. She'd never taken a bath with anyone before. Never had anyone to take a bath with. Well, that wasn't exactly true. Brent had preferred the shower. He'd said there was more room in the shower. She'd agreed. And this tub was huge, so it was no wonder that Channing had taken the liberty. Still, she wasn't sure how this worked.

It was silly, she thought as she watched his long, hairy white legs slipping down alongside hers. She'd just sucked his dick until he came while Malec had fucked her from behind. There should be no pretenses and no embarrassments at this point.

He touched her shoulders at that moment, pulling her until she lay back against his chest. It was easy, she told herself. Easy and comfortable. He picked up one of the loofa sponges, dipped it into the water, and then held it above her breasts, squeezing until all the water had drizzled down over her.

Caroline closed her eyes to the soothing warmth. She took a deep and steadying breath before saying, "It was my first time. I knew about all of it, ménages, threesomes, anal and oral sex. I knew and I'd seen it—firsthand. But this was the first time I'd ever done it."

"That's why you weren't afraid," he said, repeating the action with the sponge and the water. "That night in the bar you weren't afraid of Malec or me, but still you backed off."

"Because I had to," she replied simply.

"But tonight you didn't."

"No," she said, shaking her head. "I didn't."

It was quiet except for the sound of the trickling water.

"I wanted it. All night last night and all day today I thought about it. I knew it was inevitable, so when I opened my eyes and saw you standing there, I figured it was time to just do it and stop wondering about it," she said with a release of another breath.

"Did you enjoy it?" he asked, this time dropping the sponge and cupping her breasts in his palms.

"Yes," she whispered. "I did."

"Did you get these piercings to drive yourself crazy with pleasure, or someone else?"

His fingers were circling her nipples then, plucking the piercing until spikes of pleasure soared downward, slapping straight into her clit.

"Yes," she replied. "Both."

"I liked seeing them twinkle when I came into the room. I wanted to lick them," he told her.

His voice had grown softer, and the questions she'd wanted to ask him had blurred in her mind.

"You liked when you saw me standing there, didn't you? When you saw how hard I was for you," Channing continued to talk.

Caroline nodded, moving slightly, feeling his dick hardening behind her.

"You were so very hard. I liked seeing how you gripped your dick, how you were offering it to me," she admitted, the memory making her hot all over again.

Channing kept one hand on her breast while the other slipped down her torso, over the pouch of her stomach and down farther to cup her pussy.

"You're waxed," he said so softly she could barely hear him. "You do that so you can feel every lick and touch with more potency, don't you? You know how to elicit and receive pleasure, Caroline. You're a pro at it."

"No!" she replied quickly, vehemently. "I'm not a pro. I just know things. I know a lot of things," she told him as she looked over her shoulder.

Channing had stared at her for a second longer, his hands staying where they were. "You know how good your pussy feels to me right now?"

Caroline had been ready to get out of the tub just a few seconds ago. She hadn't liked his comment about being a pro, because she wasn't one. That was her mother. And the last thing that Caroline had ever wanted to be was like her mother. But then he continued to touch her, his fingers moving through her slit, parting her folds to stroke along her clit and down farther. She bucked beneath him, whispering, "Yes," as she laid her head back against his chest.

Channing leaned in, touching his lips softly to hers. "It feels so fucking good," he said softly over her lips. "So, so good."

"Yes," Caroline replied, her hand moving down to cover his between her legs, pressing his fingers in deeper.

He pumped into her, his tongue stroking over her lips as water sloshed around them.

"I've changed the sheets," she heard a gruff voice say, and she jumped, her gaze shooting across the bathroom to where Malec now stood wearing only sweatpants as he stood in the doorway.

"The bed's ready for you," he said before clearing his throat. "When you're done."

He walked away before she could say anything. Even though Caroline had no idea what she could have said. This entire situation was odd and new to her.

"Come on," Channing said without skipping a beat, his hand withdrawing from her slowly. "Let's get you cleaned up and ready for bed."

She didn't speak again as Channing lathered the loofa and proceeded to wash every inch of her body. He did a quick wash of himself before helping her to stand and getting both of them out of the tub. Then he took that thick plush towel and rubbed it ever so softly over every pore of her body until she was dry. She hadn't seen him get it, nor did she know how he'd known she would eventually need it, but he lifted her arms and pulled a T-shirt down over her chest. It just barely skimmed her ass, but neither of them seemed to notice as she walked out of the bathroom.

Malec had been sitting on the side of the bed, but stood when she came out. Caroline walked to him without saying a word, because still, she wasn't quite sure what she should say. He looked so tired and so sad. A part of her wanted to be pissed at him and to probably curse him out, while another part ached for whatever was going on in his mind that made him look as if he'd rather not be there at all.

"Ready for bed," she'd said as both a question and a declaration.

Malec didn't respond, but he did extend a hand to brush his fingers lightly along the line of her jaw. Channing was standing behind her, his hands on her hips. He leaned in to kiss her neck.

"Good night, Caroline," Channing whispered. "I'll see you in the morning."

She'd wanted to turn to him, but Malec's touch held her still. Channing was gone in the next seconds, and Malec helped Caroline into the bed. The sheets smelled fresh, and so did he. He'd gone somewhere else to clean himself, leaving her to Channing, and while she had thoroughly enjoyed the alone time with Channing, she would have preferred it had been with Malec.

"I don't like your plan," she said when they were settled in the bed, Malec having pulled her to lie against him.

"I did not plan for you," he said, his voice still gruff and strained.

"Fine," she said, because she hadn't planned for him either. "But I'm here now, and I don't like that you walk away instead of staying and saying whatever you're feeling. It's rude, and it hurts."

He went stiff behind her, stiff and quiet, and Caroline wondered if she should say something else or leave well enough alone, at least for tonight.

"Let's sleep," he said finally, reaching over to turn off the lamp on the nightstand and pulling the covers up and over them.

That was the end of all conversation, she knew. But it wasn't the end of her thoughts. Caroline was willing to bet that Malec didn't sleep with the women he normally took with Channing. That type of intimacy would have been left up to Channing. He was easier around women, around people in general. He was charismatic and so mouthwateringly handsome that women were sure to be eager to do whatever he asked of them. Hell, Caroline had been loving his fingers inside of her while his tongue stroked her lips, and she'd thought that spending the night wrapped in his arms, listening to the smooth and calming sound of his voice lull her to sleep, would have been nothing short of fantastic.

As for Malec. He was rough and tortured, rude and annoying. He was also too damned fine for his own good and too enticing to resist. And, unfortunately or fortunately, Caroline had just been with both of them. She'd been a part of a threesome, and she had enjoyed it. Very much.

CHAPTER 10

The sun rose slowly, purposefully, filling the sky with one-of-a-kind orange, yellow, and gold rays that stretched for as far as Caroline could see. It had peeked through the arms of the trees, intent on making its presence known until finally finding its place high up in the sky looking down on the treetops and the mountain base.

She stood on the back porch, holding a coffee cup in both hands, and simply watched. And thought. About last night.

Closing her eyes she bit back a sigh of regret, swallowing the still-steaming coffee, feeling as if she deserved the sting it produced at the back of her throat. She'd finally done it. Exactly what she'd told herself a year ago she would never do again. If anyone found out that she'd been with both Malec and Channing last night, she would be packing up and moving to another town again.

With a shake of her head she let out a breath. She didn't want to leave Blackbriar. In the months that she'd been there she found that she really liked the small mountain town. Despite the residents that wanted to know more about her—so they could talk behind her back—or wanted to pull her into their close circles—so they could talk about other people to her, behind their backs—she liked waking up each morning with the view of a mountaintop not too far in the distance.

She'd enjoyed working at the animal clinic there, taking over for the last doctor who had retired and helping the regulars with their pets. For once in her life Caroline had felt like she'd finally found the place where she belonged.

Then Malec had walked in with that buck, and Channing had stepped up behind her on that dance floor.

And then, last night.

She took another sip of coffee, staring down into the cup afterward.

"I know it's good, but it doesn't take the worries away. I haven't figured out how to put that in the recipe yet."

She didn't jump at all even though she hadn't heard Channing join her. He came to stand right beside her, so close his bare arm rubbed against hers. Caroline looked over at the arm, to the sleeve tattoo he had there. It was on both arms. An intricate design full of swirls and geometric patterns that intrigued her in the light of day. She reached out a hand and touched his forearm.

"The first month I was in the Marines, Blaez, Phelan, and I had a weekend off. The first night we went out for drinks. I had a lot of drinks," he said with a chuckle. "We ended up at a tattoo shop where I stayed until it was time to return to base getting this done. Come Monday morning, my arms hurt like hell. I thought I'd been in a battle and had them shot to hell with shrapnel."

"I noticed them before, but didn't really pay a lot of attention. They're beautiful," she said, moving his arm around so that she could see even more of the detail on the inside of his arm and his bicep. The memory of the night they'd been in the tub together and how conflicted she'd been feeling flashed into her mind. "Did the others get tats as well? Malec wasn't with you?"

She hated herself for saying his name. For still standing there and wanting to know more about him when he hadn't had the decency to say good morning or good-bye to her this morning before rushing out of the bedroom. Sure, he'd held her so close to him all night that she'd thought for a moment after waking from a deep sleep that she was trapped by some vicious intruder. It had taken her a few moments, a few deep inhales of his rich, earthy scent, and the feel of his hard dick pressing into the crease of her butt to remind her where she was and who she was with.

"We hadn't met Malec yet, and no, the others did not get a tat. But they love telling the story of the night I did," Channing told her.

She remained silent, lifting the cup to her lips once more.

"I met Malec a year into my time with the Marines. Blaez had traveled for an assignment, and when he came back he had Malec with him. Malec was also a Marine, and he'd transferred into our unit. We clicked instantly," he said.

"Are you gay?" came her next question before she could think of a way to rephrase or possibly not to ask at all.

Channing chuckled. "No, we're not gay, and we're not bisexual. Malec is like a brother to me. He, Blaez, and Phelan are my family. I would give my life for any of them. Malec and I share women. That makes us a little closer than the others but not because we're secretly in love with each other. Because we just understand each other, we understand that pit of darkness that lives and breathes inside of us each day, and we accept how we both choose to handle it."

"You don't think it's depraved?" Caroline continued with the questions because, well, it was easy with Channing.

He listened, and he replied. He didn't skirt around the questions or ignore them entirely and change the subject the way Malec had. He simply answered, whether he thought she would understand the answer or not. For that reason and probably more that she didn't quite understand yet, she felt completely comfortable talking to Channing. Even after what had happened last night.

"No, I don't," he told her. "But that may be because of my . . . upbringing, I guess you could say."

Caroline chuckled. "What? Was your mother a prostitute too?"

Her mouth snapped closed so quickly, her teeth made a clapping sound. She looked at Channing and then away, gripping the coffee cup even tighter as she stared straight ahead.

"She was a prostitute," Channing said simply. "Not you."

"It doesn't matter," Caroline said, shaking her head quickly. "Really it doesn't. I was just trying to understand you and Malec and all of you, I guess, a little better. But it's none of my business. None of this is."

She'd turned around then and was ready to walk away when Channing grabbed her by the arm. "It does matter," he said to her. "You matter to me."

Caroline paused then, looking back at the way the slight breeze had ruffled his brown hair and at his long lashes flanking those gorgeous blue eyes. Her gaze fell to his long fingers wrapped around her arm, the light hold he had on her in an attempt to keep her there.

"You matter to me too, Channing," she admitted. "I didn't want you to. I didn't want you at all. That sounds so harsh." She shook her head.

Channing shrugged. "It's honest."

"I don't know how to do this," she told him. "Is this how it normally goes on the day after? You stay and take care of the small talk, while he runs and hides?"

"We've never had a day after," Channing told her. "So this is kind of new to us too."

"Yet you seem to know exactly what to do and say," she added before stepping away from his grasp. "You're extremely versatile."

Channing chuckled then. "You have no idea. Look, there are a lot of firsts going on here. He would hate that I'm telling you this, but you matter to Malec as well. I could tell that from the start."

"Now that is funny," she said, smiling but not laughing. "I matter so much to him that he couldn't wait to get out of that bedroom this morning, to get away from me."

"He's never slept with a woman all night before. Not alone, and not with me. I told you this situation is bringing a lot of firsts for both of us," Channing continued, his face serious, his eyes still warm, but unwavering.

"Then why hurry to leave? Doesn't it make more sense to confront the issues head-on? If you don't understand, you ask the question, talk, work it out," she said because she was having a hard time understanding any of what was going on.

"It might be easier that way. Hell, it might even make a

lot of sense for someone like you. But we're different, Caroline. Not just in the way we choose to have sex, but in a lot of ways that make our lives and how we handle matters more complicated. We've both been through a lot."

Caroline shook her head, seeing this for exactly what it was. Channing wasn't just the one responsible for taking care of the women, he was the fixer. The charmer. He made everything better, all the time giving Malec the perfect excuse to be who he was without any recriminations.

"No," Caroline said to him. "You're not that much different from anyone else. I've been through things too."

"And you've figured out a way to deal with them. You find your own pleasure so you won't be mistaken for a promiscuous woman or a woman of your mother's profession. You deny your inner yearnings to please people that don't really give a rat's ass about you in the first place. So you're right, Caroline. We're not that much different at all."

She didn't know what to say to that. He'd summed up her life so quickly and so succinctly he'd actually left her speechless.

"I'm sorry," he said after a few moments of silence. "I didn't mean to be so crude. I'm just trying to make you see how alike the three of us really are and why that's probably the reason we felt so drawn to each other so quickly."

Caroline shook her head, not ready to hear any more that Channing had to say, for fear that he may be right again.

"It's okay, Channing. You don't have to apologize. You see, even though my mother was a reprehensible person and parent, according to those who judged her solely by her occupation, she taught me a hell of a lot about life and about people. So much so that I know that there are no excuses. People are responsible for who and what they are, no matter what happened to make them that way. You may be correct—the three of us are probably a lot alike. We've most likely each had a difficult time, and we've figured out how to deal with it, but you and I don't hurt other people because of it." Or at least Caroline didn't think Channing was like that.

"Malec, on the other hand, is totally responsible for the way he chooses to act. And me, well, I'm just not the type to sit back and keep allowing people to treat me in less than a way I deserve. I like you a lot," she told him. "Much more than I thought I could. But I can't stay here another second. It's just that simple for me."

Channing stood there staring at her. He slipped his hands into his pockets slowly.

"If you knew everything, you would feel differently," he said.

"I doubt it," she told him. "I think I know as much as I want to. Look, I wanted both of you last night. At first I didn't think I should, but I did and I don't regret it. I enjoyed every minute of it, so thank you for that at least," she said before turning to walk away.

As Caroline moved she wondered how she'd been able to say those words. Had she enjoyed last night? Had she really enjoyed being treated like, for short of a better term, a piece of ass? Hadn't she vowed after Brent that her next intimate experience would be with something she saw a future with, someone who could love her as deeply as she wanted to be loved?

Yes, she'd messed up again. But this time, she was owning her mistake and moving on before she could make it any worse. She was going back to her apartment for a shower and a change into her own clothes, and then she was going to work, to get back to the life she'd planned when she'd first come to Blackbriar.

"You can't run from it, Malec," Kira said from the chair she sat in on the front porch. "No matter how hard you try you can't run from it. Believe me, I tried. Remember?"

Running up onto the porch, Malec paused to look at Kira. She wore black shorts today, her top with brightly colored stripes. She looked fresh and pretty and confident. When she'd first come to this house she'd looked angry, deter- mined, afraid. All that had changed in the course of only two months. Such a short time for two people to meet, to fall in love, and to commit to each other forever. Except that those two people were lycans, and with them, he figured, anything could happen.

Unfortunately, Caroline was not a lycan.

"I don't know what you're talking about," he replied, rub- bing a hand down his face.

"She's your mate," Kira said simply, uncrossing her legs and standing. "Yours and Channing's."

Malec simply stood staring at the alpha female. His first inclination was to vehemently deny what she'd said. The eerie twist in his gut kept him from doing that. Instead, he shook his head.

"First, what type of woman do you think is actually going to agree to a ménage relationship for the rest of her life? And second, before you attempt to tell me, let me remind you that she is not a lycan. She's not a shifter of any kind or any other type of being that we're used to dealing with. She's a human, and they have definite ideas about how to live their lives."

She tilted her head. "Do you think there are no humans living in ménage relationships? Because if you do, then you're sadly mistaken. When I was in college there was a group called Swingtime. The first time I visited I was naïve enough to believe they were a group of ballroom dancers attempting to reenact that famous old black-and-white movie with Fred Astaire and Ginger Rogers." She laughed at herself. "Whew, did I get a surprise. Those couples were licking and sucking and doing any and everything they could get into. On the couch, the floor, the pool table. I had to run, stepping over naked bodies, to get out of there. Later that night I laughed at myself because they weren't doing anything I hadn't seen the members of Penn's pack doing on too many occasions to count."

"It's not the same," he told her.

"No," she replied, sobering quickly. "It's not. Because Caroline Douglas is not one of the women that you and Channing are used to sharing and forgetting. She's not a lycan that understands our sexual appetites and could easily move on to the next one, because you know what? Those females knew exactly what I'm trying to tell you now. They knew that neither you nor Channing was their mate. And since you two weren't alphas they also knew it wasn't worth trying to convince you to claim them anyway."

Malec did not want to hear this. Bringing his hands to his hips kept him from flexing his fingers, feeling the sting of the tips where his lycan nails wanted to lengthen. He held firm to the shift that wanted to break free because it was pissed as hell. Not with the alpha female, but with himself. Always with himself.

"It doesn't matter," he told Kira. "None of what you're saying matters because this is not what she wants or deserves in her life."

"Oh really?" Kira said, folding her arms over her chest. "Tell me what Caroline deserves, since you think you know so much."

Did he forget to say cocky? Kira, the lycan with the gift of vision, wanted him to tell her how he knew something that she didn't.

"She deserves a man who can love her and treat her right. A man who can walk around with her, take her out on dates, give her children, be her partner, and be honest with her, dammit!" he told her, still straining to keep his voice level.

"Oh, and she doesn't deserve to have two men who can give her those very things? Because you and Channing are both ugly abominations that can't be seen in the light of day, for fear of people turning to stone on the street."

"Stop it," he said through clenched teeth. "Just stop because you know exactly what I'm talking about. You know why this can't work."

"No," she said, stepping closer into his face. "I won't stop. You want to know why? Because what I know is that the three of you belong together. I know that there is so much more you have in here." She tapped a finger to the side of his head. "And even more in here." She flattened her palm over his chest, right above his heart. "You've just got to stop punishing yourself for something you couldn't have predicted or stopped. Mason had his own path, and you have yours."

"I said stop," Malec told her once more.

Kira nodded. "You did. And I will, for now. You have enough to think about especially since Phelan found footprints outside your bedroom window."

"What?" Malec did yell this time, taking a step back from Kira.

"He's been back there with Blaez and Channing for the last half hour. After they saw Caroline off safely, Phelan picked up a scent, and he decided to walk the perimeter. I'm surprised you didn't hear his howl the moment he found the prints. The rest of us did. Phelan and Blaez checked the monitors to see why the sensor alarm hadn't gone off and realized it had been disengaged."

"Wait a minute," Malec said, trying to wrap his head around what he'd just been told. "What the hell are you saying?"

"She's saying the Solo was here," Blaez said, stepping out onto the porch. "Caroline showed us the notes he'd left for her at the clinic, directing her to come out here. He must have already been waiting for her to arrive. When we thought it was simply her setting off the sensors he probably heard the alarm too and managed to get close enough to disengage the wires we saw ripped out on the back wall."

"So that sonofabitch was here all last night, just walking around the house like some supernatural Peeping Tom and none of us knew a damned thing! How the hell does that happen? What about our other security measures? Wait a minute. Did you say that Caroline was gone?" Malec asked, his gut tightening as he said the words.

Kira looked to Blaez, who set his lips firmly. "Yes. She went back into town."

Malec took off running into the house. He busted through the door of his room and grabbed the keys off his nightstand. He was heading out the front door again, the others in his pack standing to the side, not attempting to stop him. They all knew where he was going, and as he climbed behind the wheel of his car, they all probably had a good idea of what he was going to do when he got there.

CHAPTER 11

She was getting a headache. Tiny spikes of pin-prickling pain had taunted her throughout the ride back into town. Where before she'd enjoyed the scenery, the tall, formidable trees, the way the sunlight pierced between them, whispering at something possibly more beautiful to come, this morning she hated it all.

There was no brightness to this morning even though Caroline was sure there should be. She'd always prided herself on having an optimistic outlook, even when the doctor had told her how sick Max really was. Caroline had continued to smile each morning as she brought her mother breakfast. She was in high school then, a sophomore writing on the school newspaper because the cheerleaders and pep squad had already dismissed her the year before. Still Caroline thought she was happy as she ever would be, all things considered. She'd even started each day with the same thought.

Today is a new day.

"Remember, CeeCee," Max would say when Caroline was dressed for school and she'd returned to her mother's room to retrieve her emptied tray of food. "Today is a new day, full of fresh starts and new beginnings. You make the best of it, you hear me? Make the best of every new day you're given."

Caroline would smile and say, "Yes, Mommy," before leaning over to kiss her mother's prematurely weathered cheek.

That was their morning ritual, until the day Maxine Douglas died. After that, Caroline had looked in the bathroom mirror and recited to herself, "Remember, CeeCee, today is a new day, full of fresh starts and new beginnings. You make the best of it, you hear?"

Afterward she would nod and on some mornings force herself to smile. But Caroline would leave that bathroom with those words in her mind and the effort in her heart.

And then the world would show her its true colors. Again and again.

Well, today, she'd had enough of reality. She was going to go into her house and fix herself a big bowl of her favorite cereal and a cup of tea. Then she was going to sit on her couch and watch old movies all day because that's as optimistic as she could manage to feel after the night she'd had.

About ten minutes into her car ride Caroline had called Olivia, telling her that she wasn't feeling well and that she wouldn't be in the clinic today. There were a few routine checkup appointments on her schedule that she'd also viewed on her phone, but they could all be rescheduled. She wasn't in the mood for people today.

Parking her car in the backyard of the renovated storefront turned apartment, Caroline locked the vehicle, then walked to the back door to let herself in. Her apartment was on the top floor, so she took the stairs, feeling as if she'd run a marathon, and finally let herself in.

The chill hit her the moment she shut that door, before

she even turned around to see him standing there. The hairs on the back of her neck stood on end, her heart picking up pace immediately. Caroline clutched her keys in her hand, wishing she still had that switchblade that she used to carry when she'd lived in Portland attached. She'd decided against carrying that anymore after Brent's wife had first threatened her and Caroline had really thought she could do bodily harm to the woman. She figured it was better safe than sorry. Cursing a woman out was a hell of a lot different from stabbing a crazy, vindictive bitch to death.

Still, she was prepared to gouge the intruder's eyes out with one of the keys she held if it came to that. However, as she turned around slowly, Caroline had absolutely no idea what was standing just a few feet from her, none at all.

"I've been waiting for you, Dr. Douglas," his raspy voice said.

"You're breaking and entering," was her nervous but steady reply.

The apartment was dark. He must have closed all the blinds in addition to not turning on any lights. All she could make out as she stared across to her living room set and the small table and three chairs she called her dining room was the tall silhouette of a man and glowing blue eyes.

She'd blinked once or twice trying to figure out if that was just a play of light since she'd come from outside where the sun had been shining brightly into the room, where darkness flanked everything. But the eyes were still there, bright like the twinkle lights on a Christmas tree and eerie because they seemed to be floating in midair.

Caroline swallowed deeply, taking a tentative step forward while reaching into her pocket for her cell phone.

"I wasn't sure you would have let me in if I knocked," he continued. "Besides that, you weren't at home to greet me."

"I'm not sure I would have greeted you even if I had been," she said, chastising herself for goading him—or it.

It? She thought with a slight gasp. She'd been out at that lodge all night with five people she'd been thinking might be those infamous Shadow Shifters and hadn't dared ask them to confirm. Yet now here she stood staring at something that was obviously not human, and she wondered once more.

"What do you want?" Caroline asked, her fingers on the phone that she'd stuffed in the side pocket of the sweatpants Kira had let her borrow. "Why are you here in my apartment?"

"Because it's time someone taught you a lesson," he replied simply, "you and the company you've decided to keep."

Caroline's mind was working at record speed, going from questions about shape-shifting big cats to now, pausing as she thought about his words.

"You're the one that's been killing those animals," she said, rage guiding her forward. "You're a murderer!"

"And you're a slut!" he snapped back, flicking on a light at that moment, tossing a picture onto her couch.

Her gaze fell to the picture, and Caroline gasped. It was of her and Malec and Channing last night. She was on her hands and knees on Malec's big bed while Malec knelt behind her, his long, thick cock sinking inside of her while Channing's rigid erection was in her mouth. It was a horrid picture, and then it wasn't. Her gaze stayed locked on the contrasts in her darker complexion versus Malec's lighter one and Channing's slightly paler one. They looked exotic and erotic, and she would have been aroused if he hadn't been here and if he hadn't been the one with the pictures.

"What are you, some type of perverted sociopath?" she asked.

He growled then, low and menacing like a vicious dog. "I'm your worst nightmare," he told her.

Caroline shook her head. "You're a criminal!"

"But the people of this town don't abhor criminals. They do, however, frown upon promiscuous women who parade themselves around as upstanding citizens, a veterinarian at that," he was speaking in a level tone, but it was scary.

It was too calm and too . . . he was one of them. She knew it. He was a shape-shifter, and he was going to kill her.

"I'm calling the police," she said, finally managing to pull the phone from the side pocket in her pants.

He closed the space between them in the blink of an eye, grabbing her at both wrists until her phone and keys clattered to the floor, her gaze fixed on the long clawlike nails on his thick hands.

"Oh my. What the hell . . . you're a . . ." She couldn't get it out as she looked up at him.

Those eyes were still bright blue, like pieces of glass in the pit of his face. His brow was thick and veined, a glossy mane of black-and-white-streaked hair shooting from his head and down the sides of his face. With a look of animalistic amusement, he opened his mouth wide and growled in her face. Caroline couldn't have moved if she'd wanted to; the sight was so horrific and so petrifying it was all she could do not to wet herself.

"That's what I am," he said, his voice now filled with rage.

"And you're going to bring him to me, just like I brought those animals to you."

She shook her head, her body trembling. "Who? M . . . Malec," she murmured.

"You're going to call him on the phone and get him here, or I'm going to send that picture to every person in this town."

"What? Are you blackmailing me?"

"No!" He growled again, this time releasing her and wrapping one of his hands around her neck.

The next thing Caroline knew she was being slammed into the wall, her feet dangling off the floor, the breath squeezed out of her lungs.

"I could kill you right now! I could just snap your neck and be done with it! But it's not you I want, it's him. The beta."

The what?

Caroline blinked, her eyes filling with tears as she smacked at the colossal hand squeezing her neck. Had he just said *beta*? As in alphas and betas? She was kicking out at him even as she looked at him closely. He wasn't a big cat at all, she thought with a start. He had the distinct look of a . . . she stared at his muzzled nose and heightened cheekbones . . . he was . . . a wolf.

"No," she tried to say, but the sound barely came out. She wasn't going to call Malec or anyone else for this animal. If he knew he could kill her, then he would just have to do that. "No," she attempted to say again, this time smacking out at his face.

He growled again, tossing her all the way across the room until she crashed into the table and chairs and rolled over the floor. Caroline gasped for breath and wished her phone were closer or that she had a gun or something nearby. She wasn't sure what would work on that thing or what wouldn't; all she knew for a fact was that she wasn't going down without a fight. If he came here to kill her, then he was going to have to work hard to get the job done. Reaching out she grasped a lamp that had fallen and rolled onto her back, throwing it across the room to where he still stood.

His reply was to catch that lamp, breaking it into pieces as he continued snarling at her, his long and sharp teeth dripping some sickly looking fluid onto her floor.

She was going to die. Caroline knew in that instant. This werewolf creature was going to kill her, and all she could think about was how glad she was that Malec or Channing had not insisted on following her home.

He'd watched him. That bastard had been able to get close enough to the house without any of them knowing and watched him, probably with Caroline, Malec thought, slamming his palm against the steering wheel.

He took the curve leading to the main road back into Blackbriar on what felt like two wheels, his foot firmly planted on the gas pedal as he rushed to get to her apartment. The address as well as the phone number had been programmed into Malec's phone since that first day that he'd walked into her clinic and seen her. All the details, that's what he'd wanted to know about her, hence the look into her background he'd performed. Every detail that he could find that would go along with the picture of her beautiful face, which he could not get out of his mind.

This was personal now. The Solo had taunted him enough. Stepping foot on his personal property was like calling him out on national television, and Malec was damned sure going to show up for this fight. They should have gone with her. His nostrils flared at the thought.

Channing should have never let her go. He should have known better. And Kira, she should have seen what might happen. Blaez and Phelan knew better as well. They knew how conniving and deadly a Solo could be. Caroline should have been safe and sound behind the locked doors of the lodge.

The lodge that the Solo had been able to walk right up on. And while he was documenting facts, Malec probably should include that he should not have left her this morning. His teeth elongated, cutting his lower lip as he released a low growl.

All night long, every second until just before dawn, Malec had held Caroline in his arms. It was a new experience for him, the closeness and the warmth. He hadn't disliked it. She'd been so soft, her thighs and arms as he'd stroked softly up and down her body. He watched as she slept, saw the fluffy curve of her eyelashes as they lay against her cheeks, the rise and fall of her chest with every measured breath she took. And he'd wondered what the hell he was doing.

Was he falling for this human female?

The car came to a screeching halt in front of the building that now held two apartments. Malec jumped out, barely remembering to take the keys and close the door. He was inside the building and taking the stairs two at a time, his nostrils continuing to flare as he'd picked up the foreign lycan scent the moment he entered the building. He had that sonofabitch now! And if he'd done so much as broken a fingernail on Caroline's hand, Malec was going to rip his throat straight out with his hands.

He kicked the door in, watching as it splintered and fell from the hinges before stepping inside. It only took one glimpse of the Solo, claws bared, teeth long, sharp, and dripping saliva down onto Caroline's chest as he prepared to bite her, to send Malec completely over the edge.

Releasing his own beast with a quick tilt of his head and a howl that shook the walls of the apartment, he lunged for the Solo, grabbing him by the sweatshirt he'd worn and tossing him across the room, into the kitchen. Glass shattered, furniture broke, and the lycan stood to his feet seconds later, glaring at Malec.

"And there you are," he said with a sickening chuckle. "It's about fucking time. I thought I'd have to walk up to your door and knock just to get you to come out and play."

"That's what you should have done, you piece of shit. Killing animals, attacking a human, that's some pretty cowardly crap for a lycan to pull. No wonder you don't belong to a pack," Malec spat.

The Solo chuckled again, rolling his neck on his shoulders until the cracking of bones echoed throughout the room, flexing his fingers so that his long claws clicked together.

"Say what you want. It doesn't change a damned thing. You're still the weakest link in that charade of a pack Trekas has going on. That's why I came for you first. Once I kill you it's just a matter of climbing the ladder until the true-blood is alone and vulnerable."

Malec laced his fingers, bending them until they cracked

before faking a yawn. "A predictable plan that only proves how big a coward you are. If you want Blaez, then you should have been bold enough to come straight for him."

"No need. This way's much more fun," he said, this time planting his feet a distance apart and flexing his arms as he growled long and loud.

Malec was not impressed, and he wasn't fucking around with this creep any longer. He leapt for him then, throwing a punch that would have landed on the lycan's chin if he hadn't blocked it. That was just fine; Malec had predicted the defensive move. Solos would know how to fight, hunt, and survive. They had no other choice since they were totally on their own in the world.

Malec wasn't alone. He was a trained killer. So with a sweep of his legs he watched the Solo fall back onto the floor. Standing over him then, Malec reached down to swing his arms so that his claws did all the work, slicing at the Solo's chest and torso, his legs and arms. The Solo reached upward, grabbing Malec by the throat, but Malec grabbed one of his wrists, squeezing it so tight the bones beneath cracked, and the lycan howled in pain. When his grip on Malec's neck loosened, Malec grabbed hold of the lycan's good arm and yanked it right out of its socket, eliciting yet another howl of pain.

"Next time you think you're attacking the weakest link," Malec said, lifting his hand for one last slash across the Solo's throat, "think again."

All howling stopped as did the Solo's heartbeat.

In the distance, it sounded as if it were so far away, and yet Malec felt it as distinctly as if someone were taking tiny stabs into his heart. He heard her crying. He stood slowly looking down at his bloodied hands and claws, feeling the sharp edges of his teeth against his lip, his beast breathing heavily. His head turned slowly, knowing and regretting with every fiber of his being what he knew he would see when he turned around.

Caroline stood beside the overturned couch, her hands shaking, lifting to her face to cover her mouth, tears streaming down her cheeks as her eyes remained transfixed on him.

On the lycan he had turned into right in front of her.

Before Malec could speak Channing and Phelan came running inside the apartment.

"We came as soon as you left, but you were flying in that damned car—" Channing's words were cut short as he looked from Malec to the floor where the Solo lay in his own blood, then across the room to Caroline.

Channing immediately moved to go to Caroline, but Malec extended an arm to stop him. He did not speak, only shook his head, telling Channing to deal with the Solo. With steps that felt heavier than any weight that Malec had ever lifted, he walked toward Caroline, pulling the beast back inside and feeling his face and hands return to normal.

She was shaking her head now, wiping her hands over her face.

"Caroline," he said, his voice sounding like an eerie croak.

Her head continued to shake even as she sniffled and attempted to stand up even straighter. Dropping her hands to her side the first thing she said to him was, "I thought you were a cat. I thought all of you were feline Shadow Shifters. I had no idea there were . . . that you . . . that . . . I just, I don't know what to say."

"Don't say anything," Kira whispered, coming to stand beside Caroline, wrapping her arm around her. "Let's go into the bathroom and get you cleaned up a little. This is no place for you to be right now."

The last was said with Kira tossing an angry look toward Malec.

Caroline was a human, he reminded himself. He'd just killed a lycan in front of a human. And in doing so he'd just shown her what he really was, something he'd never, ever wanted to do.

"Did he say anything?" Blaez asked when Malec turned to see the alpha standing there, arms folded over his chest.

Malec shrugged, rubbing his hand down the back of his head. "No. Not that anyone had sent him, just that he'd come planning to take us out one at a time until he got to you."

Blaez frowned. "Was he working for Zeus's bounty?"

"I don't know. He just said he wanted to take the true-blood down. He could have been acting alone as a quasi-Hunter, or he could have been trying to collect the bounty. Either way, he's not doing a damned thing now," Malec stated coldly.

Blaez nodded. "You're right about that. Are you okay with this? I mean, how it all went down?"

Malec looked to the lycan that had saved him from himself years ago. "I'm more than okay with killing a coward-assed Solo," was his reply.

Blaez continued to stare at him knowingly. "And the rest?"

"I'll deal with it," Malec replied.

"She should come back to the lodge with us," Channing said, entering the conversation.

"No," Malec announced. "I'll take care of her."

Channing sighed. "This isn't just about you, Malec. Let's just get her back to the lodge, and Kira will feed her and I'll—"

"No!" Malec yelled. "I said I'll take care of her, and I will."

Channing's lips drew into a tight line as he moved closer, getting in Malec's face. "If you fuck this up for both of us . . ."

"What?" Malec shook his head. "I've got this."

"You don't even know what you've got, Malec. What we could have. You've been denying it from the very beginning."

"Now is not the time for this discussion," Malec said through gritted teeth. His temples were throbbing, adrenaline still pumping fiercely through his veins.

"I won't lose her because of you," Channing said sternly, his fists clenching at his sides.

It was time for Blaez to intervene.

"Malec, you stay here and clean up your mess. But keep in touch. I want to know that you and she are all right," he instructed Malec. "You and Phelan get rid of that body. And the rest will be dealt with later," he directed to Channing.

After another long stare at Malec, Channing nodded to Blaez and walked out of the apartment.

"I hope you know what you're doing," Blaez told him before clapping him on the shoulder. "Kira," he called to his mate. "We're leaving."

When Kira and Caroline came out of the bathroom the alpha female was still glaring at him. Malec looked at her feeling more than a little chastised and said, "I'm going to take care of it."

"You'd better," Kira told him before coming up on tiptoe

and kissing his cheek. "And take a shower. You smell like a dog."

She was smiling when she pulled back from him, and that simple act warmed his heart. He hadn't liked it when she'd showed up at the lodge a couple of months ago, and he hadn't trusted her at all. Now he loved her like his sister and cherished her as the alpha's mate.

"Should I be afraid?" he heard Caroline ask when they were once again alone. "What exactly does 'I'll take care of it' mean?"

Malec hung his head low, exhaling a breath and wondering how the hell he'd gotten to this point with this female. It wasn't supposed to turn out like this. He was never supposed to be in this position.

"You don't have to be afraid of me. Not now or ever," he told her, moving to where the remnants of the front door lay on the floor. "Where are your hammer and nails?"

"What?"

He turned to look at her then. She was no longer crying, but her eyes were red and puffy, her hair pulled back from her face, her hands still trembling slightly.

Malec hated himself for that. He hated that he'd ever walked into her life and pulled her into this mess.

"I need a hammer and some nails. Or rather just a screwdriver will do. I can take this closet door and put it here as a temporary front door. The knobs are similar, so I can swap out the lock as well."

He heard his own words and knew they sounded off considering what had just happened, but that was how Malec needed to play this. He needed to restore the things he'd broken, the things he'd disturbed.

Caroline moved without another word. She came to him a few minutes later with a miniature tool kit, and he went to work. Neither of them spoke until he was done, and then it was Caroline who broke the silence.

"You weren't going to ever tell me, were you? You could have, you know. I wouldn't have told anyone," she said.

Malec had just closed the new door and locked it. He stood with his back to her, flattening his palms on the warm wood. He wanted to turn around and look her in the eye, to give her the same type of honesty and candidness that she'd always afforded him. But he couldn't.

What if I find a woman and fall in love with her? What if she's a human? I can never tell her who and what I really am.

That's what Mason had said to him the night he'd died. He'd asked his twin brother how he could continue to live the life that he considered a big lie, and Malec hadn't had a response. Just like he didn't have one for Caroline now. He hated himself for that.

"I had a twin brother named Mason," he said instead, still not turning to face her. "He hated what we were, hated that we had to live under this cloak of secrecy. He wanted a better life, one where he could look forward to falling in love with a woman and being everything she needed him to be. But he knew he could never do that. If the woman wasn't one of us, a lycan, Mason knew that was never going to be possible."

"He thought a human woman wouldn't love him if she knew he was a . . ." She paused.

Malec turned to her then, knowing that his eyes glowed the blue of a lycan while every other feature of his remained human. "A lycan," he told her. "I am a lycan. A hybrid of a human and a werewolf that had been cursed by a Greek god."

She didn't speak for a few seconds, only watched him, her gaze never faltering. Caroline had more confidence than anyone Malec had ever met, even himself. She should have been running for help, calling the police, shouting to the heavens that this monstrosity was in her house, killing people in front of her. But she wasn't.

"He was wrong," she replied finally. "He was pre-judging all humans in the very same way he despised the possibility of being pre-judged."

"He was young and frustrated. I told him it would be okay, that we were here for a reason and that all we needed to do was focus on that reason. That's all we needed to worry about," Malec said. There was a tightness in his chest as the words flowed through his mind. He couldn't speak them all at once, but he wanted to. Oh, how he wanted to get this heavy weight off his chest.

Dragging a hand over his face he pushed away from the door, walking past her and into the living room that was still a mess. He lifted the couch, pushing it into the position he thought it might have been in before.

"If he'd just kept his mind on our goals, our destiny, he would have been all right. He shouldn't have been thinking about being with a human anyway. They don't deserve to endure our troubles. He should have just focused and coped with the circumstances like I did." The words came quickly and with a rush of breath and energy that had him picking up an end table and a broken lamp. After surveying the lamp he walked into the kitchen, dropping it into the trash can in there.

He went back into the living room, picking up her telephone and keys and placing them on the table.

"Why couldn't he just learn to cope? Why did he have to kill himself instead? Why the hell did he think that was the only answer?" Malec yelled, his throat stinging with the pain that had haunted him for far too long.

"Is that what you've done, Malec?" Caroline asked quietly. "You figure the way to cope is by hiding in the woods and refusing to allow yourself to feel anything serious, anything real?"

That was exactly what he'd done.

Malec inhaled deeply and exhaled slowly. "I did what I had to do."

Turning, he saw her standing closer to him than she had been before. "I'll run you a bath and finish getting things straightened out here, and then I'll leave."

Because the look in her eyes was tearing him apart inside.

Caroline took another step toward him. "What if I asked you to stay?"

His chest clenched, his muscles tightening all over. "You know everything now. I trust you won't say anything. There's no need—"

"That's just the thing, Malec," she said, interrupting him. "There is a need, and I think it's more than either one of us anticipated. More than we can even begin to consider walking away from."

CHAPTER 12

He stayed.

And they showered in silence.

Malec washed her, and Caroline washed him. When they came out and stepped into her bedroom, he sat on the edge of the bed and reached for his clothes that he'd left there. Caroline stood near her dresser, holding the towel tightly around her body.

"Can I see it?" she asked. "Can I see the lycan?"

He paused, his shirt in his hands, towel still wrapped around his waist, and simply stared at her.

"I'm not a circus animal, Caroline," he said, his words full of hurt and humiliation.

Caroline recognized that all too well, so instead of telling him what should have been glaringly apparent—that she knew he wasn't a damned circus animal—she decided to share something else with him instead.

"I was seven when my teacher, her name was Mrs. Hollis," Caroline began, folding her arms over her chest, "made me stay after class one day and asked me who I lived with. I told her my mother, and Mrs. Hollis asked who else. I didn't know what she meant because it had always been just me and Max—my mom, I mean. She didn't like for me to call her Mom all the time. Only when we were alone.

"Anyway, Mrs. Hollis kept asking me over and over again, and finally I yelled that I didn't have a daddy. You want to know what she asked me after that?"

Malec didn't reply, but his gaze was intent on hers.

"She asked if my mother even knew who my father was. I went home that night, and I asked Max that very question: 'Do you know who my daddy is?' Max's reply was without hesitation, a cool and distinct no. She didn't know who my father was because it could have been any one of her clients. I asked what a client was because that's how I've always been. If I have a question, I ask. The only stupid question is the one that goes unasked, and all that."

Caroline shrugged, the memories in her mind as clear as if they had just happened yesterday.

"Max's clients were businessmen, cops, construction workers, drunks, and druggies, any guy who could pay her fee. She explained everything to me, her six-year-old sometimes-daughter. Max never lied to me regardless of whether or not what she was telling me was appropriate or even legal for that matter. As I grew up I began to see more and more of her clients coming in and out of our apartment. One day when I was thirteen I ran out of the house too fast in the morning because Max's client was still there. I hurried to get to school, and I forgot my coat. It snowed that day, and the counselor asked me where my coat was. I told her I left it home. She asked if my mother had sold it for drugs. By the time I made it to the ninth grade the guys in school had already begun propositioning me. They offered me their allowance, their history notes, even marijuana—because of course I used drugs since my mother was a prostitute—to give them some head in the stairwell of the school or to go into the locker room with them and let them fuck me up against the lockers."

Malec growled then.

She'd heard the sound before when he'd been in her office looking down at that second buck. He was angry, she thought. But not as angry and embarrassed as she had been.

"Joey Winstadt was sleeping with my foster mother. One night at dinner, when she'd gone into the kitchen to get him another bottle of Jack Daniel's, he leaned over and whispered in my ear that he knew who I was. He'd heard all about my mother and how good she was and that he was betting that she'd taught me everything she knew. I looked right in his eyes and told him no, that I didn't know anything. How could I be a prostitute if I was a virgin? He stared at me a lot during that next year, and the morning of my eighteenth birthday he walked into the bedroom I shared with a nine-year-old foster kid and asked me to suck his dick. I told him I didn't know how, and he showed me. Joey showed me so many things and then, ten months later, he showed me the door.

"And then there was Brent," Caroline said without skipping a beat.

"Stop," Malec told her, his voice low and deadly calm.

"No, you need to hear this," she told him with a shake of her head. "You need to hear how Brent was a businessman and he wined and dined me, filled my head with everything I thought I wanted to hear from a man just before he had sex with me at every opportunity. It was the perfect relationship until I opened my door one day and got slapped in the face by Brent's wife. You see, Brent had taken pictures and videos of us together. He loved to see me, he'd said. Wanted to be able to see me at any time, in any place. Well, apparently he'd been looking while he was at work, and he was fired. Someone on the staff e-mailed the pictures to his wife. And you know what he said when I went to him looking for answers and support, asking him what the hell we were going to do?"

Malec shook his head. "You don't have to do this."

"Oh yes, I do," she told him. "Brent said, 'Do I look like the type of man to leave his wife for an easy slut like you?'"

"Bastard," Malec cursed, his fingers tightening on the shirt he still held.

"When I saw that first news broadcast about the Shadow Shifters I was astonished. For about an hour I thought of all the people that may have been walking beside me on the streets that I had no idea who or what they were on the inside. I figured, wow, they're just like me. Every human looked at them and thought they knew the truth, when really they had no idea."

Caroline shook her head and continued, "All my life I knew what people saw when they looked at me, Malec. And still, I managed to put myself through college, to become a very talented veterinarian, and to move myself to a town where I was needed. I did that because, just like you, I felt like I had no other choice."

"I'm sorry all that happened to you."

"Don't be sorry," she said, shaking her head. "Just don't sit there and presume you know what I'm thinking when I look at you. I want to see who you are, Malec, not because I think you're some kind of freak, but because think I may be falling in love with a lycan."

There, she'd said it, and her stomach quivered with the admission. She wasn't going to tell him this, wasn't going to put herself on the line like this again. But she hadn't been able to stop herself. Looking into Malec's eyes, whether it was the blue or the brown ones, that hurt and disappointment was still there, and it pierced her soul to know that he wouldn't allow her to do anything to make it better.

Malec didn't speak. He dropped the shirt to the floor and stood, removing the towel next. In an instant his hands moved, long, sharp nails extending immediately. His forehead stretched and protruded, the close-cut black hair he normally sported grew a little longer, standing straight up, stretching down the sides of his face, and his eyes, they were blue again.

Caroline went to him. She touched a hand to his cheek and smiled as he leaned into her touch. "Still sexy as hell," she said. "Now that should be a crime."

He bared his teeth then, his dick jutting forward with the action.

"I didn't want to want you," she confessed, flattening another palm on the hard pectoral muscle of his chiseled chest. "I told myself over and over again that it wasn't going to work. That I could not possibly want him . . . and his friend. I was making a mistake again."

He lifted a hand, carefully slipping one of those long, clawed fingers beneath the binding of the towel, flicking it open with one quick motion. When it was on the floor he lifted those sharp nails to her nipples, tapping them against her piercings until they clicked. Her nipples grew hard instantly.

"You didn't want to want me either," she continued, her voice going lower, both her palms on his chest now. "Even with Channing, you were certain that this human couldn't possibly be what you needed."

Caroline leaned in, licking her tongue around his nipple while he still toyed with hers. His breathing hitched, that growling sound rumbling from deep in his chest. It was like a message, a special lycan Morse code that went straight to her clit, causing it to throb and harden.

"But you do want me, Malec," she said, letting her hands slide down to grip his thick cock. "You want to take me by yourself, just as badly as you needed to take me with Channing. I know because I feel the same way."

This time Malec moaned and gripped her breasts. Caroline looked down to see that the claws had retracted. She looked up at his face to see his brown-eyed gaze staring back at her. She smiled up at him and whispered, "Sit down."

Of course he hesitated because he was the one used to calling the shots. But this was her house and her rules. "Sit down right here," she told him again, this time gripping his cock and rubbing her thumb over the tip.

Malec sat dutifully, and Caroline immediately straddled him. He placed his hands at her hips, his mouth closing over one dark nipple. She slipped her hand under that breast, lifting it higher to feed him, loving the sight of his lips on her skin. With her other hand she went straight for her clit, rubbing the tight little bud frantically while he suckled her.

He pushed that hand away, pulling his mouth from her tit to say, "I'll do that."

And she let him, arching her back so she could continue to enjoy his hot mouth on her breast and his finger working her clit. She was wet, could feel her essence dripping from her pussy, and when Malec let his finger glide back to dip into that sweet nectar, then lifted it to her lips, she sucked that finger as if it were his cock. He moaned, and so did she.

Then she was the one moving his hand away, grasping his dick and positioning the tip at her entrance, sinking down on his length slowly, deliciously. His teeth held on to her nipple then, applying just enough pressure to have her screaming his name before she began riding his cock.

Malec kept his face between her breasts, moving his hands to her hips, lifting her and slamming her down on his length in sync with his quick thrusts. Caroline's nails dug into his shoulders, the feel of his thickness slipping in and out of her intoxicating.

He rubbed all the right places, until she felt like exploding. She yelled his name, "Malec!" with her eyes closed, still seeing him in his lycan form.

She'd been telling the truth when she'd said he was still sexy as hell, even as a wolf. Not only had his facial features and his hands changed, but his body looked more buff, stronger, his dick hung longer down his thigh, still thick and oh so damned enticing. She'd wanted to go to her knees and suck him off while he ran those clawed nails through her hair. It was strange and yet so fucking sexy at the same time.

Just like now. She touched the sides of her breasts, squeezing them together while he licked both of them, one and then the other, letting them rub along his cheeks while they fucked. When he abruptly pulled back, saying quickly,

"Turn that shit around," Caroline immediately did as he asked.

She lifted up off him, climbing onto the bed, this time kneeling with her back facing him. Malec grabbed her hips once more, slapping her ass while she reached between his legs to grab hold of his cock. Positioning him at her entrance again she slammed down on him this time, loving the sound of her flesh slapping against his.

Malec immediately pushed her forward, his hand pressing strongly at the base of her back. Caroline leaned in until her breasts were rubbing against his thighs while Malec pulled her cheeks farther apart. She continued to pump him while Malec's fingers reached down to touch her clit. He circled the nub until Caroline was moaning and mumbling something incoherent. He continued that sweet torture until Caroline was biting her lower lip, it felt so good. Then he moved those devilish fingers back to circle around her anus. She bucked at first, and he smacked her ass again. "Bring it back," he told her. "Bring that sweetness back to me."

Caroline loved the sound of his voice, the way it stroked along every nerve in her body, coaxing and begging her to acquiesce. She did, leaning back, arching so that her ass was up even as her pussy continued to move over his cock. Malec slipped in one and then two fingers, thrusting slowly in and out of her anus while his dick still worked inside her pussy.

Caroline couldn't see; hell, she could barely breathe. There was nothing but pleasure. Nothing but the sweet, delicious buzz of complete satisfaction ripping intensely through her body.

"You like that, don't you?" he asked her. "You like double penetration."

Caroline continued to ride him fiercely, wanting that release more than she wanted her next breath.

"Answer me, Caroline! Answer me, my sexy little vixen," he whispered, thrusting his fingers with a little more pressure in and out of her.

"Yes!" she screamed. "Fuck! Yes!"

Malec worked her pussy and her anus until Caroline bucked over him, squeezing his legs as her release ripped through her like a torrential storm. She yelled his name and heard him coming right behind her, making another sound . . . a howl, she was sure.

CHAPTER 13

Channing was there, standing at the bathroom door with Caroline's robe when she stepped out. Malec had handed her the towel when their shower was complete, but now, to her shock and yes, pleasure, Channing was wrapping her in the warmth of her terry cloth robe.

"I made tea," he told her. "Chamomile because my mother insists it's good for calming the soul."

Caroline could smell the tea, and a smile slowly formed. "You're the best," she told him, not even bothering to ask where he'd come from.

She should have known he wouldn't have left. Channing was a nurturer; he had an instinctive need to take care of the people around him, the ones that he cared about. As he tied the robe's sash tightly at her waist she felt a little giddy at the fact that she was now included in that group.

"That door's not sturdy," he told Malec with a grim glance over Caroline's shoulder.

"It was all I could do for the moment," was Malec's deep retort.

They were both standing close to her. This time Malec in the back and Channing in front. It was warm here and more comfortable than she'd ever thought possible. Right in this spot, positioned between these two intriguing men, or lycans. There was no fear and no trepidation this time, only comfort. How often had she longed for this feeling, Caroline could barely recall. And when she wanted to question whether or not what she was feeling was right or wrong, Channing's palm cupped her face.

"Let's get you into bed. You could probably use some rest," he told her.

"I'll get the tea," Malec said as he leaned into her other cheek, kissing her there softly before walking away.

She followed Channing's lead as he moved her toward the bed, gathering the sheets that she and Malec had mussed and fluffing her pillows.

"You stayed outside even though you knew what we were doing," she said as she sat on the bed and looked up to him.

He held his head down for a brief second, then looked up to her with those sexy-as-hell eyes.

"I gave you the space you needed," he told her.

"And what do you need, Channing?" she asked. "When do you get what you actually need?"

It was an important question for her, one that she'd been pondering more than she'd been willing to admit.

He sat down beside her then, wrapping an arm around her shoulders. "I get to be right here with you. I get to look at you and know that you are safe."

She smiled at him because that wasn't the answer she was expecting, and yet it was the one that made her feel the best.

"You have a dimple," he said, touching her left cheek. "It peeks out right here when you smile. I saw it that first night when you were at the bar with your girlfriend, and I liked it. I knew I wanted to see it every day for the rest of my life."

"Here's your tea," Malec interrupted.

Caroline hadn't even heard him return to the room, but there was now a cup of hot tea in front of her. Channing took the cup from Malec's hands and held it to her lips for her to take a tentative sip. He did that until she motioned to him that she was finished, moments later.

"I did some more work on the door and propped a few things in front of it," Malec said. "It'll do for tonight. Besides, I'll be right here, so everything will be fine."

Channing made a move like he was going to stand at that moment, saying, "That's fine. I'll be in the living room keeping watch."

"No," Caroline said, reaching out a hand to touch his arm. "Stay. Here in the bed with me. I want you both to stay."

Malec did not leave Caroline. He couldn't.

He held her throughout the night again. This time the thoughts flooding through his mind were different from what they had been before. He was no longer trying to figure out if he were falling for her and if that was the biggest mistake of his life. It was no longer a question.

For the first time in he didn't know how long, Malec had made it through the night without remembering and regretting. He'd lain there with his arms wrapped loosely around her, not tight as he had the last time when he'd thought if he let go she might actually slip away. No, throughout the last few hours he'd felt her steady breathing as her hands lay against his while they slept. When he kissed the top of her head, she nuzzled closer into him, and he felt a warmth and satisfaction that he'd never experienced before.

Channing did not leave her either.

The lycan that Malec had known and come to think of as a brother had slept on the other side of Caroline, his front to her back, his hand on her hips, while Malec's circled her shoulders. They'd kept her like this, between them, protected by them and . . . cared for by them, throughout the night.

This was different for Malec, the sleeping arrangement and the feelings that swarmed through him as a result. It was more than he could have ever wished for with any female, and it had happened with a human. With an inward sigh he'd watched as the soft, golden rays of the sun poured through the thin curtain at the window in her bedroom and noted that the light did not bother him at all.

He'd preferred it dim in his own bedroom because it had been morning when he'd found out that Mason was dead. Sunlight had poured through the windows in his parents' house as Malec had awakened to his mother's screams, and when he'd stood there staring at his brother's hanging body in the bathroom the fluorescent light combined with the sun had made it so blindingly bright he hadn't been able to avoid seeing the body, or that his brother was gone forever.

He closed his eyes to that thought right now, noticing the pain that normally cut through him like a knife had subsided substantially, as with each breath he inhaled the scent of her hair, and it filled his senses. The feel of her softness beneath him, the warm brush of her breaths across his bare chest, all covered him in a blanket of satisfaction. A feeling he'd never thought was possible to achieve.

There was a soft moan and the feel of her shifting slightly

beside his gaze dropping down to her face. There was a small smile, even as her eyes remained closed. Channing was kissing the back of her shoulder, his eyes closed as his tongue slid over mocha-hued skin. The sight was erotic and intimate and had Malec's mouth instantly watering to do the same.

He ran his fingers through her hair, loving the softness of the loose curls and the way she arched her neck upward at his touch. Her lips were parted slightly as her eyes fluttered open to meet his gaze.

"Kiss me good morning, Malec," she whispered to him.

There was no way in hell that Malec was not going to oblige her. Lowering his lips to hers, he touched them quickly in a light kiss, then went in deeper when her hands flattened on his chest. His tongue delved deeper, stroking over hers with languid movements that had his dick instantly hardening, his mind filling with thoughts of her and her pleasure.

"Good morning, beautiful."

Caroline heard his voice seconds after she felt Channing's hands slipping between the crevice of her bottom. His tongue had been tracing lacy circles over her back, warming and arousing her with slow and undeniable precision. As she'd slept through the night she recalled the feeling of intense heat surrounding her. It should have been uncomfortable and annoying, but instead it was relaxing. She was safe here, in this bed, between them. Nowhere else and at no other time had she felt this way. That thought had roamed in and out of her head while she'd slept and dreamed of them touching her, kissing her, wanting her in the exact way they were now.

Her mind sighed a good morning in response to Channing, because her mouth was otherwise occupied by the sweet and intoxicating efforts of Malec's tongue. Channing's hand cupped her cheek before sliding down her thigh. His teeth nipped the tender skin at her spine as he lifted her leg, sliding it upward until Malec reached down grabbing the back of her knee and locking her leg to his side.

Channing continued to move lower as his fingers slipped between the already-moist folds of her vagina. Those clever fingers moved slowly but provided instant and potent jabs of desire that shot through Caroline's body like hot spikes. She gasped at the touch and moaned when Malec bit her bottom lip in response. With her back arched Caroline's blunt-tipped nails dug into Malec's chest. Channing continued his assault by pressing two fingers deep into her aching center. She bucked against him, wanting . . . no, definitely needing more.

And Channing gave it to her.

"So hot and wet for us," he whispered. "You were dreaming about us taking you, weren't you, baby?"

His voice was so smooth and yet so sexy as he whispered, his breath fanning warmly over her bottom, where he kissed and licked insistently. Caroline was on fire, as Malec had released his hold on her leg—probably assured that she wasn't going to put it down for fear of severing the delicious torture that Channing had begun. Malec's hand was now cupping her breast, kneading the heavy mound before taking her piercing between his fingers and shaking until she gasped.

"Yes!" she moaned. "Yes! Both of you!"

It was true, she had been dreaming about them, ever since that first night at the bar. She'd seen Channing's alluring blue eyes and heard Malec's deep, sexy voice. She'd felt them surrounding her, enticing her, welcoming her. Her first instinct had been denial. Now, all Caroline could think about was the need, the desire that threatened to strangle her and the two gorgeous men that were intent on giving her everything she never knew she needed.

"Let's give her what she wants, Malec," Channing whispered, just before he'd moved so low that his tongue could now slip into the moistened cove where his fingers had just stroked.

"Everything she wants," Malec replied, moving his hot kisses down the line of her neck and then to finally, blessedly, cover her nipple.

As Malec's tongue worked over one nipple, his other hand squeezed her opposite breast. Channing's tongue thrust deep into her center while his thumb flattened over her clit, rubbing until Caroline was pumping fiercely against his ministrations. She couldn't open her eyes, couldn't say anything more than their names, over and over again as her head thrashed against the pillows.

She was on fire, her body and mind screaming in ecstasy as their mouths and hands worked on her. With a moan from each of them, almost orchestrated into a sort of erotic rhythm, Caroline felt sexier and more desired than she ever had before. These two men, these two lycans, wanted her. They were telling her with their mouths and their hands, and the sounds of their desire echoed throughout the room. They wanted her and—god help her, as her body tensed, ripples of pleasure soared through her as the most intense orgasm she'd ever experienced overtook her—she wanted them in return.

"Good morning," Channing said as he'd slid his naked body along hers.

With a finger to her chin, he turned her face so that she could receive his kiss, his lips still wet with her sweet-as-honey cream.

She kissed him back, letting her tongue rub along his, her eyes still dark with the release she'd just experienced. It had been that way for him too; that's why he was able to see it so clearly in her eyes. The moment her body had tensed, her muscles contracting, Channing could do nothing but continue to stroke his tongue along tenderness. Her taste was beyond anything he could have ever imagined, sweet and thick and all for him to enjoy.

He'd loved holding on to her throughout the night, feeling the curve of her ass cradled against the hard length of his cock. It was exactly where he'd wanted to be. And when morning came he hadn't been able to resist. He'd wanted to taste her and he had, and now he knew without a shadow of a doubt that she was meant for him. And for Malec.

"Good morning," she replied with a smile as she lay back on the bed.

Malec continued to toy with her breasts while Channing stared down into her face.

"Thank you for staying," she said to him, lifting a hand up to cup his cheek.

Her touch was warm and genuine, and Channing turned his face into her palm to kiss her there.

"You are so very welcome," he replied.

"We won't leave you again," Malec said. "You know who and what we are now, and as long as you are okay with that, we want to stay with you."

The words were different and sounded strange to Channing's ears, but they were also true. She belonged with them, and Channing wasn't about to let her go.

"Come back to the lodge with us," Channing said to her as he watched her look from him to Malec and then back to him again.

"You'll be safer there," Malec added.

"We'll take care of you there," Channing continued, this time touching his hand to her face, letting his fingers slide slowly along the line of her jaw. "We want to take care of you, Caroline. To give you all the pleasure you desire and to make you happy."

There was no doubt that Caroline would be safer at the lodge with the entire pack there to protect her, even though the threat of the Solo was now over. But after hearing her speak about what she'd endured throughout her childhood and into early adulthood, Channing wasn't positive that telling her to pack up and move out there with them was going to go over very well. Malec, of course, would not have thought of it that way, which was why Channing was the seducer.

She stared up at him, blinking for a few silent seconds before replying, "What if I say no? What if I would rather stay here in my own house and continue going to work at the clinic that I believe is just beginning to get used to me being here?"

Channing could hear the immediate thumping of Malec's heartbeat only seconds before his reply came.

"Then I'll just have to move in here," Malec told her. "Me and Channing."

Her eyes grew a little wider as she looked at both of them

once more. "Are you serious? You *and* Channing would move in with me?"

Channing nodded as he had been considering his response carefully. The bottom line was he had no intention of letting her out of his sight from this point on—even without the threat of some maniac lycan trying to make her a pawn in his game. He simply did not want to be away from her, but he wasn't sure that was going to be reason enough for her to pack up and move with them.

"We're dead serious," Channing told her. "Last night with you was wonderful, more gratifying than I know either Malec or I have ever experienced, and we're not about to walk away from you or from what we can have together."

"I . . . I don't know," she said, shifting so that she could sit up in the bed.

Channing moved over, as did Malec, but they both still stayed on the bed with her. Caroline pulled the sheet high up on her chest as she used both hands to push her hair back from her face and attempted to smooth it down.

"I've never considered anything like this before. What if it doesn't work? What will people say?"

Channing took her hand then, lacing his fingers through hers. "This is just about us, baby," he told her. "It's about us taking care of you and pleasuring you."

"Is that all it's about?" she asked as she looked over to Channing.

He opened his mouth to speak and then, for the first time that he could ever remember, he closed it, unable to reply. What did he say to that question? How did he tell her that he felt deep down in his soul that she was their mate, that he'd felt that the moment he first saw her? Would she believe him, or would the doubt already clouding her eyes continue to bloom?

"This is new to us," Malec intervened. "There are no rules and no expectations. But we want you with us."

She'd looked to Malec as he moved off the bed. He didn't know what to say to her either, and Channing knew that meant they were in big trouble.

"Caroline," Channing started to say, but she held up a hand, effectively silencing him once again.

She grabbed the sheet, wrapping it around her as she moved off the bed.

"Before either of you says another word, just listen to me for a moment. I want you both to know that it's not just been since I met you that I've been trying to fight this. I've always known," she said with a sigh. "Not that I would end up in bed with two men, but I've always known that my needs and desires were not like other women's. I thought I was dealing with that in the best way that I knew how. Then the two of you came along."

Channing rubbed a hand down the back of his head as he continued to watch her. He wanted to touch her, to reach out and take her into his arms, but he knew that this was something she had to do on her own. He couldn't decide this for her, and neither could Malec, although Channing was sure the other lycan was quickly trying to come up with a way that he could change that.

"Do you believe in fate?" Caroline asked Malec, who shrugged in response.

When she looked to Channing, he nodded, because he absolutely believed in fate. Or rather, he'd known, as the lycan being that should not have been on this earth in the first place, to accept what the Moirai, or the Fates, had planned for him.

"I do too," Caroline continued. "I think that everything in my life happened to lead me to this point, and possibly to you. Max, my mother, she believed in fate, saying that whatever was meant to be for your life, would be." She shrugged. "I don't know how else to explain it, just that I wanted you both immediately, and I think you felt the same about me. Last night was different, but it felt right. It felt good. Still, in the light of day, I just don't know about this other thing . . . this ménage. I don't know how to even consider something like that. What would people say? How would we go about doing this? Would both of you take me out to dinner? And how about our sleeping arrangements? Do we all climb into your king-sized bed? We could never fit into that small car of yours, Malec, as gorgeous as it is. And, Channing, I don't even know what type of car you drive."

She was exasperated now, her fingers scraping along her scalp as she thrust them into her hair. They were pushing her, and it wasn't fair. Channing and Malec had known for years that this was what they wanted in their lives. They'd only given Caroline days to figure it out.

With that in mind, Channing moved from the bed and went to Caroline. He kissed her on the forehead and smiled down at her.

"Why don't you get a shower and get dressed for work. Your entire life does not have to change because we came into it," he told her sincerely.

"I'll drive you to the clinic, in my small car," Malec said with a wry chuckle. "'Cause I'm betting that this guy rode his superbike here, and I know you're not getting on the back of that."

Caroline smiled over at him and then gave Channing a questioning look.

"It's a Kawasaki Ninja, and she'd be welcome to ride on the back anytime she wanted," he told her.

"That's a pretty sweet ride," she told him. "What color is it?"

"Candy-apple red," he replied, a little surprised that she knew the type of bike he'd been referring to.

She nodded, then came up on tiptoe to kiss him softly on the lips. Before Channing could say anything in response she was pulling away, stopping in front of Malec and placing a hand on his chest as she kissed him too. It was when she disappeared into the bathroom that Malec and Channing both finally released the breath they'd been holding because the worry that she would toss them both out on their asses was real.

Luckily, Channing thought, the Fates had intervened.

CHAPTER 14

An hour and a half later, Caroline stood on the steps of the clinic watching as Malec pulled away in that sleek and sexy car. Her argument that she could drive herself to work had been completely ignored and when she'd brought up how she would get home, Malec had immediately announced that he'd be picking her up. Originally, she'd been upset by his presumptiveness, but now, she'd smiled as she realized how good a match man and car were. Channing had looked deliciously handsome sitting astride his bike, Caroline recalled as she'd climbed into Malec's car. They were two hot men, and they were all hers, she'd thought with a nervous giggle that had her immediately looking around to see if anyone had seen her.

Had Nora seen her getting out of Malec's car? What would she have said if she did? And why should Caroline even care?

With a sigh she unlocked the door and let herself into the clinic, gasping loudly when she turned on the light to see pictures taped along the front of the receptionist stand. They were taped around the window. She turned and saw them on the file cabinet, all along the walls. Lifting a hand she covered her mouth to stifle a scream as the pictures were the same as the one that crazy lycan had in her house last night. It was of her and Channing and Malec.

"So you decided to come back," Martin said, walking slowly from one of the back offices, using another picture to fan himself.

"What the hell are you doing? Where did you get these pictures?" she asked.

"Did you know that I've worked here for sixteen years?" Martin asked.

For the first time since she'd taken over as the head doctor of the clinic, Caroline really looked at Dr. Martin Woods. He was a tall, thin man, in his late thirties, his face sallow, eyes bulging slightly. His hair was graying at the temples, and the earring in his left ear that at one time might have given him an edge of sex appeal just looked odd on the otherwise nondescript man.

"Yes, I read your résumé, Martin," she replied in a stiff tone.

After she was hired, Caroline had the option of keeping the existing staff or hiring new people—her people. She opted to keep the existing staff because she hadn't had the heart to fire anyone. She also figured it would help her make more friends in town if she remained friendly with those who had worked for her.

As far as Martin was concerned, that philosophy had never worked. She had a feeling today was a prime example of that fact.

"I've been living here in Blackbriar all my life. We're good people here. We take pride in our land, and we love our animals," he told her, slapping that picture down on Olivia's desk. "Then you come along, and all hell breaks loose!"

Caroline was already shaking her head because she had an idea of what he was thinking.

"Where did you get these pictures, Martin? Who gave them to you?" she asked, still keeping eye contact with him, but backing up until she was closer to the door.

"Nobody gave them to me," he told her, his face twisting with disgust. "I took them myself!"

"What? Why?"

"Because you're a whore and a slut, and I knew it from the first time you stepped into this clinic," he spat. "Oh sure, Dr. Willoughby thought you were hot stuff coming from that fancy school back east with all those recommendations from other doctors. But he had no idea what you really were. You hid it from him, but not me. Not for one minute."

Had the lycan that was at her apartment last night taken Martin's camera and then developed the pictures? Why would he have done that? Just to get her to bring Malec to him?

Caroline felt her cheeks heating, her fingers clenching and unfolding at her sides as she struggled to keep her composure.

"So you followed me out to someone's private property and took personal pictures of me. Now what's your plan, Martin?" she asked, wondering how that lycan had gotten the pictures if Martin had taken them.

"My papa always used to say that karma never forgot an address. What goes around comes right back around," he said with a sickly chuckle. "I snapped the pictures, but my camera got stolen before I could have 'em developed. It's so damned creepy out there in the woods. I thought a damned dog or wolf was howling behind me, and I decided to get the hell out of there quick. That's probably when I dropped my camera. Anyway, when I got home last night there was my camera and my pictures, and I knew I had you then."

Caroline was shaking her head. "You're sick," she told him. "Sick and delusional. Who I choose to have sex with has nothing to do with how I perform my job."

"Oh, you're a performer, all right, and I'm going to let everyone in this town know just what kind," he told her, moving to the desk and pulling out even more of those pictures.

At that moment Nora came through the door, almost knocking Caroline down as she pushed past her.

"You!" she shouted, and Caroline wondered what the hell was going on now.

"You must be one of them! Abomination! Atrocity! Animal!" Nora yelled, pointing her finger at Caroline, as if that were really necessary.

It was obvious she hadn't come in there to accuse Martin of anything. Of course that wasn't possible because he was one of them, and Caroline was not. And she was beginning to think that she never would be.

"My goodness. What is this?" Nora asked, turning around to see the pictures. "You are one of them! Just look at you!"

"Yeah, they're all filthy heathens," Martin added.

"And they're those shifter things like they said on the news. All of them! Jeb heard them yelling and howling and carrying on over in her apartment. We went over there this morning, and it's got the wrong door on the hinges and it's a foul smell, like something died in that alley behind her place," Nora announced. "We all know it now. We know just what you are. Poor Olivia couldn't even come in here today to face you. She feels so betrayed. I told her not to be—that's how you things work. But I won't have you here. Not in my town!"

"That's right," Martin chimed in. "Whatever you are you need to go and take those others out with you."

Caroline's head was spinning.

Was this really happening to her again?

Were these people actually standing there judging her for things they knew absolutely nothing about?

"We don't want your kind here!" Nora had just yelled and lunged.

Caroline had been standing there not really sure of what was going on, but she looked up just in time to see the crazy platinum blonde coming at her. She pulled an arm back and punched Nora the second the woman was close enough, knocking her straight back onto the floor.

"Bravo!" Caroline heard from behind and whirled around to see Channing walking into the office.

"Oh shit! He's one of them! He's . . . I gotta call the police . . . he's one of those shifting things," Martin was mumbling hysterically.

Channing shrugged and reached over the receptionist desk to pull the phone cord from the wall.

"You can call them after we're gone," he said, baring his teeth to Martin and causing the man to fall back into the desk chair, letting loose a high-pitched scream.

Channing turned to Caroline, extending a hand and asking simply, "You ready to go now?"

Caroline hadn't spoken a word in response. She first put her hand in his and walked out of that clinic, knowing she'd never step foot in that place again.

Channing had just pulled his shirt over his head when he heard the door to his bedroom open. A deep inhale told him exactly who it was, and he continued to snap his jeans and slip his feet into the boots that had been sitting beside his bed.

He'd returned to the house hours ago after taking Caroline back to her apartment and packing up all her clothes and belongings. She'd left the furniture and some pictures on the wall that she'd said were ugly. Other than that, all she had in life had fit into Channing's second mode of transportation, a shiny black Escalade. When he'd decided to go back to the lodge and switch vehicles that morning, it had been with the intention to come right back and watch her while she worked at the clinic. He wanted to be sure that the danger of the Solo was definitely over. He'd had no idea what he was going to return to, but was damned glad he'd made the decision to return to town.

They hadn't spoken much on the drive back to the lodge. Channing had suspected Caroline needed time to wrap her mind around all that had happened and the huge step she was taking in deciding to move into the lodge with him and Malec.

The huge step they were *all* taking.

"You went back to the clinic to watch her," Malec said, stepping into the room quietly.

Channing tied his boots and sat up straight in the chair. He looked at Malec, his pack mate and best friend. Then he stood, going back to his dresser to slip his watch onto his wrist.

"You were able to convince her to move back here," Malec continued. "I knew you would. I was going to talk to you about what our game plan should be when we got back."

"You shouldn't have left her alone," Channing replied. "Those people were vicious assholes to her. You knew that there had been witnesses last night, that our secret was out, and yet you left her alone."

Through the mirror he could see Malec standing with his hands thrust into the front pockets of his jeans. He looked so cool standing there, so aloof and in control, the way he always looked.

Malec nodded slightly, holding Channing's gaze. "I got Blaez's text message about some of the townspeople trying to come out here last night. So, yes, I knew that someone had seen something and that now the humans were reacting. That's why I was trying to convince her to come back here this morning."

"Is that the only reason why?" Channing turned to him and asked. "Are you only trying to protect her from the backlash of the situation? Of our fucked-up situation?"

Malec inhaled deeply as Channing crossed his arms over his chest. To a passerby they might have looked like they were in a standoff, two strong and virile men, facing each other with the fate of their future hanging like a weight between them.

"We've already fixed the sensors that the Solo damaged when he was out here. Phelan's commissioned more intricate software from some of the people he's still connected to at the Department of Defense. The people from town don't know exactly what they saw; they're thinking we're just

Shadow Shifters, just as Caroline had thought," Malec informed him.

Channing gave a tight nod before saying, "That takes care of the fact that they now realize they've been living close to shifters, but what about the fact that one of those nosy-assed townspeople was also out here taking pictures of me, you, and Caroline?"

Malec's hands came out of his pockets as he took a step closer to Channing. "What are you talking about?" he asked, the tone of his voice shifting immediately to that of ice-cold rage.

"That's right! Pictures that were plastered all over the clinic walls when she got there this morning. Two of them verbally attacked her right there in the receptionist's area, calling her names and doing everything but holding some type of ritual to cast her out of this damned town!"

Channing knew that his tone of voice had changed as well. He'd felt his heart rate rising as he spoke, remembering what he'd witnessed just a couple of hours ago. He'd wanted to break that guy named Martin's wrists for daring to spy on them. Who the hell did that, taking pictures of others having sex in the privacy of their own home? And these humans dared to call their pack savages? They were possibly more fucked up than the other species roaming the earth that they were so afraid of.

It was Malec's turn to yell now. "What the hell? Pictures? Dammit!"

"That's what convinced her to move out here, Malec. Not anything I said or you did. She had no other choice. They were going to physically remove her from the town or possibly treat her like they did those others during the witch trials. I got her out of there as fast as I could," Channing said, his temples throbbing with the memory.

Caroline, on the other hand, had looked so calm. She'd told him to take her to her apartment so that she could pack, and she'd done so with steady, organized motions, speaking as if she'd been planning the move for months. Channing hadn't seen her since they'd arrived at the house because Kira had whisked her away somewhere. All of Caroline's bags and belongings were still stacked in the living room.

"Ignorance," Malec sneered. "This is exactly what Mason predicted. What he knew would happen eventually."

Channing shook his head. "We've been watching it unfold for the last year, Malec. Since that fiasco in Washington, D.C., when the Shadow Shifters were unveiled. It was just a matter of time."

"That had nothing to do with us," Malec countered. "Those shifters were fighting a totally different battle than we were."

"Sure," Channing said, drawing a hand down his face, the hair of his beard prickling his palm. "They may not be up against the god of all gods and all his mythological powers, but they didn't want to be outed either. So now the government's forming task forces and armies to find and capture all the cat shifters they can, while Zeus has commissioned an all-out hunt for Blaez. And Caroline has just been swept onto a side of this supernatural war that she's not prepared to deal with."

Channing paused then, considering his words carefully. He'd been thinking about this all afternoon as he'd unpacked all the boxes of food and other supplies that he and Kira had ordered online. This was the only responsible answer. It was the best way to keep Caroline safe while the pack continued to figure out a way to keep Zeus and all the other bounty hunters from finding Blaez.

"We have to change her," Channing said finally, his words lingering in the silence of the room while Malec stared angrily at him.

"No," Malec replied only seconds later. "That's not an option."

Channing shook his head. "It's the only option, Malec, and you know it."

"I won't do that to her," Malec insisted. "I won't take away everything she knows, everything she's worked so hard to become. All that those dumb, narrow-minded humans told her she would not be. I won't sentence her to this."

Malec had finished with a vehement slap of his palm to his chest. Channing knew exactly what the other lycan was thinking and possibly what he was feeling. Being a lycan wasn't easy. Learning that he was totally different from the parents he'd come to love and all the people around him had been a tough pill for Channing to swallow all those years ago as well. But he had adapted, because he'd had no other choice.

"She's stronger than you think," Channing told Malec. "You weren't there today to see how she handled them, how she simply walked away, looking at them as if they were the ones with the problems, not her. She had pride and strength, and she held her head up high. She didn't beg them to understand or try to negotiate with them; she simply left, with only pity in her gaze for them. She's meant to be here with us, Malec. I know you feel that as strongly as I do."

At his sides, Malec splayed his fingers out wide, bringing

them back together slowly, all while a muscle in his jaw clenched. Channing had known this would upset him, but he didn't give a damn. It was the only choice, and he planned to move forward, with or without Malec's consent.

"This will end her life," Malec said, his words tight and restrained.

"Her life is here now," Channing told him. "It's with us."

Malec looked up at him, their gazes holding for silent seconds.

"She's the one for us," Channing continued. "You felt it that night at the bar, just like I did. As we stood there, you in front of her, me behind. I know you felt that connection, as if the Fates had finally brought us together."

"Don't give me that fate shit," Malec said, shaking his head. "You know I don't believe in it."

"But you do," Channing told him. "You have been believing in it since you walked out of your parents' house and joined the Marines. Since the moment you decided that you would not take your life the way Mason did. You made those decisions because you knew you had a greater purpose, a destiny to fulfill. And how could you fulfill that destiny without the Fates?"

"Fuck the Moirai!" Malec yelled. "They do Zeus's bidding, and they fuck with our lives, the ones that were already messed the hell up! They don't give a damn about us!"

"And yet they brought Kira to Blaez and Caroline to us. That was no mistake," Channing continued even though he could see Malec's body shaking with rage.

He knew he was pushing him, knew that this entire conversation was one Malec had never intended to have. But there was no other way.

"Aleya killed herself. Do you remember that, Channing? She put a blade in her chest because she didn't want to be the creature that Nyktimos had changed her into with that one bite on the night of the full moon. I won't . . . I can't . . . do that to Caroline. I just can't," Malec said quietly, shaking his head as he started to leave the room.

"But I can," Caroline said.

She stepped through the open adjoining door that connected Channing's bedroom to the sitting area on the other side.

"I can decide if I want to remain human or if I want to be changed to a lycan," she continued with her shoulders squared, her gaze now level with Malec's.

"No," he said slowly. "I won't sentence you to this life."

"It's not a sentence, as you put it, if it's what I want," she told him. "There's nothing for me in that world anymore. I've learned all I could, tried all I know how, and they're still determined to cast me aside. I'm tired of begging and pleading to be accepted. I just want to be . . . I want to be with you," she told Malec. Then she looked past him to where Channing stood. "And you."

Caroline and Channing stared at the doorway that Malec had just walked through. Phelan's text to Malec requesting he come see him in the monitor room had come at the most inopportune time.

The fact that this was also the most eye-opening moment of Caroline's life and that Malec had played a big part in her transformation hadn't escaped her either. Still, Malec had exited to carry out his duty, and she was left standing in

Channing's room, trying to grasp everything she'd just heard and what she'd just declared.

"Do you know what being with both of us will entail?" Channing asked from where he stood behind her.

Caroline let out a slow breath before she turned to face him, shaking her head. "All I know is that this is where I want to be. I have no idea how this . . . ah . . . the relationship with all three of us will work, but I don't want to be without either of you," she said to Channing.

He was watching her as if he wasn't certain her words were true, or that she actually knew what she was saying. But Caroline was perfectly clear on what she wanted, and she was determined to convince them of the same.

"We've never done this before," Channing told her. "The relationship or . . ."

"Or changing someone into a lycan," she finished for him. "Then I guess we're all going to be broken in together."

She tried for a little humor to ward off the tiny remnants of anxiety she'd felt as she'd listened to Malec and Channing discussing her future without her.

"One of the first rules will be no discussing me or anything that concerns me behind my back again. I'm perfectly capable of making my own decisions," she said, taking another step closer to him.

He nodded, his lips suppressing a smile. "I'll just bet you are perfectly capable, but I'm not the one you need to convince."

"I shouldn't have to convince anyone," she said. "Hell, I'm so sick and tired of fighting this battle. Of trying to prove myself to people who don't give a damn and trying to fit in where I obviously don't."

"You know, I can totally relate to that feeling," Channing said, coming closer and taking her hand.

They had moved to the sitting room after having followed Malec in an attempt to continue their conversation. Now Channing led Caroline to a sage-colored couch, which, as it turned out, was just as soft and comfortable as it looked. She sat down, leaning her elbows on her thighs.

"I never had any delusions about my life," she confessed. "I've been overweight since I was a little girl. The doctors never hesitated in telling me and my mother what I should weigh and how I should look. But Max was convinced that I should be whoever I was meant to be without anybody telling me anything." She shrugged. "So that's the same outlook I adopted. I'm proud of every ounce of my body, proud of the fact that I put myself through college and became something other than the prostitute that they thought I would be. And I'm more than the slut that these repressed and judgmental people of Blackbriar now think. Maybe I was always meant to be right here, in this place with you and Malec. What if my destiny was to be a lycan all along?"

Channing had been rubbing his fingers over the back of her hand. The motion had been consoling, the look he gave her not at all judgmental, but of compassion. Just as she had come to expect from him.

He said, "I thought I knew who and what I was up until the night I turned sixteen. I'd been laid up for a couple of days after getting into a fight with these guys in the neighborhood. And I remember lying in my bed, staring up at the ceiling. We lived in a pretty rural area. There wasn't another house for miles down a long, winding road. My mother had opened the window because I'd been sweating when she came in to check on me. So I'm lying there, and a breeze is coming in the window—some light too because it was the full moon, and it was late—probably sometime around midnight."

Caroline touched his hand this time, taking it in hers as he talked.

"In the past days since I'd been in the fight I'd been thinking, why did Zane and his friends love picking on me so much? What was it about me that they didn't like? And then I felt it. Right along my spine it felt as if something were crawling there. I wiggled a bit and then finally turned over on my stomach when it didn't stop. I thought maybe a fly or some other insect had flown into the room and gotten into my bed. So if I rolled over, it could get up and go on its merry way.

"But the sensation along my spine didn't stop. I tried ignoring it, but that only seemed to have made it spread. My arms tingled, and so did my feet. My head started to itch, and I scratched and scratched. I rolled over on the bed again and looked straight out the window, to the moon. And just like that I knew."

"You knew you were a lycan," she said, a little breathless as she'd been so intent on listening to his story.

"No," he replied with a shake of his head. "I knew I was going to die."

She must have had a crazy look on her face because Channing smiled and quickly added, "I knew that boy that had tried to stand his ground but still took the beating from those three older boys was going to be no more. The shift overtook me, and in the next couple of days I was adjusting to the new things my body was feeling. I snapped a picture of myself when I'd had the guts to look in the mirror, and then I began researching because I knew in my gut that this was not just happening to me. Just as I knew kids like Zane were all over the world bullying other kids that were like me . . . like the old me."

Channing all of a sudden looked very serious, his gorgeous eyes pensive. "I killed Zane. On the next full moon when I'd learned more about who and what I was. I'd decided to hang out by the lake because there was a wooded area that was close. I wanted to shift and run through those woods just to see how it felt. I hadn't yet figured out that I could shift anytime I wanted, just thought it was on the night of the full moon like most of the werewolf legends stated. Zane was there, and he was smoking marijuana. Earlier in the day when we'd been in school Zane and his friends had put Fred Hampton's head in the toilet. They did that for all of ten minutes with other guys in the bathroom, taking bets on how long it would take before poor old Fred passed out. Well, Fred didn't pass out. He finally made it to sixth-period English and had a seizure from all the stress and the adrenaline rush during Zane's little stunt. Fred had been rushed to the hospital, and Zane and his friends had laughed the rest of the school day. The minute I saw him I pounced."

"Oh, Channing," Caroline said, her heart heavy from his words.

"I just did it, and then I left him there. They found his body weeks later, after some other animals had gotten a chance at him." Channing lowered his head then. "I've never forgotten that day. Never forgot what I was capable of."

Caroline could only shake her head. "He tormented you for no good reason but that he could. It was shameful and inhuman. For all that they accuse the shifters of being beasts, the humans aren't any better."

When he didn't speak, she cupped his face in her hands. "I know you told me that story because you want me to know all that goes with being a lycan. And I'll just tell you that what you've said doesn't stop me from believing you're a terrific guy, or lycan. You're honest and caring, and that's more than I can say for those 'superior' humans that you knew and the ones I ran into this morning."

"You're right about that," Channing said, touching her hair lightly. "You're beautiful, and you're spirited. You know who you are, and you're not ashamed. I think that's what I love most about you."

Caroline had opened her mouth to say something . . . she was going to thank him and to tell him how handsome he was, but she stopped.

"Don't worry. You don't have to love me. Not yet anyway," Channing told her.

And to make that point clear, he leaned in, touching his lips to hers. It was a tender touch in comparison to the instant heat that always came with Malec's kiss. And yet, it still stirred her immediately. So much so that she laced her arms around his neck, pulling him closer, parting her lips in welcome.

When his tongue touched hers there was a spark of pleasure that soared through her like it had a mission. Channing tilted his head, stroking his tongue over hers expertly before licking and sucking her bottom lip. Caroline raked her fingers through his hair, following his lead, releasing her hunger for him in a guttural moan.

He moved faster than she anticipated, pushing her back on the couch and pulling at the buttons of her dress until they popped free.

"I want to see those pretty breasts," he whispered before thrusting his tongue inside her mouth one more quick time.

When he pulled away his hands were busily working, ripping the bra apart next. Caroline heard the material tear, and her clit throbbed instantly. He cupped her breasts with both hands, pushing them together so that when he licked one nipple, he only had to move slightly to the left to gorge on the other. For what seemed like an eternity of pleasure, he toyed with her nipples, sucking, biting, and sucking again.

Caroline grabbed at Channing's hair, holding his face between her breasts as she thrust her hips upward, her pussy aching for attention.

"More," he mumbled. "I . . . want . . . more."

Caroline's head thrashed against the back of the sofa. "Yes. I do too."

He stood then, his fingers moving lightning fast as he pulled the snap of his jeans apart, unzipped his pants quickly, and freed his thick cock. Where Malec was thicker, Channing was longer, and she immediately recalled the smooth and delicious taste of him as he'd moved in and out of her mouth.

Gripping the base of his cock Channing stared down at her. "Show me," he told her.

Caroline had been so busy looking at his cock, watching the way his hand gripped so tightly at the base and then moved up the shaft, his thumb rubbing along the tip. Her mouth had watered and he said, this time with a little more force, "Show me that sweet pussy, Caroline. I want to see how wet you are for me."

Already breathless from watching him, her breasts bared, the dress ripped and twisted around her waist, Caroline leaned back on the couch, spreading her legs wide.

"Yeah," Channing moaned as he watched her.

She slipped the thin lace material of her underwear to the side, baring herself to him, and when she saw his tongue licking over his lips, his hand moving faster on his cock, she used two fingers to separate her already-damp folds.

"I love seeing you like that. So open and ready. I dream about it every night," he told her.

"Channing." She said his name slowly while pushing two fingers deep inside her pussy, her gaze dropping once again to his rigid length.

He came for her then, taking the steps to close the distance between him and the chair, bending down to touch the tip of his cock to her entrance. He moved there, up and down her slit, coating his dick with her juices and then pulled back.

Caroline whimpered, "Please."

"Here you go," he told her. "Open wide."

When she opened her eyes to see his dick only inches from her face Caroline did not hesitate but took him in, tasting herself on his length, driving her wild with desire and need. Channing moved in and out of her mouth, stretching his arm down and between her legs to rub over her clit. Caroline bounced on that couch, her hands cupping Channing's ass.

"You're so ready for me," Channing whispered. "So fucking ready."

He pulled out of her then, her mouth and her pussy, and Caroline moaned with disappointment.

"Oh no, baby. We're not through yet," he told her as he positioned his dick at her juicy opening and thrust quickly inside.

Caroline gasped and looked up at him. "Promise?"

He grinned then, that sexy little smile she was beginning to adore. "Your bet that sweet ass of yours, I promise."

And damn, did he deliver. By the time they both reached their release, Channing was nipping along her neck, tiny little pricks of teeth she knew were too sharp to be human. Sated and probably about ten seconds away from falling into a nice deep sleep, she whispered, "Will it hurt?"

"Will what hurt, baby?" Channing asked, his tongue stroking along the skin he'd just touched with his teeth.

"When you turn me into a lycan," she said, her eyes closed, legs still wrapped tightly around him.

"I won't let anything hurt you, Caroline," Channing vowed. "Not ever again."

CHAPTER 15

Three weeks later

The full moon

Blaez had chosen Blackbriar as the place to build this log fortress and to hide from Zeus because the town was located at the base of Blackfoot Mountain. Its summit reached straight up to the sky, and thus Zeus held it sacred, as he also held eagles, the oak, and feuds that made no sense at all. For these reasons, Blaez had assumed he would be safe.

He had assumed wrong.

In the past weeks Caroline had learned a lot about the Trekas pack and what their purpose was in this world. She learned about the other supernatural beings that walked the earth and how one day she too would learn to protect herself from them. Because as a member of this pack, they would soon be coming for her as well.

It wasn't like the years she'd studied to be a veterinarian, she'd thought a few nights ago when she and Kira had been sitting in the massive library going through books and talking about the possibilities to come. No, studying to become a lycan was a much tougher task. Just as keeping up with the insatiable sexual appetites of Channing and Malec was.

"It's worse as we get closer to the full moon," Kira had told her. "That's just how we're made. The moon feeds us in a way. Our power, sexuality, and sanity rest there because when Zeus was wreaking his havoc on Lykaon and Arcadia, Selene was the only goddess powerful enough to intervene."

"But her intervention didn't stop him," Caroline added. The story of how the lycans came to be was the first thing she'd learned when Malec had come around to agreeing that she would be changed. He'd been the one to tell her the story one night while they shared a lounge chair on his deck. He'd called it a bedtime story, but what they'd done after he'd finished talking had really been what put her into a deep and restful sleep.

"No, it did not," Kira replied. "But it gave us a fighting chance against what she knew would eventually come."

Caroline had nodded. "And that's what we're preparing for now? Zeus's wrath?"

"He wants Blaez dead. It's not so much about his revenge against Lykaon now, but his own ego. You know the god of all gods has to be the best at everything, and he has to be feared by all."

"Is Blaez afraid of him?" Caroline had asked.

Kira had grown silent, staring off at a section of books that she'd already told Caroline were written in Greek.

"He's afraid of what will happen to this world when he finally has to face Zeus."

And tonight, as the full moon shone brightly in the dark sky, and lightning crackled and flashed intermittently through that darkness, Caroline thought she might just be afraid of when that happened too.

"Normally when it rains like a monsoon and there's thunder and lightning the sky is filled with clouds," she'd said while they were all sitting at the table having dinner.

When the bright and fierce-looking white, gold, red, and orange streaks split through the sky, they illuminated throughout the house. And when the thunder roared and rumbled so loud and hard it shook the windows only the moon's luminescence showed through them.

"He's angry, and he's showing it," Channing replied.

Phelan scowled. "He's a bully, and he's showing that too."

Kira nodded to Caroline. "You know who they're talking about."

It had taken her a minute, but yes, Caroline knew. It was all any of them had talked about since the Solo had appeared and the citizens of Blackbriar had been made aware that the pack of great-looking men that lived in the woods were not just great-looking men, after all.

"More bounty hunters will come, won't they?" Caroline asked.

"You bet your ass they will," was Phelan's quick retort.

Malec set down his fork and used his napkin to wipe his hands. "Favor from Zeus is worth a lot to some."

"And I'm worth a lot to him, but only if I'm dead," Blaez added.

Kira reached over to take her mate's hand. "That's why I was selected for you, so that together we could deal with Zeus when the time came. We'll get through this, and we'll make things better for the lycans because of it. It's our dest—"

Kira's words tapered off, her eyes widening. Everything went quiet at that moment as all gazes went to her. She did not speak, only blinked, attentively, as if someone—who was not visible to the rest of them—was speaking to her. When she lifted her hands, placing them flat on the table, Blaez stood.

And then there was a knock at the door.

Phelan scowled.

"Why is the alarm not going off?" Channing asked quietly.

Malec stood then as well, reaching for Caroline. She stood up from the table and didn't speak as he pushed her behind him. Channing had stood by that time as well. He and Phelan had nodded to each other and appeared to be moving toward what Caroline now knew was their weapons and security room at the far end of the house.

"No," Kira said finally. "It is a friend."

Blaez put his hands on her shoulders. "Are you sure?"

She nodded, her eyes blinking as she seemed more like herself at this moment. "Yes. Open the door."

Phelan took the liberty, moving past Channing and all but stomping toward the front door. When he pulled it open, a bright bolt of lightning crackled, casting an eerie glow on the man standing there.

"Hell no! This is not a friend," Phelan said, grabbing the front of the man's shirt and pulling him into the house.

He had the man's back slammed against the wall before they could all run into the living room in an attempt to stop him. Caroline had stayed close to Malec, but she was looking directly at them when the growling began. And this time it wasn't just Phelan. The man he was holding had growled as well, his sharp teeth bared, eyes glowing a fierce green as he stared back at Phelan.

"Enough!" Blaez yelled as stepped over to where Phelan held the other man.

No, Caroline thought as she continued to stare. This was definitely not just a man. And it wasn't a lycan because nothing had changed on him except his eyes, and they were a different color than Phelan's and the rest of the pack's.

"Let him go, Phelan," Blaez said, standing beside them. "Let him go now!"

Phelan growled as he let his hands slide from the man's shirt, and then the man roared back, loud and long, in Phelan's face. At his sides Phelan's nails broke free with a sickening clicking sound, and Channing and Malec went to stand beside him, grabbing his arms.

"Move him back," Blaez told them, and they did what the alpha said.

Kira came to stand beside her husband. "You are a Shadow Shifter, and you need our help," she said to the man. "Come inside and tell us more."

So this was a Shadow Shifter, Caroline thought as she watched them walk to the couch and take a seat.

"My name is Jace Maybon," he spoke once he was seated. "I am the Pacific Faction leader of the Shadow Shifters. I am looking for my friend and fellow faction leader, Cole Linden. The scents surrounding this place are strong for other species, so I figured it was safe to stop and ask you if you've seen any feline shifters in this area."

"No," Blaez answered. "Did you pick up a feline scent as well?"

"There are many scents," was Jace's reply. "It's hard to separate all of them."

"Because they're coming!" Phelan said, still growling and baring his teeth. "They're coming, and you're letting his kind in! We wouldn't be in this predicament if they'd been able to remain a secret."

"That's not true," Channing added. "Whether or not the human world found out about the Shadow Shifters last year or two weeks ago, we would still be facing the same issues we have with Zeus."

"We are not involved in your otherworld feud," Jace said. "But our leader, Roman, knows about the evolving situation. We're all in a precarious situation at this point."

"That's all the more reason why we shouldn't be sitting here acting helpless and letting in something that might very well be an enemy! What if he's accepted Zeus's bounty offer as well?"

All eyes went to the man who called himself Jace Maybon until again Kira spoke up.

"He is not, Phelan. Trust me."

Phelan easily yanked away from Malec and Channing's grip, his lycan in full form as he growled once more, his speaking slightly distorted as he talked over his elongated teeth. "I don't trust anyone."

He opened the door and ran out into the rain before anyone could stop him, and Caroline gasped, lifting a hand to her mouth in an attempt to mute the sound.

"I know that you're not here to harm us," Kira said, touching Jace on the shoulder. "Why don't we go somewhere a little more private, and I will try to see if I can help you locate your friend."

Jace nodded to her. "Thank you," he said. "I appreciate your efforts."

Blaez walked with them toward the library. "We don't want any other species to be lost or captured out there in this world the way it is now. There's no telling what will happen if we cannot account for our own."

"I agree," Jace told him.

When they were gone and only Malec, Channing, and Caroline stood in the living room, she looked at them and sighed. "I think I need a drink."

Malec handed Caroline her glass of wine.

"Well, it's certainly been an eventful couple of weeks," she said, staring out the patio doors to the still-raging storm.

"More like a couple of months," Channing added, filling his own glass and taking a quick swallow.

Malec downed his entire glass and refilled it. They hadn't turned on any lights when they'd retreated to his room. The dark was still his preference. Besides, there was enough light coming from the moon, as if in stark reminder of what tonight was and what needed to be done.

It had taken him a while, but he had come to grips with what he felt for Caroline. It was because of it—the strong emotion that he accepted but still had not spoken of—that he would give Caroline what she wanted. He would do anything to make her happy and to keep her with him and Channing. She said she wanted to become a lycan, and tonight she would.

"It's been a rough and sometimes delectable road up until

this point," Malec said, letting the taste of the wine settle over his tongue.

Channing stood close to Caroline. Both of them had been looking out the window. They turned when he spoke.

"I can definitely vouch for delectable," Channing said, slapping a hand to Caroline's ass. And watching it shake in response.

Luckily, she'd just finished taking a sip of her drink. She smiled at Channing in response as she moved the glass from her lips. Caroline knew they both liked to watch her ass, which was why she took an extremely long time adding lotion to her body after a bath or shower. Since Channing spent a good bit of time in Malec's room with them now, he was often there to see her getting dressed and to watch that magnificent ass.

When Channing took the glass from her she continued to watch him, her hand moving to rub along the bulge of his cock when he was moving away to set the glasses on the table. Malec had smiled. Caroline was extremely receptive. There was never a cat-and-mouse game with her, only want and take. When they wanted they were able to take and when she wanted, oh hell, they'd better be ready to give. There had been a couple of times when he'd thought she was already a lycan because of how insatiable she could become.

He hoped that was the Caroline they would get tonight. Malec had been thinking about this moment for days now, just as he was certain Channing and Caroline had too. It was finally time.

"Undress her," Malec told Channing as he walked to the nightstand and took a bottle from the drawer.

He pulled his shirt up and over his head, pushing his

shorts down his legs and stepping out of them, he walked over to where Caroline and Channing had been standing.

Channing had already pulled the dress Caroline had been wearing up and over her head. But he made sure she kept the shoes on, five-inch-heeled sandals with straps that wound straight up her calves. Caroline loved shoes, and Malec realized early on that he loved the shoes she wore.

"You look like you're ready," Caroline said to Malec as he came to stand in front of her. But when she reached out a hand to touch Malec's thick cock, Channing grabbed her wrists, holding her arms straight down by her side.

"The question is, Caroline," Malec said, lifting a hand to quickly undo the clasp in the front of her bra, "are you ready?"

Her unbound breasts jiggled, the new rings he'd bought for her piercings—sterling silver circles with a diamond that dangled from the center—glistened in the moonlight. He couldn't resist. He leaned forward, kissing each piercing, loving the background of her wide, dark areola. She arched back against Channing, and Malec could hear him placing kisses along her cheek.

Malec snatched the thin wisp of material from her juncture, dragging his flattened palm over a thick, soft thigh. She moved then, opening her legs as if inviting him in, and Malec groaned.

"You want me to check and see if you're ready, don't you? Naughty, naughty girl," he told her as he went to his knees, tongue extended as he licked her tender lips.

Channing released one of her hands to lift her leg up, giving Malec even better access to her wet and waiting pussy. He dove in like a starving man, licking every drop of her essence as she bucked between them. When he was ready to thrust his dick inside of her Malec forced himself to pull back. It couldn't happen this way, not tonight.

Coming to his feet, Malec wrapped his arms around Caroline's waist, pulling her against his naked body and kissing her with every bit of emotion he possessed. She was everything to him. Her presence helped him heal from the past, embrace the present, and look forward to the future. She was his mate in whatever form—human or lycan. She was the woman for him. And tonight, with the power of the full moon, he planned to make that official.

Channing had undressed by the time Malec ended the kiss, and he took the bottle from Malec, opening it with a resounding click. Malec kept his hands on Caroline, kneading her breasts, his thumbs flicking her nipples as Channing poured the oil down her back. She sighed and leaned into Malec when Channing stroked her ass, being sure to get a good amount of the oil back there, down into her crease.

He gave the oil to Malec, who poured it quickly over her heavy breasts, loving how they looked all shined and enticing. When the bottle was empty, Malec dropped it to the floor. He looked at Caroline and thought he'd never seen a more alluring goddess flanked in glowing moonlight.

He lifted her leg and positioned himself to slide deep inside of her. She'd grasped his shoulders, moaning as she took him greedily inside.

"Oh, Malec." She sighed his name, kissing him this time as he began to move in and out of her.

Channing moved then, lifting Caroline's other leg so that it wrapped around Malec's waist. As Malec stroked inside of her he felt the moment that Channing's length pressed firmly into Caroline's ass. She bucked slightly, then settled onto him as she had been used to doing in the past weeks. Malec deepened their kiss as he thrust in deep, then pulled out so Channing could go farther into her. They worked in sync filling her, pumping her, pleasuring her. Caroline's nails dug into Malec's shoulders, her moans filling the room.

She sounded heavenly and felt like sunshine on every single day. Malec's muscles bunched as the pleasure increased, her essence dripping down on his cock, her nipples scraping against his bare chest. When she pulled her mouth away from his and let her head fall back against Channing's shoulder to take his waiting kiss, Malec watched her.

He pumped into her pussy and watched her tongue dueling with Channing's. His dick grew harder, slipping in and out of her with the slickness of her arousal. Tearing her mouth away from Channing's, Caroline began to moan, her pussy tightening around Malec's cock. He loved when she did that and knew her release was coming soon. Glancing over her shoulder to Channing, who also knew Caroline's pleasure signs, Malec tensed only slightly as they both nodded.

It was time.

"Hold on to me, sweetheart," Malec told her.

She gripped his shoulders tighter as Malec and Channing began pounding mercilessly into her. Their strokes were still synchronized, moving in and out of her slickness with a glorious sound. Her breasts moved up and down with the quick motions. Sweat ran down Malec's back, and Channing's face contorted with pleasure. Behind them, through the window, the storm—Zeus's performance—raged on while the moon sat high and burned bright.

It was time.

Malec struck first, lowering his mouth to Caroline's shoulder, biting down with his elongated teeth into her skin. She stilled, and Channing bit down into the back side of her opposite shoulder. They both held there for a moment, tasting her blood against their tongues. When she arched between them and screamed, Malec's release exploded into her, Channing groaning as his did as well.

Caroline screamed again, the sound echoing into the night, her neck arching back as their teeth sank deeper into her. "I love you," she whimpered. "I love both of you so very much."

"I love you, baby," Channing whispered, his tongue flattening over the bite to the back of Caroline's shoulder.

"Caroline, my heart," Malec had said immediately after. "My life, my destiny, I love you more than I ever thought possible." He'd licked his bite until the flesh was now sealed, his DNA already seeping into her bloodstream, changing her from a human to a lycan, even as they continued to hold her, together.